THE SMUGGLERS LAMENT

DOUG CHESLER

LifeRich
PUBLISHING®

LifeRich Publishing books may be ordered through booksellers or by contacting:

LifeRich Publishing
1663 Liberty Drive
Bloomington, IN 47403
www.liferichpublishing.com
844-686-9607

ISBN: 978-1-4897-3376-4 (sc)
ISBN: 978-1-4897-3377-1 (e)

Library of Congress Control Number: 2021902375

Print information available on the last page.

LifeRich Publishing rev. date: 08/29/2023

Contents

Chapter One

THE BASICS

"The Army teaches boys to think like men."
Elvis Presley

The transfer cases were never supposed to be stacked higher than 5 feet so they did not draw attention to themselves. This was the height of the Vietnam War so we were receiving over 100 cases a day. These transfer cases were considered top priority cargo so we had to keep them moving until we got them home. This was a major part of my job to get Sgt. Donald Scarborough from Russell, Mississippi back to his hometown so his family can bury him. The cases were a brushed aluminum and a lot of airmen working on the flight line were spooked by them and couldn't muster up the strength to lift them even when they were empty. I was used to them so we used them as a table or a bench and on night shift we would even get some shut eye on them. But when I had to pull their orders to identify who was inside and where they were going was when it got more personal. If it was Lieutenant Thomas Murphy from Dover, New Jersey who died in the line of duty during a firefight up north in Danang, then I had to make the connecting flights to get his remains home, ASAP. It was a sad job but somebody had to do it. The worse detail was having to accompany the dead soldier all the way home and to be the one to deliver the body and the bad news. My home base in Northern California was receiving over 500 transfer cases a week; so many that we would have to fill in for the Chaplains and accompany the bodies to the funeral homes. I am sorry to inform you Mr. & Mrs. Lee but your son died bravely during combat in Vietnam defending the United States of America. In reality, him and his squad were way up north in Cambodia where they shouldn't be and they all got hit by an incoming US rocket. Friendly Fire is what we called it. We found his dog tags mixed up with his squad's all over the side of the hill and we really don't know who or what is in this box. Sometimes the dog tags were all we had to go on. Our bombs blew everything to smithereens

Back in the Fall of 1969 everything was going really good for me as a freshman at one of the big partying schools on the east coast. I was, at this time, a young hippie type going to UMASS up in Amherst, with about 10 other good schools in the area, it was party city. It was getting hard to wake up for my 8 am statistics class so I figured I would drop the course and just take it next semester. But next semester never came. The hardest thing in my life came as a result of dropping that course because by Christmas I was at Lackland Air Force Base in southern Texas in basic training. One of the stupidest things I ever did was drop that math class and lose my 4-F deferment. My draft number was 37 so the government grabbed me just like that. I had to go to Fort Hamilton in Brooklyn to get my physical and I enlisted in the Air Force to get out of the draft. I spent Christmas down in San Antonio, Texas and this wasn't quite how I planned to spend the holidays. We had the choice of getting drafted into the Army or the Marine Corps for 2 years or enlist for 4 years in the Navy, the USAF or the Coast Guard. I just couldn't see myself crawling through the rice paddies with the snakes and the leaches in the rain. Then there was the problem of those Oriental people hell bent on trying to kill you. Boot Camp was a far cry from The University of Massachusetts-

A good night sleep was always just a short dream in basic training, there was the Vietnam War going on so things were taken very seriously. We didn't get enough sleep as it was, and the days were long and challenging. Just about every other day your tour came up to pull a 3-hour guard duty during the night protecting the guys from the threat of communism. Armed with my rifle and flashlight I had to keep moving so I didn't fall asleep standing in one spot. The rhythmic sounds of the snoring would sometimes reach the pitch of the cicadas scream and how it drops off into the night only to then notice the constant farting noises of my sleeping comrades. I wasn't really scared armed with a flashlight and an M-16 military assault rifle and, at 18, I was in the best shape of my life. Listening to the guys yelling out from their crazy dreams and talking in their sleep entire conversations was always unsettling and when you started trying to answer them you knew you were in trouble as well. The reality check came from the constant yelling and screaming from the Tactical Instructors that were supposed to break you down and then they start to build you up again. The first month was absolutely insane until we started getting the hang of things.

Three times a day we had to march into the mess hall and all the companies strutted in the order of their training. The company that was getting ready to graduate looked like some drill team, they looked like they were a well-oiled machine. Since we were the "rainbows" we looked like a can of worms, our TI's would bark "Company Halt" and we would all bump into each other. Our TI would yell "Right Face" and some of the guys would turn left so the TI would yell "YOUR OTHER RIGHT ASSHOLE"! It took a long time to get this regimental thing down and some guys had it easier than others. It was grueling to watch the weaker, dumber guys get a ton of crap. The TI's had about a month to send the guys with more serious issues home so that the Air Force didn't have to own them and pay for them the rest of their lives. You could tell the guys who weren't going to make it as they looked ready to pop and it was a sad process to weed them out. They were going to be a lot better off going home and then the instructors could concentrate on busting our balls big time. I felt sorry for the guys that looked like deer in the headlights, but I couldn't spend much time with them because I had enough problems of my own. Then there were the guys trying to walk over me like they thought we were playing "King of The Hill". That is what we had to learn, teamwork, and how to help each other reach the teams' goals. But some guys didn't know and some didn't want to know. We all fall short and that is when we are supposed to help each other up.

We were called Rainbows because we had not been issued our green fatigues yet so our clothes and hair had some color to it. Soon we got our GI haircuts and the barbers shaved our heads bald. I looked like Uncle Fester on the Adams Family. When we got our fatigues and our white underwear, we all looked the same. It took me days to recognize the guys that I came down with from Ft Hamilton in Brooklyn. When we had to hit the showers at night, we had two minutes to shower and dry off. The weird thing was that the only thing we had on was our dog tags and we sounded like a bunch of cows in a barn. Eventually we bought the little rubber jackets so they didn't make such a racket all the time. A lot of basic training was about stripping you down and then starting to build you up, their way. To fall in and drill together as a team we had to lose the "I" by surrendering some of our ego and learning how to take orders from our superiors, even if they were assholes. A hard thing to have to swallow was when we were really right but we had to act like we were wrong to avoid any confrontation with our superiors. There were always some show offs that wanted to look good in front of the instructors. When we ran in formation, a few guys thought that they should run way out in front of the pack. Our Tactical Instructors made sure that they were rewarded with extra work and they lived at the back of the line.

I was standing on the chow line at attention (of course) and I heard this commotion coming from around the corner towards the other chow line. It was some prisoners all chained up to each other and standing heel to toe so that the first guy was commanded to take a step forward, and one by one, they all did the same. They were forced to move looking like a crawling centipede. I figured that we had it hard enough so I couldn't imagine what these poor bastards were going through. Just then a TI was walking by and he started screaming at me and the guy in front of me on the chow line. He was yelling that "it looks like you two dumbasses want to join them over there!" And just as he was about to walk by, he stops and gets so close to me that I could smell and feel his bad breath on my face and as he is yelling, he is spraying spit all over me. Now he is screaming how us hippie freaks look like we were growing beards. I hardly thought I had to shave but me and the guy in front of me had to report to the latrine and learn how to properly shave. Well it turned into a real shit show as a few TI's were screaming at us to keep shaving and the guy in the mirror next to me was freaking out. He was a bleeding mess as he was chopping the crap out of his face and his acne made his face look like raw meat. The poor fuck had a couple of TIs screaming right in his face. He was shaking so bad that he kept dropping his razor so they screamed louder. I couldn't take it so I yelled to lay off the guy and give him a break. I figured I would get an Article 15 and could get a few days of marching the athletic field for yelling at an instructor or worse yet to be put on their shit list. They had to send the guy home and I am sure he was better off as it could get very ugly, it would be absolute hell for the poor bastard. The next day they assigned me as a squad leader for my bravery and compassion I guess!?

One night as I was sound asleep this big, black lummox named Clarence Moon Harrison from Waco, Texas woke me up thinking he could get me to suck his big black schlong. It was 2:00 am and the horny asshole had his dick on my pillow pleading with me to help him out for he won't" say nothin" if I sucked him off. He was supposed to be on guard duty and here he was trying to get a nut from his sleeping brothers. He wouldn't leave me alone so I had to jump up from a deep sleep and quickly get this guy off of me. In the middle of the night with the whole barracks sound asleep I knew that shit was gonna hit the fan. So, here was this big black dickhead from "Wack-O" Texas trying to get over on me. I was a pretty laid-back hippie type always laughing and fooling around and I was the flight clown even able to mess with the instructors. Because of my easy nature, maybe old Moonie thought I liked to suck dick but it wasn't happening. I boxed PAL and Golden Gloves in

NYC in High School, so I knew how to dance as Moon Harrison and the barracks soon found out. The entire barracks was up and around us in a circle and at 2 AM the whole thing felt like West Side Story, but in Texas. Moonie was big and strong and he rushed me and knocked me down. With everyone in our skivvies and dog tags it really did seem like some strange play. Our dog tags had a way of counting cadence and keeping score. The real reality was this huge guy had me by my ears and was trying to bash my head on the floor. I was able to get in a punch from the floor right in his nose that let me get up and beat the living daylights out of him in a barrage of good jabs and hooks. After a big roundhouse, I knocked him down and he begged for mercy pleading with me to stop. As he laid there, he looked so pathetic that I helped him up as he started to cry. I felt bad for him as he not only got beat up but got exposed as a predator. And he cried like a little girl.

We found out that Harrison had been trying to take advantage of other guys sound asleep in the night. Our Flight Leader wanted to report him to our Instructors but I asked to let him slide, for he would be court marshaled and thrown out of the service. We never heard about Moonie trying any more night riding after that and he would go out chasing the ladies with the other dogs, so it was eventually forgotten about. But

I still wasn't going to drop my soap in the shower. I don't think I am homophobic but the idea of having my mustache velcroid to some guy's butt hole wasn't a big turn on. There were a lot of gays in the service, both men and women, but it was still a court martial offense to have gay sex. Supposedly they put salt peter in our food to help curb our raging hormones but I heard that was just a myth. Salt peter is a meat tenderizer and does nothing to retard prisoners or soldiers of their wild desires. But late at night a lot of guys could be heard jacking off in the latrine as the three months of basic training was a long time for a guy to be horny and alone, especially at 18. But even though I was dead tired I spent a lot of late nights laying in my bunk, tired from a long day's training, listening to the San Antonio rock station. I had to fall off to sleep with my earphone in my ear. I still needed to soothe my soul late into the night. I had this little transistor radio that looked like an Esso gas pump that I hid under my pillow. Back home we had Allison Steele, "the night bird" on WNEW 102.7 FM to get us through the night. Some nights even the San Antonio broadcasts seemed so very far away.

On about the fifth day of training we were abruptly woken out of our bunks by the usual screaming of our drill instructors. I don't know why they were so mad all the time? They woke up angry and we heard them coming down the hallway with their metal taps on their boots. Hopefully, they didn't knock my bunk to the floor with me in it. If you were on their shit list, your bed, footlocker and your locker could be thrown out the window and it would take hours to put it all back to pass an inspection. I looked out of the window and saw that it was raining and no one was on the PT field. The Sargent yells to be in our PT uniforms after breakfast. We put on our jock strap, blue shorts, yellow USAF shirts and combat boots. He also said that by tomorrow we will we be praying for sunshine. At first when I saw that no one was out doing calisthenics my heart skipped a beat, thinking that it would be an easier day. I was relieved that we would not have to run laps in the hot Texas sun; but our TI's had other plans for a rainy day.

First, we had to line up next to our footlockers and do some warm-ups as the hot muggy barracks quickly got up to a hundred degrees. Starting with some push-ups, sit-ups, jumping-jacks and squat thrusts, we were all sweating like pigs. One of their favorite tortures was having us lay on our backs with our hands under our butts and lifting our legs up six inches with those fricking combat boots on. If our boots touched the ground, there was hell to pay, we would have to run the stairs. The barracks were five stories high and we would have to run down the stairs, across the barracks and back up the other side for say a half hour. Running up 5 flights of stairs 20-30 times stopping to do pushups sucked big time. The worst was doing reverse pushups by sitting on the edge of our footlocker and then lowering our butts to the ground and back up again without touching the ground. I could feel my arm muscles ripping. We had to keep working on all these cruel calisthenics all day. A really sick one we had to do, especially late in the afternoon, was the squat thrust push-up which is exactly what it sounds like. Twenty of them could make you want to puke, give up and cry. Having to pull up my boots back up to attention seemed like I was in quicksand. Each boot probably had a pint of sweat in them to go along with some blood blisters. We wore a lite nylon sock under our wool socks but the beating our feet took was brutal.

By late afternoon I was so light headed that I felt like I was going to pass out, many guys did. If the TI's thought that a guy was faking it, the whole team would have to pay. Sometimes the entire Flight had to do the guys punishment, it got mean. The TI would say, "Gentleman, thanks to Private Fuck-Up, after dinner we will meet for a 5- mile run. Be sure to thank Private Numb-Nuts after every mile!" The TIs took advantage of every teaching opportunity to prove the point and sarcasm and repetition hammered the point home. Having to do more then what was thrown at us was so hard to swallow. We hated it and swore at the fuck-up all the way. The next morning, I was happy to get outside and take my salt tablets to try and work out my cramped muscles. We prayed it would not rain for a while. The whole day so far was sit-ups, push- ups, squat thrusts, running and marching. Sometimes the South Texas sun we would lose 5-10 pounds of sweat a day. At night guys would jump out of their bunks yelling as they tried to work out a leg cramp. It was weird to see guys all wrenched up and twisted trying to find the right position to end the cramp. By the end of bootcamp the obstacle courses became easier, almost fun. Marching double time and doing the Queen Anne Salute with our rifles made us look pretty sharp. After a while I was able to push through the pain and after a half hour of running or swimming, I was able to go into that anaerobic cocoon. We said it was like getting your second wind as it triggers endorphins and dopamine in your brain. That was our optimal physical training along with class time and repetition until we got it all down. Some drills we were blindfolded so we could strip down our rifles and put them back together in our sleep. Being able to stand at attention while holding our rifles out was a mental challenge as much it was physical.

Standing at attention while holding an 8-pound rifle straight out until the drill instructor says at ease, was nuts. If we were standing at attention or at parade rest with our rifles, the TI's liked to sneak up on us from behind and kick our rifles out of our hands. And of course, there was an unwritten law that a soldier never lets his rifle hit the ground. If it does you will run laps while guys were sleeping. Another law was that you didn't call your rifle a gun. "This is your Rifle and this is your Gun, one is for killing and this one's for fun". And then you grab your crotch! After three months of this crap we started getting pretty sharp. They broke us down and built us back up to be a United States soldier. When we graduated from bootcamp we started more technical training and I started learning about planes. I was also starting to believe I was "a tough- mo-fo, maybe even a tank!"

The sole purpose of the drill instructor was to ride our asses 24/7 armed with the old slogan that for all the sweating done during training saves the blood from flowing during actual combat. If we called our Tactical Instructors drill instructors, we would be doing guard duty for a week. A DI was Army and Marines. And if you had to pull extra details you were a sad sack that got no sleep! The TI's were hardened lifers that were trained to give us as much grief as possible. When their

Adam's Apple was pressed up against our faces and they were screaming something unintelligible, we had to stand there and take it like a man. If you were called a Mary or the TI was making some reference to you wearing panties then you just hope it didn't stick as they seemed to love calling you names. Everyone had a few nicknames to put up with and if you showed that it bothered you, you would probably have to wear a new name tag taped over your real one. So, you try to be cool and not let them see you sweat. When the TI's were standing around with us, they liked to call out our new names for our failures and misfortunes. Everyone was FUBAR "fucked up beyond all recognition" and one of my personal favorites was the philosophical question asking us if our mothers had any kids that lived?

But the meanest groups of sergeants were the Cro-Magnons that were the mess hall sergeants that ran the kitchens and dining halls. They had to cook and feed a lot of troops and they were always under the gun to get the 3 meals served and cleaned up. The Air Force had the best food and there was always a separate line that served breakfast day & night to feed the evening and night shifts. Each kitchen served a thousand guys and the kitchen crew were working from 5 AM till 9 PM, 7 days a week. Then they had to train us and prevent all of us from messing up the place. They made it hard for us to carry a big tray of lasagna while they were riding our backs for 17 hours. Thank God it was only for two weeks at a time. These guys were in for 20 years yet kept getting busted for drinking or insubordination for telling some Lieutenant to fuck off. I don't think that there were any actual qualifications or tests to pass for these guys but being mean and ugly. These cooks always thought they actually owned these kitchens as they were always screaming at us to get out of their goddam kitchen. They were constantly telling us not to walk on their motherfucking clean floors or we would be washing them all night with a toothbrush and a bottle cap. Our first Kitchen Patrol detail was over at the off-limits section of the base. This was the fenced off corner of the base that was for the poor souls that were facing special assignments such as the stockades, Article 15's, and foreign military dudes getting trained usually in communications. Anyone could get an article 15 as us new recruits had to have one hanging out our fatigues so some TI could pull it and then we were in a special world of shit. Thank God I never had one pulled on me. So, for two weeks we had to get up at 3:00 am and double time it in the dark over to that mess hall to work in the greasy and brutally hot kitchens. The ovens were hot, the serving areas with the steam serving warmers were so hot that you were drenched in sweat by 6:00 am. But the worst area and job was the dishwashing room called "pots & pans" as then you had to deal with a steam room type of atmosphere with your rubber gloves and plastic overalls on, slipping and sliding on the wet greasy floors.

On my second morning working KP, I was starting to get the hang of things, and putting up with the cranky mess hall sergeants yelling at us for fucking up his kitchen, I had a bad snafu. I was sweeping up a pile of dirt from the storage room floor when I heard the sarges barks to get on our serving station line. It was 6:00 am and it was time to open the doors. I had to quickly sweep up and get the pile picked up, I found a shovel and lifted up a garbage can cover, tossed in the dirt and closed the top. The bad thing was that it did not sound right so I looked back inside to get the sickening realization that it was not really being used as a garbage can, it was filled with flour! Since I had to run to my spot to serve the scrambled eggs, I had hoped to get back to clean up the mess I made before the lunch time baking begins.

We served about a thousand troops and yes there were WAVES and WACS as well and we gave out seconds and even third helpings. They say that we all balanced out on the physical training and the "three square meals and a cot" philosophy. If you came in thin you gained muscle and if you tipped the scale, you lost and were in the best shape of your life. Some guys never ate so good in their lives. After a couple of months, I was turning into a lean, mean fighting machine. We could run the mile in combat boots in under 7 minutes and do push-ups and sit-ups and hours of marching and calisthenics. But, getting back to my breach of kitchen protocols, I was just finishing up with the serving line when to my dismay I hear the screams coming from the dry supply room. I heard the Mess Sergeant yelling the question "Who is the mother fucking dumbass who shit on my flour?" With his hideous drawl it sounded like I really did take a crap on his floor! I tried to suppress the reality of the situation and assess the possible ramifications for a few moments. I had to come clean with my confession that I was the "motherfucking dumbass" that apparently took a shit on the man's floor! When getting berated by these maniacs we had to stand at attention and take shit even if it was not true and they had to exaggerate everything to prove a point. Of course, I didn't really shit on the man's floor but since he said it, I might as well have. This was not a court martial so I had no rights and no excuses or defense. If a guy tries to get out of it by making excuses or whining about it, he will learn quickly, to zip it. After having to clean up "his flour", I was assigned to pots and pans for the week. The worst attack would be to be called a pansy as that would open up "Pandoras Box" so to speak! It always had to do with our manhood or our lack of guts. Being called a worthless puke with no balls could get to you when they are screaming in your ear in front of the whole Flight.

The pots and pans were always stacked up to the ceiling with burnt and caked on foods and grease that had to be scraped off before being soaked in 200-degree tubs. If it was the baked and burnt lasagna we were screwed. We had to have a guy monitoring the garbage cans so we could separate the silver wear, from the paper goods to the leftover food. The paper goods were burnt in the incinerators and the food was delivered to the pig farms. I slipped around in my rubber suit with the goggles fogged up for 14 hours a day all week with blisters on my feet from being wet and full of the funky detergents we had to use. And I had to wear this stupid paper hat that kept falling off my head. Because my boots never dried each day, they felt like they weighed about 10 pounds each as I was hobbling around on the sloppy floors all week. I had some nasty blood blisters and soggy socks that turned my feet into big prunes. I prided myself with the best spit shine shoes on the base. Even in my year at Eastern Military Academy in

9th grade, I could get $5 for shoes and $10 for boots. The officers got me out of details and paid me to do all their boots and even tipped me if they had to attend a special function. So, I really had the spit shine down as my combat boots usually looked like black and shiny patent leather glass. They had a professional shoe shine stand out in front of the Base Exchange (the BX), but they were just shoeshine boys compared my fine leather work. It would take me hours to get my boots looking good again. I made a lot of money and it got me out of a lot of bull shit details. After making tiny circles with a cotton t-shirt and Kiwi polish all of a sudden it popped into a deep shine. I swear it had to do with my saliva as it looked like magic as they turned into patent leather. Officers would pay me $5 just to do their hat brims.

The only redeeming factor of working KP was having good food to eat as the cooks all competed on their specialties like wings, chili and bar-b-q. But, the general rule of thumb, was to stay away from the Mexican cooks and their hot sauces and hot peppers! Let's be real, these guys are not your friends or "amigos". If some gold-tooth smiling man pulls out a pouch of dried peppers from his waistband, he has to be packing some very serious heat to burn your mouth with. The general rule of thumb was that the smaller the pepper, the hotter it was. This one time their trick was to try to get you to just touch this little pepper with your finger and then taste it on the tip of your tongue. How bad could that be, Right? Well Fuckin-A tweet, it felt like a nail got hammered to my tongue and it lasted about 15 minutes with nothing but burning hot pain. These little guys would be laughing and hi-fiving each other on how they fooled us "el stupido gringo madicones," once again. Later at night when a lot of tequila was being consumed and things were not so jovial the MP's had the Mexican areas around the base off limits so there would not be bloodshed. Some of these little shit kickers would like to have the top of their switchblade showing out of the back pocket of their jeans, just to let you know that they might be small in size but big on machismo. Their gold tooth smiles were questionable.

Northport was a quaint little town that boasted a beautiful harbor and miles of beaches on the bayside and on the Long Island Sound. Our high school had very good sports teams and when we played at other schools, we realized that we were the only all white school in the league. It was especially obvious at basketball games and in their home gyms the teams and the stands were a lot more colorful and we were the minority. Our arch rivals were another great sports program that we were always battling for the title. In baseball, basketball and football their teams were all Black and Spanish and we looked like ghosts or ducks out of water. The thing is that once we got into the game, playing our sport, it was a fight to the finish and the fans went wild. The problem was that after the games, we all rumbled. During one of the rumbles, knives were drawn and baseball bats were swinging. They had to cancel the next game so we didn't do any more damage. So, that's the way it was in times so close to the race riots of the late 60's. Growing up in Northport did isolate us and most of the kids took on their parent's political views. Many of us learned tolerance in college as it was hip to be open minded and to try to embrace all races and religions. It was even hip to believe in nothing at all, as long as you didn't hurt anybody. When I entered military service, it was quite an eye opener to how different we all are. The military way of life brought us all together and we realized that we all bleed red and now we all have to make the best of it. It is just that at all meals we all sat in our own areas. The chow hall had three sections and the whites sat on their side, the blacks sat on theirs and the Spanish guys had the rest. Then there was still the rebel's vs the yanks and all the other stupid divisions.

My first black friend was the guy on my top bunk. His name was Terrence Wade from Philadelphia. Since he was the shortest guy in our flight, he was assigned to count cadence. We lined up in formation according to our height and I must have grown some as I was in the second row. The shortest man was in the front row all by himself to set the cadence and the stride. The TI's were always yelling at him to quit marching like he was marching in the ghetto. There was no mercy anywhere to be found. We had a lot of fun entertaining the troops with our nonstop banter. We even took on making jokes about our differences and we made fun of our own kind. Laughter had a way of breaking down some of the hate and prejudice that we carried around with us. My new friend looked like Flip Wilson and we ran with some of the characters from his TV show. Not everyone felt the same about our friendship. A few good ole boys pulled me aside and asked me why I was hanging around with the little nigger boy. I told them that he was not a boy, he was a GI, just like us and they laughed and said I was nothing but a nigger lover. The next night these ass holes tried to jump us outside of the barracks and we all got into it. The TI's broke it up and we had to run laps together holding hands well into the night. The only thing that became of it was that my buddy Flip and I got closer and the three haters got a ton of crap from two of our black TI's. All three of those guys eventually got held back and had to repeat basic training with the fuck ups and we were glad to leave them behind. They were all Southerners, some kind of white supremacy group.

We had the Black Panthers and these white Nazis, all passing out their tracks and preaching their prejudices. Everywhere there were groups like the Buddhists or the Moonies, all trying to gain new recruits. There were all sorts of Christian missionaries out trying to spread the Word. There were Mormons on their two-year missions going all over the place and the Jehovah witnesses knocking on everyone's door. The MP's had to throw most of them off the base but they were all a dedicated and committed bunch. We all petitioned for peace but we lived in a violent America. We killed the Kennedy's, Martin Luther King, Jr., Malcolm X and we were just getting over the Detroit, Watts and the Newark riots. We had the Black Panthers, the black Muslims, and even the KKK and other hate groups all on the news. There were the white supremacists and the neo Nazi's still wanting to kill the Jews and the non-whites. Every evening we had Walter Cronkite on the news delivering the war and the chaos and the violence in our country and it wasn't pretty. Because we had to follow orders and fall in line with military protocol, we had to learn to work together as a team. We all had to learn that there was no I in team. The common bond was that we were Americans and we could all join together to go fight and kill other people of the world. Once again, the rally cry was "kill for peace!" But there was no peace to be found, only wars and rumors of wars.

If you weren't working or sleeping or eating, you were hanging out with 10,000 young guys on or around the base. There was always something going on and plenty of guys to do it with. Since our room and board were paid for, we could do whatever we wanted with our monthly paychecks. There were always guys hanging around the rec-halls selling life insurance policies or some financial investments and other guys would send money home. You could always buy some jewelry for your mom or your girl back home on payment. There was always someone selling something. Those guys were good. They played cards or shot pool with you and they knew how to play the homesick or guilt card on you. They would ask you if you told your mom that you loved and missed her or if you wonder if your girlfriend is staying true blue or not. They knew how to put a package together to take care of them and they knew what you made and when you got paid. So, I ended up buying my mom a gold necklace on payments, it was a four-leaf clover with a diamond and she wasn't even Irish.

There was always some kind of game being bet on whether it was sports, card games, pool & ping pong, or the daily numbers. We bet on anything and on pay days there were guys going around collecting their bets and some guys lost their whole paycheck before they even got them. Off base there were pool halls, strip bars and of course the seedy motels to rent and party in. On our first base liberty we all got a few rooms to hang out. Everyone chipped in and we bought some pot and some uppers and the elevator operator said he would send up some ladies in an hour or so. We went out to buy some Jack Daniels and some snacks, and a box of Trojans. It was our first time off the base in months so we were pretty excited. We came back to the hotel and started passing around some "Old #7" and some beers, and we passed around some reefer and shared the uppers. By the time the women came up I was on the bathroom floor praying to the porcelain gods. I had not drunk any hard liquor in months. My girl cleaned me up and made me some coffee. She was from West Texas and had been "hooking" for a couple of years and she wanted to save enough money to move to LA. I was still pretty drunk so we hung out for a few hours and ended up walking around San Antonio holding hands on the River Walk. She was all paid for the night and she told me that a lot of guys just wanted the company. The next time we all went out I asked the bellhop for her, but he said she had gotten beat up really bad, and had to go back to West Texas. She said her name was Jenny but they called her Ginger, she had pretty red hair and freckles. All she wanted to do was get out of West Texas and go to LA to become an actress. The odds are, they will probably eat her alive and spit her out. She was a sweet girl and she seemed to laid back to be a good hooker. Hopefully she will stay home and find an easier profession.

If you weren't interested in the strip bars and the sex shops or that kind of partying you could do some really cool stuff out doors. You could rent a jet ski or a boat and go fishing. We rented motorcycles and rode up to the mountains or out in the desert. A lot of guys liked to go out dancing trying to meet the local girls. Besides the huge Lackland Airforce Base, Fort Hood was north of the city and there was a Strategic Attack Base a few miles away. The tiny little stone Alamo could fit in one of the aircraft hangers. With so many troops hanging around there was plenty to do and most servicemen knew how to have a good time, the ones that didn't stayed by themselves and read books or watched TV. There were always the base movies. But a real bummer to having time off was getting picked up on a jack shit detail being organized by some dick head Staff Sargent looking for volunteers. It could be policing (picking up cigarette butts and papers) the grounds, or mowing lawns, or painting offices, or moving stuff from one place to another. Have you heard the saying "if it moves pick it up, if it doesn't move paint it -"? We always had to field strip our cigarettes by ripping apart the filters and shredding out the tobacco. If you were caught littering you would have to do the policing detail for days.

Like anything in the service, if you looked busy and kept moving you were left alone. I had a stoned-out buddy who worked as a heavy equipment operator and he use to like to look busy by digging a huge hole with an all-terrain-bulldozer. Then he would roll a big doobie, smoke it, and throw the roach in the hole and cover it up, at least he looked busy. Well to get out of these bull shit details we would actually sign up for an assignment called a PC- the Perimeter Check. Each base had to have an on-going guard duty and there was a sign-up sheet in the Flight Office that we would sign up for in 3-hour segments during the night. We would sign up in pairs to sign out a jeep and a hand gun & rifle and get our flashlights, our yellow helmets and our armbands so we could take slow patrols around the base perimeters. Each guy would bring a small cooler with some beers and snacks along with a big fat doobie to smoke. Since we were armed and dangerous and all alone on the outside perimeters of the base, we pretty much had the whole area to ourselves. Who was going to mess with us? They didn't have guards to guard the guards! This was a good way to hang with a friend and get us off those bull shit details cause if you were signed up for a PC you were good for the day. Since it was during the night it was usually pretty quiet and we were all about getting a nice high and sharing some good shit. I liked to bring salami, provolone & Italian bread with my canteen filled with some Valpolicella, but sometimes I had to settle for Slim Jim's, Cheese Wiz, crackers, and Boones Farm Wine. Texas wasn't Arthur Avenue in the Bronx so we had to improvise, but we were close to the Mexican border so there was an abundance of Acapulco Gold to help balance things out.

This was 1969 and if we were wearing our civvies, we were wearing bellbottom jeans, Fry boots, pearl buttoned denim shirts and a denim jacket. We would wear hats to hide the fact that we had military crew cuts instead of long shoulder length hair. No matter what amount of leather fringe we wore, we were dead ringer for GIs with our dog tags and our marching postures. And usually our clothes were pressed & pleated from the base laundry, and it sure is true that some girls liked men in uniform! When we would go to the local dances, we would definitely wear our dress blues, Lt blue shirt and tie, blue slacks and dress shoes, blue hat with a black spit shine brim to help stand out from the local boys. I was 18 and in great shape and feeling my oats, and getting to be sowing my wild oats as well. All small excursions to get a buzz were called PCs as you always drove around and kept moving. The key was not to be stopped somewhere looking suspicious. That is why the actual PCs were so safe as all the cool heads had them locked down, nobody wanted to mess with the MPs or us guards. We had the whole base perimeter and the stars and a radio. Some great conversations of the existence of God and the universe took place out there under the stars with hardly a care in the world. We were still so young yet we were being trained to be soldiers, being trained to be fearless, even though we were scared shitless at times. But there was strength in numbers.

We joined the Air Force to avoid having to be a grunt in the Army or worse off being a Marine and being FUBAR for life. Those Jarheads were so tough and some had to be controlled with electric cattle prongs so as to not try to screw your younger sisters or kill guys that were screw ups in friendly fire. Some of our special outfits were training some very tough guys and the Marine training was so much harder than our Air Force training. But late at night getting a buzz with a buddy was such a good release and sharing of home life sure helped pass the time even if the stories of bravery or romance were somewhat fabricated. The goal was to entertain and paint a great picture of your home life, your High School and your girlfriend or even your car all left behind waiting for your return. Telling stories about homelife was always seasoned and colored with exaggerations to make them more interesting. The old six-cylinder Mustang in the barn just sounded better as a Mach 1 Mustang specially when your buddy told you he has a 327 Camaro SS under wraps back in his garage.

I went to Tech School in north Texas to become an Air Cargo Loadmaster, math was my strong suit. That was the difference in our training. I was sent to school and went through another training period on the job for the first year. The funny thing about being in the Air Force was that only a few guys had actual air status as pilots, crew chiefs (the mechanics assigned to the plane), the navigators and the load masters that took charge of the shipping assignments. Everyone else was ground support on the flight line or in the hangers or the offices. Besides shipping weapons and supplies my number one priority was being responsible for the complete delivery of the transfer cases to escort the body bags inside them. We couldn't stack more than 3 high out on the flight line so it wouldn't show how bad it really was. This was the height of the TET

Offensive and some days we had dozens coming back at a time. The orders were kept in an inner tube at the head of the case like at the bank drive throughs that showed the poor bastard's information and final home destination. If it was Donald Scarbrough from Russell, Mississippi then we had to make all the connections to get him home A.S.A.P. There was a pre-morgue in Nam and another at the three main bases in California and Seattle, Washington. Lots of guys couldn't deal with the transfer cases as only we knew if they were full or empty. Some guys just lost their strength when they felt the weight of them and it affirmed that there was a dead GI inside- Because the transfer cases were the top priority, they had to go on the next available flight to get them home A.S.A.P.

With over 500,000 troops in Vietnam in 68-69 we had "buku" transfer cases coming and going every day. Empty cases were always stacked all over the flight line as occupied case didn't hang around as we had to keep them moving. Just like some Military Chaplain and another escort have to personally visit the fallen angel's home to deliver the bad news, the proper procedures had to be made to get the body & personal affects home as well. The Air Force hid things being shipped like weapons and ammunitions to look like food and medical supplies. We once shipped a two manned submarine in a big container looking like a huge freezer for a mess hall. Supposedly this little sub was meant to go up the Mekong River to do some recon and search & destroy way up in Cambodia and Laos where we weren't supposed to be. So, on the flight line or inside the hangers when we were shipping back cargo to the States, we would see so much contraband hidden amongst the manifested cargo. I was stationed at the coolest base in the states, Travis AFB was located in Northern California, one hour outside San Francisco, Haight Asbury, North Beach, Fisherman's Wharf and the last part of the summer of love. It seemed like all the dumb ass fucking servicemen were partying and getting high or trying to experience some mind-expanding drug. Heck, the Beatles were doing it as well as all the rockers and Jimi Hendricks asked, "if we were experienced? "

Travis AFB was the main destination of illegal drugs as well as other contraband that was being shipped for free by the Air Force 's air express. In 1969 it was the busiest airport in the world as planes landing from South Vietnam and bases in the Pacific were averaging an arrival or departure every 10 minutes 24/7. It appeared to us that practically every GI was bringing back something illegal. Electronics from Japan, silk suits and custom orders from Bangkok, and anything you could want or imagine from Hong Kong. But the big money was all the drugs from south east Asia. Ty-stick, opium & hashish, cocaine and heroin and all the variations of drugs were coming in on every other pallet. When a pallet broke in shipping there was always drugs laying on the ground. We would throw all the undocumented cargo in a back room and if it went unclaimed, we would get rid of it. With the cargo planes coming and going around the clock, the amount of questionable cargo was staggering. We could just help ourselves to the point of starting to make some serious side money. Our base pay was around $ 200 / month and we were making $ 500 to a thousand a week on just the spoils of war. There was so much stuff that some guys stuck to cameras, stereos or jewelry & clothes. Things being smuggled could be anything from an NVA handgun to a shipment of stolen medical supplies. And my job as a Loadmaster was to keep the stuff moving between the Orient and wherever home was and back again. Cam Ron Air Base was the main base that shipped to my home base at Travis, they had their own morgue so that was our main shipping assignment and a constant reminder of the 58,000 deaths and over 300,000 injuries that led to thousands of deaths later. The statistics showed how many more amputations there were due to the jungle tactics of mines, bungy sticks and death traps being set by the NVA. One of my ultimate horrors is how they shipped drugs inside the dead bodies from morgue to morgue as part of an organized crime network. We were doing our little things within the big shipping routes of the Military Airlift Command right alongside of the evil workings of the Mafia and other subversive groups. A troop returning from overseas would be paranoid about a hash pipe and some hashish he has hidden in his socks in his footlocker when another pallet could have hand grenades and C4 explosives. Let's face it, if something isn't bolted down, it grew wings.

My roommate was with me since we started Tech School together. He was a fellow Loadmaster from the rich area of North Jersey called Far Hills. He was a good looking, muscular, Italian kid named Anthony Costa and his father owned a big construction company doing big projects in Jersey. Tony would get these big plans in the mail of blueprints of projects being planned for Atlantic City. There was talk of opening up legalized gambling casinos in AC and Tony and his father Angelo Costa were going to cash in on it. The reason Tony was serving his country was to get out of prison having to serve time for some kind of racketeering charge. Because we were both Italian and working & rooming together, we became good buddies. Tony was actually a cool guy with a big heart and a love for fast cars, women and rock and roll. Being 18 in 1969 we were either cool or we were square. If you were square you didn't get high, take chances or buck authority. If you were cool you "thought you were cool" and you could coast by a lot of crap. Our saying was that "it's cool & it don't mean shit", nothing did and that offended the hard asses- we tried not to sweat the small stuff. We were just cool like "Cool Hand Luke" was cool! Tony had a lot of connections and we were able to jump on any flight in the world as it was technically part of our job. But there was no way I was involved in smuggling the hard drugs, I was just a hippie that got drafted and now was in the middle of all this crazy shit. The service did change us all, we got smacked with a lot of reality and we had a lot of growing up to go through. We were no longer school children but property of the United States government, we were GI's, Government Issued! Some of the training films brought up the fact that we could no longer run to our mommies and daddies as now the Department of Defense owned us and we had to fall in line and follow orders.

Another good buddy of mine was a friend from New Jersey that grew up as a mechanic in his father's garage. Charley actually enlisted for the love of his country. He was a straight-shooting conservative who loved

Corvettes, girls and drinking his beer and shots of Jack Daniels. Charley was on his second tour of duty; he was regular Army and he was a few years older than me. He survived over 600 missions on his Huey search & rescue helicopter. There were 4 personnel assigned to each chopper; pilot & copilot, crew chief and gunner. Charlie was the crew chief assigned to keeping the helicopter in good mechanical condition and operated the other machine gun while in the air. He survived two mid-air collisions that he had to jump out of before they crashed wildly to the ground. They were sitting ducks when they picked up or dropped off our guys. At a hot LZ (landing zone), they would shoot themselves out (spray gunfire to clear a landing) then pick up the wounded to deliver them, then turn around and go right back to the hell hole they just left. It was insane and one of the most dangerous jobs in the Army. How he survived over 600 missions rescuing thousands was a miracle every day. When he got out of the Army 6 years later, he wasn't that crew cut kid that enlisted to serve his country but rather an alcoholic drug addict suffering from "shell shock" as they called it back then. He was forever getting busted for drinking & driving and in and out of the VA Hospitals to get clean & sober. We didn't call it DWI or rehab or PTSD back then and guys didn't know that Agent Orange caused cancer yet.

Charlie was a product of the war and the high times of the 60's and yet he was a bona fide hero as he was so into getting back up in the air to save another wounded serviceman. 635 missions and life deep in the Mekong Delta. One of the toughest jobs he had to do was to get in and out of the LZs fast as he could to not get shot down by the bullets flying all around the cabin. This meant he had to keep a rubber mallet with him to hit all the guys trying to hang on to the ship and pulling it down while taking back off. He had to hear the men screaming to get them the hell out of there as some would have to fall back to the ground in hopes of getting rescued on the next chopper. Can you imagine having to bash your own men's hands so the chopper wasn't pulled down and everyone dies in a fiery crash or by the guns of the NVA? There were times that 10-15 men would have to be knocked back down so he could save the wounded and half dead. This is why many guys spent their down time sleeping or getting as high as much as they could because you could seriously die or worse be mangled for life. There was no guarantee of tomorrow so they lived like there was no tomorrow. Nothing really mattered so things took on a bad I don't give a fuck attitude and "I don't give a rats ass about it".

To compensate for the actuality that life could be over in a flash of time, we all tried not to think about it.

This was accomplished by keeping busy and filling our minds with other things like sex and drugs and rock and roll or having that relationship with God and other believers. Some guys said if they hurried up and died at least they got over the suffering and the constant fear of getting captured and getting tortured to death. It seems the worst fear was getting captured as it almost seemed dishonorable. And getting so messed up physically that you wished you could die was a fate worse than death. The choppers blades didn't even stop churning and Charlie was already getting laid in the hooch's in the jungle set up for the men wanting "some quickie poontang". Talk about not practicing safe sex! Charley said he would rather die getting some nookie then being captured and to be stuffed in some bamboo hole in the ground- With so much death & misery around the common attitude was fuck it, let's get high -What is that thing in the Bible about the Epicureans, "they ate, drank and made merry for tomorrow they surely die".

The late 60's was a wild time to be alive with the war and the cultural revolution going on. I had already been somewhat politically active attending some marches, demonstrations and local debates. I had attended the Woodstock festival and would hang out down in Greenwich Village to make the scene. Going to UMASS at Amherst was very cool and the liberal curriculum stressed anti-war. They did have an ROTC program that the peace-nicks were already demonstrating against. Everything changed when I got my draft notice. I remember a big song at the time was about leaving on a jet plane and not coming back again and 58,000 didn't come back so suddenly I was forced to take some things very seriously. In the service it was the old slogan of "Kill or be Killed" and the most absurd slogan was "Kill for Peace". On the college campuses it was "All we are saying is give peace a chance," but the Democratic National Convention showed how split we were. I figured it was better to enlist in the Air Force for 4 years and get some decent training then go in the Army and crawl around on my belly in the jungle for 2 years.

My original technical training was in aircraft refrigeration & air conditioning which I thought was a good one because I could work at any airport in the world after active duty. About 2 months into the tech school, they come and tell me that there was a mistake with my records and I am actually too colorblind to work with all the color combinations needed for all the wiring. I actually lucked out by getting my new orders for Air Cargo Loadmaster School, an important job. The Air Force had their "up and away into the wild blue yonder" pride and most airmen loved planes & flying. The sad reality is that 90 % of air personnel are ground support services as only pilots, navigators, bombardiers, crew chiefs (head mechanic) and Loadmasters actually had flight status. I lucked out with my new training which was to learn the whole aspect of moving cargo all over the world. If I had to get Lt. John Jackson and his personal affects home from South Vietnam to his mom & dad in Cape Elisabeth, Maine, I had to make the right connections on the right planes. We learned how to make the daily manifest reports so we knew all the cargo that was supposed to be shipped. The new C- 5A cargo plane was just short of a football field and a wing span just as wide, the entire first flight of the Wright brothers could have flown inside its cargo bay! One cool maneuver was getting to jettison whole pallets right out the bays door as they parachuted safely to their landing zone. It could be a jeep, food & supplies or weapons & ammo, or it could be of the living being variety when we send out paratroopers. This is part of the reason why we got involved with the shipping of undocumented cargo as well. Everybody we came in contact with would ask about a certain planes ETA because they all would be waiting for something, whether it was cookies from home or contraband from the wild blue yonder. And with the sex, drugs and rock and roll of the times it made the whole smuggling thing that much more exciting!

We had it made as we got to fly all over the place, sometimes on our days off duty we could hop a flight to any air base. My favorite hop was up to Norton AFB near Seattle as we knew a lot of guys to party with up there under the patient eye of Mt Rainer and the Puget Sound. Mt Rainier was absolutely incredible as it stood out 15,000 ft all by itself. When I first saw it, I thought the snowcap was a cloud. As beautiful as the Rockies in Colorado are, the high peaks are viewed from a mile up already (Denver is the Mile-High City). Some fellow airman had a cabin up in the San Juan Islands up on the Puget Sound that we would have a blast at. We could howl at the moon, go out for moonlight cruises or just sit around big bonfires on the beach and get high as kites. We were young and restless and we were searching for all life had to offer.

We were inspired by the music, the books and the notion that we could change the world. It was a revolution that gave us this feeling that we could open up our minds and raise our consciousness. A lot of us still believed that all good thoughts came from God and I believed in Jesus Christ as that pathway. A lot of people were looking at eastern religions and even the Beatles were tripping with the gurus up in the Himalayas. We were all passing around books like "The Doors of Perception" by Huxley, "Siddhartha" by Hesse, "Don

Juan, a Yaqui Way of Knowledge" by Castaneda, "On the Road" by Kerouac, "The Prophet" by Gibran and of course the Bible by God himself. But as much as we liked to explore the existence of the spirit, sometimes we were way too high to make any real sense, but we were legends in our own minds. We got a buzz on beer or wine, stoned out on marijuana & hash, then there was opium and pills like THC and uppers and speed so you could stay up all night talking a mile a minute!

But the ultimate head trip was the hallucinogens & psychedelics like peyote, mescaline and the ultimate trip of lysergic diethylamide (LSD!). Two Harvard Psychiatrists heading the psychology department, Timothy Leary & Dick Albert did the research and became self-advocates for the "turn on & drop out" philosophy of the LSD trip and expanding your mind & perception. Once again, the Beatles sang to us about this high life in songs like "Lucy in the Sky with Diamonds", (LSD), and acid rock and psychedelic music and art was the rage. Music like the Moody Blues were the ultimate head music that somehow came on late at night to hopefully soothe the soul and inspire the spirit. All this was part of the experience that was sublime to the craziness of the partying as a lot of us drank, puffed, snorted, and dropped all sorts of combinations looking for some kind of nirvana. What the hell, the Indians took peyote and mushrooms and cut their thumbs off to commune with their spirit guides! We stayed away from the narcotics and needles as the heroin junkies were in their own class of dopers and could be seen nodding out or slurring their speech or falling down. The guys doing the downs for pain or for the rush seemed to get hooked on such a physical addiction very quickly and then the most efficient way to get off was to shoot up with a needle and a spoon, so it scared the bejesus out of me. My group of knuckleheads usually stayed away from it, we had trouble enough functioning as it was. For some unwritten reason it was better to jump out of a plane high on LSD then to be fucked up on smack as we felt it was better to freak out then nod out and not open your shoot. I guess you could say we were nuts but we weren't as FUBAR as the junkies.

Chapter Two

TONY AND THE TWINS

I am a GI- Government Issued
(I don't work for the Mafia)

CALIFORNIA

The Endless Summer

Tony was my best bud all the way through Loadmaster Tech School and then on to our first assignment. The Air Force had our training figured out to be able to work together on the same details and on the same planes to be able to cover special cargo and stuff that needed security clearances. Sheppard AFB was in Wichita Falls, TX on the Oklahoma border. This was the southern region of the tornado belt as a few years earlier the whole town was practically leveled by a string of twisters. We had to watch all these made for the Army documentaries about the threat of natural disasters and the threat of war on our own soil. We lost as much to drinking & driving and speeding as we did on the front lines so we had to continue with the driver safety courses at every new assignment. And my roommate was in constant auto safety class. He was always in trouble with the MPs for speeding. The fact that he had a '67 Corvette Stingray roadster with a 427/440 hp engine with full power options, black with red leather interior, didn't help. He was pulled over as much so everyone could get him to pop the hood and show some chrome, but I think they had to draw the line at 100 mph - on the base! Tony was so cool that he would let me borrow it all the time. I could get rubber in third gear at 75 mph and with the top down at night I felt like I was flying on my back 4 inches off the road. We thought nothing of going up to 140-150 on the open roads. But that was Tony, he had a Donzi speedboat with big Mercury cruisers on the back so we just had the need for speed! He worked for his father since he was a kid so he was able to have good toys and the good thing for me was his generosity as we shared everything we had, and Tony seemed to have it all.

My first trip back home to NY was to Ft Dix/ McGuire AFB in South Jersey. We had to first go to Atlantic City to see Tony's father and all the work building casinos on the new board walk. It was an incredible project and the Italians sure knew how to work with concrete. The whole city was being rebuilt as a renaissance of sorts. It seemed like Angelo Costa's only son was going to be in pretty good shape after he met his military obligations in a few more years. The irony was that Tony was getting the best training in smuggling that the Loadmaster job had to offer and I worked right next to him. I got along with his whole family and his two younger twin sisters were Siciliano hotties in which I didn't dare get caught even looking at; they had a lot of uncles & cousins. I was just meeting the family so I didn't want to get caught drooling over Tony & Anne Marie so soon. Tony was named after her mother, Antonetta so they called her Tony or Tina. The family was named Angelo, Antonetta, Anthony, Anna Maria and Antonetta-del (little or young). The family dynamics was so warm and passionate and it didn't hurt that I was mostly Italian.

Since my mother's maiden name was Rosmunda Immaculata Norelli, my father could have been Khrushchev and I'd still be Italian. As a matter of fact, after my mother got out of the Korean conflict and had me, she did private duty as a nurse at the home of the Castellano family when their son was gunned down on the street. His name was Paul and he did live but needed full medical attention. Because my mother was a young pure Italian that spoke the language and went to mass and was an army nurse, she was offered a lot of money to stay on as a permanent nurse for the family. They probably knew they would need her as there was a turf war going on with the families all over NY & NJ and as far away as Nevada and Sicily. The knew it would be good to have a nurse that was proficient in gunshot wounds. On her last detail she was sent to Hawaii where she met Gen Douglas Mc Arthur in the officer's mess hall and he told her she had beautiful eyes and looked like Elizabeth Taylor. I don't think anything became of it as she met my father after the war, but I was named Douglas a few years later! I hoped it wouldn't go bad for my relationship with the Costa family in this day and time. I didn't want to get labeled as some kind of military narc or straight shooter that couldn't be trusted. So far everything was going well. I was their son's good friend and we worked together and had it made in the shade.

Everything in the Air Cargo Loadmaster job was not what it seemed to be; deception ruled. The flight line was shipping tons of cargo all day and night and even the Air Force was using deceptive tactics to hide many different types of cargo. Since we had a top-secret clearance and a license to smuggle so to speak, we would joke about being somewhere between James

Bond and Maxwell Smart. We could fly anywhere the planes could go and places like Hawaii, the Philippines, Saigon, Bangkok and Japan were all part of the routes. Our big cargo planes were always filled with everything that you could imagine and a lot of things were unbelievable and we were flying under the radar. I mentioned shipping a two- man sub disguised as a big refrigerator, and all sorts of military hardware was disguised so it wasn't recorded. What we didn't handle the Navy did. We set up entire military bases right down to toilet seats and the MASH units were makeshift hospitals. The number of barrels we shipped back & forth were staggering, some were medical supplies and others contained Napalm. There must still be thousands of striped 55- gallon barrels all over Southeast Asia along with tons of other rusted twisted metal by -products left behind from the war, and war has been going on here for centuries. In Vietnam we still saw rusted out machinery left by the French from 20 years ago.

The reason we enlisted in the Air Force for 4 years rather than be drafted in the Army for 2 years was simply due to the fact that the Army & Marines were the "Grunts" that were trained to crawl around on their bellies and fight in the jungle. They were the real heroes that sacrificed their lives everyday fighting for our freedom. Working around the big cargo planes gave us the protection because we were on the bigger bases and pretty far from the actual war zone up north and closer to the DMZ. Our assignment to work on the larger planes kept us from having to go further in country as they needed the larger air strips to land these big suckers. Some Loadmasters were assigned to planes and choppers that went deep into the jungle and towns & villages up north. Down south in Saigon was another center of death and misery that was out of control. They say that hell is the absence of reason and this war was total chaos because, let's face it, all war is insane and we were even killing our own troops in "friendly fire". That was one of those oxymorons that is totally without reason like, "KILL FOR PEACE" or "CIVIL WAR", there is nothing civil about war.

My time and duties during the Vietnam war was very different then my friend Charlie who had over 600 missions in a helicopter that the life expectancy was about a month and all that he wanted was to be in the air and rescue our troops. He also was the gunner on a M-80 machine gun and had to kill or be killed to protect his ship. I did my job and although it wasn't as glorious as some it was still an important part of the military operations. Charlie somehow survived and was a hero that suffered for years from all he had seen and been through. He took hundreds of photos from the air and showed an incredible firsthand account of the wild, crazy, tragic and glorious time he spent in Vietnam, and it sucks that he was never the same from all he went through. Going for those PC s and drinking and getting high is his way of trying to cope with all the death and destruction that he had seen and the other horrors of war. That is why he jumped into any makeshift brothel in the bush as he figured he might as well die with his boots on high as a kite. He was so gun-ho as a young man that he enlisted in the Army for 4 years so he could defend our country and fight for our freedoms. I think Charles John Bonham loved being a soldier and he certainly liked being up in the air in his Huey attack & rescue air Calvary helicopter. He left 6 years later a long-haired bearded hippie with an alcohol & drug problem that put him in and out of the VA hospitals. What Tony Costa and I did was on a totally different level and function. We were responsible to move things around to support and supply the troops. Without the shipments of food, medical supplies, fuel and ammunition the war would be over in a few days. The final days of the war with Hitler's Germany was accomplished when we shut down their supplies during the battle of the Bulge as they simply ran out of gas.

I never had to fire my weapon at anybody but I was still very much involved in the war. We took most of our duties very seriously but like most of our comrades, we lived life on the edge. Can you imagine being up in a C-5A cargo plane equal to the huge 747 Jumbo jets high on LSD and having the time of your life?? There were many experiences going on in our young minds as we were thrust in to this war and still searching for our own existence. We were searching for God and the way to find some sort of harmony despite the fact that we were locked into the process of destroying other human beings and their cultures. So, we did our thing, we also had a lot of things going on. We did our best to live and experience the life of being a soldier in these insane times. Tony would someday get back to his father's business in Atlantic City and I would continue my search for my place in this world. But for now, we felt on top of this world at only 18 years old and being able to do whatever we wanted. The service did train us to have a certain order in all our procedures as we did everything in rank & file. We were just supposed to follow our orders and there was a natural order in the platoons, companies and battalions that we were assigned to. In being a part of this order, we trained and drilled so that we would know how to do what we do as a habit. We were told that it takes about a month of training to get or break a behavior. We believed that our soldiers were the best trained outfits in the world. This is why all the different outfits had their own honor & glory and a lot of pride. Because of that training the "Fighting CB's" would stand up to the "Air Calvary" on Saturday night at the local saloon. So, when the going got tough the tuff got going. Army life was a stabilizing force in an insane world.

With all the order and protocol we had, we then had the freedom of being out on our own to do our jobs. The officers in charge were the pilots and co-pilots that flew the planes. They were the best pilots in the world, the Navy, Air Force & Marines fighter pilots were just awesome in their abilities and training. There was so much trust and confidence that they displayed that made us believe we were the force to be reckoned with. The Russian Migs were big powerful jets but the edge went to our pilots training and their abilities to take chances and fly outside the nine dots. So, we just did our jobs with good teamwork and then we could enjoy the ride. The lifestyle of the late 60s was tumultuous as we had the war on one hand and the so-called Cultural Revolution on the other. It was so common to see a heavy hitting soldier with a big peace sign on his helmet and the picture of the flower hanging out of the barrel of an M-16 was a sign of the times.

The big common denominator of all the baby boomers was “sex & drugs and rock & roll!!” The lure of smuggling was the counter cultures answer to supply & demand and we not only made a lot of tax-free money but got to sample the goods. Every transaction was made by the ritual of smoking a joint, having a snort or dropping a tab. Quality was always sought after and promises of this particular sample was always of Primo Grade, it was good shit!! In the beginning we had enough product just in what turned up in flight line and in the hangers. A lot of cargo would just go unclaimed or untagged and we would throw it in the dead-end holding area. It could be drugs, electronics & cameras, gold or silver, watches & jewelry or anything of value that was desired and could be turned to a profit. It wasn’t uncommon to find a bale of marijuana or a package of cocaine that we could stash to sell later. That is why powders and pills were smaller and easier to conceal. With the raw tonnage we shipped 24/7 there was no way for the authorities to control it. Every once in a while, the Department of State agents would come by on a tip but we knew they were just going through the motions to make it like look like they had a grip on the war on drugs, which they didn’t. The supply sergeants were the guys that would hook you up on the bases but it was the Loadmasters that moved it all over the world.

Our country's drug habit was so huge that not only did we have hundreds of planes and ships coming in every day in bases and ports all over the west coast but we had many other smuggling routes from South America, Europe and places like Afghanistan. A good buddy of mine bought a fishing boat in Tampa-St Pete when he got out of the service. He bought a 65' Criss-Craft and got his Captains license so he could charter fishing trips and do commercial fishing on the Gulf. Places such as Tijuana Mexico and Key West Florida were big smuggling ports as well as New York and Miami. My friend found it easier to just buy the fish from the Mexican fisherman and double the price back at the Miami docks. It wasn't long until he got into the really profitable import business of drug smuggling. He took his boat out in the drop off spots in the Gulf and picked up the shipments of marijuana and cocaine from the small planes coming from Columbia and Mexico. All he had to do is fish it out of the water and deliver it to the guys waiting at the docks. This was such a big operation that they had men at NASA using satellite maps of the area so they knew where the Coast Guard cutters were so they had a safe spot to make the pickups. One time they came upon someone else's stash and loaded up the boat so that it started listing to the right. My ingenious friend went into the water and repainted the water line so the boat looked better in the water. But it was so loaded down that he could barely get the load in. When the Coast Guard came in the area, he decided to strike first by radioing in a destress signal and he got the Coast Guard to tow his boat in with a ton of drugs in the hole!! More on my friends story later on. We would hook up with him and party with him. He was a real character and a party animal.

Another friend from Northport High was my friend Buzz who was a shipping manager of a large import -export company out of the port of Miami. He would ship those large shipping containers that could go from ship to rail from points south in the Caribbean and South America. They would export down manufacturing goods and import fruits and vegetables. He too would have bales of Colombian pot and cocaine in amongst the containers of bananas. If we were ever someplace that we needed something to party with say at a hotel in Vegas or a beach resort in Hawaii all we had to do was call Buzz and it would be delivered under our hotel room door in the morning! That is what good friends were for and you needed people you could trust. My connections seemed light weight compared to Tony Costas connections with his family, and he had a big family. His ties were in New York-New Jersey, Miami and Las Vegas and the whole state of Nevada as they seemed to own all the casinos and whore houses everywhere!! Tony was just a kid my age but he was connected so we were really in the thick of a lot of illegal activities. I never really saw anything illegal; his family was much too smart and slick for that. I did meet a lot of well-dressed guys with pinkie rings in stretch limos that would take Tony out to dinner or bring him to their homes for meatballs and cannoli's. When Tony's sisters would show up to party with us it was an added treat, they were so young and hot. They were turning 18 soon and they were off to college and they sure looked good in Daddy's red Mercedes 450 convertible. I think a little something was starting to spark with Tony. We gave each other the little flirting signs of interest, and her sister was pretty sweet too. Did I mention that they were identical twins? Tony had some connection to a casino in Lake Tahoe that was about a 2-hour drive away and we could make it in 90 minutes in the Vette. We were comped in a big suite and I was hoping to spend time with Tony then but the problem was that the twins were inseparable?! I might have to woo both of them!! Our home base was an hour away from San Francisco and two hours from Lake Tahoe and the Nevada casinos so we could go in either direction and go to the ocean, the mountains or the city on our pass days. Northern California was a blast as there was so much going on and "The Beach Boys" were always singing about those California girls!

San Francisco was definitely the heart of the "sex and drugs and rock & roll" scene as the hippie culture was still centered in Haight Ashbury and places like the Fillmore West and North Beach were the center of the psychedelic rock music. Groups like the Grateful Dead, Jefferson Airplane and Big Brother & the Holding Company were all hanging out and playing regularly. Being from New York made San Francisco just as special, both cities have a lot in common and were the center of the cultural revolution, if there really was such a thing?! New York had the Hamptons, Fire Island and the Jersey shore but the California beaches and bays stretched for a thousand miles and we had the Big Sur just 2 hours away. We spent many good weekends partying in the city or gathered around a big bonfire on the beach singing and dancing in the moonlight.

So many times, we swore that we would stay back in the barracks and get a good night's sleep only to be lured out by the promise of a great time with a bunch of party animals. Some work nights we were able to get some shut eye by stacking up the empty transfer cases and sleeping on them. They also made good desks or tables but like I said, some guys were creeped out by them since they were like coffins. A lot of times we were awake all day and night and had to take some speed or diet pills to get through. A lot of guys liked to take an upper along with some pot to get that balance so to speak!?! So many guys did "recreational drugs" or they "partied" as we called it, you were either a "head" or you were "square" and it seemed the heads outnumbered the squares 2-1!?

One thing to mention is that we were only an hour away from Oakland and the headquarters of the Black Panthers. Black Panthers were always on the base recruiting new members and preaching about their revolution. The race card was always being played as the white boys and the black boys still didn't play together and the Spanish guys usually had their own section in the big mess halls as well. The Watts, Detroit and Newark riots were only a few years ago and the country was still divided, me being a hippie of sorts tried to embrace all people but it wasn't easy. Hate and prejudice still loomed everywhere and just because we listened to the Temptations and or Sly & the Family Stone didn't mean we were embracing our brothers- We did hang out with some cool black dudes that liked to party, that was a common denominator for all of us. I had gone to an all-white high school back in Northport NY, not until the service, did I hang out with people of different colors. No matter how I felt, in these large mess halls we all sat with our own people. That's just the way it was.

We had a small seaside hotel that we use to stay at down the California coast in the Big Sur in the town of Avila Beach. It was a sleepy little town with fantastic sunsets looking over the bay and the big blue Pacific. At night we could hear the seals and the sea lions as they barked at the moon and the stars. We would rent the entire 3 story hotel and the beach for the weekend and the owners were these older hippie couple that became like family. They just loved us and our good Acapulco Gold and Lebanese Hashish that we would give them for our ongoing bill. Guys would come down there to hang out and relax and then sometimes we would get wild. We would have these bonfires on the beach and we would keep the fire going all night. Most of us slept on the beach until the sun woke us up and we went back to sleep in our rooms. We had guitars, bongos and harmonicas and we surfed and played volleyball and got very high all day and night. We made these special fire pits and cooked lobsters, scallops and crabs. We washed it all down with a good local wine and pitchers of Pina coladas and Strawberry Daiquiris. These parties were some of the best times of our lives. We all split the cost for the weekend by about 20 guys and Tony usually had some extras treats like, fireworks, a sailboat or a wave runner to play with. We had a lot of toys in a beach shack with a huge cooler filled with beer and snacks. We had scuba gear, surf and boogie boards and hammocks and floats to lounge in. The cool thing was that we had the little hotel and beach all to ourselves. No one hassled us, and the town had a few restaurants and bars. We really did try to be polite and we paid in cash and tipped well. The couple that owned the Sunset Hotel was Bob and Madge and they were great folks that treated all of us like the kids they never had. It was a perfect relationship.

Heck, we were the United States Air Force and we were on an R & R on a beautiful California beach and we didn't have a care in the world. There would be plenty of time to fret and worry about things later on. Being in the Air Force is what we were supposed to be doing, for now. And the girls were almost as wild, it was the late 60's in the days of "FREE LOVE". There weren't any STDs that penicillin wouldn't cure and we never did catch anything anyway, thank God. Our rule was that we could love these young ladies but we couldn't fall in love with them because we shouldn't get tied down, there was plenty of fish in the sea. And besides, we were too damn young. We had bases and ports all over the Pacific theater and the good old USA.

But things did not all work that way as guys would get all serious. They were lonely and missing their homes and families. Even our Company Commander would try to discourage guys from getting hitched and we had to watch these training films about sexual transmitted diseases, drugs and dating the locals. Some of us were still just 18 and we shouldn't be needing to get married so young. We had plenty of time to grow up and settle down as we just got to vote, fight and kill the yellow people and in most states, we couldn't even drink yet.

The general idea was to go through the service or college or both before settling down and we still had to start a career and put some money together. The more technical life becomes the more is it required to get training, schooling and job experience. Back a hundred years ago in farming and an agricultural society the kids married and worked in the family business and started their families by the time they were 20. This is what we see in all the "Third World" countries where families live and work together. In our technological society the young people need to go for continued education and training. Now kids will go through graduate schools and still live home into their late 20s and woman put off having children into the mid-thirties. But the pressure to grow up and settle down is always a part of this thing we call life; we are to conform to the way “they” say it should be. But we wanted to break that mold and push the outer edge of the envelope and experience life in all its manifestations. I was being called to something magical and I knew there was much more to this life then a 9 to 5 job and a house in the suburbs. I wanted to take the road less traveled like in Frost’s poem, and that will make all the difference---

A bunch of us were all out together at a nightclub over at Stockton about 20 miles away from our base. It was a wild place that was popular with the bikers and the “fast” girls. We all rode our bikes over to have some fun and they had a live band and a big dance hall. On a Friday night they probably had over 500 partyers so it was a pretty cool place to hang out. Tony, me and a couple of our buddies met some girls that wanted a cruise on our bikes. The four of us took the girls out for a ride around town. The chick with me was cute and after a few dances she organized for her girlfriends to hook up with us for a ride. It felt good to have her arms around me as we toured Stockton. I drove fast so she had to hold me tight. The girls told us about a good place that was a rest stop to get high at. So, we went maybe 10 miles away. We pulled into the overlook and there was a few cars and bikes parked, probably all getting high or couples making out.

We jumped off our bikes and sat together to look over the valley and we lit a joint to pass around. Just as we were enjoying the scene another group of bikers pulled up, maybe 8 guys. All of a sudden one of the guys started yelling that one of the girls was his old lady. We shrugged it off but this big drunk biker wanted to make a thing of it. The girl said that Snake didn't own her and she didn't have to listen to him. We started to realize that this wasn't going to go well and we were outnumbered two to one. Snake and his buddies were big, ugly, greasy guys. The one girl wasn't going to let it go and she was screaming and carrying on. She was riding with Tony so big Snake tackled him and knocked down his bike. Just like that, shit hit the fan and we were in a free for all. A big knucklehead jumped on my back. He had a chain on his wallet that he took off and started swinging at me. I gave him a kick to his gut and pushed him backwards but him and another guy came back at me. The other guy had brass knuckles and I tried my best to fight back but we were out- numbered and over matched. They pulled out chains and I was able to take a helmet and bash two guys but then I was overcome. I was on the ground and we were getting kicked and hit so we had to cover up and take a beating. The cops pulled in and dispersed the crowd and we had to go to the local hospital to get stitched up and treated. The girls split and we had to get back to the base and report to the Company Commander. We found out later that Snake and his boys were part of a local gang called the Outlaws. The cops wanted us to press charges but we told them we were all GI's from Travis and we were shipping out soon. Next time we all went out together we went up in the opposite direction to Sacramento.

Every weekend we had something planned. We made enough money selling whatever we received in our little side shipping business and we had fast cars and bikes to get us there. If it wasn't on the coast or in San Francisco it was over at Lake Tahoe. Northern California and the wild state of Nevada had so much going on. If we wanted to go further away, we could hop one of our cargo planes and we would even get a box lunch. Any air base that was on the routes that we flew to in the states was available for a hop. As long as there were seats, all we had to do was sign up and be on time. We could make connections to more than one base and plan a round trip itinerary. Since we worked with all the flight logs, we could take advantage of traveling throughout America, and even Hawaii & Alaska. Because of our flight status and the opportunity to grab hops all over the country we were just the luckiest guys in the service. All the planes were exciting and since our planes were well protected, so were we. It was very cool to lay back in the net chair floating in space and high in the sky.

Back in the states we were planning a weekend party at the Lake Tahoe Golden Casino. Tony was having a party for his twin sisters 18th birthday and people were coming from as far away as New Jersey. We had around 30 guest all staying at the hotel and it was going to be a wild time. By Saturday night we were all dancing and partying and things were heating up for me and the twins. After midnight I was handed a note from one of the birthday girls, Tony, telling me to meet her up in her suite in an hour. This girl had it all going as she was sexy, smart & rich and now technically an adult in most states!! I slipped away to shower and get dressed excited to see how this was going to play out. The crazy thing was that when I got up to her room both sisters were there and I didn't know what was going to go down. We drank some shots of Sambuca and did some lines of coke and they told me that since it was their birthdays, they were ready to lose their virginity!!?! The music was loud and I had to ask them if I was really hearing this right? They smiled and said that I heard them right. They had planned this for a while and they thought I would be the right guy. That's when I knew that there was a God and he loves me and wants me to be happy!! We sat together on the couch and I was trying like mad to take my time. I never was in a ménage e trois before and this was some kind of a dream come true. The girls were purring like kittens and they were ready, willing and able and we were caressing each other and holding each other tight. After about an hour of kissing, caressing and exploring it was getting time to go in the bedroom. The girls thought it would be good to get in the hot tub. Who was I to resist, so I opened some champagne, rolled a doobie and the twins filled the tub and lit some candles?

Just as we were in the warm bubbly tub and all turned on for a fabulous encounter the pounding on the door shattered our dreams. It was Tony yelling that the narcs were here and they were trying to shut us all down. I breathed a sigh of relief that it wasn't about this secret tryst taking place and we were just being hassled by the Man. But we had to stop and get dressed, the ATF guys were making their rounds. Tony's family owned the joint and took care of this as, apparently, they just had to donate to the agents on hand. But it was almost morning by the time everything cooled down and this magnificent night would have to be put on hold - we slept late on Sunday and we all had to leave by the evening so I hoped that this opportunity would be rescheduled soon. This really was like a dream that most of us guys fantasize about and the twins were so cool and beautiful making me one lucky guy.

I didn't get to see the twins until we went back to AC for a funeral. Tony asked me to take a 3-day pass to go with him. They found his favorite cousin in a dumpster with a bullet in his head and his tongue cut off and given a necktie. He was supposedly stealing money from the Atlantic City casino to support his $500 a day habit and after many warnings his luck ran out. Tony was devastated, they were like brothers but Tony said no one could tell him anything, he was a train wreck and didn't want to listen. The guy was so drugged out that he lost his cool and ran up tabs and owed the drug dealers and his family. He even started stealing from his own people and that sealed his fate. That is what made Tony so cool as he had his wits about him and although he liked to party like the rest of us, he was always in control. We spent the time at the Costa family home which was a beautiful mansion on the ocean beach with all the trimmings, including the twins down the hall. No way were we going to continue our budding romance in the family home but we did get to hang out on the beach one evening and have some sweet time around the fire.

When we got back from our pass, we had to ship out to Norton AFB up in Washington to escort some

Marine Major, or what was left of him, back to his mother in Wisconsin. The guy was 36 with 3 kids and his chopper was shot down as he was rescuing some marines pinned down in a shit storm. He was a highly decorated Purple Heart recipient with over a thousand missions with 3 tours of duty. He was on his way to making Colonel or even General, if he lived. We were required to stay for the funeral and then we get the news that a carload of our guy's buddies was on the way up to his funeral when they got hit by a drunk driver. We learned early that life is never fair and you just never know how it's going to go. We got 4 of his fellow pilots who survived years of fire fights and were trained to fly their helicopters through hell and back and now 2 of them are dead from a drunk driver going the wrong way on a divided highway. Life just isn't fair -The driver training films we had to watch at every new assignment showed that more GIs were dying on the roads than in actual combat.

Life is not fair and it isn't very predictable as situations change with the wind, we just never know how things will go down. I think that is why life in the military appeals to certain individuals. There is a certain stability to the routine of everyday life in the service as you have a rank and file in the way everything follows in its own guide lines. Everyone knows their position and their place; you followed your orders and you operated within your assigned responsibilities. But life can still throw you many curve balls and change ups. My longtime friend from high school was living out his dream of having his boat and living off the water. He got bitten by the lure of the fast money and the high life of smuggling and making the big deals. He started by fishing the Gulf of Mexico but soon saw it was cheaper and easier just to buy the fish from the Mexicans. Then he got involved with a big-time operation. He would make 10- grand in one day for picking up a shipment in the Gulf and bringing it to the Tampa docks. The fact that he carried a Barretta & a shotgun was just for precautionary measures and didn't bother the crew, it was really just for show, wasn't it?? Everything was going pretty good for him and as soon as he finished paying off the boat, he was putting down the deposit on that house on the bay. Since he was a good husband and father, he couldn't say no when his family asked him to take in his 15-year-old nephew who was getting into trouble back on Long Island. He enrolled him in school and got him a part time job down at the boatyard. The kid was doing okay and Flash was doing a couple of runs a month and taking out fishing charters on the weekends. One day Flash had a couple of keys of coke in the trunk of his Caddie to deliver after dinner. The thing he didn't know was his stupid nephew had made a key for his baby blue Coupe de Ville and stole the car that night to go joy riding. Unbeknownst to the kid was that there was 40 grand of Columbian pink cocaine in the trunk!! The fool got drunk and ran the car off the road into a swamp and left it there. The local Clearwater police had it towed out and busted Flash for possession and sales and he got 15 years as drug smugglers got more time than many homicides. Another bummer for Flash was that he wasn't working for the local Boy Scouts and even though he was going to do hard time in a Florida jail he still had to pay back the 50 -K as they would probably kill him in prison if he didn't. He did 7 years and got off for good behavior but lost his wife and family and his boat and his dreams.

One day I was breaking down a pallet so I could ship some of its cargo to another base. When cargo comes in from overseas, we then have to re-ship the contents to the next base until it gets to its destination. As I was looking for a package, I came upon a box with no name or address so I knew it had to be something interesting. I brought it to the holding room and opened it up. It was 40 lbs. of Columbian cocaine probably worth 50 grand, street value over a hundred thousand. I gave it to Tony as it was way too much for me to sell. He made some phone calls and a few days later we split 25 thousand dollars. By now we had one of Tony's dads' accountants investing for us so an E-4 Airman making $300 a month could hide some serious doe re me. I figured it was time to buy my dream car so I put a down payment on a brand new 1969 Corvette Roadster with a hard top and a rag top. It was equipped with a 427 / 420 hp engine with a tri-powered carburetor and it was fully loaded, black leather, mahogany steering wheel, side pipes and fiber optics lighting. Black on black. Top speed 165+. Northern California and Nevada roads were calling my name- I had a rich grandfather so I told everyone I had gotten some trust money!? Being a two-seat sports car, I figured I could still fit both of the twins in the passenger seat as they probably only weighed about 115 pounds each. It was going to be a great summer in a place where summer never ends. Shifting gears with two girls sitting next to me was great fun.

Our next weekend party was a blowout over at Yosemite National Park in this outrageous hotel overlooking Half Dome Mountain. We invited the usual suspects and I flew in the twins and Tony flew in one of his main squeezes. We had a penthouse all set up and we were going to try some hiking and fishing on Saturday & Sunday. I could hardly wait till Friday night to resurrect the ménage e trois in the hot tub that was so rudely interrupted by the DEA in Lake Tahoe. After eating and dancing to a great house band we ramped it up with some good pot and some mescaline and everyone got pretty stoned and a little trippy from the mescaline. The twins looked even more beautiful in my altered state and the room was spinning as we danced to some Van Morrison, the Young Rascals and Vanilla Fudge. We were all so high and loose so nobody seemed to react that I was slow dancing with both girls - It was a magical night and we were staying in the old Majestic Hotel. Tony brought his girlfriend to our hot tub so I had to cool it for a while. He had sort of given me his blessings but I don't think group sex was going down with all three siblings involved. But under the bubbles I wasn't quite sure who was touching who? I was pretty sure Tony's girl had her foot between my legs but we were all too high to care at that point. We all ended up sleeping in the living room with the panoramic view of the mountains & the Yosemite Valley out the windows.

We slept late and after a good brunch we all headed out for a hike up the spectacular trails looking up at the famous El Capitan & Half dome Mountains. We stopped for a rest on an overview and some joker foolishly yelled out "Look out, rattlesnake!!" Well some of the girls screamed and one of our buddies stumbled backwards and fell off the cliff. He fell about 20 feet and landed on a small tree growing out of the rock below. If he had not landed there, he would have fallen a thousand feet to his death below. He was hanging on for his life, and worse yet, he had a huge rattlesnake curled up next to him. We had to move fast so Tony let down some rope and started to repel down to the ledge. When he got close enough, he took out one of our guys handguns and blew the snake right off the ledge. We had to have the Park Rangers call for a med evac to rescue our friend. He was messed up as a sharp branch impaled his right side, which is how he was able to hang on until they rushed him to the hospital. We stayed with him until after surgery and he finally fell off to sleep very baked out on the morphine that he was given.

We then got back to the party, the evening activities were getting under way and it was a beautiful night. After dinner and a little music, I took the twins out for ride up to an overlook called "Lovers Leap" and we put a blanket down and looked up at the moon and stars. I brought some fruit and Sangria and it wasn't too long that we were feeding each other grapes and mangos and drinking the wine off of each other!! Soon we were all tangled up together and we were all making love to each other. The girls were amazing and so damn willing. Good thing I had stashed a few lines to help us get even hotter so I could take my time with these young flowers. We went back to our suite and pretty much spent the rest of the night locked in a three-way embrace. We didn't leave the suite all day on Sunday as we ordered-room service and we all held on to each other until it was time to leave that night. I could hardly believe this was happening, the twins were amazing and we were zooming down some wild roller coaster ride as we broke all the boundaries. I was only out of high school for two years and I had no idea that I would be living this kind of high life and traveling all over the world. I was still learning about the art of love so I was just getting started and I had much to learn. Now I have this crazy romance going on with identical twins that should be against the law yet it drew us together like a magnet. It was good that we lived on opposite sides of the country yet I was going to places beyond my wildest dreams and fantasies. We said our goodbyes to Yosemite and we all had to get back to the base. It wasn't easy to drive the twins to the airport as we were all joined at the hip for the weekend but we will make plans to be together soon. Tony and some of the guys got back to Yosemite and we did some trout fishing and had a blast. We caught some big Rainbows right under a waterfall that was just incredible.

It was good to wear our uniforms when we would go out to certain places, especially to dances, casinos and parties where other servicemen were present. Maybe because we were serving our country during the war, we were treated a little special and we would get a lot of free drinks, introduced to a lot of young ladies and get comped at hotels & casinos. Some women really do like guys in uniform. The bad thing is that a lot of the local boys didn't like us being around. They thought us to be rude and we were invading their bars, their woman and their action. They were always challenging us to some local contest or tests of strength or they just wanted to fight on a Saturday night! I didn't look for trouble, some GIs just liked to fight. A truck full of local-yokes driving around with gun racks looking for a fight was somewhat intimidating and you were always outnumbered. When 4 Yahoos jump out of a truck looking for 3 servicemen to harass, it's fight or get beat up, there wasn't many choices. One rule to these stupid fights was that you had to strike fast and get it over quickly because if you were too cautious and held back you were going to get your ass handed to you. If you tried to pussy foot around and fight like you were duking it out with your sleeves rolled up you are giving it all away to chance. We learned to punch and kick with everything you got cause most guys run out of steam quickly and you didn't want to give them enough time to grab a weapon. A good swift kick to the balls and a couple of uppercuts should knock them down, it is very difficult to fight back when you are doubled up with your nuts in your hands and your eyes bulging out.

Here we are out some night looking to have a good time, do some drinking or gambling, maybe do some dancing or shoot some pool and all of a sudden, we have to fight for our lives. We don't know if the guys got a blade or a gun and we had to be careful that they didn't hit us with a beer bottle or a pool stick. That is why we try to take it outside so there was more room to dance. A lot of times they would be fighting over some girl or for losing money on a bet or a game. I didn't look for trouble but it surely found me and my New York accent didn't help as everyone thought that since I am Italian, I must be a gangster. We did learn some self-defense; we weren't the Marines or the Special Forces but we learned basic moves. I got involved with the PAL in junior high and even went to a military school for a year and learned to box and protect myself. After high school I grew to 6'1"/ 180 lbs. and I boxed some tough guys. I took my lumps but managed to not get killed. I lasted a couple of rounds in the NY City Golden Gloves Tournament and continued on the Air Force base team. The greater thing I learned was to be able to diffuse a potential crap shoot so we didn't have to go rogue, the best thing we could do was to be peacekeepers rather than baby killers! Trying to break up fights could be very painful as you were bound to take an elbow to the nose and if you were breaking up a couple, you could have the loving wife on your back trying to gauge out your eyes.

One night we were trying to mingle with the local cowboys and a skirmish broke out back by the dart game. Tony and I got pinned down in the corner and we had to take cover as the jerkoffs were throwing darts at us. Looking like Captain America, Tony picked the round table up like it was his shield and pushed us forward through the crowd. We got almost to the front door when we lost our shield and had to fist fight our way out. Tony was good, we managed to take a few guys down each. Lucky for us a bunch of Marines came in and they helped us kick ass and take names. The MPs came in and since we knew them from our PC patrols, they helped us restore order. Saturday nights out with the guys in these local honky-tonks, there was a lot of testosterone ramping up. With the loud rock & roll on the juke box or a good band playing, boys will be boys and some just wanted to fight.

We were coming out of a bar outside the base one night, when all of a sudden, a black limo pulls up and two prostitutes and their pimp jump out and attack this MP that was walking past us. The pimp was a tall black guy with a red hat and a long fur coat on. The two women looked Russian and they had on their fur coats and tons of jewelry and high heels, the three of them were quite a sight. Apparently, their limo got so close to running over the MP that he had to pound his fists on the hood to get the tire off his foot. Then the pimp draws a switch blade and starts to swing it at the MP and his girls start swinging their pocket books at him. By the time we got close to them, the ladies were on the poor guy's back and it was a real shit show. We knocked them all down and got the GI out of there, we were able get the knife loose before the pimp stuck the MP. The twisted trio was screaming threats and promises but we were on them like a cheap suit. They were assuring us that we didn't know who the fuck we were messing with, we snickered that in truth, they certainly didn't know who the fuck they were messing with!! We made them sit in their car and gave the car keys to the city cops. We had to show up in court for the MP and the three shit heads were still harassing us and even swearing at the judge and the cops. They threw them all back in jail and we had to come back to testify again in 30 days. We got a Letter of Commendation for helping the MP from the city and a plaque from the Military Police so we were glad to help. A few months later a Marine that I was boxing in the ring, caught me with a roundhouse and punctured a piece of my retina, so I had to shut down my pugilistic activities for a while so it would heal.

With a war going on and violence in our cities we lived in turmoil and there was a lot of assassinations and racism. Then we had the Peace Movement and the anti-war protests and demonstrations so we were a divided nation and Vietnam was a very unpopular war. I didn't really know what was a popular war, was it killing the Nazis or the Japanese? As an enlisted man I was caught somewhere between the Hawks and the Doves. I identified myself as a hippie who was a part of the sex and drugs and rock & roll philosophy but I still could not take off my dog tags or just take off to join a commune in Canada. The Mei Lay Incident when Lt. Calle ordered all 280 people in the village to be killed gave a reason for us to be called baby killers. The problem was that the village was hiding Czechoslovakian machine guns and ammunitions but shooting the little children was a horrible war crime. Sgt. Charles Bonham had to make some fucked up decisions in the thick of the fight to ensure his missions safety.

One of the worst realities of military combat was the search and rescue missions that their main objective was to flush out the enemy and then be hung out to die.

Can you imagine the bravery of these soldiers knowing that you probably will be killed or captured as you're being used as the bait??! The men in charge knew that a certain amount of our men will be killed and maimed and that is just the way it is. There was so many fucked up things about the war that seemed to defy any morality or reason. They were killing their own officers because they were so inept that they put the entire unit in danger. Our own officers were getting shot in the back from a kangaroo court out in the bush or by a guy just so messed up that he kills his own soldiers. There were so many of our men so high on drugs that clouded their reasoning & decisions and the guys hooked on heroin were a mess and they couldn't shoot straight if they tried. Most guys waited until they were back in camp to let loose and everybody reacted differently to the different drugs they were doing. Reefer was being smoked like it was cigarettes and getting high helped dealing with the fact that we were in South-East Asia trying to kill these yellow communists.

The psychedelic drugs were in another category all by themselves. The most popular ones were psilocybin (Magic mushrooms), peyote, mescaline & LSD. Lysergic Acid Diethylamide or LSD is a chemical discovered in the 1930s and made famous by guys like Aldus Huxley who wrote "Brave New World" and "The

Doors of Perception ". There were the two Harvard psychology professors, Dr Timothy Leary & Richard Alpert (later known as Ram Dass), that were the vocal leaders of the psychedelic movement. The author Ken Kesey "One Flew Over the Coo-Coos Nest" and leader of the Merry Pranksters (a group of psychedelic trippers traveling the country in a hippie school bus) was the subject of Tom Wolfs book "The Electric Kool-Aid Acid Test".

Rock & Roll groups such as The Beatles, The Stones, Lead Zeppelin, Jefferson Airplane and The Grateful Dead were all a part of the psychedelic experience. The Grateful Dead would have these huge concerts and give away acid trips as part of the show that would last for 4-5 hours. My personal favorite head tripping band was the Moody Blues as their style and sound effects were tailor made for enhancing the experience. Jimmy Hendricks anthem "Are you Experienced?" and "Purple Haze" were classic hallucinating songs. LSD was clear & odorless and easy to smuggle as thousands of "hits" could be held in a small suitcase. Mescaline, peyote & shrooms were also popular hallucinogenic as well, and could all be easily obtained. Peyote, psilocybin and magic mushrooms grew in southern pastures and were a part of Mexican Indian cultures.

I first tried LSD back in high school as all the Heads were trying it, we would also go into the city to the "Village" and concert halls like The Fillmore East (I got to the Fillmore West in San Francisco as well) and The Bitter End and the Academy of Music were around since the beatnik days. Being outside with my friends was the best way to trip as we would ride our 10 speeds, hang out at the beach, go surfing and the best times were watching the sun rise as the colors were far out man. Our senses were highly tuned as hallucinations were very visual & and we seemed to have some sort of connection to spiritual phenomenon. We had a higher consciousness and awareness. A lot our perceptions were altered and it gave us this "all truth" connections to each other or to a butterfly or the thunderous sound of a breaking wave. Square bricks on a building would turn into diamonds, you could see the musical notes as well as hear them. Rock & Roll was absolutely incredible as I tripped all 3 days at Woodstock. Where did all those freaks come from wearing American flags, peace signs and beads? Some of the girls wore long flowery dresses or tight jeans with holes in them and some didn't shave their underarms! I didn't think it looked attractive as I didn't want to be kissing somebody's hairy arm pits. Then I saw that most women in the world didn't shave at all. So, when high on hallucinogens everything looks different so you look at everything in a new light.

The Beatles song "Lucy in the Sky with Diamonds" (LSD) said it well about being high on the hallucinogenic and experiencing visions and mind expansion. In Joni Mitchell 's song Woodstock she sings about getting back to the Garden of Eden. We thought we were going to change the world. Many a morning as the dawn started to bring the nights wild visions into focus, we would be sitting on a cliff or a beach and as the sun appeared on the horizon, we would have tears streaming down our faces. The morning sun shined on our faces and through our hair illuminating a golden aura. We knew there was a God and we felt so connected to our souls and to our spirit. And then there were times that it was absolutely insane and you thought you could hear the trees growing or your dog had extra sensory perception to go along with his footlong whiskers. But you could also be positive that your best buddy was going to kill you as that was a bad trip with bad vibes!! If we were tripping in a bar or at a party, things can get out of hand as people can be a real bummer man. I, fortunately, had many great vibes and I witnessed many great sunrises coming up out of the Atlantic as well as great sunsets out in the Pacific.

Tony and I spent a weekend pass tripping up in the Big Sur and we had to return to work the Sunday night shift. The problem was we had done some very strong and pure LSD - 25 and we were still very high from the night before. The only thing we knew to do was to do some more. Usually we could get through the night by making up some reason to go to a quiet loading dock or a cargo warehouse but this night was special. That particular night the base was expecting the first landing of the biggest plane in the world, the C-5A Galaxy which was the new plane to its cousin the Boeing 747. The Air Force was making a big reception so a lot more brass and big shots were out that night to see the big beast come in for a landing. I knew things were getting weird when a 4 stripe Staff Sargent looked like they had 20 stripes on their arms and the officers looked like Nazi Storm Troopers?!? Guys were talking in foreign languages and in secret codes and spies were listening to us through the intercoms. When we worked on the flight line, we wore headphones to protect our hearing and when a big jet or an F-15 was coming in or taking off we just stopped talking until the blast of the engines subsided. High on drugs amplified all these sounds to a fevered pitch. Just as I was thinking that we were shipping an entire zoo in the back warehouse, or something equally absurd, the C-5A was coming in to its landing pattern. It looked like a spaceship that had about 20 headlights and wings stretched out about a quarter mile long. But as it landed and it put its brakes and drag down the noise was deafening. So much that the reverb actually cracked the wall and guys were holding their ears and grimacing. Well that was enough for me and I dove on the ground looking like some freaked out asshole!! The guys covered for me and said I had some food poisoning as they saw me curled up in the fetal position looking like I was going to deflate or implode. This was after 3 days of pushing my senses to the limit and the biggest plane in the world almost crashing through our flight line?!

There were other times that we got to go up in the air and really fly high in two realities. We gave the mile-high club a whole new meaning-we were in an incredible situation as we were cruising along at 500 mph at 10,000 ft and we were tripping our brains out!! The views were always incredible anyway, that is why we joined the USAF, but now the hallucinations were some seriously insane shit and not for the novice or the weak hearted. The Birds spaced out song "I can see for Miles and Miles" was a big song at the time and we were going through the Doors of Perception -

The twins grew up like they were the jet set and they loved fast cars, boats and bikes and they didn't seem to be afraid of anything. They loved getting high and they loved to trip like the rest of us. They were even more beautiful when their eyes were wide open and they had that look that the whole world was being pealed back like a flower for their inspection. Since the girls were inseparable it almost made sense that they wanted to share my company and I guess that since I was their brothers' best friend, they felt safe with me. The few times I was alone with just one of them was strange as we definitely felt like we were the 3 Musketeers. I never got intimate without both of them. I think they felt that it would be cheating if it wasn't the 3 of us. We so tried to push the outside of the envelope in everything we did so there wasn't a boundary on our intimacy as we explored this wild relationship and lifestyle. Oh, and by the way, trying to make love on LSD was insane, it can happen but there is so many wild sensations and distractions and with 3 of us it is just plain crazy!? These two sisters had such a bond as it was, so the extra sensory revelations we experienced together was electric to say the least! Under the psychedelic influence, at times we believed we could communicate telepathically as that was a part of the hallucinations and twins are born with an innate sense for each other as it was. We were so fascinated with the whole higher consciousness thing as we read and shared all we could on the subject. And these ladies were super smart as they were headed to the University of Florida State, after a year off to travel and explore. They were going to major in marine biology because they loved the ocean, they were competitive surfers and they were scuba diving since they were 13.

Papa Costa was probably going to buy them their own Sea World just so they can play with the dolphins. Lucky for me I was laid back and I could handle the twins being better than me in a lot of sports & competitions. In high school they had a straight A average and they were both cheerleaders, and on the gymnastics and soccer teams. Tony even had them take kick boxing so they could take care of themselves. What can I say, these gals were beautiful Italian hotties that were smart and athletic, and it seemed there was nothing they couldn't do? I didn't know what Tony & the family actually knew about what was going on between us but I certainly wasn't going to tell them either!! Tony knew that we were getting high together and he knew experientially how a lot of drugs we did made you extra horny so I was hoping that he didn't judge. He was a very cool dude and at 20 years old he had already been around the block a few times and he seemed wise for his age.

Even though we were involved in the war and we are still classified as Vietnam Veterans, not having to actually fight made the Air Force seem like a good job. Guys like my friend Charlie were Regular Army and his chopper flew combat missions as well as troop transport and medical evacuation. I had another friend from home who was a Marine and both (named Charlie) were in the thick of combat. By the way, they couldn't be called "Charlie" because that is what we called the NVA and the third letter in the Army alphabet was Charlie as in Alfa, Beta, Charlie so they were called many other names. In fact, we gave names to everything as the services had official names for everything as well. Everything had a classification code and its official nomenclature. We had given nicknames for everyone and everything and you called the enemy Charlie, the people Gooks, you didn't kill someone you fragged them, you didn't go nuts you were just a little shell shocked (we didn't even have PTSD yet) and the horror and the bullshit was blown off as "it don't mean nothin!"

Another friend from Long Island, Cpl. Rex Hillman that was a Marine, spent most of his time crawling around in the jungle and in constant danger having to engage with the enemy and always on guard and on maneuvers. He spent many nights on point hoping not to set off a trip wire, fall on a bungee stick or walk into an ambush. And he would be ordered to get some shut eye sitting in his fox hole in the month-long monsoon filled with rain and mud, snakes and leaches. If he had to pull guard, he set his claymore mines and wires and hoped he could hear them coming on their patrols, as you couldn't see them and if you did it was probably too late. Like the saying went, "we owned the day but they owned the night". One particular night when he was just in country a few weeks he was in his fox hole on guard duty. He was looking out over his perimeter and he was on the edge of a large rice paddy field. He had his claymore mines set up inside an area enclosed with razor wire. In the moonlight he could see a small hooch about 100 yards across the field. All of a sudden, he sees a guy come out of the hut at 3 AM and Rex sits up and sets him in his M-16 sights and sees the guy walking towards him. The man shimmies under the razor wire and Rex gives him a few more yards and he then he is going to shoot him. Just as Rex was squeezing the trigger, the guy raises his arms up and yells "Don't shoot, I'm a marine!" Being new Rex didn't know that the hooch was a small whorehouse right in enemy territory and the marine was out getting his jollies. The guy could have been killed by the VC or by Rex. Apparently, these prostitutes were an equal opportunity agency as they serviced both the NVA and our troops at the same time. Rex didn't know how many gooks he fragged because in a fire fight he shot everything that moved. On a bad night his platoon got overrun and Rex took one in the hip and leg. If that wasn't bad enough while he was being hoisted up to the chopper during the fight and the wind blew the Huey through the trees and the cables took down a large branch and ripped up his face. They had to lower him down and start all over again. After a couple of months in an army hospital in the Philippines he was right back with his unit hooked on morphine and then on heroin. He had to battle shit way after he was back home and he took all that hell home with him.

In the height of this "Vietnam Conflict" we were shipping home an average of 100 transfer cases a day (AKA our fallen causalities, our dead). Mostly young men that were just starting to live and now their remains are pushing up daisies at some National Cemetery still in their rows and in order with the names and dates as a reminder of their ultimate sacrifice. Over 58,000 dead and 300,000 wounded and we pulled out and let the communists take over the country anyway. We had to account for every death and we had to hope that some of the MIAs would be found alive. We heard reports that a fate worse than death was to be tortured and held captive in some rat hole until you did die of disease or starvation. The Geneva Conference was established by the UN to try and protect all the POWs but our prisoned GIs were treated worse than animals. The prisoners we detained were usually treated fairly, unless they were holding back important military intelligence. A brutal form of interrogation was being waterboarded which was a cloth over the face and having a steady stream of water flowing on the rag as you were bound and hung upside down. After an hour most prisoners were ready to spill the beans before they drowned. The pictures we saw of our POWs looked like the pictures from the concentration camps from Nazi Germany. As a Loadmaster I was trained to fight but since I was assigned to the big cargo planes, I was safe as they were well protected and not sent deep in the jungle, they needed long runways to land and take off. Deep in the jungle and up north there were bad reports of MIA's being held in bamboo jails out in the rain with the rats and snakes.

A sad thing was to go to the VA hospitals and see the guys that wish they were dead and God bless the men that were trying to make the best of their disabilities. But every VA Hospital has that ward that cares for the poor souls that are neither dead or alive with little brain activity and not much reason to be kept alive. When one of these fallen vets did finally die (or falls asleep as some like to say) the families had to be notified and many would be so relieved that they didn't have to suffer anymore. Isn't that where we get the term "Rest in Peace" from? The worst suffering is the constant pain these veterans are in and the hopelessness of the reality that things are only getting worse. The Bible says that if we have no hope in the resurrection, we are men most miserable. We all need hope or we wander around without vision in a messed-up world. Somehow the survivors that got to go home and resume their lives without too many physical, mental and emotional scars were the real lucky ones.

Most guys were trying to substitute the crap in their heads with alcohol, drugs and isolation and found it hard to trust people and have healthy relationships. Let's face it, wars were being fought all over the world all the time since we were thrown out of the Garden of Eden. And people have been killing each other since Cain killed his brother Able. We say we want peace but we steal from, lie to and hate our neighbors. Even married folks kill each other and we hate anybody that is different. We kill in the name of God and religion and we hate people for their skin color or their beliefs. We believe that man's true nature was created in the image of God but we have fallen so far away. This is why we needed the Messiah to save us and cleanse us of our darkness. These were some of the things we would discuss on our PCs or getting high listening to some head music rocking out some Steppenwolf or some Crosby, Stills, and Nash (or "Cocaine, Pills and Hash" as we called them). Since we were all involved in this war, we tried to make some sort of sense of what we were doing just like the politics, the college campuses, the press and the church. We all want peace and when you get down to it the Communists and the Vietnamese people love their children and families just like we do. Back in America we had people killing each other and the generation of love didn't lower the crime rate either. Everyone wants to go to heaven but nobody wants to die.

When I took a step back for a minute to catch my breath, I realized how much the military service forces a kid like me to grow up a little. Of course, a 19-year-old man thinks he has grown up because he is physically mature and, in the service, you were trained to be able to work together as a team or at least follow orders. I did feel that I was a part of this cosmic consciousness that made me understand things and experience things on some kind of higher plane. I knew that with all the bad things we saw that evil did exist but I also was positive that love was still the bottom line. We were to love God with all our hearts & minds and love our neighbor as ourselves. At 19 I wanted to experience this thing we called love and half the music we listened to was about searching for that love. The Beatles told us "All we need is LOVE" and we were to "Make Love not War" and we were supposed to be in the sexual revolution as well. I had a few girlfriends back home and seemed to be getting the hang of things so to speak. Then things all changed when I met Tony & Ann Marie. We didn't know the rules or guidelines, there wasn't a manual for a guy involved with identical twins. Amazingly, I was intimately involved with these very special young women who spent their whole lives together and seemed to have a magical relationship as it was.

Now with the lifestyle we were living and sharing we were going through an incredible emotional and physical fascination for each other. We were all looking to try to raise our consciousness by looking at life in a new way by breaking down preconceptions and judgments. The girls told me that they never were sexually attracted to each other beyond enjoying their natural beauty and their tender hearts. And it was more a sharing of tenderness as they made it seem natural to caress and to love each other, and they said it was me who turned it all on! I was the straw that stirred this drink and it was a delicious intoxication at that. These two young flowers got so into my heart and senses and the passion was thrilling as their smell, their touch and their taste were all aphrodisiacs. When we got together somehow all our energies came together and all our walls broke down so that we could just flow together. It was like the energy of three streams flowing together to form a river. Mixed with some love stimulating drugs such as pot, coke, mescaline and a good bottle of wine, we swirled together as in some wild dream and sexual fantasy. It has been said that life is wasted on the young but we were like sponges, we would soak up anything that held our interest. We tried to take every day as a day to learn or experience some new thing. The twins and I were into sharing life not only in the fast lane but we also slowed things down to be able to grog life's wonders. The girls were so in to nature and the ocean and they examined everything quizzically. They made a big deal about a bug or a flower and swam with Pilot Whales, they were fearless. It was good that we weren't together all the time for it would be to intense and someway we would swallow each other up! These 3-day lovefests were intense enough as we needed a few days to come down from the high and get back to normal, whatever that was? Besides we needed time to reflect and start to plan our next rendezvous.

The hard part of our relationship was trying to hide all the hanky-panky going on, especially around the family. Everybody could see that we were close so when we were around any of the family, we tried to cool it the best we could but it was hard (sometimes literally!) not to hold an embrace or give that telltale look that lovers share. The saving grace was that it was nuts to think that we would actually be doing all these incredible things! We started planning more of our 3-day adventures so we could be free to do whatever we wanted. We didn't just hole up in some hotel or resort, we also enjoyed exploring and fortunately the girls drove their Mercedes 450 SL all the way cross country just to give me a run for my money on those winding Highway 1 roads. We went boating and surfing and the girls were like fish in the water. They took me scuba diving and they showed me all sorts of wild fish and water plants and they were the most beautiful species in the water and on the beach for that matter!! They were two sun-kissed and healthy beauties that drew a crowd of onlookers whether they were waterskiing behind a boat or surfing a breaking wave. Until they started school in the fall it was going to be a great year. Like I said, it was good that I had my job on the flight line so I didn't burn out or die trying. When the girls decided to stay a few more days down at the beach I was driving like I was Dale Earnhardt after my shift was over, only to drive back to the base before I was AWOL in the morning. I was burning my candle at both ends and after a long day I swore I was going straight to bed after my shift had ended. It only took one of the girl's phone calls to get me speeding down the highway for another rendezvous. One morning I almost wrecked as I skid off the road to avoid hitting a zebra! Apparently, a real-life zebra had escaped from the Hearst Castle down the Pacific Highway on the way back from seeing the twins. I wasn't tripping but I still couldn't tell if it was white with black stripes or black with white stripes as we once tried to figure it out tripping down at the San Diego Zoo?!

Crazy unexplainable phenomenon always seems to happen when under the influence. Once out at night walking in the Golden Gate Park, we met a man that was out strolling with a pure white llama and some kind of large dog at his side. We were all in awe of the strange looking llama but I kept getting distracted by the strange looking dog. I asked the guy what kind of dog it was and he replied that it wasn't a dog at all, it was a Canadian Timber Wolf! Only in San Francisco did this make sense! Then there were the drag queens up at North Beach and the spaced-out freaks in Haight Ashbury walking around in robes and wizard hats. It was crazy times. I came back to the base after a weekend furlough with the girls down at Avila Beach. They were staying there and doing some work and play, tagging the big sea lions for some summer school credit.

I met Tony at breakfast and he told me it was time to shut down again. You see Tony was smart as a whip and he knew to shut down all of our underground activities from time to time. Sometimes it was on a hunch or a tip and other times we did it to break any routines to throw off the guys in the government Fords, Wingtips shoes and Ray Bans. We were always being watched so it was good to move out whatever was around and shut down for a while and then change how we do things. As the saying goes "you got to know when to hold them & know when to fold them" so we shut down and got back to shipping back the dead and doing our jobs. Besides we didn't want to get too greedy as that will lead to trouble and Tony didn't want any more trouble by us showing off our booty. This time the entire base was on alert. There was a lot of military types looking around and it was a good thing that we were clean as a whistle. We didn't have a paper trail so we were able to walk away without a trace since we never talked on the phones on the base and we stayed out of sight of any cameras. Nobody was getting popped for smoking a joint so we continued to go out and have a good time. I couldn't do my mad dash to see the girls. I couldn't take the chance of showing some pattern leaving the base at night for a secret rendezvous with Angelo Costa's twin daughters. Something was up, some of the guys that we met at the casino & hotel in Lake Tahoe came to talk with Tony out at an Italian restaurant down the highway. They were trying to get him to take over some heroin that they couldn't ship back from Thailand but he said he was sorry that he couldn't help them as we were shut down due to some investigations. And besides we stayed away from the morphine and the opiates - we drew the line in the sand.

Back in New York, at the newly named Kennedy International Airport, shit came in from all over the world on the international flights. Guys would rob the express trucks and a lot of people were ingesting bags of heroin and cocaine working as mules from places like Columbia and Afghanistan. There was a lot of smuggling going on everywhere. Then it broke down the pyramid to the streets so a lot of people were involved in this until your friend would score a bag or a gram or a few hits of something so everyone could get high. We liked to say that a person couldn't just buy all this good stuff at the local 7/11. We were all piggy-backing the biggest shipping company in the world, the United States Air Force and the US Navy. But I did have some code of ethics even if it was not on par with the US Government. I did not want anything to do with the hard drugs like heroin. This drug was so addictive and people just had to have it so they would rob and steal and they could not be trusted with anything, they were junkies. I know they were somehow thought of as artists and musicians and talented people but if you were injecting the shit in your veins every day you were in big trouble. Many good men came back from overseas in pain from an injury and when the pain pills ran out, they turned to the needle and the spoon. When a person was doing 10-20 pills a day it was getting cheaper to do smack at $15 a bag. I never heard of anyone smoking too much pot and overdosing or driving recklessly and killing anyone but people did get too high on drugs and crash and burn. I liked driving and we could drive for hours on some speed & marijuana listening to some good trucking music. Driving when you are nodding out on opiates was an accident waiting to happen. We just had nothing to do with heroin and the bad energy around it, we were "up heads" and hoped for a positive experience.

The Guido's from Las Vegas showed up again to put some pressure on us to reconsider the offer to move some heroin and they were offering a suitcase full of cash. When Tony asked them what part of "no" did they not understand, the big dude pulled a knife on us so we had no choice but to kick the crap out of him and the other two hoods with him. Now I was afraid of what was going to happen when they come back to retaliate as these guys weren't the local jokers, they killed guys. Tony went and called his dad and his dad said that he would take care of it and not to worry about it, easy for him to say, he was on the other side of the country. About a week later a limo came and took us to Lake Tahoe and I figured we were done for but we actually were guest of the place and we were given a formal apology from the ass holes that tried to rough us up. There was something to be said about 3 men in black suits with butterfly bandages and bruises on their faces trying to apologize to two 19- year old kids. But this wasn't our first rodeo, of course the fact that Anthony Costa was Angelo Costa's only son and nobody should be messing with him was the bigger issue here. A few days later the black suitcase was delivered and we split $ 50 grand as a peace offering to the Costa family back in Atlantic City. The casino threw us a huge weekend party as a gesture to the men in uniform and we all had a blast getting the full service and treatment. We had speed boats and ski jets to play with all day out on Lk Tahoe and they made us a luau Saturday night and we hung out in the heated pool and jacuzzi. We woke up to a brunch and then spa treatments and we gambled with their money.

The girls must have kissed my "boo-boo" I had over my eye 100 times as I did catch a few zingers in the dance with Pauley Knuckles and his apes. By the end of the weekend we let bygones be bygones. We were the property of the US Government so we had to fill out a report with the MPs on how we got jumped by "a bunch of local punks coming back to the base from the movies". By the way, we did see the new movie, "2001-A Space Odyssey" stoned and again the next night tripping and it was incredible! The scene where the ape picks up the bone and gets the revelation that the bone is a tool and then a weapon is excellent. He then stands erect and becomes man and right away attacks the apes and bashes their leader's skull in with his new weapon. Before that they just screamed and yelled at each other. He then triumphantly throws the bone in the air and it turns into a space shuttle headed for the moon. The movie was ground breaking in special effects and gave us plenty to think about. I would like to say that this was the end of our relationship with the boys from Lake Tahoe, but their mission was to get us to ship their shit, but it just wasn't going to happen as it wasn't our mission.

We took it easy for a while, there was a lot of security going down and we needed a break as things were too hot and dangerous on the base and the flight line. We had an increased amount of work as the war was escalating and our body count was way out of control.

It was getting harder to transport over 100 body bags a day and we had to keep them moving to places like Biloxi, Mississippi or Boise, Idaho and the peace- nicks were shouting how we are in an unjust war and we were killing babies and shit. The thing is, I don't recall what a just war was, maybe when you had a madman like Hitler or the ruthless Japanese who snuck in and killed over 2,000 Americans in a few hours at Pearl Harbor you had a "just war". Dropping an A -Bomb on Hiroshima and Nagasaki and blowing the two cities off the face of the earth was justified as it put an end to the war, I guess? This Vietnam War or conflict, as it was called, should not have been our war but we had to stop the spread of communism somehow as it ultimately came down to US verses the Russians, like it was in Korea almost 20 years ago. Whoever had the biggest army ruled the world, then it was the biggest navy, and then the most fighter jets and now it is whoever had the most nuclear weapons. And soon it will be whoever wins the space race as we just put a man on the moon and I am sure it won't be long until we have a space station that can send lasers down on our enemies. When Alfred Nobel invented dynamite he thought he was inventing a great tool for construction and mining but soon man figured out how to make it into a destructive force. It made Alfred so disgusted that he established the Nobel

Peace Prizes to help counter the offenses of dynamite and nitroglycerin and other implements of destruction.

Since we had more time and more money than we knew what to do with, we took some of our stash and went out and bought two 1969 Harley Davison Sportsters, 900 cc to tool around on. California didn't have helmet laws so we looked pretty sharp with our mirrored Ray Bans and combat boots on. No way were the girls riding on the back or in a sidecar as they had 2 -750 cc Yamahas and they liked to shoot by us at 100 Mph. One time we were all out cruising out in the desert when a caravan of bikers pulled up and parked with us for a rest. It wasn't long before we were all sharing some weed and lines of speed. Some of the bikers were veterans so when they found out that Tony and I were Loadmasters and current enlisted men there was cause for a celebration! They took us back to their camp up in the hills. They numbered about 70 men & women. We were glad to see more women so we didn't have to worry about our 3 girls. We partied with them into the night and got stoned and drank Jack Daniels, some biker had scored some peyote and we got very high and howled at the moon until we watched an awesome sunrise come up over the desert sky. We got a couple of rooms at a motel and spent the day in bed and around the pool. The twins never looked bad as they always seemed so up and ready for anything and I called them the "Eveready Bunny Rabbits" for more reasons than one. I spent a night partying and I looked like hell in need of a shave, a shower and some rest for my bloodshot eyes. The girls looked so beautiful and I don't know how they stayed so delectable even out riding in the desert. A month later we delivered a car full of Hawaiian Gold pot we had intercepted and we gave it to the Desert Rats for a great price and it didn't cost us a dime! We kept telling each other it was time to quit but it was so easy to make a few deals and it was a thrill to live the life.

Some of the bikers wanted go for a midnight ride because it was a full moon and the desert sky was radiant and the Milky Way looked touchable. The desert and the mountains looked like an x-ray with a silver lining. We stopped to take some more mescaline and pass around some mushrooms and then a small group of us headed out into the night. We headed towards the mountains and the desert became a giant mirage. At times the road would shift so we felt like we were going straight down on a roller coaster. The sounds were deafening and the wind was reshaping our faces like in a fun house. Our new friends took us up in a canyon that had a rock formation they called Beatnik Rock. It was a stream cutting through the rocks that turned into a waterfall and a pool. It had a long waterslide and places to dive and hang out. The rock formations had incredible paintings and gardens; clothing was optional. Between the mescaline and the rushing water the place was like an oasis. The hills and rock formations took on so many different shapes and sizes and our bikes felt like chariots blasting through the night. With the first signs of light on the horizon the wild images became more in focus and the morning light gave us a whole new pallet.

We had to attend the Memorial Day Base parade and all the day's activities. We invited the town people to come and see some of our hardware and ways to keep us safe. I had to demonstrate the way we could shoot pallets of food or weapons out the bay doors and parachute them right down to the LZs. We showed some documentaries on our firepower and capabilities that was so impressive to us. The wild thing is, at the end of the presentation, they showed us that everything we saw was already outdated and obsolete. We had things like a halftrack vehicle that could go into a river and then open up on both ends so that other vehicles could drive over it. The fighter jets we had were equipped with such sophisticated "smart bombs" that were heat seeking and automatically on target. We had planes that could fly through radar and missiles that could travel at

MACH 3 speed. The frustrating fact was that we had enough firepower to level South East Asia. But just like a boxer being held back, we were getting beat at their own game! We were fighting a jungle war that they have been fighting for years, they were so dug in that they had underground tunnels and underground fortresses running all through the country and into Cambodia & Thailand. A month of Navy & Air Force fighter jets doing sorties 24/7 would end the war fast but we didn't want to escalate the conflict to an all-out war with the Russians and or the Chinese. It seemed we were happy to just fight a defensive battle. We would take the hill in the day and they would take it back the next night. That is the balance of power we maintain with the Russians on the arms race and now the space race. If we have 15 hundred nuclear warheads each there lies a balance of power, but it also means we have a total of over 3,000 nuclear warheads that could knock the whole world off its axis. The Bible tells us that someday the weapons of war will be made into plowshares to tend the garden and we won't be killing each other or dying anymore.

Charlie Bonham loved helicopters since he was a young boy, he even made models and had them hanging in his room. Growing up in his father's Esso service station he became a good mechanic and when the time came for his draft notice, he enlisted and he ended up in helicopter crew chief school. He got assigned with his Huey to the north near and around Danang, close to the DMZ and the heavy action. As part of the air cavalry as a med - evacuation unit Charlie was in the thick of the battle. Charlie was devoted to keeping his bird in the air but when he was on the ground, he was a party animal and the funniest troop around. He could be seen flying his imaginary chopper around as he pretended to be holding the rudder in his hand and imitating the sounds of the blades as he bopped around the base. Everybody liked Bonham and he liked smoking pot, drinking beer and snorting speed. He had a little mutt named Roach who was addicted to eating the roaches that they would flip to him. When they were all passing around a doobie, little Roach would go crazy waiting for them to toss him the roach, hence his name was ROACH! Old Bonham was a big dog himself. He was famous for knowing where every hooch in the jungle was located so he could knock off some quick poontang. The man had some appetite and he liked the girl sons as they were the young girls about 16 -18, as the momasons were a little older and you could buy them for the month for about $20 and they would "fuckie-suckie" you and cook and clean your clothes. How he managed to keep his wits and his sense of humor was beyond me but he did suffer and never could return to normal later on. I guess he left his best parts all over Vietnam and I am sure there was a lot of little hairy baby sons growing up around too.

Since we shut down all our extracurricular activities for a while at Cam Ron Bay AFB. The agents would break down a pallet and would find all sorts of things being illegally shipped but they seemed to be looking for something more. When our so-called friends from Lake Tahoe contacted Tony again, we knew something was up. They wanted us to inform them as to what was going on with the investigation but didn't tell us why. We told them that the Hells Angels volunteered to go fight up at Hanoi just as long as they could bring their bikes, and that the government was looking for other clubs to volunteer. They weren't buying this and were not pleased with our jokes. But something big was going to go down and we did not want to be near it when it does. Another limo was sent for us and this time we met Tony's father at the casino and we knew this could not be good. We found out that the reconstruction of Atlantic City was costing more than planned as they were behind schedule and over budget so they needed to raise some capital. The best return for your money was the import and export business of heroin and cocaine and it was a cash business that you didn't pay income tax on. What they were asking was that Tony and I would supervise and guarantee a ton of heroin to be shipped over and right under the authority's noses. It was way out of our league and comfort zone but with thousands of tons of cargo shipping every day we could come up with a plan and we were pretty resourceful. They offered us $ 100,000 for just 2 days work and with all we had invested already we would be set for a very long time. My accountant wanted me to invest in this new restaurant that was going to go public and open up as a franchise all over the country. I figured the twins would like it as it was a seafood restaurant called "The Red Lobster". Tony and I had to accept the challenge and we didn't think we could just say no – It was not like we had a choice, specially Tony.

This whole deal would not be such a risk if it wasn't for the G-Men all over the base. We had heard that the Russians had intercepted our communications involving the fail -safe daily defense systems. Every day we had planes making high altitude surveillance and attack maneuvers that were set in place in case we had to actually bomb sights in Russia, Cuba, Beijing, North Korea and other enemies of our country and our allies. There was always doomsday theory scenarios and other Cold War paranoia going on as it was spy vs spy on the international level. We knew this was big as there was always some high- level espionage going on between the Cold War countries and the NATO forces. I did have a security clearance for the sensitive cargo and documents that we shipped. We decided that we would take the obvious route and smuggle the shit back inside the transfer cases as we were bringing back over 100 cases a day. Since they were transferred by us from morgue to morgue, we were responsible to get them all the way home. When we shipped the transfer cases back to Travis, we used the C-141 Lockheed Star lifters, with 4 underwing jet engines that carried 90,000 pounds of cargo as well as 185 troops and 60 medical stretchers. The C-141 had a back- door ramp that was used for ejecting cargo and paratroopers. We had 285 in service C-141s along with the giant C5As and hundreds of C-130 cargo planes. We had such a huge operation so it was kind of easy to hide a few tons of contraband among all this raw tonnage. We insured the Priority 1 transfer cases by flying along with the shipment and deliver it straight to the morgue at Travis. We could avoid the whole customs and the surveillance checkpoints by just doing our normal duties. We could make up some fake shipping manifests and add at least ten empty cases per flight. We could move a ton of drugs at a time and with over 100 cases coming back every day we could get this whole thing done in just two days, right under the authorities' noses-

We had trucks coming & going with food deliveries from the docks in Frisco to the base and out to food warehouses everywhere. Feeding 20,000 troops three times a day was quite a huge operation as it was. We could have a truck pick up bananas from the docks in San Fran and deliver some to our warehouse. We replace it with cases of the white powder and deliver it right to the hotel kitchens loading-dock in Tahoe. As Loadmasters working for almost 2 years shipping cargo for the USA, Tony and I were getting to know the ropes. And since we could ship weapons and ammo and make it look like food & medical supplies, then we could ship drugs as well. We were shipping morphine and other pain medications and Napalm & Agent Orange were even more deadly so it all amounted to the fact that there is safety in numbers. We weren't the only game in town and we were just small change compared to what was going on and we had the Navy, the Merchant Marines and the US Postal Service all working together shipping millions of tons of cargo. Then we had outfits like UPS and gigantic freight companies that were shipping all over the world. There were the big containers ships like Maersk and the Greek lines that shipped everything from diamonds to stolen Rolls Royce's so we were not even a big fish in a small pond -There is a phenomenon out in the forest and woods that takes place between crows and owls that illustrates this strength in numbers theory. The crows so fear the owls that they bunch up and cohabitate with them sometimes a hundred to one. They figure that it is safer in the long run to keep the owls close to their vests as it increases their odds of survival. If the owl kills and eats one crow a day there is still 99 that have survived, go figure? So that is why we could pull this deal off right in front of everyone by just blending in with what we did every day. In the back of my mind I remembered how my friend Flash got popped by a freak incident when his nephew decided to steal his Caddy for a joy ride- you could never be too careful and you had to know how to roll with the punches when things go bad. We knew how to operate without leaving a paper trail.

We met with the head honcho at Tahoe to go over everything with his apes. Tony and I tried not to tell them too much as the secret to our success so far is the secrecy of our moves. We were firm believers that "loose lips really do sink ships" so we didn't use the phone or leave a paper trail. Having to do anything with these monkeys was so against our better judgement. If it weren't for Tony's dad, I wouldn't touch this crap with a ten-foot pole. Having to make an alliance with these goons can only be a big mistake, it could cost us our lives. The one good thing is that for two days we make $ 50,000 each. I kept telling myself to just be cool, it really did not matter if we got busted with a pound or a ton but it was a lot less stressful to hide a couple of pounds than a couple of tons! We took a flight over to Cam Ron Bay with extra transfer cases to get things started. We loaded up the two planes with all the cargo going back to the States and secured the extra transfer cases. I wished Tony Godspeed as we always do and hopped on one of the hammocks for the long flight across the Pacific. After a few hours of nervous sleep, I was startled when all of a sudden there was an explosion on the port side of the plane. It rocked the plane so much that I thought we were hit by a missile. I looked out the window and saw that one of the 30,000 pounds of thrust General Electric engines blew up and was on fire on the port wing. I was never so scared in my life and the plane felt like it was going down. The pilots announced that we will be making an emergency landing at Hickman Field in Pearl Harbor in Hawaii. Our pilots were tough as nails and cool as cucumbers and they acted like this is just normal procedure. This is why we all trained so hard, they levelled off the plane and a lot of turbulence steadied. Thank God we still had 3 engines that still worked and we could land in Hawaii in one hour. But now I thought it might be better to crash in the Pacific then to crash & burn in Ft Leavenworth for the rest of my life.

Our pilots knew their shit and we landed without another problem but we were all still shaking as the wing was smoking and the big jet was making a hell of a racket on the landing. When we reported to the base commander and filled out the reports, he told us we would be able to transfer on to another C-141 in a few hours so he told us to go get some chow and report back to secure our cargo on the new plane. The air cargo crew at Hickman Field had the pallets all loaded up by the time we got back to the flight line. I was freaking out but our flight crew had that right stuff attitude that everything was under control and it was business as usual. I told myself that nobody really gave a damn about the transfer cases but me. I felt like the guy in "The Tell -Tale Heart" as the cases had a heart beat and they were about to split open and blow heroin all over the fuselage. The pilots notified our base of the situation and I left word for Tony of our snafu. I hoped this would not ruin our plan and cause any suspicion to our manifest. The mechanics told us that the engine took in a flock of birds and almost blew the wing right off. It was easy for them to say but I was still in shock from the explosion and there was no way I wanted to go back up after all that we just went through. The pilots said they could fly with two engines if we had to. These guys were trained to be steady and deal with every situation so they were ready to go right back up and continue the mission.

This reminded me of the time we had a Volkswagen van filled up with surfboards and 10 speeds for a weekend down at the beach and the rear end, air cooled, engine seized on us. We got out to investigate and the whole engine was on fire and about to blow. Since we didn't have any water, we all had to pee on the engine to put out the fire. The next day the guys replaced the engine in a couple of hours, it was held in place with 4 bolts. The only problem was the engine smelled like pee and we had to steam clean the engine compartment. Because the flight line at Hickman Field was so efficient, we were only grounded for 2 hours and we were back in the air without anyone even considering our cargo. There was still a chance that we could pull this whole thing off. When it came down to it, we were just another plane coming in from overseas that was running behind schedule, but with over 2,000 pounds of illegal drugs aboard it felt like the plane was painted yellow with a black stripe down the middle of it waving the Jolly Roger flag! I finally arrived at about 4 in the morning and although the guys waiting were all freaking out, we still got the other truck loaded up and on the road before the sun came up. We went to sleep knowing that 100 -grand was coming in cash and we swore it was our last dance.

We put in for a 2- week furlough and we had a few days of R&R coming as well. We both went back home to get away from California and the base and the smuggling and after a couple of days of home cooked food with my mom I was anxious to meet up with the twins. We booked a few days at the Plaza Hotel in Manhattan and painted the town red. We dined at some great restaurants and saw a few plays and got to see the Allman Brothers at the Fillmore East high on acid and it was the best concert I ever saw. The girls were wonderful, we went to the Met and saw the Impressionist and we saw the play Jesus Christ Super Star on some mescaline and we all felt like we had a deep spiritual experience. We watched the sunrise out on the beach at Coney Island and held on to each other like we were in love for the first time. We finished out the first week at my stomping grounds in the Hamptons. We rented a little cottage and watched the waves roll down the beach. Because the girls were so comfortable with each other, I was able to slide right into their hearts and bodies. Making love with them was like a wild dream. It was a ride on a magic carpet and if I closed my eyes, I lost my sense of time and space. The twins were so identical that it further messed with my ability to identify them, in my altered state it was impossible. When we shared some good pot or something to give us a little kick it would put us on the edge of shear ecstasy, we were so into pleasing each other.

Every day the girls would be giggling about some new thing they wanted to do and the right drink or tote on something would break down any possible hang up or reservations we still had. We were all thrill seekers, speed junkies and now love monkeys. Because we were having the time of our lives we decided to fly down to the Keys with Tony and his gal Jessica. We rented a charter to sail out to a few Islands. By now the cat was out of the bag. Tony knew what was up. Fortunately, he was still cool and would pat me on the back and tell me what a lucky bastard I was. When your libido is at a high point your attraction energy is strong too. I swear Jessica was warm for my form also and I was wondering if she was going to put her foot in my crotch again! We toured the Caribbean and stopped at St Thomas & Martinique and there was a hot tub on our yacht- I had my hands full with the twins and I didn't want to push my luck with Tony's good nature so I tried not to respond to Jessica's hot body. I would not do that to Tony anyway, we did live with certain morals. The girls were so sexy and so sweet and the smell of their hair and the coconut oil was intoxicating. We took in the sun and the salt air. We did some scuba diving and got to see an old wreck from a ship that went down when the Rum Runners were sailing the seas and I felt a certain connection to them.

We had to eventually get back to California and back to work as there was still a war going on and someone had to support it. We were still enlisted men so we had to say goodbye to the girls and make our way back to the base. I had to suppress the desire to go AWOL and escape with the twins to a little island somewhere in the Pacific. But I knew they were starting school in the fall and I still had two more years before I was free to buy a yacht and sail around the world - I was so knocked out by our time together that I just could hardly wait to see them again.

When I got back to my room at the base there was a note from Tony telling me that our money is in our accounts and we should celebrate! I figured it was time to hang it up and quit while we were ahead but Tony said that the boys from Lake Tahoe had other plans. I just couldn't see myself as an international drug smuggler as this whole thing had escalated to the point of insanity. It all started as a way to get high and make a little cash as the drug culture was a part of the times, but I was in the USAF and I didn't work for the Mob.

We had agreed that we would do this one big deal but now these guys wanted more and I wished they would take a hike and leave us alone. I was starting to realize that Tony was much more connected and I knew it was only going to be trouble. We had more money than we knew what to do with, we were almost set for life.

My money was invested in the Red Lobster restaurant franchise and they had just gone public. They were starting to open restaurants in every mall being built around the country. I had enough money to have all my needs met, I couldn't even spend it as it would wave a red flag to how I got so rich? I kept insisting that I was done and that we should stick a fork in it but I could see that my friend had bigger ideas. I tried to tell him that the odds were against us and we were bound to get caught and spend time in jail or get thrown in a dumpster, but he didn't want to hear it. His family's connections put him in a larger capacity then what I was doing and I was getting close to the danger zone. For a while we put it all to rest. We had a lot going on, the Military Airlift Command (MAC) was increasing our work load. We were shipping everything under the sun to South Vietnam as the war was escalating. We were even spreading out to Cambodia and bombing the hell out of Hanoi and places up north. The body count was getting ridiculous. We were recording more and more serious injuries. The political unrest was dividing our country back home. We figured it was time to plan a blowout 4th of July party to let off a little steam and celebrate our big deal.

We decided to book a resort over in Sausalito, a rich little town across the San Francisco Bay. We found out about a place on the harbor that was a bunch of houseboats with all the luxuries and amenities. We had boats and jet skis to tool around the bay. We even made plans to spend a night over at Fisherman's Wharf and we invited the gang to help us celebrate our country's birthday. Tony promised a fireworks display that would give the city competition. By now a lot of the gang was wise to the notion that the 3 Musketeers were sharing more than a little swashbuckling as we were carrying on for months now and we were hopelessly in love with each other. Between the service, running drugs, the flights all over the place and the money being stashed away we were living the dream. But my relationship with the twins was the best thing that I ever experienced and it was so hard to control ourselves. Most guys would be bonkers over either one of these beauties and I was involved with both of them! The sad part was that I knew it wasn't going to last forever and we weren't going to move to Utah to do the polygamy thing -So we lived in the moment and took things day by day.

We had a poster in our office of a group of paratroopers all holding hands in a circle over the ocean and it was titled "Carpe Diem" and that was our motto "SIEZE THE DAY".

The base temperature was really heating up, crawling with Military Police, custom agents and ATF investigators. They were looking for even more then drugs and the stolen surveillance reports. We found a whole pallet of AK-47 assault rifles abandoned in the warehouse, and if we found 100 rifles there must be thousands that we didn't have a clue about. With all the agencies snooping around we would think that the Guido's would be scared and just go lay low but they were relentless in their pursuits. They were on us like a cheap suit and they weren't taking no for an answer. I wanted to tell them to go fuck themselves but these guys weren't the local Boy Scouts so I had to put up with what was now harassment. They were really leaning on Tony as they probably had some shit on him and it seemed like he was going to start back working with them. I was starting to think that it might be time to start looking for a transfer. The twins were going to start school at Florida State in Tallahassee. I didn't want to leave this base and Northern California but with all the crap happening, it might be time to take a permanent vacation, before I get one!! There was a good base down on the Gulf Coast called Kessler AFB in Biloxi, Mississippi that was only a 4-hour drive to Tallahassee (If I hop a flight to the Pensacola Naval Base it would take about a half hour). Biloxi and Gulfport were cool towns with great beaches, good fishing and big casinos, and there were plenty of nice places to shack up with the girls, so I could make the best of it if I had to.

Tony was getting stuck between a rock and a hard place. He had to stay loyal to his father's business but asking him to smuggle was the reason why he had to enlist to begin with. I didn't tell Tony any of my thoughts or possible plans. This mess was starting to cause a rift between us. Tony didn't tell me what they had on him but when they started to threaten me, I went ballistic. I was going to go rogue on the next guy that tried to muscle me. They tried to tell me that Mr. Costa would not like it if he found out that I was doing both his daughters and I freaked out wondering if they had any pictures of us? That is what these guys do to get the point across before they break your thumbs and then throw you in the dumpster (which they owned as well). I should have never gotten involved in the first place. They have Tony by his balls and they are starting to tighten up mine as well. I was starting to get serious about getting a transfer out of here. Who could I complain to? My drug dealers are being mean to me and could our Base Commander go talk to them for me? Maybe I could just tell them that I don't want to play with them anymore or tag them and say that I quit and they are it. I knew it was time to make a move to transfer to another base and quit while I was still ahead, while I still had one.

It was coming time for the twins to start college; it was late August and their parents were hosting a going away party at the new Silver Dollar Casino in Atlantic City. Tony and I caught a flight through 4 bases to get to McGuire AFB/Ft Dix, just 20 miles from AC. I had to sneak the girls up to my room after hours and after we got stoned, we all got very paranoid that there were security cameras spying on us, and it was probably true so we turned the lights out and turned up the TV. The next night we had to get out of there so we went up to Seaside Heights to get a motel on the ocean to have some privacy as we were sure our room was bugged. When I got back to Travis, I found out that my transfer was approved but sadly I wasn't going to Mississippi, Florida or any other continental base; I was off to Vietnam! I knew the time was coming for my tour of duty to Nam so it was time to go and serve. Maybe it was a good thing to get as far away from Travis as I could, to save my ass from jail and who knows what the boys in the black suits were going to do to me, because I continued to just say no.

I did not tell the twins this sudden change of plans. Cam Ron Bay was literally half way around the world from Florida. I was also thinking that after a year off to live the high life the twins would have to buckle down and hit the books, so I had a lot of thoughts spinning through my head. South Vietnam could be a buzz kill like the heads would say and I could really get killed over there. Now I was going to be a love sick - home sick fly boy like all the other sad sacks. I don't think I could be like a Charlie Bonham and actually love it there. Most guys had pictures of their sweetheart from back home and if you were flying solo you had Playboy centerfolds up, and we all had the Barbie Benton pictures up regardless. We all swapped Playboys and girlie magazines and outside the base was plenty of sex shops to comfort a lonely guy. In South Vietnam you could get anything you wanted for 2-5 dollars and for 5 dollars you could have the guys younger sisters who were still virgins. And for 7 dollars you had them all night. After being passionately in love with the twins for 7 months there was no way I would want one (or two?) little girl sons. But just thinking about my little bunny rabbits being 10,000 miles away was making me sad and I haven't even said good bye yet-

There has been a real problem with the girls that I have had since I've known them and especially since we have been so intimately involved, is that after all this time I still can't tell them apart? I don't even think that their mother can even tell them apart and they have been playing off this all their lives. They are so pretty to look at and then you start to notice just how identical they are. When they dress alike, even down to matching bras & panties, and then act and talk the same, it is just plain nuts. They have done some real switch-aroos, and they confessed they did it to me and I didn't have a clue. So, with all the smuggling and the subversive activities we were involved, the twins were amazing. They could change their identities so I couldn't tell who was who so they could pull the wool over everyone's eyes. They could work a big deception and the joke was on us. These girls were so incredible and I had to say goodbye to not one but two of them. I started to plan a good scenario to how it should go down and I decided that I would go to Florida and spend our last weekend together for a very long time, maybe forever. I knew of a cottage down in Treasure Island on the coast that I could have for a few days. A buddy of mine was a lifer in the Navy and he had a cottage right on the beach. He was always out to sea so he let me use his place. We had to have a great last hurrah to hold each other tight and say something meaningful and if it gets to sad, we will have to get very high and screw like bunnies-

By now the whole company knew I got my orders for a permanent assignment at Cam Ron Bay AFB, so of course we had to go out partying a few times and I figured that we have some kind of Bon Voyage gathering down at our hotel at Avila Beach. Even though I would still be flying to Travis my new assignment would have me shipping to the three main bases on the west coast and bases and ports all over the Pacific rim. Riding on smaller planes to go to one strip airfields in active areas was always an experience. We would get a squad of choppers escorting us and the thrill of one of our fighter jets buzzing by at 700 mph was a real head turner. No matter how many times you see one, a fighter jet loaded with air to air missiles, Napalm and machine guns was a pretty formidable weapon. If I was the enemy I would run for the hills. We all loved planes and my barracks was out by the end of the runway and we used to sit on the back steps blowing weed and watching all the planes come in. They would all be stacked up in the sky and they would be coming in so low that we could read all the numbers underneath the fuselage. If we were looking into a big sunset, we could see the heat from the engines making mirages on the tarmac. If you were high you would be sitting there holding your breath enjoying these incredible flying machines. The sound of them taking off right above you rumbled through your entire body and shook your very soul. I got to sit up in the cockpit on a lot of rides in the helicopters and sometimes they would let me play pilot as they instructed me to just hold her steady as she goes. On the shorter runways it was such a wild ride as the planes seemed to be flying straight up, if you looked out the window the ground was behind you and you lost your bearings. We all were here with the common bond of flying and just being up in the air far from the rat race below-

The last few weeks stateside was spent getting everything squared away and packed and some stuff had to be stored like my car & bike. I only packed a duffel bag, because, once there, everything was cheaper to buy. I spent a few days training my replacement who was on his second tour and had just come back from South Korea so he knew the ropes. He was hitting it off with Tony and I am sure they would be working all our monkey business without missing a beat. His name was Jack Murphy from Hell's Kitchen in Manhattan. Jack was from a big Irish family, 8 brothers and 2 sisters and his father was a union rep in the meat packers of lower New York. Jack fought with the NYC Athletic Club, he was about 6'3, 225 and he had hands the size of two canned hams. His only loss was to a young heavyweight named Larry Holmes.

I took care of all my transfer duties and when I went to check out with my Company Commander, he told me that I did a good job and he said he would send a good recommendation, (if he knew half of what I was doing I would be in the stockade waiting for my court martial !!). He let me sign out early. He knew I was going home and then 10,000 miles cross country and the Pacific to beautiful Vietnam. I could see my mom, see the girls, and hang with the guys down at Avila Beach before I shipped out. This time it was all round-trip courtesy of the USAF & Pan American as they flew right to the base.

I got to stay with my mom a few days and she had me go to mass with her so she could show me off to the "Prayer Warriors" that she was saying the rosary with. I would write these long letters to her and she would read them to her nurses and anyone else that would listen. With all the shit I put her through growing up she was still my biggest fan. She laughed at every joke I ever told and loved my crazy stories. On Easter Sunday a few years ago, I came to dinner still a little tripped out from the night before. We watched "Jesus of Nazareth" and I had a religious experience and started crying. My mother must have known I was a little-nuts, as if she didn't know years ago!? I saw a few old friends from my hometown and then I flew to Pensacola to meet Tony & Ann Marie in Tallahassee. It was a 3 to 4-hour ride to St Pete so I rented a big Coupe de Ville and we drove down singing songs with the radio. A great oldie came on that the girls made me stop at a record store to buy it. The song was "You belong to Me" by Patsy Cline and one of the verses was "Fly the ocean in a silver plane, See the jungle when its full of rain, just remember when your home again, you belong to me -" we also got the Peter, Paul & Mary song "Leaving on a Jet Plane" and we listened to them all weekend.

We went out to the boardwalk for a nice dinner and then we had a few drinks at the bar. These two jerks were trying to hit on the girls as usual and I finally had to tell them to please go fuck off. They gave me the usual baloney about how it ain't fair that I should be with two women and they had none. The girls told them that the way they were behaving it's no wonder they didn't have a date and I figured it was time to pay up and split. We took a walk down by the water and the ladies surprised me with some blue mescaline that we were able to snort a few lines to start off the night. We walked along looking at the stars and checking out the pelicans when all of a sudden, I was grabbed from behind and pulled down by one of the morons from the bar. He was trying to choke the crap out of me and his buddy was coming at me with a big piece of driftwood. Just as he was going to beat me in the face with his stick, Ann Marie squares off and plants a flying kick to his nose and sends the guy flying into the surf. She must have broken his nose as he was bleeding like a pig and screaming that "she broke my fucking nose". Tony meanwhile gave the other dude a roundhouse kick to his chest and sent him flying in the sand. I picked up the piece of wood and I chased them down the beach and they didn't know what hit them as they ran away, they probably couldn't believe that my two little cuties could pack such a punch. The girls were so awesome and I was one lucky guy to be with them. They had my back, it seemed they would do anything for me. We went back to the cottage and did some more mescaline and the girls were extra excited, I guess beating up on guys was a real turn on. Sex that night was the best ever but the next day was bittersweet. We knew it was our last night together for quite a while. We drove back Sunday and the girls were crying and punching me for leaving them-we drove to the airport in silence. I took the red eye all the way to Frisco and I had to put my sunglasses on so the stewardesses didn't see the tears in my eyes.

Chapter Three

VIETNAM

"War is not heathy for children and other
Living things"

I returned to the base and it seemed so strange not to have my room so I split with Tony to the beach. The guys all came down and we had a little farewell party and we howled at the moon and I said my good-byes. I spent the final day with Tony and that was the last time I saw him alive - I flew the 10- hour flight in my fatigues and was to bummed out to talk with anybody. I had a lot of time to think about things. I was too excited to sleep so I took a check-up from the neck up and tried to evaluate my crazy wild life. Now I was going to Nam for a year and there would be new challenges and the GIs and the civilians were even more insane then the people I left. I couldn't stop daydreaming about the girls and the wonderful love we shared. I noticed my smile in the reflection in the window as I thought of how they kicked the shit out of those two clowns at Treasure Island and how they just laughed it off like it was nothing. We finally flew through some clouds to see the panoramic view of the Cam Ron peninsula and the mountains out in blue South China Sea. The harbor looked weird as the big battleships and tankers towered over the various shapes and sizes of the smaller fishing boats all around the bay. It was a clash of cultures and history and some of the fishing boats were over a hundred years old and the way of life hadn't changed for centuries. Then, to see the destroyers and aircraft carriers from our Pacific fleet looming over everything was a sobering feeling that we meant business.

The airfield and the naval port were active since the French built them in the 40's after the big one. Now the USAF & the US Navy have a huge operation that was the biggest installation that I had ever seen. We had the Marines, the Navy and the Air Force in full strength and it just didn't seem possible we could ever be pushed around or take any shit from anybody. The big guns on the USS Missouri could shoot a bomb the size of a Volkswagen 50 miles away like it was nothing, but later I would find out that they weren't allowed to use them. What the fuck is with that? We had to pussyfoot around and fight with one hand tied behind our back. The base was a sprawling complex of tents, barracks, fuel depots & equipment yards and hangers all surrounded with sand bags and bunkers. We had rows and rows of planes and choppers and acres of army vehicles. The Vietnamese people were everywhere riding bicycles and pulling their carts and the preferred mode of transportation was the small Hondas & Suzuki motorbikes. I was assigned my own jeep to get around, my duties were spread all over the base and the harbor. The mountains, the sea and the beaches were in constant contrast to the camp & the town that was built and fortified for war & peace, the problem is that there hasn't been any peace here for a long, long time-

I had not been here a week when I heard a familiar greeting in the morning mess hall. It was Charlie Bonham's famous saying "Heh man, wow man, what you going to say man, what you going to do man?" what ya gonna drink man, what ya gonna smoke man, or what ya gonna snort man? Far out man." But there he was, larger than life and we had a lot of catching up to do. He was here to get some medical attention. He had burned himself working on his engine and his arm got infected. He said he "better take care of it" before they saw his fucking arm off and he would have to wipe his ass like some Gook! (These people wipe with their left so they eat with their right) Charlie-son was going to be here for about a week. He showed me his arm and it did look "pretty gnarly"!?? Old Bonham was one of my best friends. We knew each other for years and he was so entertaining. He was the funniest guy around. Somehow the Army was letting the combat vets grow their hair long, CB had a beard, headband & beads and to quit smoking he was doing coke snuff. Coke snuff was a strong tobacco that he carried in a pouch and took a little snort on his knuckle and made all these snorting sounds like he just sniffed ground glass. He was the cat's meow, he looked like the poster boy for "The Village Voice" or "High Times Magazine". And if you didn't know that he survived 2 mid-air collisions looking like John Wayne in "The Green Berets", you would think he had completely lost his mind. He was two sandwiches short of a picnic and one can short of a six pack. He had more sayings and stories than you could shake a stick at and he liked to mix a little truth with a lot of fiction. If he wasn't such a hero saving people, he would be locked up in the nut house-

Charlie-Son was a partying fool, he was stoned all the time just like most of us were. His problem was that he liked his beer & shots and he had this ridiculous theory as to the "proper alcohol & marijuana maintenance!" He would take me on a short PC so we could share a bowl and then we would stop at his favorite watering hole. He would shoot back a few stiff ones and get that buzz going pretty well, so then he would have a little something to eat to settle down his head. He would order a little bar food that he could pick on slowly, he didn't have much of an appetite when he drank. Next, he would seriously get snookered and then he would go out to his car in the cold and turn it on and open the windows. He would turn his tape deck on and listen to some Steppenwolf until he rested and woke up freezing cold. He would take a couple of hits on the pipe and go back inside to start the whole process over again! He really believed that he had this all figured out and he thought that the pot got him high and the booze brought him back down. That's why he was always getting popped for drinking & driving. One time he was back home in North Jersey on leave and he was out on a Saturday night drinking and driving from bar to bar when he was told the cops were performing checkpoints after midnight. So about 2 am here comes Old Chaz flying along the back roads to avoid the road blocks on the two highways through town. He comes barreling up Schooley's Mountain and plows right through the two police cruiser barricade. CB fought in missions all over Vietnam and kept his Huey in the air for two tours yet back home he couldn't have a driving license on the east coast. One night he was pretty lit up and he was out driving from bar to bar after partying all day. He had signed out a jeep earlier from Transportation for a detail he was on and he still had it hours later. He heard that the MPs were conducting road checks at checkpoints on the main road coming back to the base. So, Charley-Son decides to go all around the back roads and ends up driving into a ditch. He gets tossed out of his jeep and comes out of the ditch without a scratch. It is said that God protects babies and drunks.

I was getting some chow at the mess hall when I ran into a couple of pilots that I knew from Travis. They sat down next to me and told me the bad news. They told me that the whole base was in shock and the news spread like a wild fire. It was reported that Tony Costa and Jack Murphy were caught in a shootout with the Nevada ATF agents at Lake Tahoe. They were supposedly caught with a suitcase full of cocaine on the way back to California. The police and the agents were set up to ambush them at the border. One of the cops jumped the gun when he saw that the guys were still armed and shot Tony in the shoulder. Jack shot back and the agents unloaded on him. Tony was able to jump back in his Vette and he took off spraying gravel in his wake. Four police cruisers took off after him and the chase was on. The government Fords were no match for the Corvette for Tony was going like a bat out of hell and back on the highway he was roaring at 170 MPH. He was able to get off the freeway on to a two-lane highway. He was bleeding so bad that he had to pull over to wrap his arm with some tape. He had parked on an overpass over the Black River so he ran down to the waters edge to wash some of the blood off of himself. He heard some sirens off in the distance so he decided to jump in the river. The river was treacherous from the spring rains so Tony was bouncing off the boulders and getting beat up badly. He grabbed on to a floating branch and saved himself before the river went over a raging waterfall.

The cops eventually found his car still running by the bridge and they must have figured he jumped off into the river. His car was shot full of holes and they saw all the blood on the driver's seat. Jack Murphy was shot dead with 15 bullet holes and three agents were shot and one had died on the way to the hospital. They found Tony's bloody leather jacket by the water fall and they recovered the cocaine behind his seat. The Nevada police combed the area and they decided that Tony lost to much blood and died in the freezing waters. The entire incident was all over the news and the report stated that Tony was in the Air Force and he had ties with the big hotels in Tahoe and Las Vegas. SGT John Murphy, AKA "Big Jack" worked with Tony at Travis AFB and was a part of the gang. I was safer to be in Vietnam then in California.

After I got set up and started to adjust to this foreign land, a couple of new buddies asked me if I wanted to go with them to Bangkok. I worked with these two guys on the flight line and they were cool guys. Cpl. Joe Russo was from Philadelphia and Sgt. Ian McIntosh from Columbus, Ohio. They were in country for about six months so they wanted to show me the ropes. Both guys had been to Bangkok, Thailand a couple of times, it was close enough to go on a three-day pass. Bangkok is considered one of the wildest and crazy places in the world. It is known as the Venice of the East. Bangkok is made up of little islands, canals and waterways and the main area is called the Floating Markets. They had gondolas and everything that floats to travel the waterways. Many types of crafts were houseboats and everything is tied up together. The main markets sold everything you could imagine and back up in the canals there was things that you couldn't even imagine. They were famous for imports like electronics; Sony, Mitsubishi, Panasonic, Nikon, Minolta and imports from Germany and Swiss watches. They were known for silk dresses and custom suits and dyes and prints.

Whole markets were specialized in gold and silver and the food markets were filled with all sorts of exotic foods, some still living. The back markets had opium, ty-sticks (a combination of strong marijuana & hashish woven on sticks looking like an appetizer but you smoke it), cocaine, heroin, and all different potions and elixirs.

The big deal here was opium, and opium dens were legal bars and clubs. The Opium Wars with China have gone on and on for a couple of hundred years. The battles were fought against the British and the French against the powerful Qing Dynasty. These wars led to the start of the Republic of China where opium is still legal. My boys were going for one of the private clubs to spend the night in sexual fantasy. The beautiful Polynesian girls were trained like the Geisha Girls in seduction and service. They were trained in potions and teas and many ways to bring pleasures. They were proficient in the Kama Sutra and they can bring you up and down like a yoyo. The drugs and teas were all designed to bring you pleasure and they gave you baths and massages and kept you going all night. In the morning you got a final bath and breakfast. Some guys spent the entire weekend there. We left in the morning to go out exploring the enchanting place that use to be called Siam.

We rented 3 Yamaha 500s so we could tour the countryside. But first we had to get out of the biggest traffic jam I have ever seen. Just like the harbor, the roadways were crowded with everything that had wheels. Some had engines and some were powered by oxen or horses, some by men and some by elephants. The main vehicles were motor bikes and bicycles and people walking every which way. The place was just plain nuts. The city was the size of New York City, about 8 million people. We were in the old city that had Buddhist temples and gardens everywhere. The downtown was a big modern city. Once we got out of the city, we were going through miles of rice paddies shaped in circles like they were floating entities. Water buffalos, oxen and elephants roamed freely. We rode down into the jungle and I was glad the highway was safe to pass. Now we rode through different troops of monkeys. They would steal anything they could get their hands on. They would be swinging from the trees and perched everywhere. They were so crafty that they could steal a wristwatch right off a person's wrist. In the jungle was also home to snakes and snake charmers. This place was no joke, it is bad enough that there is a war going on but you could get wrapped up by a python or mauled by a Siamese Tiger. A 300-pound, 20-foot snake could sliver up a tree and drop down on you, wrap you up and squeeze the life out of you. Huge vultures were seen on all sorts of carcasses and it was survival of the fittest. I guess because we had the best weapons, we were the fittest and on top of the food chain. Once man learned how to make a spear, he was the smartest and now we could go to the moon and back.

We pushed through the jungle to start going up into the mountains. We stopped at an overlook to see the jagged mountains and I was reminded that we were in a far-far-off land. We started up a mountain road and when we went around a turn we came upon a bad accident. A farm truck filled with animals ran into a van that was filled with women. A lot of animals were dead and a few women were dead. We pulled over and tried to help, everyone knew we were US Military but we see that some gorillas were guarding the women. It didn't take us long to figure out that the women were being smuggled for the sex trade business. They were all young good-looking women. Joe, Ian and I had our service revolvers but these guys were heavily armed so we had to play it cool. Soon the Thailand police showed up and they looked more like soldiers then cops. Now we all had to show our papers and they let us go. The thugs obviously paid off the cops as they helped them clean up this mess. We were pretty sure they threw the dead women off the cliff with the dead animals.

We took off glad to get out of there, we rode back the 3 hours to Bangkok and some sort of civilization. We bought some gold jewelry and I went back up to get a real flying carpet. My flying carpet was from the 40s and was well used. Flying carpets are 3 by 6-foot prayer rugs that have places for opium pipes, incense and opium. My rug was very worn at these places. The owner would sit crossed leg in the lotus position and smoke opium until he could go to la-la land. The dreams and visions would take them on journeys and they would fly on their carpets. This was in line with the snake charmers and the magic that was part of the culture. "Ali Baba and the Forty Thieves" comes to mind, "Open Sesame"! The South & North American Indians were very into prayers and visions using all types of drugs and potions. They had underground ceremonial chambers to smoke the peace pipe and have visions. Siam was and is a very enchanting place. Bangkok is everything they say it is and not many places can you walk around with elephants, when their trunks are up it means they are happy and that brings good luck.

My long-time buddy Charlie did not have these perks as he was assigned to a combat attack and rescue Bell Hu-1 Iroquois (Huey) helicopter. He was the Crew Chief Mechanic and even though the pilot flew it was considered Charlie's bird because he was responsible for keeping it running and up in the air. He was located way up north near the DMZ and the base was at Da Nang where fighter jets and Strategic Air Command were on attack. From there Charlie went deep in the jungle to small camps and bases that only helicopters could go, the helicopter replaced the jeep as the way to get around. In the hot spots they didn't land but could hoist up the wounded in stretchers under attack as Charlie had an M -80 machine gun mounted on his port side. He had to lay down a constant spray to protect any ground fire so close to the landing zone. Up in the air he would sit on his helmet to protect his ass from being fragged from below. He also had the basic medical skills to help the badly wounded. He was able to assist the medic to stop the bleeding out or give them some morphine to help them with the screaming pain. When a medic was aboard, they would start IV bags as time was critical to get the wounded back to the MASH unit. And it was right back to the hell hole they just left to pick up more. This is why Charlie and his fellow soldiers were some of the bravest outfits in the war, as the natural tendency is to get down and take cover, these guys ran towards danger and never backed down. And they did this every day and Charlie loved what he had to do and never got tired of the WOP -WOP -WOP of the chopper blades. Back at his base at night he would drink beer, smoke pot and talk about how awesome these helicopters were. They were the backbone of this type of fighting and when the choppers were making their assault it was a flying wing of Wup-Ass!

A major destination in the Pacific was Clark AFB in the Philippines. It was a big stop on the way to South Vietnam. This was an R & R location along with Japan and Bangkok Thailand. It was a close enough place to get some Rest & Rehab or, along with whatever else a guy wanted or thought he needed. The biggest base in South Vietnam was Cam Ron Bay as all branches operated there. It was the port and destination of most shipping and passenger transportation and even some civilian airlines were used to transport personnel. Since 1945 the Flying Tigers Airlines operated passenger flights throughout the Pacific and transported troops and after the war they were bought by Federal Express. The base had two 10,000 ft runways as everything from smaller planes that go further in the country, to F -15 fighter jets and our big football field size cargo planes landed and departed around the clock. The Navy's 7th Fleet was in the harbor so it was a big stronghold for the US military operations. A few years later when the collapse of Saigon took place the base was rocketed until the end but we were long gone by then. It turned into a Russian installation and it is still one of the bigger military bases and port in South East Asia. Over 58,000 Americans died and with all the other countries on both sides the death totals were estimated to be that over a million communist military died, and 250,000 South Vietnam troops died. The estimated civilian death count was over 2 million. We took over after the French fought there for 20 years and American forces were fighting there for almost 10 years for what? The communist took over the country and killed many more dissidents and even renamed Saigon to Ho Chi Minh City.

When Charlie was getting his arm taken care of, he reported to the base clinic so the nurses could treat his infection. One morning he was having breakfast in the mess hall with one of the MASH nurses so I joined them for some coffee and SOS. Charlie introduced us, she was a combat nurse working in the OR and she also went out on rescue missions and she was absolutely beautiful. Her name was Nancy Barret, a second Lieutenant from Baltimore Maryland. We all hung out for a while having coffee and listening to Charlies' stories. We were laughing and having some fun and when Nancy smiled, she looked radiant. There is something about a pretty nurse in uniform that made them so special. With her nursing hat and white uniform on she looked like an angel. We decided to meet for breakfast the next morning. Charlie was going to be here for a week so we met some new people to hang out with. The next morning, we had a couple of tables filled, Nancy invited a couple of her girlfriends and I invited Joe and Ian and we all had a good time. Charlie still held court, the guy had so many incredible stories and he managed to put a funny twist on some of the gruesome "war is hell" ones. We decided to all meet out at the night club in town the next night. We all danced and hung out together and I was starting to feel something sweet for Nancy. I was pretty sure she was starting to feel the same.

Beatle nut was a hard berry that the Vietnam woman would grind down and chew like chewing tobacco but it gave them a buzz and rotted their teeth. "Beetle-nut" is what the older woman were called and they were the women that would do the little jobs now that they were no longer desirable for prostitution, for most guys that is. It was more about their teeth rotting out of their heads. So, they would take care of a guy's hooch and cook and run errands for 5 dollars a month. They made their entire livelihood off the GI s and they loved anything American. They worked in these old army tents doing production work on long tables with no chairs as they could squat on their heels for hours. This particular tent had about 20 women, 10 on each side to repackage consi (marijuana) with Marlboro cigarettes. The woman would first open the cartons of Marlboros and sift out the tobacco into large bowls. Next, they would fill the empty paper and filters with finely grated marijuana and pack it in tight. Then they put the marijuana cigarettes back in the pack and sell them to the GI for a dollar a pack. The Marlboro tobacco was then rolled into cigarettes. The women liked to smoke the American tobacco or sell them for 25 cents a pack. Five dollars would buy you a big bag of grass and the beetle-nut momma-sons would go buy you whatever you needed. If you wanted a young woman it would cost you as much as 2 dollars and if you wanted her for all night it cost you 5 dollars depending on your tastes.

I never went that route, I never thought it was that good without it meaning something. We didn't have to buy company back in the states, we had plenty of young ladies to hang with. But Charlie lived everyday like it was his last and he was one of the funniest characters in the Army. He was very hairy chested and since the Vietnamese people were practically hairless, they would always want to touch his chest or stomach and say "same-same monkey" and Charlie would make a monkey face and everyone would laugh. Sometimes he would have an orange wedge in his mouth and he would chase the kids around pounding his hairy chest like an ape. The kids would shriek and howl as Charlie-Son chased them around the tents. Like I have been trying to say, Sgt. Charles Bonham was a hero, a larger than life character and he saw more horrible shit then I could ever imagine. This is why I take offense when people call him a burned out drunk or pot head when he had to endure all that he went through. How many normal people have tried to rescue an injured soldier only to have their skin fall off from being severely burned by Napalm? Or having to shoot down a woman who was running at you with a baby wrapped up with a grenade!! There were so many orphan babies to use as decoys as life for women and children had little value. Charlie had to do many unimaginable things for 3 years in the jungle against an enemy that was trying to kill him and leave him with his tongue & eyes cut out. A lot of GIs said they wish they would just die and get it over with as the men that got shot down didn't have to suffer night after night. But guys like Charley Bonham couldn't wait to get back up in the air and go to save our guys from the jungle. The knuckle head even re-upped for 2 more years.

Charly-Son told me about large poppy fields that he had flown over the border into Cambodia that he took pictures of. Since the fighting was overflowing into

Laos and Cambodia our guys were fighting in all three countries. Charlie had detailed pictures of the heroin being manufactured and distributed. He showed us acres and acres of the white poppy flowers and long tents to process and package the product. They used fans and heat lamps and they had women raking and spreading out the heroin until it turned into powder. The women wore plastic suits and face masks and had to rotate every 15 minutes to prevent overdoses. This particular camp produced thousands of pounds every week and they operated 24/7. This camp supplied the United States and Europe and there were hundreds of camps all along the border of Cambodia and Laos. Of course, a lot of people were addicted and seeing people with collapsed veins was gross.

I asked Nancy out on a date and told her I would pick her up for dinner Saturday night. I wanted to do something special so I decided to cook up a dinner that I could take out in the jeep. I could tell her I was taking her to a cool restaurant that opened up the beach that I wanted to go to. I made some chicken marsala over noodles with big mushrooms and broccoli. I bought a bottle of wine and I kept the dinner warm with a warmer from the mess hall. I packed up everything and hid it all in the back of the jeep. I picked her up just as the sun was starting to set and we drove up the beach to where the restaurant was supposed to be. I went around to open the wine and serve her a glass. She still didn't really understand what was going on so I unveiled the evening dinner plan. When she sat back to be served, she actually had a few tears in her eyes. My plan could not have been more romantic and we had a marvelous night. For dessert we had some fresh fruits that we fed each other. After dinner we sat under the stars and had a great talk. She told me that this was her first date since nursing school. I asked her how could this be since most of the guys on the base would gladly ask her out. She said that her assignment as a MASH nurse was overwhelming so she never had time to do much of anything. But she said that I had knocked her socks off with my charm and this date was the best date ever.

After hearing stories of great Perimeter Checks, Nancy asked to go out on a real one. We signed up at the Flight office for Saturday night and we each bought some favorite snacks and drinks. By the time the night came we were pretty excited and it was a beautiful night. My buddy Ian lent me his telescope and tripod and we let down the windshield and set it up on the hood of the jeep. In with the telescope was a map of the stars so we could locate the constellations and planets. We felt so small and insignificant yet the love we felt in our hearts was beating out of our chests. We took a slow lap around our section and passed by a man riding on a bicycle that we passed going the other direction not more then 15 minutes earlier. He had a couple of boxes on his rear fender so we stopped him to investigate. It turned out that he was stealing car batteries from the motor pool. We confiscated the batteries and let the guy go. He was so thankful that he had tears in his eyes and he kept bowing to Nancy and saying "cam on ban" (to feel favor).

The Air Force and the Navy shipped more 55-gallon drums then Carter has pills. On every base, fort or camp there were piles of barrels everywhere you looked. They were shipped by the pallet and stored at fuel depots and were filled with good stuff like gasoline and drums of oil and tons of Napalm and Agent Orange. The red and white barrels were kept under wraps as all weapons were disguised as food and medical supplies so they weren't such an easy target. We used the Agent Orange which was a lethal exfoliant that was sprayed by helicopters and smaller propeller jobs dumping it on the vegetation and pretty much killing all life. It was used to kill the trees, the fields and the rice paddies as well as the livestock and the people. The combination of Agent Orange and Napalm so raped the land causing widespread famine and starvation. Agent Orange left offspring, both human and animals with birth defects and our troops came home with it in them causing sickness and death.

Napalm on the other hand blew the hell out of anything in its path. Napalm was a combination of gasoline and a jelly that made it sticky and gave it more firepower as gasoline would give it the bang and the jelly would make it burn longer and a thousand degrees hotter. It would now stick to any surface and burn right through flesh like rocket fuel. Napalm burned at 3500 degrees which melts through steel and gives off carbon dioxide that kills all life, one of DuPont's great inventions to further destroy the land and all living things. We had more ammunition then was used in all of WW 2 and we dropped tons of bombs on Hanoi 24/7 for the rest of the war. The Ho Chi Min Trail and the DMZ were rocked with everything we had to back our outnumbered ground troops. If we lost 58,000 troops then the Vietnamese, Cambodian, Laotian and Chinese people lost a couple of million. The amount of heavy artillery we had was staggering as we shipped pallets of rockets, missiles and bombs. We had plastic explosives like C-4 and claymore mines and grenades and we had flame throwers and a plethora of guns and ammo. We probably could blacktop the whole damn place and put up a McDonalds and sell water buffalo burgers. We all feared that we will have lasers out in space soon able to pinpoint targets all over the world and we pray that we don't destroy the entire planet. With thousands of nuclear weapons, we can destroy the earth. Jesus come quickly.

Cam Ron Bay had both SAC (Strategic Air Command) and MAC (Military Airlift Command) squadrons in place. We had a lot of planes in the air so we felt fairly protected. Down in the south, Saigon was a hell hole and up north Danang was getting rocked all night. Our surrounding area was fairly safe, we were lucky to be stationed at Cam Ron Bay. It was a huge base protected by army and marine camps and on base, we had some formidable aircraft all lined up and ready to go. There is nothing more formidable then an F-14 all loaded up with missiles. But one evening just at nightfall the alarms went off and we scampered to our bunkers. Incoming rockets took out part of a hanger and a hit on the makeshift hospital. Fortunately, nobody was injured, Nancy was with me going to the motor pool and we were close enough to get our eardrums blasted and we saw double for a while as the sky lit up like lightning. We probably had concussions. A squad of Apache helicopters took off followed by two F-14 Tomcats and they flushed out a group of rocket launchers from an NVA camp up north a way. We could see and hear the thunder as our guys hit their marks.

As they were working on putting the MASH unit back together, Nancy got the word to come in as they had suffered injuries, a pilot and his gunner got hit from shrapnel when their bird got hit. Both men were hit on their left side and were badly burned by the explosion. They operated on them and put them in baths of ice, medicine and morphine to keep their temperature down. Nancy stayed with them all night doing what she could to take care of them. The gunner was short, he was getting ready to go home, hopefully he will heal enough to get home soon. The pilot was so tough that all he wanted to do was get better so he could get back in the air. He was shipped to a hospital back in Japan. More causalities were coming in so Nancy worked all night and day. I worked on getting some new equipment for the emergency room and when I got together with Nancy later that night, I rubbed her feet until she was sound asleep. Sitting there for a while watching her sleep, I knew that I was with an exceptional human being.

We had a few days of R&R coming up so we decided to hop a flight to Hawaii and live it up a little. We were able to book a round trip flight on a regular run on a big C-141 and we even got 2 bag meals. The Air Force did it right, we had two ham & swiss sandwiches, an orange and a banana, a bag of gorp and a yogurt. Once we got situated the two pilots came around to secure the plane. We were greeted by Captain Eric Richter who was one of the pilots on the near disaster when the jet engine exploded from sucking in the seagulls. I told him once again that he saved our lives when he was able to get the plane under control as it was nosediving to the ground. He told us that part of his training was to practice taking off and then landing while losing power. He added that in Nam he took a lot of flack and was glad when the Apache choppers and our jet fighters escorted him. To witness the F-15 Hornets with 4 underwing Stinger air to air missiles and 2 M-80 machine guns was an awesome display of military power. Captain Richter flew over 300 missions over all the South Pacific and South East Asia. When we talked to him about the birds, he told us that some migrating birds can fly up to 35,000 feet. He told us we were only at 18 to 20,000 feet when we took in the birds. This just blew our minds that he was able to pull the plane back up before it crashed into the ocean. He said that he was just doing his job, he said the real heroes came home in the transfer cases.

We flew to Honolulu and stayed on the island of Oahu. The first day we rented scooters and toured some of the main attractions. We got to see Pearl Harbor, Waikiki Beach, Diamond Head and Kailua Bay. We stayed at a resort on the beach at Diamond Head right on a lagoon. The Hawaiian Islands are made up of over 150 volcanic islands stretching 1500 miles in the South Pacific. We got up the next day and took a flight to Maui to try some surfing. We took a surf clinic and rode some 5 to 10 ft waves. We rode up a 10,000-foot peak of an active volcano that had such a beautiful view of the island and the ocean. We stayed for 2 nights in a Yurt right on the cliffs looking over the bay. We fell asleep in the warm ocean breezes still rocking from the waves. We ate great seafood dishes and drank exotic rum and fruit drinks. The islands were so romantic and the weather was perfect. The one bummer was seeing the devastation at Pearl Harbor and visiting the sunken memorial of the USS Arizona. The Japanese snuck in that Sunday morning and killed over 2400 servicemen in just a few hours. We ended the war by dropping 2 atomic bombs on them.

Between learning the Bible and trying to connect with God and getting inspired by Nancy's example of excellence, I was on a strong high. Life was a wild ride through all this power and energy unfortunately designed to annihilate the enemy and save our world from Communism. As Americans, we felt we were always on the right side and even in our own civil war, I was a Yankee. I couldn't understand how we were catching a beating here in Vietnam and it just wasn't our problem in the first place. We were being held back so we were in a no-win situation and our hands were tied to really go on a full throttle attack. Back home in the States our country was in a big ruckus over what we should be doing and how we should be doing it. The only thing certain was that people were dying all over the world. There were times that Nancy worked around the clock with all the injuries and I was shipping over 100 body bags a week. We all try to love our families but it seems we hate our neighbors. Hopefully mankind has more good attributes than bad. I always felt that mankind would be able to figure all this crap out but the bible shows us the way it really is going down. Right now, this age is controlled by Satan and his Devil Spirits. Not until Christ comes back as the first one resurrected from the dead will he resurrect his church to eternal life. Christ is coming back on his white horse to defeat the god of this world, AKA Satan, the Devil.

When I was a child, I played Army, Cowboys & Indians, Cops & Robbers and watched it all on TV. When I got a little older, we would attack the boys up the street with sticks and garbage can lids. Later we rumbled with the towns around us. Ever since grade school we knew the pecking order of the toughest kids and who was the toughest guys in school. The varsity football team was a barometer to how tough we were. If we lost a game, then the next practice we had to do head-on drills for hours. Head-ons were a punishing drill consisting of two lines 20 yards apart. Our coach would spin the ball on the ground and two guys would run full speed at each other like rams on steroids. If you didn't recover the fumble you had to go again and again until you did. Coach was somewhat sadistic, he liked to have a 140- pound Freshman line up against a 250- pound Senior lineman. It was always about having to prove how tough you are. Then at 18 we could go in the Army and really fight and kill.

Christmas was especially tough; there is no place like home for the holidays. The service did do a good job for we had a sunrise service looking over the bay and then a big turkey dinner with all the trimmings. Later we had a USO party with some Vietnamese rock bands singing "Light my Fire" and "The Green Berets" with their Oriental accents. They had lights set up and a Christmas tree and some marines put up a giant cross over the mess hall tent with a banner saying GOD BLESS AMERICA: JESUS LOVES THE MARINES!! It was so good to have Nancy by my side. We exchanged gifts. She gave me a special black Swiss Army knife and matching watch that she ordered from

Geneva. I got her a matching set of pearl necklace and earrings from the divers here in the South China Sea and a couple of custom-made silk dresses from a guy I knew from Bangkok. It was a wonderful Christmas and we were in love. Nancy was such a good nurse for she had to be to be in a MASH OR. There were many times when three or four medivac choppers were bringing in GIs all at once that badly needed lifesaving procedures. The OR staff sees so much blood and guts and a lot of guys don't make it through surgery in that they had been bleeding out since they got blown up in this fucked up war. The incredible motivating factor that pushes the staff is that they get to help save lives and that is priceless. A lot of people in medicine know that we can sew people up and put them back together, but only God gives us life. "All the king's horses and all the king's men, couldn't put Humpty Dumpty together again." If people cannot handle this then sometimes alcohol, drugs and sex become a big substitute to try and fill the void. The suicide rate of the GIs was a sad reality of just how bad things are. Nancy and I were starting a spiritual journey together. The bible shows us that we will be transformed by the renewing of our minds. We had to stay positive to do any good so we can use that positive energy to break through the bad energy of death and destruction.

Our base Chaplin was a seasoned veteran serving since WW 2 so he has witnessed so many signs, miracles and wonders as well as the evils of the god of this world, Satan. Coronel William Thompson preached a great sermon about the working of Holy Spirit by believing the bible teaches us how to manifest the power of God in Christ. All the bigger bases had a chapel or a place to worship. Out in the bush they had itinerant priests, preachers and rabbis that held their services on makeshift altars and podiums. It was always good to see guys huddled up praying together. Like I have said, we need God more in these hard times as it is a matter of life and death and we need to believe in the resurrection or we are "men most miserable". It was a good thing that Charlie, Nancy and I were all being drawn to the higher power. As for me, I was starting to realize that this was the truth I had been searching for all of my life. Nancy and I were even starting to pray and read the bible together and we were starting to get a real natural high from it. The bible was showing us how to walk with God and unlock the great mysteries of life. Gods holy spirit gave us power to live an abundant life.

The good Lord was obviously looking over Bonham as he survived his third midair collision. They were evacuating troops up north when they started taking flak and bullets were flying all through the cabin. They got on the guns and the pilot maneuvered about to go on attack. As he swung around an incoming rocket took off most of the tail section and they started spinning out of control. Before they crashed the crew bailed out except Charlie who went down with a badly wounded marine. The fuselage blew sky high in a large firebomb and the report was that Charlie comes out walking through the smoke and fire carrying the wounded marine on his back. The crew said that they all witnessed another incredible miracle. We heard that the CO put Charlie in for a Purple Heart for his bravery and lifesaving actions. It was a damn shame that Charley-Son could not defeat his worst enemy after all he's been through. Drinking and smoking kicked his ass and held him back all the rest of his life. Many men left a good part of their lives in Southeast Asia and some didn't come back at all. Life just ain't fair as Charlie survived all those combat missions yet wasn't allowed to operate a motor vehicle in four states up and down the east coast. He was an alcoholic and a war hero.

Bonham, Nancy and I were all serving our years assignment in country. Bonham was on his second tour, he wanted to go back in being he just loved what he did. Now we all had about six months to go, I had a little more and Bonham had less. You were not officially "short" until you were under 50 days when could start counting backwards. Nancy and I were doing great together, if she wasn't on duty and if I was not on the flight line, we were together. Nancy loved to listen to Charley's stories and we all spent most of our time together laughing and joking. He had so many incredible stories and sayings and he had a wild imagination to boot.

Ever since we both were in boot camp all we have done is train. We all started with physical training and continued on with more in our tech schools. Seeing a company of nurses running by in formation was always a good thing. No one dared made a sound or a cat call because their Company - Commander taught self-defense and lifted weights. She supposedly liked to grab a stupid private running by to make a teaching example of some choke hold she was trying to show. The women in the service today were trained just like the men and were a lot tougher than they use to be. We were told that women had a much higher threshold for pain. If it were up to men to have babies, we probably would not procreate.

Nancy started working 12-hour shifts and she started working the 4 days on and 3 days off rotation and I had some air time scheduled to deliver to some bases in my section. We were shipping home a lot of bodies and Nancy was taking a beating in the OR.

We had over 500,000 troops in country and the dead and the wounded were at the highest count in the conflict. When I went to some of the bases to pick up and deliver various priority cargo, I saw a lot of GIs getting wasted. Most guys were drinking and getting stoned but many more were doing heavier drugs like speed and amphetamines and pain pills and morphine. I think that with all the bad shit these guys have been through the heavy partying and drugs are a way to deaden the pain. Guys would really let loose on their down time and it wasn't unusual to see 20 guys dancing in their skivvies with their dog tags swaying to the beat. Everyone was very high singing along to the Four Tops or the Rolling Stones and for that night you tried to forget that you were far away from home.

Besides the emotional stress and thoughts of war and destruction there was still the fact that many men were injured and physically hurting. Pain pills lose their effectiveness quickly and after a few weeks a guy needs more and more. When the addiction starts taking over, the tail wags the dog. People start feeling worse as now the drug starts calling the shots and it creates its own desire to relieve the pain. When a person addicted is not high, they are usually miserable because now they suffer from different types of pain that only another hit can relieve. When somebody was coming down from the drug they were "crashing" or eventually "nodding out". Heroin is so strong that when injected into the vein it hits the brain and the nervous system so the user gets that big rush that they are chasing. But smack does pack a punch that can take away all your pain and problems till you come back down again. I am not trying to judge any one as I don't walk in their boots. Eighty percent of these soldiers were drafted so they didn't want to even be here, no less having to kill these oriental people. They came in fairly straight and now they leave as addicts and junkies. And many more have demons to battle and to be tormented by. Everyone wants to go to heaven but nobody wants to die.

I was breaking down a pallet to ship back to the States when I came upon some gruesome souvenirs that some troop was trying to send home. A footlocker had been damaged and as I was trying to tape it together, I was freaked out to see 3 human skulls inside. Some guys were really into the skull & crossbones trip and I had seen a lot of skulls being used as ashtrays and even as hookah pipes. I thought that smoking weed out of an M-16 rifle was kind of fucked up (is that where we get the term "shotgun" from?). But no way am I going to smoke anything out of a human skull. I would wonder about the bad vibes surrounding the whole thing. One night I was out tripping with a buddy in the woods when he freaked out and had a bad trip. He stumbled in a rectangular hole and as he crawled out, he thought that he fell into his own grave, and it was I that led him there!! For hours he was freaked out and paranoid and he started crying about his father's death years ago. That is why we tried to be positive and do cool things outdoors so our surroundings didn't close us in. Music was so important too. Some music can drive you crazy. Even the difference of two Beatles songs can affect your head. The difference between "Here comes the sun" and "Revolution #9" can mean a blessing or a bummer. So, LSD lets you step back and take a look at yourself and you better like what you see or you better change it. I just wasn't into the skulls and dead stuff. We also saw guys having these custom-made rings with human (V.C.) eyes in them. Some dudes had really evil looking tattoos with sculls and crossbones and even pictures of the devil. Since we were the property of the US Government, we were technically not supposed to desecrate ourselves!? A majority of GIs got some sort of tattoos representing their time in the service. I was thinking about getting another one of a small (1 inch) jet plane but now I want a small holy spirit dove over my heart.

The Colonel was holding meetings and Bible fellowships around our section and we were shadowing him and his aide around the area. We met out in a bombed-out village in an old abandoned Buddhist temple. We stayed there a few days and we had a good group of GIs and even some local villagers attending. The final day we all left after the morning fellowship to drive back to the base about 20 miles through the jungle. Nancy and I stayed to clean up and talk to a few guys and then we went to meet the Colonel back at the base.

We drove through old pathways that the jungle was taking back, nature was claiming the air and the land. We came to a river and a wooden bridge that was filled with Siamese crocodiles. We crossed the bridge and came to a better road that bordered a swamp. We came around a bend in the road and almost drove right into a dead water buffalo lying in the middle of the road. There was one of our red flares still active so it was `not more than 20 minutes ago. We looked to the right and saw a bad accident. The Colonel's jeep had flipped and was lying upside down in the swamp. His aide had left a flare burning so we figured he must have gone for help. We found the Colonel lying face down under the windshield, we lifted up his head and Nancy wiped off the mud on his face. He let out a choking cough and vomited up some swamp water that at least showed he was still alive. He was trapped under the jeep's window frame and the faster I was trying to clear away the mud, the faster it was filling up with water.

I ran back up to my jeep to get a shovel and the come-along. I attached the come-along to the frame of the jeep and we could see that it was sinking into the swamp. I cranked the canvas straps as hard as I could to try and shore up the jeep. The window frame had the Colonel's arm pinned to the dashboard and he was bleeding profusely. Nancy had her bag so she put a tourniquet above his elbow. The jeep sagged and fortunately the Colonel gained a little separation from the mud. I had to be careful that I didn't slice him with my spade. Nancy yelled that the Colonel's arm was very messed up. He also had a compound fracture and we could see the bone sticking out. All of a sudden Nancy lets out a scream," Watch out for the crocodile!" I turned around just in time to bash his head with the shovel. I sliced him right in his eyes and cut off his forehead. He retreated back in the water and his two buddies beat feet back into the swamp. I gave the chords a few more turns and we almost had the Colonel free. I used a tree branch as a fulcrum to pry up the jeep a little more and freed the Colonel from the jeep and the mud. We couldn't see just how bad he was because he was covered in blood and mud. We had to drag him up the bank and in to the jeep. I drove as fast as I could but

Nancy kept yelling for me to slow down so she could hold his arm in place.

We finally got back to the ER on the base and Nancy stayed with him through surgery. The doctors told us he had a collapsed lung and broken bones and a huge gash on his arm. They put his shoulder and his arm in a cast and he needed over one hundred sutures to sew him up. He was back working in his office after three weeks with his arm in a cast and a brace. No one was going to call him an old tough son of a bitch, not to his face that is. We did tell him that we loved him and we were glad he didn't die in that swamp to be eaten by the crocodiles. His aide ran 10 miles back to the base and passed out from losing a lot of blood. We all gave blood for these guys, I have AB- so I had to do my patriotic duty every six weeks. Second Lieutenant Haywood Jenny from Bullrun, Mississippi was the Colonel's aide and driver. He worked out and ran cross-country and it was obvious that he was in great shape, he was able to run at least 10 miles bleeding like an Arkansas hog. He needed bags of plasma and blood and 20 stiches on his thigh to repair an artery. Both these men wanted to be back in uniform as quickly as possible, that is just how they roll.

I took a ride with an Airman from the flight line in a flatbed to go back and pick up the flipped jeep. His name was Pfc. Van Decker from La Jolla, California and he had thick blonde hair like a surfer. He wore some beads and a leather chord around his neck and he had a small sunrise tattoo on his shoulder. He said he got drafted and that if God was willing, he would survive to surf the Australian coast by next year. He also said he would rather wipe out on a forty-footer then die in the Vietcong jungle. By the time we returned to the dead water buffalo it was being devoured by vultures and big water rats. The Water Rats were as big as small dogs and we had to be careful because they were not afraid to attack us. We pushed the half-eaten water buffalo off the road and picked up the jeep with the power winch. When we got back to the base, we found Nancy right by the Colonel's side. The kitchen sent over roast beef with mashed potatoes and gravy and Nancy looked like an angel feeding the Colonel until he fell back to sleep. It was quite an amazing day. Even though the Colonel almost died, God is good, all the time. We felt so good to be able to save a life with so much death around. Every life is special, it is just that the Colonel's life affected a lot of people.

Charley was officially short as he went under 50 days in country, he can now start counting backwards. In 7 weeks, he will be transferring to a better location as a lot of guys got to choose to go to Europe or Turkey. I could see myself going with Nancy to say, Puerto Rico or in Panama. But we would probably go to Europe and we could see Rome and the Sistine Chapel and all that art. I think Chaz would like to see England and Germany but I don't know if we could see Gay Paree as de Gaulle had recently sent the US forces out of France! I thought it was only 25 years ago that we liberated France from Nazi Germany? Wherever Charlie went would be a hell of a lot better than here. A big ongoing debate we had here was what is the harder time, your first 50 days or your last 50 -you certainly didn't want to get fragged when you are so close to going home. A great thing about completing your tour of Vietnam was the 30 days leave you had saved up! So those first days and weeks were especially hard and if you were out in the jungle, they said it didn't count as you didn't know what the hell was going on anyway.

In that great book about WW-1," All's Quiet on the Western Front", this soldier survives the entire war only to be shot in the head while picking up a flower by someone who didn't know the war was over. We really started praying for Charlie that he will make it home safe after all this time. The ongoing debate included the ideas of fate, chance and destiny. Some guys figured that when it is your time to go you would be a grease spot by midnight. Other people think it has something to do with a random chance like walking under a ladder and getting hit by a paint bucket, or having a tire fly through your windshield. I guess we all wish to die in our sleep at the ripe old age of 90. I believe there are angels to protect us from some of this bad crap and will protect us from demons and evil.

So, Charlie-son, same -same -monkey, made the final countdown as he completed his second tour in Nam. He must have done boom-boom a thousand times, 645 missions, survived 3 midair collisions and smoked a hundred pounds of consei. His crew put on a farewell party that was a hoot, we said our goodbyes and we hoped to see each other in Europe or back on the east coast. "Here, there or in the air" was another great saying of ours. His plan was to get back to California, buy a Corvette with some of the money he saved and drive the southern route across the country. He planned on going down Highway One along the Ventura Hwy to San Diego, over to Tijuana and up to the Grand Canyons. From there he was taking Route 66 and over to the Gulf, he was going all around Florida to the Keys and up the east coast to North Jersey to see his mom. There is definitely something to be said about a veteran touring the USA in his convertible Chevrolet- I planned on a different route when I drive my roadster back in about 50 days!! Before Charlie flew out, he got his orders and he was going to Germany to a cushy assignment at a helicopter training base.

I got a couple more letters from the twins. They were done with their first year at FSU, now they were doing a summer school course studying the manatees along the Gulf coast, I figured it was with those two barracudas as they still were all hanging out together. They hoped that when we came East, we would celebrate their birthdays at a big party they were going to have down in Key West. They told me that it was going to be a big blowout like we use to have at the beach in the Big Sur and they had some surprises for me when we come. I still think the twins were so awesome, they didn't have a mean bone in their bodies and they did everything with passion and gusto. Because of my love and commitment to Nancy I hoped we can all still be tight but in a different way. So, I hoped that our new friendship would continue to be special and that Nancy would be cool with the whole thing. If you looked up cool in the encyclopedia you would see Nans picture next to it! She was smart, she was cool and she loved God and his Son Jesus Christ, so who can be against her?? Spent some of my last days going on my final inspections of the flight lines around my area. Nancy was detained waiting on her replacement who hadn't reported yet, and she had to train her. This was ok with me, we will be getting to "deede mowe" close to each other, We had some great plans for our furlough. We were going home and I was going to meet her family in Baltimore. Then we were going to Long Island to see my mom and some old friends. After all that for a week, we were going to cruise the coast all the way to the Keys, stopping at a few points of interests along the way.

My final assignment was to deliver some priority one cargo to a few bases around and I had a little time to reflect on this foreign land. I was fortunate to be assigned to Cam Ron Bay for it was pretty safe place at that time. Up north and down south the main cities of Da Nang and Saigon were getting rocked. War had raged here for years so the countryside and the towns and villages were all torn from the bombings. A lot of the roads and bridges were ripped apart with burnt out vehicles blocking the way. That is why the helicopter was so important as the way to go and the "wop-wop-wop" of the rotors were a part of the landscape. But the sound of the fighter jets doing their sorties flying in formation was an incredible sound and display of military power. The noise these two aircraft make have a duality in their emotional impact. On one hand the sound of the choppers flying in their thunderous formations and then the fighter jets loaded with missiles and firepower are a bastion of power and victory. And on the other hand, it sounds like a lot of shit coming down, death and destruction, same sound but two distinct meanings. All depending on which side of the fence you are on. As good Americans we hope and believe that we are on the right side of the fence.

Nancy wanted to go out on one last PC as a celebration of our time here. We were able sit for a while overlooking the bay, the harbor and the beach and it was a beautiful view. In contrast to the mountains and the sea was a big part of our Pacific fleet hanging in the harbor. The huge destroyers, 1000 ft long tankers and the floating military bases we call aircraft carriers, loom over the waters like sleeping dinosaurs. The antiquated USS Missouri where McArthur signed the peace treaty with the Japanese, had those humungous guns on deck. The 3 guns could shoot 2,200-pound bombs 50 miles away, that's like shooting a Volkswagen to Hanoi. All this hardware built to annihilate the enemy and we have been trying to kill each other since Cain killed 25 % of the population by fragging his brother. Now we are so good at this killing thing that we can drop an atomic bomb and wipeout an entire city with one punch. Between the USA and the USSR, we have enough atomic bombs to knock the earth off its axis.

So, this is what we see and feel looking over a military base out under the moon and stars marred by the" rockets' red glare and the bombs bursting in the air." It isn't thunder and lightning or fireworks going off on the horizon but the real war raging through the night. We held each other tightly and we were so glad to be getting the hell out of here, or getting out of this hell hole.

With the north Vietnamese people killing the south Vietnamese people for generations it is a wonder that they can fall in love, have children and live some kind of life. The universal bond is the love that we share with each other that transcends all this hate. The last days being short were especially tough. All the emotions of being here a year were coming to a head and the thoughts of the future was exciting. We really do get extremely anxious about the chance of getting rocketed or getting blown up on these last days. Men out in the jungle were never safe and the NVA didn't stop fighting just because you were going home, there was no time outs in the fight. So, we did start thinking about the odds and the dangers of being involved in this conflict spurred by the exhilarating energies of flying out of here soon. A big song at this time was the Animals' "We Got to Get Out of This Place" and Grand Funk's "I'm Getting Closer to My Home" and were being sung all the time, especially at night being high with the guys. We had that saying that "it don't mean nothin" and you could add your own slant to it like "no big deal" or "don't sweat it" but my favorite was "one billion Chinese don't give a crap about it!" The final factor for me was that we were in a war zone and death and disaster was a lot closer hanging out like a shroud around us and 58,000 of us didn't make it home.

It was Nancy's time to say sayonara as she trained her replacement who happened to be a male nurse. People were snickering about a nurse being a man but I figured that if a woman could be a General or a fighter pilot then a guy can be a nurse. The Pentagon was thinking about having women fighting on the front lines so the feminist movement was starting to take off. I wondered that since we have mail women delivering our mail, will we have garbage women picking up our trash? What's fair is fair. The OR staff threw Nancy a good party and we said our goodbye that night. Our plans were for her to fly back to LA and then back to her family in Baltimore. Nancy got her orders and after 30 days of freedom and a few TDY travel days she was going to Germany. She was going to the biggest military hospital outside of the states at the army's Landstuhl Medical Center and she was very happy to get assigned there. My first choice was the Ramstein AFB which happens to be 3 miles from the west gate of Landstuhl!! So, Nancy "was leaving on her jet plane and she didn't think she would be back here again". The Army was right about joining and seeing the world, within the next month we were going to fly over two oceans and drive around on 3 continents. When I saw her off on her plane we prayed together before we kissed goodbye. I would pick her up in Baltimore in about a week. This will be the longest we've been apart since we met last year so I guess we can say that we have grown on each other.

I was finally down to "two nights and a wake up" so I said my farewells to the flight line crew and to my friend and advisor Colonel Thompson. I thanked him for his prayers and fellowship and I hoped we would see each other "here, there or in the air!" This Chaplain was a true Man of God. His last salutation to me was "Vaya con Dios" or go with God. I knew that the good Lord had a lot in store for Nancy and I if we stayed faithful. I checked out with the CO and he gave me my orders although I already knew I was going to Germany. I had met the CO in the latrine and he asked me if I could "speckenze Duetche "so I had a good idea where I was going. In the morning I was up in the air in a Boeing 727, when I looked down on the bay and the ocean, it looked beautiful against the green mainland. At 10,000 feet you could not see the troubles the people were having down below. It was a great flight as most flights over the ocean are. I survived a flight in a C-141 with a blown engine and a cargo that would put me away for life. In a commercial flight the takeoff and landings are so much more gradual as the military planes get up quickly and you feel the added g-force as you climb or assent. First time I rode up on a C-141 I looked out the window and couldn't quite find the ground, it was behind me more than it was down in front of me. I said goodbye to Vietnam for now, I still had another year to serve and I was an Air Cargo Loadmaster so I will still get my flight time.

Chapter Four

GERMANY AND THE WALL

"99 Luft Balloons" by Lena

"Using balloons to fly things over
the wall was brilliant"

I touched down at Travis AFB and the California coast looked awesome after being away for a year. I took my Sting Ray out of storage and I shipped the hardtop home. I would be riding straight across the country with the top down. In fact, they had just completed US 80 connecting the George Washington Bridge to the Golden Gate. In Nevada and Utah, I had my 427-roadster cruising at 150 mph and with the top down and the fact that I was stretched out 4 inches off road, I felt like I was flying on my back. I roared through the Rockies and down Monarch Pass in Colorado Springs. I decided to put my dress blues on and stop at the US AIR FORCE ACADEMY. I got the tour and was invited to the evening meal as a returning Vietnam veteran and it was a gas. They asked me to get up and say a few words so I spoke about some of the duties the Air Force had at our base. I got up the next morning and hit the plains. I crossed the mighty Mississippi late that night and knew I was on my way home. The Corvette was an animal, it didn't even get going until 4th gear at about 75 mph. When the secondary carburetors kick in, I get shot back in the seat and get rubber going quickly to 100 mph. It was the true American sports car and late at night driving with the top down I felt like I was in a rocket ship, and life was good. I stayed on RT 80 through the Midwest and stopped in Pittsburgh to see a buddy of mine going to school at Pitt and stayed the night. My friend was graduating from Pitt and was in ROTC to go in the Navy. He was going to fighter pilot school in Pensacola and he still had models of jets hanging from his dorm room. Between wearing my fatigues and my spit shined combat boots and popping the hood to show the 427 -engine, I was having fun at every stop. Nancy and I shared that attention to details that we could we fine tune our looks and behaviors. We called this that certain je ne sais quoi that gave us a stagger and confidence. If we felt good and looked good, we were on top of the world. The final day I drove to Maryland to meet up with my sweetie. It was good to get back to the east coast and far away from South East Asia.

I finally pulled up to Nancy's house, she must have heard the Vette pull up because she came running and she jumped into my arms and knocked me down. I could have stayed there making out all afternoon if it wasn't for the fact that we were on her parent's front yard. It had only been 8 days apart but we knew we were seriously in love. The next thing she does was call dibs on driving the roadster. I put the top down and off we go. Sitting back so low, looking over the big block hood, made Nancy look like a little kid. But boy could she drive. She threw shifts and took flat spins and she put the Corvette through its paces. She drove us out to the beach and took me to a beautiful spot she knew of. We practically raped each other out on the beach and some kids walked by and we had to scramble under our blanket. Here we were back together on another coast and our relationship was going intercontinental once again. We stayed for 2 nights at Ocean Beach, Maryland before we said bye to Nancy's folks and took off to Florida for the twin's party at Key West. We made it down to Myrtle Beach and we decided to stay at a motel on the Grand Strand so we could play a round of golf in the morning. It was good to go for a long walk as I have been driving for days.

We then cruised down Interstate 95 to Miami to stop and see my buddy Buzz and his wife Maria. They belonged to the Miami Country Club's two courses started by Jackie Gleason. Buzz and Maria were scratch golfers so they had to give us 20 strokes to make it fair. The good thing about playing with them was that they showed us little pointers to improve our games. When Buzz said he thought Nancy had a great swing, I gave him the look to let him know that I wasn't trying to grab Maria from behind to help her swing. There is an unwritten law that we could flirt with a guy's girl but we better keep it in our pants. If your lady wasn't being hit on you would wonder what was wrong. In the lobby of the clubhouse was this awesome picture of Arnold Palmer walking up a fairway with his "Arnie's Army" behind him. The reason they were all stopped was that the "Great One" was getting ready to tee off and he was dressed up in all his glory. He was wearing his floppy hat, striped shirt and plaid pants and his golf cart had a bar built on it. We had a nice day even though they still beat us by 3 strokes. The only bummer was that Buzz just didn't want to hear anything about God and the bible. He couldn't understand how there could be a God when his little baby girl was born and died from a birth defect. There was not anything we could say to comfort them. We said farewell and headed down to the Keys.

To be with a beautiful woman on a sunny hot day driving through the Keys in a convertible was almost perfection. The 120-mile long archipelago consists of 42-Cays and 42 bridges through some of the bluest and clearest water in the world. When we were out in a runabout, we had to keep pulling up thinking we were running aground, but when we tested the depth with an oar, we were still in 15 feet of water. We decided to spend the first night at Key Largo to recoup before seeing the twins and the big weekend party. We stayed at a little cabin on the beach and Nancy looked stunning with her sun-tanned body and her tiny bikini. After a swim and shower we ate dinner on a little wharf watching the sunset with the pelicans. We walked along the beach hand in hand and we thanked God for His ocean, His stars and His love. It was a magical night. We fell asleep out on the porch enjoying the warm ocean breezes.

I woke up in the warm morning sunshine with Nancy's warm body under my arm with her head on my chest and my arm between her legs. We made love in the water bouncing along together in the waves. We went back in the house and showered and I rubbed down her slightly sunburnt body with oil. It was a coconut oil and it tasted pretty good when I licked it off her delicious body. We drove down to Key West and met the twins for brunch. They weren't teenagers any more but sometimes they looked 15 and sometimes they looked 25. They were still with the two marine biologists and they were actually ok guys. The twins were so excited, they had a lot planned and some special surprises. They have a great local reggae band for the Saturday night luau and beach party. We all went out for dinner at the Green Parrot and did some dancing and drinking. There was a fire going on the beach and there was some guitars, bongos and harmonicas and we all sat under the stars singing in the moonlight. We were staying at the old Rumrunner Hotel that Hemingway would stay at. The twins told us about the plans for Saturday and it looked like it was going to be an awesome day. Nancy and I spent the rest of the night in this cool porch and bedroom restored like you were smuggling rum and setting out sometime later in the night. We planned on visiting the Hemingway House & Museum sometime over the weekend as he wrote a lot of great works here. He was also famous for his fishing trips and drinking rum and Nancy and I were into his writing. He wrote about both world wars so I was a big fan of his style and his quest for adventure. We slept late and met the gang for a breakfast buffet down at the docks that the twins arranged. There was already about 20 of us with more arriving today, like I told Nancy, the twins probably spent 30- grand of their daddy's money. To rent an Inn, a yacht, a beach with top shelf booze & drugs, a band, lobsters and steaks and water toys for the weekend in Key West had to add up.

After breakfast we went back to put on our bathing suits and to get together a day pack. The twins really were doing everything over the top. They chartered a 75-foot sailboat as our floating base for the weekend. We had some wave runners and Boston Whalers to go waterskiing, scuba diving and exploring. There was plenty of food and drinks and it was an absolutely beautiful day. The twins told me about a small cay they found with an underground cave and grotto to explore that they wanted to show us. We loaded up a Boston Whaler with some gear and the six of us headed off to explore a key called Sandy Cay. It was a small island the size of a football stadium with a rock formation on the side, some palm trees and a white sand beach. The rock formations must be where the grotto was and there was a small runabout beached on the shore. I thought of the days that pirates hid out on these islands with ships full of booty. Small cays with caves were perfect to hide the gold and jewels that was stolen from the Spanish. The Spaniards stole it from the Incas who built their altars and temples out of solid gold and silver so they could make human sacrifices to their gods. The only thing I could have done better would be to give us an old pirate's treasure map to follow. Even in more recent days the rum running and now the drugs still give this area a sense of danger and mystery.

We walked around to the opening of the cave that was hidden by vines and ivy. Inside was a large cavern with what looks like a deep pool in the middle. Standing in the shadows on the other shore was this long-haired bearded dude tending to a small fire. He was wearing a cut off pair of jeans and around his neck he had a gold cross and chain. Even though it was dark and he was on the other side of the cavern, I could see it was Tony by his shadow on the cave's wall. It was the exact shadow I use to see when we were out late looking around for something and his shadow reflected off of a hanger and out to space. Yes, we use to trip together a lot. We ran around to meet each other and Tony dives into the pool and swims out of sight. I look over to Nancy to see if she was ok and she gives me a thumbs up so I dove down after him. Swimming through a narrow but deep passageway I could see light at end of the tunnel. I entered another incredible grotto with some flora and a waterfall coming down the rocks. We sat on the rocks and talked for a good hour and the girls and guys caught up to us and played on the rocks diving in the pool.

I knew that Tony swam down that river and hid out even with some bullet holes in him. He told me how he commandeered a canoe at a boy scout camp and floated down river for about 20 miles. By now the whole group of us were sitting around listening to Tony's tale of being a modern-day smuggler on a worldwide scale. He continued down the river until he floated under a highway bridge where he hid the canoe so he could walk up on the road. He came upon a service station so he could call his dad for they already knew the FBI was looking around for him. Within two hours he was in a limo heading down to Tijuana to make it over the border and points south. At Juarez a plane picked him up and took him to Buenos Aires where they took him to a hospital to nurse his wounds and pull out a couple of slugs from his back. After a couple of weeks of laying out on the Mar del Plata beach he already had a new passport and identity building hotels in the capital. The real Anthony Costa died in the river escaping from the law in Nevada, his body was never found in the raging waters.

After lunch on the beach, everyone wanted to go with the twins to explore caves that are around some of the islands near us. We loaded up some scuba gear on the bigger Boston Whaler and we all headed out in the crystal-clear waters. We saw a plethora of fish, but the big predators swarming around made us hold our breath. The barracudas were awesome and with three rows of razor sharp-teeth and their sleek silver color they looked like eating machines. They are so fast that with one shake of their tail they come right to my face, I wouldn't stand a chance. And then fortunately they are gone like magic. When a fish is cut in half by these big predators, within seconds there is nothing left. The waters boil with swarming fish and then the 8-foot Bull Sharks come through and they will attack anything in their way. Recently, one of our guys got too close to a 6 ft barracuda and he got sliced by its fin and had a nasty gash on his leg. Just brushing next to it could slice your leg off. Shit happens as we are invading their fishing grounds. I really was scared of diving down into caves or old wrecks as you never know what you are going to find. My fears are to come face to face with a moray eel or a giant Sting Ray so I stayed close to our group. We went inside an old wreck and it scared the crap out of me. The cave we found was closing in on me and I felt claustrophobic and couldn't regulate my breathing. I came back to the boat and realized I would never be a SEAL.

This fear goes way back to 5th grade summer camp. I was down at the shoreline one evening thinking about the swimming test I had to take in the morning. I was already the youngest Bass in the camp and tomorrow I should become the youngest Barracuda ever. Suddenly I heard a sound like a large animal trudging into the water, kerplunk, kerplunk, kerplunk! I looked over and saw this prehistoric beast going into the water. It was a giant snapping turtle with at least 10 nylon hooks hooked into its mouth like long whiskers. It stopped to look at me and it was the size of a big coffee table. It let out a hideous hiss and sauntered down into the deep. It was big enough to snap off a finger or a toe and I was sure it would be waiting for me down in the murky waters. Bad enough is that for the test I had to swim down to the deepest water to retrieve a five-gallon container and push up with my feet to the surface. It was then I was positive that the beast would be waiting for me to snap off an appendage and pull me down to its lair.

The next morning it rained and I was so relieved that I went to arts & craft all morning. The following morning was bright and sunny but I got myself so worked up that I decided to go to arts and crafts again. Within the hour the announcement came over the loudspeakers for me to report to the lifeguard station.

I spilled my guts how I saw a giant snapping turtle right in the swimming area. Well I got laughed at and called a chicken and I was worse off than the poor kids that couldn't swim that were called the salamanders. I came up with a great idea to try and get a picture of it with my new Polarized Land camera. The next night I took some beef jerky and put it out on the shoreline where I first saw it. I sat there with my camera and waited until it started getting dark. I waited so long that I started falling asleep. But just like that, he was out of the water eating the jerky right next to me. I fumbled with the camera and he started to charge me. I stepped backwards and tripped and as I started to fall the camera went off a few times. The flash went off and scared the ugly bastard back in the water and I swore he looked back at me with a sneer. But fortunately, I caught him on camera and his mouth was open to bite me. The lifeguards took my picture away but I kept the other one. I went from zero to hero and they had to dredge the lake. They never found that monster and they had to give me a test in the pool. But to this day I still think of him waiting down in the murky waters for me.

As beautiful as the colorful fishes and coral was, the deeper down we went the creepier it got. How the twins and the marine biologists and even Nancy all seemed fearless was beyond me. I had to push through so I didn't look like a salamander or worse, a chicken. It was all about conquering our fears and going on attack. When the book Jaws came out that summer, everyone was sitting on the beach reading but only the brave were going in the water. Even the sound of the fish coming in the water evicted fear, Dunn, Dunn, Dunn, Dunn, Dunn. Sea monsters have been around since the world was flat and we just fell off into the abyss. Every fear I had was deep down in that murky water with that ugly beast with those long nylon whiskers. We found a large sea bass with an octopus wrapped around it and that was so disturbing but it was survival of the fittest just like us. Sharks are on the top of the food chain even though they have things like lampreys and other succors attached to them. It's a dog eat dog world and it is truly amazing what you can find in the big predator's stomachs. They can swallow fish almost as big as they are and it can go on and on with more fish inside of them. An octopus has no bones or cartilage yet they have eight arms with succors and they can fit through tiny holes and can twist off a lid on a jar like it is nothing. Fish are pretty smart and that is why they hang out in schools.

We left the caves and Sandy Cay and joined the other partiers on the sailboat. We spent the afternoon snorkeling and diving over an old Spanish galleon wrecked on a reef from the 1740s. We stayed out on the water until the sun started going down and we saw a purple, pink and orange sunset hanging out with the pelicans on the dock. We went in to shower and change and we met back on the beach where there was a stage set up for the band. They had a big fire going on the beach and they were serving tables of lobsters, shrimp and scallops. They had big bowls of paella and jambalaya and some conch soup that was to die for. We had blenders of Pina coladas, strawberry daiquiris and Navy grogs flowing. Once the band started rocking and everyone was dancing in the sand the party ramped up a notch. We had about 50 people partying on the beach and they were being ferried out to the sailboat to do some serious partying. Tony and his sisters were having a blast driving around in the moonlight in a speedboat and Tony had some awesome fireworks he was shooting all over the bay. I had to stop calling him Tony as his name was now Angelo Augustine from a large Italian family from Argentina. This family was Tony's cousins on his mother's side and they were involved in the construction on the governmental buildings in Buenos Aires. So, we knew Tony was going to be okay and he was still living the life we all knew he would.

Later on, we hung out with the band sitting around the bonfire playing guitars, bongos and steel drums as we all sung along and passed the pipe. Even Nancy took a few tokes as it was a magical night and by tomorrow, we would be returning to places all over the world. Angelo would be returning to South America and the twins and their boyfriends were going back up to Tallahassee to start another semester. Nancy and I were off to New York where we were going to store my car back home so we could fly together to West Germany. We wanted to get there early to tour a little bit of Europe before we had to report back to our bases. Sunday morning as Nancy packed up our car, she urged me to go say goodbye to Tony and the twins. I walked with the girls on the docks and we gave each other some warm hugs and kisses for old times' sake. I am sure we were all still in love with each other and I hoped we always will be. Angelo and I said our goodbyes and we planned on seeing each other somewhere in the near future. We talked about our spiritual journeys and Angelo said he was going to a good church in Buenos Aires.

We split after lunch and made it all the way up to Captiva Island to stay the night at the South Seas Plantation on the Gulf. We played some golf and got to dine at some great restaurants on the Sanibel - Captiva Islands. We took a boat ride to a small island that had the local attraction called Rumrunners that had a bar on the beach that we could watch the sunset over the Gulf. The bar was an old hangout from back in the days that they did run rum and other treasures of the sea. There were even stories of the Underground Railroad taking escaped slaves south to Jamaica and Haiti. We ate on the beach with a luau of shellfish cooked on the fire wrapped in seaweed with corn and potatoes and then we walked around the island in the sunset. We held hands and stopped to hold each other and take it all in, we could see lights from other fires and parties around the bay. The sunset and the reflections on the water was glorious yet when Nancy would lean back in my arms our bond felt very warm and strong. With the horrors of war all around it was times like these that soothes our souls and took away some of the pain. Late at night during restless sleep Nancy started having nightmares that I could see and hear and I know it was similar to my demons chasing me like a one headlight car. When my body would twitch or jump, I would be helplessly falling from a rooftop or a cliff and it would wake me up in a sweat. But the deep, dark and twisted nightmares were so sick and fragmented and were absent of any reason, like hell was supposed to be. Some of my nightmares recurred all day like bad memories that would make me ashamed of myself. How could I have these horrible thoughts and feelings. It was all the blood and guts we have seen and the evils that followed. We would try to remember that this was a good time to pray and find some peace with God and Christ.

As time went by, we kept seeing that Nancy and I had a very groovy thing going on. Nancy was so understanding with so much great energy and spirit and she was so unselfish. She was a good witness of the fruit of the spirit and God working in her life. She was kind and patient, she showed goodness and joy and she loved with gentleness, and she was always in control. She was so easy to get along with that it seemed that everyone loved Nancy! We slept late and ate brunch on the dock overlooking the marina and we saw a bunch of huge manatees in the harbor. The startling sight was that the manatees were all sliced up from the motorboats running over them. We decided that we would have to tell the twins about the manatees and to ask their boyfriends to do a study on how to save them from the engine's blades. Nancy wanted to find out what can be done to protect these awesome animals. We got to play another round of golf on the resort and somehow Nancy got me to give her a stroke a hole. She ended up beating me by 10 strokes and now I owe her an hour massage. We left Captiva and headed up and around the Gulf to New Orleans. We got as far as

Gulfport, Mississippi and checked into a motel for the night. Nancy told me that it was time to make good on our bet and took out some lotion and oil. The problem was that when Nancy took off her clothes to lay down, she looked absolutely incredible. We had been driving all around the east coast for days with the top down, out in the sun golfing and boating and laying out on the beach so we were both quite bronzed. Nancy looked like she was still wearing a white bikini and she was a big turn on, not that she wasn't anyway. When she turned onto her back her luscious white breasts and tan stomach was all I could take. She just has it all going for her, she was soft and yet athletic, and she took me places I've never been before. I tried my best to give her hours' worth of massage but I got lost in her sex and her love. I ended up trying to make love to her entire body and her soul and she had to take a rain check for the rest of the massage. We got up late and after a swim in the Gulf and a brunch on the beach, we continued on to "The Big Easy".

We went over to Biloxi Mississippi to Keesler AFB to look up a Loadmaster buddy of mine. We met him for lunch and he filled us in on all the shit going down. He told us how the MPs and custom agents were using German Shepherds at all the bigger bases and in country to sniff out bombs and explosives. By accident they uncovered a shitload of heroin at Travis and I couldn't help but think of the goons from Lake Tahoe. My friend Bob told me that it is a cat and mouse game as now the smugglers are using strong chemicals to throw the dogs off. I was once again glad that Tony and I were out of the whole business cause the odds were against us. As we were getting ready to go, Bob tried to give Nancy a beautiful gold cross and chain that she declined telling him that she only wears the cross that I gave her last Christmas. He also wanted to give us a Nikon SLR worth about $500.00 but we said we had one of those too. She figured that wearing a stolen cross lost any spiritual energy it could have had in the first place. My buddy Bob was no longer moving drugs so he adapted to the times and started collecting precious stones and expensive jewelry instead. They say that diamonds are a girl's best friend but they are also the smugglers friend as a small pouch of them are worth a ton of drugs taking up a lot of room. A small pouch of diamonds was worth more than a ton of marijuana or a shipment of cocaine or heroin. I don't think that dogs could smell a shipment of diamonds soaking in Napalm.

There was a great old song that we all sung, "When the Saints go Marching in,' that has a powerful meaning that now rings out to us. "O when the saints come marching in, I want to be in that number. When the Stars fall from the sky, When the moon turns red with blood ... ...When the trumpet sounds its call ... ... When the fire begins to blaze, I want to be in that number, when the saints come marching in". We are the saints, the times are the start of the thousand-year reign of Christ's return, the trumpet is the last trump when Christ returns in the sky on his white horse. When the moon turns into blood and the stars fall from the sky is the start off the destruction of this world as we know it, and the creation of Paradise with Christ and YHWY forever. I must have said the Lord's Prayer thousands of times; but never understood its full meaning. "Our father who art in heaven, hallow be thy name. Thy kingdom come, thy will be done, on earth as it is in heaven." The prayer starts right off with God first, and praising His name. God will get His will and his kingdom will be established on earth. We ask for our daily bread and for forgiving us are sins as we forgive others. Deliver us from evil and the prayer ends like it begins with praises to God. This is a model of how we should pray and the bible is filled with great prayers. The more you pray, the more you learn how to listen. That still small voice inside us.

Christ is the first one to be raised from the dead and the bible tells us in great detail that he is sitting on Gods right hand. The angels were headed up by Michael, the Arc Angel, Gabriel, the messenger and Lucifer, the bright morning Star. We learn how Lucifer wanted to be like God and falls from grace and takes a third of the angels with him. His name is now Satan and his angels are the Devil Spirits. The Bible tells us that besides God and His son, the only other spirit entities are the 40 elders and the spirits that guard the Tree of Life. Not until Jesus Christ, the Messiah, returns do we the believers meet Him in the air and reign with Him on earth. During this thousand- year reign he will restore this world to Paradise. This is when there will be no more death or sickness as Satan and his followers will be thrown in the fiery pit. In the end God gets his will and it will be Glorious. A lot of religions believe that when you die you go straight to heaven but the bible tells us that we are all dead until Christ returns and resurrects us. It says that there is no memory in the grave so whether you died yesterday or a hundred years ago your next thought will be that you are raised from the dead. For the thousand-year millennium, Jesus Christ the Messiah will restore this world back to Paradise.

By nightfall we were having crayfish stew on Bourbon Street and we stayed at an old inn in the French Quarter. We walked hand in hand on Canal street and saw the Mississippi along the docks. We stopped and held on to each other watching the paddle boats and the barges going by and when she leaned back to kiss me, we melted in each other's arms. I loved her so much that it hurt! After spending a year together in Vietnam witnessing all that horrible crap, we were now going through a healing time together. Sometimes when I hold her, I think of the many times she held a young soldier as he died in her arms in the OR. She had to keep working day after day with all that blood and guts and men screaming out because they lost an arm or a leg to a bomb. Nancy had to try and comfort the poor souls that were now missing major body parts and were so messed up and didn't want to live anymore. Not only did they have visible scars but deep emotional scars as well. We called the guys going through this "nervous in the service" or being "shell shocked" and we all got jumpy to loud noises. If the loud noise is a truck backfiring, we would dive for cover from all the times we had to bail-out into a bunker during an air raid. A lot of these soldiers went through hell as they were deep in a jungle of misery and death. Some men just wanted to die to get over all the harrows. We both knew that our trust in God has helped us to change our hearts and minds as we walk in His love. We thanked God for our lives and His spirit and we believed for great things as we stayed faithful. We left in the morning for Memphis as it was time to start heading back to New York so we could fly to Europe.

From Memphis we pushed to Baltimore so Nancy could get her things shipped and spend time with her folks. Nancy's parents were pretty cool people, they both worked in medical research for Johns Hopkins. She had 2 younger twin brothers that were in their second year at the Naval Academy at Annapolis. Both parents were activists involved in the political and current social causes. They wanted to dump Nixon, end the war, help the starving children in Africa and they were health nuts and ran in marathons. I was thinking of the saying "like mother like daughter" as they could have been sisters. We all went to Annapolis to visit her brothers and Nancy and I wore our uniforms so we could get into the Naval Academy 's mystique. I don't think I've seen anybody look as good as Nancy wearing their uniform. The way she had it pleated and form fitted to her body was so sexy yet she still looked sharp as an officer in the USAF. Since I didn't have any gold or silver on my shoulders, I did take a little flack, especially when I escorted Nancy to a military function. The way I rationalized this disparity is that if the government hadn't fucked with me by drafting me, I would have finished college and gone in as an officer.

Now as a Vietnam veteran and a Loadmaster, I had air time, and a fine-looking Lieutenant on my arm. Driving home from our little tour we looked like the cat's meow in the Corvette with our flight sunglasses, suntans and Nancy with her scarf on her head. It never got old to pull into a truck stop and pop the hood and draw a crowd, some to check out the car and some checking out Nancy's fine ass!! I put the car in storage and we started to get ready to fly to Europe. We still had some time before we had to report so we decided to go to Paris. Even though De Gaulle threw our military out of France, we now could go to visit on a Visa. We flew to Paris, the City of Lights, and stayed in a wonderful old hotel right across from the Moulin Rouge. We spent our time touring the city on rented bicycles and then we rented a car to tour France as we headed to Germany.

We couldn't get better assignments then what we had. Our bases were 3 miles apart and we were right in the middle of Europe. We were about a half a day from France, Switzerland, Brussels, Amsterdam and the Berlin wall. Our bases were the headquarters to the United States operations in both Europe and Africa so we hoped to get around some. Places like East Germany and Romania were behind the Iron Curtain and part of the Soviet Union. The communist block divided Europe in half and there was a lot of terrorism and anarchy going on. Even the IRA was killing other Irishmen and north Africa was a mess. The USSR did not allow religious freedoms and they even burned bibles and other classical books. Their stores were empty as you were put on a waiting list to order a toaster or anything aluminum and getting a steak or a roast beef was practically impossible, unless you knew somebody down at the docks. West Germany had a strong economy and right in Stuttgart was the home of Mercedes and Porsche and I was already thinking about buying Nancy a classic old MG convertible to tool around in.

When we got to "The City of Lights "we decided to just stay there until we had to report. Paris was so magical and there was so much to see and enjoy. We both liked the Impressionists so we spent two mornings at the Louvre and we spent time walking along the Seine and window shopping the West Bank. We ate at little cafes and danced together in the discos in the night. Our only hassle was that this kid ran by and snatched Nancy's gold cross and necklace. I chased him down the street and down an alley right into Nancy as she went around the block and close lined him and knocked him down. When shaking him down for Nancy's chain we also found 5 more gold chains and 3 watches. He told us that he was 14 and has been working the streets for

2 years and makes most of his money servicing men in the alleys. We turned the jewelry in to the French police station and they told us that these kids work for pimps that make them steal and prostitute for a little bit of drugs. They are kept working the streets 20 hours a day. When they stopped producing, they were found in a dumpster or floating down the Seine. This sort of thing was all over the world and woman and children were exploited everywhere we went.

We left Paris and France and headed towards West Germany. We already started following major roadways and we were looking forward to getting on the Autobahn as a lot of our new assignment was learning the lay of the land. Since the Autobahn didn't have a speed limit, neither did we and the two seat Volvo we rented was put through the test. Europe was so far an incredible place filled with so much culture and wonders. With all the countries trying to coexist and the ancient and modern history all melded together, there was just one big problem at hand, the Berlin Wall dividing Europe in half. We checked in at our bases and reported to our Commanding Officers and given our new assignments. We had to report to the NATO HEADQUARTERS as per order of Colonel Thompson, we were getting assigned together for a special detail working with the CIA. We were to spend time at NATO headquarters here at Stuttgart and learn about our new assignment and duties. We learned that the Colonel was serving as the head of the Chaplain services but he also coordinated the activity between the CIA and NATO. We were informed that we had been on a need to know status but we will be getting security clearances. We will be starting a very special series of missions as Nancy and I will not only be working together but will be doing it as a couple to best get around Europe. The great thing is that we are assigned to Colonel Thompson in a clandestine project that will give us the ability to go rogue as couriers and agents. We will get training back in the States for a couple of months and get more training in PT, firearms and CIA protocol. This was so incredible but it seemed like it was something that Nancy and I were called to do. The Colonel and his staff said that we were naturals for this assignment and we spent the next month getting our lives together and getting situated as a couple from Canada working here in Germany. The CIA is setting us up with new identities, passports and papers so we can go through all the countries and especially through the checkpoints into the Communist Occupation. The part about Nancy and I working together as a couple was of course a dream come true. Like everything else we did, we will go through a hell of a lot of training.

The first month was a gas as we spent most of the time getting used to our new identities and connecting with the destinations that we would be making. Nancy started to find us a place to live and we were assigned a new BMW 2002 convertible to cruise around Europe in. Another fine car confiscated by the CIA. We started by delivering different packages to the major cities in Western Europe and we stayed at some wonderful hotels and inns to get used to being a newly married couple. This was all such a fantasy and a dream come true and we got a lot of practice in making it some kind of crazy reality. We felt like we were watching a movie and we were in it, sometimes we both would get that strange Deja-vu feeling. Touring around all the cities they all started looking familiar and even the same but it was that weird feeling that we simultaneously got that was questionable. Could it be from God? Or from the dark side, or was it by mental telepathy or just a big coincidence? We also started to know how to cover each other and know each other's moves, kind of like getting good at dancing together (or cooking a big dinner party). Like most of our training, practice makes perfect and if we could break down an M-16 with our eyes closed, we could rebuild a carburetor. Nancy was in a whole other league as she could work at putting an injured person back together again. We seemed to share in an energy that drew us to all the events we were involved with and everything was connected and exciting. It was further fueled by our love we shared for our Heavenly Father and for each other. After some intense training here at NATO headquarters and then back at Langley, Virginia we will be going through the Wall and into Berlin and the Soviet Union.

The situation on both sides of the wall in 1972 was very dangerous as acts of terrorism were all over Europe. We were on a routine swap of information. We could pass off our suitcases at the hospitals we were going to. The "war of words" between the KGB and the Radio Free Europe people was getting ugly. They caught spies working inside the radio station and they even caught them trying to poison the food in the cafeteria. The Russians were trying to jam the broadcasts and we sent over more and more pamphlets and my car was filled with flyers and information in 10 Slavic languages that I would leave for the freedom fighters in various places. Once we were way too close to a suicide bombing right at the Brandenburg Gate. We were leaving to go back home when somebody tried to take out the checkpoint. We were parked on line and getting some coffee when the whole place rocked by two Palestine terrorists with C5 explosives, 15 died and 25 injured. We had to wait in Berlin for 3 days until we got clearance to proceed. We were in the cafe but our car's windows were blown out. If we hadn't gone for coffee, our heads would have been blown off. We had to have a new convertible top put on and a new paint job. We had over 300 acts of terrorism reported in West Germany that NATO had dealt with. A lot of violence was from the division caused by the Wall but there were also many other reasons for people wanting to kill each other.

We had been going over to East Germany for a few months and we were getting around pretty good. We were able to make deliveries and swaps all over Berlin and we went to state run hospitals and clinics. Nancy's involvement as a nurse gave us access deep into the Soviet Union. We did a lot of trades with other agents that were deeper behind the Curtain and even working both sides. We couldn't even imagine just what the information the CIA was moving between the embassies and as a courier I was more concerned about keeping things fluid. We knew that everywhere we went we were under surveillance so we just kept moving and we tried not to get pinned down. We were always looking for a way out and once we were in our car, we felt a lot better. The blast at the Brandenburg Gate was a sobering reminder that we were still in a war zone and that we were the enemy. A big difference between the East and West was the visible presence of armed soldiers and guards at every public area and German Shepherds sniffing about. We had safety in numbers at all the stations and terminals and everyone had to show their papers on command. We could feel the oppression as people were much more cautious and walked around with their heads down and didn't congregate like in the West. Everything from the East was done in secret and the whole underground was operating like it always has. Things were not so bad when we stayed overnight at some of the inns and old hotels, but we had to proceed knowing that big brother was always watching. Again, we waited to be out driving as if we could flip a switch of consciousness to freely be able to communicate. We could finally unload to each other all the things we saw around the city. When riding on the public bus we would sing the Simon & Garfunkel song "America" Now the man on the bus could really be a spy and everyone was under suspicion.

We were on a train going north to a hospital in Nuendorf, about 40 miles from Berlin, and Nancy was wearing her nurses' uniform. As we were walking to the front of the train these two Russian cops decided to grab Nancy and haul her into one of the private compartments. Suddenly I had a Luger in my face and a soldier yelling for me to back the fuck up. I took a step back and had enough room to kick his gun to the floor. He lunged at me and I was able to guide his face right into the wall. As if on cue, Nancy stomped the other guys foot and followed with a knee to his crotch and as he doubled over, she uppercut him and snapped his head back. Just like that we knocked them both out and threw them on the floor of the side compartment. These Russian thugs messed with the wrong girl. We ran out leaving them on the floor and we were able to quickly get off at the next station. The element of surprise caught them off guard as we knocked them into tomorrow. My heart was pounding hard but I was in awe of just how skilled Nancy was. We wondered if the two pricks would think twice about messing with another woman but, unfortunately, they will probably be coming on even harder next time. I couldn't help but to take the guys Luger and then throw it in the river so he would be in a real mess losing his piece. Raping and God knows what else they were going to do with her was probably taking place all over this police state as they were short on human rights. Like the war zones we have seen, the rape or death of one person can get lost in all the horrors of war. So many citizens were arrested and jailed and taken to places like Siberia and never seen again. So many children, the real flowers of war, were left without families and homes. The street kids usually were pimped by men with no value for their lives and if they didn't produce, they were eliminated. Their lives were so terrible as they were made to do horrible, degrading and very sick things. The cops, the soldiers and the KGB had free reign on most matters so we tried to stay away by becoming invisible. But as our saying goes, some things just had to be done. We didn't really have much of a choice as they backed us up against the wall, literally. Thank God we got protection from NATO and the CIA and as a couple we prayed to God for His protection.

We got off public transportation and rented a car and Nancy changed out of her uniform. When we finally checked into an inn up north of the city, we settled in for the night so we could go to the medical center in the morning. We had a good meal and some Chianti, and we retired to our room to plan out another day. We laid in front of the hearth and eventually fell asleep in front of the fire. Nancy was an amazing woman and at only 24 years old she has already been around the block a few times, and now we are getting around the world together....In just a few years together we have already seen so much. We met and fell in love at Cam Ron Bay in Vietnam and got to some big ports in the south Pacific. We got around to see some of our big country and now are here together in Cold War Europe. There is talk of us going to Africa to help with the war in Nigeria. The biggest transformation has been our journey and walk with God and there is a lot more to come. Here we are getting trained by the CIA and we have a great mentor in the soon to be General Thompson. We hoped to get more involved then all this intelligence & surveillance phase but it was a duty that had to be done. We continued on to the medical center and decided that public transportation was out and we will be driving and walking from now on. Besides, the public terminals were getting bombed everywhere we went.

Nancy and I were able to have a bird's eye view of the summer Olympics in 1972. West Germany hosted the Olympics in Munich during a troubled world view. The venues were all around us and we were signed on by the Colonel as security, especially after the raid. The Black Friday attack took place just as the Israelis athletes got to their dorm. It was such a horrible act of terrorism to take it out on the Olympic athletes, but it sure got the world's attention of how heinous the terrorists are with no regard to human life. The tensions were so bad that the games were more like battles then athletic contests. As GIs we all were big fans of our American team as if it really was our team, and in some ways, it was. We got to meet some of the athletes and I got to work out with some of the boxing team as they were mostly army guys. Nancy ran some cross-country training with the track team and she showed some serious time trials. I got my head handed to me as our boxers were great and I was glad I was wearing head gear and chest pads. In the 180 - 200-pound class these guys were monsters and I was glad it was just sparing practice. Our boxing team was practically at war with the Cuban team, the Cubans had a great team and won gold in a lot of weight classes.

Being with the American athletes was a great experience. We could feel the camaraderie and the commitment to excellence that they all shared. It was the same for our fighter pilots and chopper pilots and our special forces teams, that would take a bullet for their brothers in a second. Like we would say that some people run from danger and some people run towards it. So, with all the various rivalries and actual wars and hating, these Olympics were like the Roman and Greek gladiators against the lions and the slaves of the early games. The Russian, East German and Romanian teams were all together for a long time and competed all over the world. There was a lot of talk about these teams being professional. There were reports of doping and even accusations that some of their woman's teams had men competing on them! Even the communist's referees and officials seemed to be on the take as well.

They looked as if they made the fair call they would be sent to Siberia and our officials were outraged and could only file meaningless protests. The Americans asked why the communist gals were so big and ugly, and why did they have to shave? It was a very intense competition and it made some of us patriots hate our enemies even more. So, our day rooms and recreation rooms were filled with our screaming fans and the competition was fierce. Out at the bars we had the local Germans and other Europeans to contend with and our passions were all very patriotic. Since we were guests in their country, we had to eat some crow and try to be good sports at least. The American swimmer Mark Spitz won and set all the records in swimming but was getting constant death threats and had to leave early because he was Jewish. Some wished the leaders of all the countries could just duke it out but we all know that the old men make the wars and the young men fight and die in them.

After the attack on the Israeli athletes the security was increased to a feverish pitch as every country that was competing bolstered their staff. The West German, the Munich and the Olympic police also stepped up security so there was more security then Olympic athletes and their traveling teams. We were falling over each other and everyone had to be fed and housed for 3 weeks. Fortunately, Nancy and I had a room in a hotel right in Munich and had some friends right down the hall. It didn't suck that we had potato pancakes with fruit compote for breakfast and sauerbraten with mashed potatoes for dinner all paid for by our TDY money. The number of items on the supply and demand list had to include things from all the participating countries. The Cubans were going through withdrawals because they were out of Cafe Bustelo coffee and we had to get a special shipment from Cuba for them. Since we had a blockade on them for 10 years, we heard that Fidel personally had the coffee shipped so his athletes could enjoy the caffeine buzz as well. Fidel like his coffee and cigars, but loved his teams, especially the boxing and baseball teams. I had to pick up 200 pounds of Cafe Bustelo from Havana. We had it flown to the Stuttgart AFB and we delivered to the Cuban delegation. The coffee from Cuba was even stronger than the Cafe Bustelo they made in Brooklyn and could keep you up all night. I first got turned on to it my freshman year of college. All the serious students would pull all-nighters in the library drinking Cafe Bustelo and doing uppers, or Black Beauties to study. Every time I tried it, I got too jittery to study so I just partied all night. But I do think that Cafe Bustelo was habit forming and it gave me the buzz after a couple of cups!! It must be good as it almost caused an international incident -

When we received the coffee shipment for the Cuban team, we actually got it from the Dominican Republic. Ever since the embargo against Cuba, the Cuban government set up plants in neighboring countries that shipped their best exports. Besides coffee they had cigars, rum and sugar cane confections. The best cigars were Montecristo # 2 hand dipped and rolled and shipped all over the world. Bacardi Smugglers Blend Rum pre-WW2 and El-Tosaro Premium Tequila were highly favored all over the world. After we delivered the cigars another big package was sent to "THE AMERICAN TEAM". It was a large box the size of a large suitcase filled with Montecristo # 2 cigars and Bacardi Smugglers Rum. It included a hand written thank you note from Fidel Castro. The embargo was starting to lift and goods were starting to be traded again. The bigger issue was the number of Cuban refugees coming to America in boats, cargo ships, rafts and anything that floats. It was 90 miles from Havana to Key West, but many folks were intercepted and sent back. And some died in the sea.

Since Nancy and I have really been getting to see the world and getting to go behind the Wall we see all different types of people. The truth of the matter is that people are just people and we might look a little different but we are basically all the same. Only on maps do we see the boundaries but family life is not all that different all around the world. Most people love their families and their countries. The boundaries change all the time, 40 years ago the Russians were our allies and Germany and Japan were our enemies so nothing makes sense in the big picture. Way back in the Bible a great account was when Babylon was a great Kingdom and attempted to take over the world as a One World Government. The problem was their pride as they tried to make a better world without Gods help. The Tower of Babylon was built to reach the heavens without Gods blessings or help. This is why God confounded their languages, hence the "Tower of Babel". Later, the great Patriarch, Abraham, spoke that he looked for a city whose founder and maker is God. This will be the new city of Jerusalem in Paradise. Then we will all be one and there will be no more wars or death. So nowadays we see how the communist's countries belief is that the country is everything and there is no God so it is the opposite of Christianity. The thing is that true communism is that all things are shared by the people. True Christianity is that we are all equal and that we all share everything in common. Then we distribute our pluralities to those who have need. “If God takes care of the birds, will he not take care of you, oh you of little faith?” The work that Nancy is involved with transcends borders, political agendas and nationalities and focuses on family dynamics and treating the individuals in need. Nancy focused on each person and didn’t care what color or nationality or whose side they were on. Every Combat Nurse took on the spirit of Clara Barton from our Civil War as she cared for all soldiers going through horrid conditions of amputations and infections. She later started the American Red Cross that Nancy is still affiliated with a hundred years later. Nancy just wants to see her patients get better and it didn’t matter what they did or didn’t do. When an enemy is on the table being sewed up, he doesn’t look any different, especially on the inside.

The Colonel liked to show us the historic accounts in the Bible and the Old Testament prophecies that have come to pass and how some are yet to be fulfilled. The Old Testament prophecies that pertained to the coming of Christ are written as well as when he returns in the future. It is written that Abraham is the Father of many nations as the Christians, the Hebrews and the Muslims all are traced back to him. The big deal about Christianity is that through believing that God raised Jesus Christ from the dead we shall be saved. Through this faith we are connected to God through His Holy

Spirit. We believed in a monotheistic God and not a triune three headed God. The concept of the trinity was not added until the treaty of Nicene in 325 AD. Jesus came to forgive our sins and he died on the cross to pay the price so we may have eternal life. Satan's plan is to steal, kill and destroy so the spiritual battle will end when Christ comes back to defeat the Devil. The last enemy to be defeated will be death as we will be resurrected in Paradise. This is why all the Christian groups are in all these countries trying to spread the message so people can learn how to believe and get that spiritual connection to God. The Bible tells us that for every life that is saved, the Angels dance in heaven, so once again I ask what is the value of one life? For God, he sacrificed His only begotten son, The Lamb of God. This is why Christians all over the world are spreading the good news of the Bible so people can believe and be saved. Nancy and I have great joy seeing people get turned on so they can know the truth and be set free. What we are doing for our country trying to save some lives is an excellent privilege but helping people to gain eternal life is priceless.

Then we were all excited about the Munich Olympics starting right near us in venues all over West Germany. The amount of smuggling was insane as supply & demand was all over the black market and now with the Olympics, people were coming from all over the world. Then just as the Olympics were starting, the massacre of the Israeli athletes went down and all Europe was in turmoil. This terror attack was between the Palestines and the Israelis but everything was then further divided between the USA and Russia as who was backing who. They came very close to shutting down the Olympics but they didn't want to give in to the terrorism. The Olympics were getting so political that big countries were taking turns boycotting the event. We had to shut down our trips for a month as the temperature all along the border was too hot for going in to Berlin. We did a lot of work with Radio Free Europe and I got to send a lot of info over the wall in balloons. I sent hundreds of balloons up all along the German border. Other groups were sending them down in Southern Europe along Yugoslavia and from boats out in the Mediterranean Sea. Even up north along Latvia and Estonia and along the Baltic Sea, all the way to Leningrad, there were speed boats zipping through the night just like it's been done for centuries. The balloons were set to deflate at different times so they could be sent to different destinations according to the wind. Each balloon would deflate at set times and send out thousands of tracts promoting democracy or exposing the perils of communism. Propaganda was a war of words and the Soviet state tried to control the people's thoughts and actions and the KGB enforced it.

We thought that using balloons, kites, carrier pigeons and hooking it all up with Radio Free Europe's broadcasts was the coolest thing we were involved in. We learned how to set the timers on the balloons so we could send them over in the wind targeting major destinations. We could send out thousands of tracts giving out our slant on life in the West. The satellite countries such as Poland, Yugoslavia, Czechoslovakia and Romania were basically cut off from the rest of Europe and the free world. The people were isolated from our way of life and any information or exchange of ideas and resources were squashed by the KGB. It was our job to keep the underground pathways open to connect the people with the rest of the free world. So, we were part of the underground and we tried to sneak in and out of places and deliver our goods and information. Now we are involved in the Cold War and doing all sorts of wild things playing cat & mouse with East Germany and the entire Soviet Union.

Another great part of our duties was to make pickups and drops all around Europe in our BMW and we got to see some pretty incredible places. We made runs to London and Copenhagen as well as to

NATO bases around Europe. NATO and our CIA were working with all the allied countries who had their own intelligence as well. It really was spy vs spy. We just didn't spy against the Communists, as every other country were all playing the game. In the capital cities there were countries' embassies on every other corner, except if the countries broke diplomatic relations with each other. If there was an embassy there, they had that country's version of the CIA or KGB and whoever they were doing business with. Nancy and I were still soldiers working for our country but we were now a young couple from Canada visiting our family in Germany. Since we didn't really exist, I wondered how many people were working on and off the grid like us? We didn't get our mail nor did we get paid as money just showed up in our account for our expenses. Our monthly pay was being put away for us back in the states (if I didn't own the Red Lobster stocks it would have meant more) as Nancy's First Lieutenant 's pay has been building up for her for almost a year now. Getting to travel around Europe and stay in these great places has been a dream, and doing it all with the woman I love is incredible. Col Thompson was starting to work us about how much more God can bless us when we get married. The closer we get to God, the closer we get to each other.

Nancy was so into her work with "Doctors Without Borders" and the American Red Cross and other German medical teams. And it was also a great cover to move about the various countries and far into the Eastern Bloc. She was concerned by the lack of medical treatment in East Germany. The differences of the medical community were so much better in the West. Like in the markets and the stores, the medical supplies and equipment were depleted and way behind the West. Nancy's team said that the hospitals in the Soviet Bloc were years behind in procedures and their equipment was antiquated. By the end of the year in '72, trade agreements were made between East & West Germany so that the East Germans could cash in on some good ole capitalism. We played the point that capitalism was working a lot better than communism and the Radio Free Europe broadcasts worked on hitting this hard as the West was looking so much better than the East. After all, not too many West Germans were trying to go back over the wall, except knuckleheads like Nancy and me!

During the Munich Olympics the East German and other communist bloc countries such as Romania and the USSR were practically at war with our American team. Some of the East German women's team were accused of being men and some of the officials were accused of taking bribes. And then the doping and steroids were out of control and there was widespread cheating and athletes were getting hurt. The Russian red army teams were actually like pro teams all playing together for years. This was the start of new Olympic rules on what is pro vs amateurs as it was always the best amateur athletes in the world competing. The Russian basketball team beat the American team for the first time in a game. The Russians got to replay the final play 3 times to win. The average age of the Red team was 30 and they played together for years and the American college kids average age was 22 and they played together for a month. It all seemed like this was fodder for the Cold War, as everything seemed to count. Just like when Hitler's Germany hosted the Olympics and tried to show how the German Arians were the superior race, the USSR was trying to do the same in the '72 Olympics. It was hard to tell just who was fighting who as there was fighting all around the world in places like SE Asia, the Mid East and North Africa. Right here by the Wall of Shame, with its own DMZ and armies guarding both sides ready to fight seemed like war as people were getting shot. With the failsafe bombers going back and forth doing surveillance and ready to drop nuclear bombs, we were always in fear of a nuclear war. Sometimes we were playing a propaganda game against the Soviet Ministry of Information and the KGB. Our Central Intelligence Agency was involved with the governments of all the countries for we had an ongoing courtship to give aide, military support and arms to back up our promises. It wasn't a game and our cover as "Eric & Gisela" could now be shot or hung as spies for getting caught transferring secret documents and other crimes against the government. One of the biggest protest songs and social commentary of the times was the song "Eve of Destruction". It was about being close to the nuclear annihilation of the world and all the hate and violence and people wanting to kill each other.

All the big bases on the coasts usually had a big terminal for international flights. I would go the base cafeterias when working nights to get something to eat and watch the world go by. It was so good to see couples reuniting after being away from each other when one was deployed. When a soldier was finally home and safe from some life and death situation, they are usually met with shrieks of joy. It gave me great feelings to sit and watch couples and their families celebrate. But the disrespect of people against the war was a sad event. They would protest by taking it out on the returning vets and hold up signs calling us baby killers and war mongers. They would burn the American flag and effigies of Uncle Sam and President Nixon and publicly burn their draft cards. This is not what the Vets need to see as they were bringing home a ton of crap as it was. There was a lot of hate in the world and at every parade we saw people protesting and hating the opposition. It seemed that everybody had some sort of cause so that nobody could come together. To see violence back home certainly made our country in turmoil and people claimed to move to Canada. As always, we wondered what we were fighting for and why can't we seek peace. History shows that WW2 bailed out the great depression. I can't understand how we were stuck in a ten-year depression and all of a sudden, we were pumping out jeeps, trucks, tanks and battleships and guns and weapons. When a newly built squadron of fighter jets would fly over, they would darken the sky. So why could we not generate that energy in peace time. Why do we need a good war to strengthen the economy? And it just wasn't right to see a vet drunk and out of work. We were supposed be helping our brothers in the service and in the churches, and the peace movement was supposed to be all about love.

In Biafra things were still so bad that even the livestock was starving. The food had to be shipped in every night and there still wasn't enough to go around as many villages and areas did not get fed. There was a ceasefire but there was constant fighting over the next of the food and medical supplies and thousands of people were starving or sick with diseases. The current epidemic of malnutrition and the spread of sexual transmitted diseases were spreading at an alarming rate. Some of the early detection of autoimmune diseases that were being isolated as the HIV and AIDS virus was taking its toll in central Africa and the medical staff did not have clue to a cure. Nancy's team was inundated with long lines of patients needing medical treatment and they worked 18-hour shifts. Nancy would work nonstop treating the people with vaccinations, birth control and education. Many tribes were still under the control of the shamans and the witch doctors and they feared the foreign intruders. I feared that our medical volunteers were susceptible to all the diseases as well. One of the hard comments was the question of why do we continue to haul in all the food to the desert where nothing grows when we should be trying to move the people to where the food is. But that was not going to happen either. Another great term we used was that everything was just one big cluster fuck. Many people believed that the ground was cursed.

As soon as Nancy got to work at the Landstuhl Medical Center she started getting close to another army nurse. Her name was Jane Miller from Columbia,

Missouri and she was a widow with two kids. Her husband died in his Huey in a fire fight in Nam in 69 and she was stationed stateside at Ft Hood in Texas. After she buried her pilot, she transferred to Germany to get away for a while. Jane was quite a strong woman and she was raising two good kids on her own. Nancy and Jane worked 50 hours a week together and they covered for each other. Nancy liked being with her kids and taking them places. I tried to help the little boy catch a ball and play some soccer and I just had to take him out fishing. Nancy would look at me all goofy eyed when I would take him under my wing. His name was Joey and he was going to be 7 soon, his younger sister was Clare and she was almost 5. I liked kids but no way was I wanting one of my own for quite a while. Working to save some kids is our big maggilla at this time. We wondered about introducing Jane to Charley-Son but it could be too soon for both of them. Jane's husband and CB both had their other mistresses that they loved, a Bell HU-1 Iroquois helicopter. Nancy said it was good to have another female friend as the boys in the agency were all Alpha males. The main attribute was that we were all committed to the common goal of completing our mission and helping each other get home safely. Jane was a good-looking lady and she was tough as nails and we were glad that she loved the Lord. Jane and

Nancy were bonding and becoming good friends, and we all loved her kids.

The "Drs Without Borders" recruited Jane to go to Biafra with Nancy on their next good will mission. Biafra was a small newly formed country on the south corner of Nigeria and it was taking a beating by the Nigerians and the tribal warriors. The government was starving the people as it was estimated that 10 - 15 thousand people were dying a day. They would shut down the food and supplies by the Red Cross to further starve their own people. Millions of people were refugees in their own country and by the end of 1969 Biafra was taken back over by Nigeria again. Death, misery, disease and birth defects continued to destroy the land. It practically killed us to see the news of the warlords stealing all the food and supplies. They had to burn the bodies and bury them in these big open graves.

Jane and Nancy were so brave to push through all the horrible conditions to try and minister a little hope to mothers and their kids. The lines went on forever and they got little sleep for days. We shared some bible about reaching out to the poor and Jesus healing the lepers in the market place. After we receive our Holy Spirit we are commissioned to walk like Christ. In Biafra we have no choice but to pray and believe.

The Christians we met said that they were amazed that we believed in God as we had so much, what do we need God for? But in reality, it was amazing that they believed having so little. The Biafrans only hope was to believe in Gods power as they had nothing else. There was no hope or vision. The little children that limped around with no limbs and deformities ripped our guts out literally. With all this grief and the smell of burning flesh in the air, it was common to see people puking. We put toothpaste in our nostrils to mask that horrible smell from the mass graves that burned 24/7. The burning smell of the fires darkened the sky and made us sick from the stench of death. Over in Vietnam and in Biafra the smell of burnt hair and human flesh is so disgusting and violates more than your senses. It goes deep in our soul and desecrates our life force. The devastation lasted for years and without food and supplies the relief efforts were too little and too late. We were just putting band aids on open wounds. The whole country was a gruesome display of mankind's hate and greed against other human beings. The Biafrans were being slaughtered and starved to death and an entire nation of people were being wiped off the face of the earth

Our crew of volunteers did the best we could do but it was only a drop in the bucket as for everyone we could help, there were thousands dying in the streets. There was no clean water or food and we all had to ride shotgun on the trucks from the airport with our rifles to deliver what we had. We used tanker trucks to deliver water where we could. The domestic and wild animals were starving from hunger and thirst. The draught turned the ground into a dessert so nothing could grow. It was also over a hundred degrees during the day so we worked more during the night. We were fortunate to be NATO and US forces as they didn't attack us out on the routes from the airport. When we got back to West Germany it was another world and we needed to throw away our clothes and it seemed that we just couldn't get clean enough as it was badly imprinted in our minds and in our pores. We all lost weight. It was hard to eat, different smells would still make us sick. We made a total of 8 relief missions in the 6 months we could get in and out without having to fight the Nigerians, the warlords or other murderers, mercenaries or freedom fighters. It was just another place that was hell on earth. Once again it was hard to have meaningful relationships as we were callous and separated from anything that was good. We needed to go to God in prayer and we took some R & R to try and get away from our own torments. It was all about the love and compassion we still had deep within us.

We hoped that time did heal our wounds, it is just that a lot of crap gets repressed deep in our psyches and continues to haunt us for the rest of our lives. How does one get over the mind picture of dead bodies being bulldozed and the smell of death was so bad we could literally taste it? Months later we would still gag on some smells triggered by our memories. Once again being out together with the fresh air rushing in our faces was very healing and I thanked God I was with Nancy. Love trumps Evil.

The medical staff that Nancy would go to Biafra with, had a couple of big orphanages that they would go to. They were so overcrowded and short on supplies and sterile procedures. Because of the wars, starvation and disease, many children lost their parents and entire families. They had birth defects that could be due to villages staying close as the big families had many cousins and extended relatives. Because of the tribal wars they had a tighter gene pool and the men did not go far away to find their mates. A birth defect that seemed to be on the rise was the children born with cleft palates. The Doctors and operating staff took on the surgery to repair a lot of the really bad cases that needed skin grafts and major dental work. The whole process required hours of surgery and more operations later. Because this was part cosmetic the doctors and their team had to do the surgery on the fly and we brought them back to Italy to an actual hospital. To eventually see their mouths put back together was so wonderful and when they could smile it was so beautiful that it would bring tears to our eyes. Not only could they eat soup and drink liquids but they could start to learn how to talk. Over the 6 months that Nancy was going to the orphanages the Doctors did over 100 of these surgeries which saved a lot of their lives. A lot of these orphans were left to starve to death as they were considered hopeless cases until these doctors got involved. Again, I would hold Nancy as she cried herself to sleep with all the suffering she dealt with. Somethings just ripped our hearts out and you don't see the good through all the bad.

Another one of our great sayings was that when we are ass deep in alligators it is hard to remember that the original objective was to drain the swamp! When we remove ourselves from the dark energy we are in, we can see some of the good things we did accomplish. The devil and his boys have a way of belittling us and what good we do, but light dispels darkness and good does overcome evil when we remain strong. With the death and destruction in Central Africa it might look like we were only scratching the surface but we have to start somewhere and again what is the price of one life? One life is priceless and so many people I am with would sacrifice their lives for you. The men and women that run towards danger instead of away from it are the real heroes.

Back in West Germany life was a lot more peaceful, at least we were not starving or dying in the streets. The Landstuhl Medical Center and my base at Ramstein was dealing with more deaths and injuries from terrorism and political espionage. The Cold War was in full stride and we had political assassinations and other covert actions as it was "Spy vs Spy" like in the Mad magazine cartoon. We had secret military intelligence, the CIA and national security police forces that were all involved with gathering, deciphering and exchanging information. We were living in the age of "James Bond" and Scotland Yards, the Russian KGB and the Israeli Mossad were highly trained and all countries had their own intelligence. Even back thousands of years ago the bible had many accounts of spying. A famous account was when Moses sent Joshua and Caleb in to the Promised Land to spy out the land and to report about the giants that lived there. We are asked not to forget the political and religious persecution's (espionage), the mock trial and the crucifixion of Jesus Christ. The Mesopotamians dating back to 6,000 BC were still in the bronze age and they are responsible for inventing the wheel, written language, planting and cultivating crops and they are considered "the cradle of civilization". They have written accounts of forgers that could reproduce the signets and seals to spy on an official letter from the king to his generals!! The book of Ecclesiastes tells us that "nothing is new under the sun as all is vanity and vexation of spirit".

Our base in south west Germany was less than 100 miles away from the Iron Curtain and the Berlin Wall yet the differences were astronomical. We enjoyed a thriving economy; an abundance of food and products and we were free to come and go as we pleased. Not so in East Germany and the satellite countries as the government controlled everything and gave back nothing. It was all for the Republic as individual rights were sacrificed for the good of the State. If you spoke out for your rights you were classified as a political dissident and you could be arrested in the middle of the night, never to be seen again. They say the biggest jails and labor camps in the world are in Siberia. The freedoms we take for granted were all censored by the state. The rights for free speech, religious freedoms, the right to peacefully assemble, to bear arms and to travel outside of the country, were squashed and thrown out the window. The state even controlled and censored the TV, the radio and the books you could read. They had book burnings of the bibles and the classics and having a rock and roll record of Elvis or the Beatles could get you a one-way ticket to Siberia. Because of the propaganda being fed as constant diet, that is all that most people knew. If you did try to complain they would be knocking on your door late at night, and arresting you in front of your family and your loved ones. An important point that we do all share is that the Communists love their children too!! We all pray that this basic love will supersede all politics, race and religions.

Nancy and I have seen the family dynamics of people on five continents and when it gets right down to it, family is all we have. I've seen little children playing on the stoops in The Bronx and I've seen kids playing together in the bombed-out towns in Vietnam. They look about the same as families vacationing at Disney World or running to our Jeep in Biafra. Kids are kids and they are not only our hope for the future but they are life longing for itself. The real big issue is why they must suffer with cancers, life threatening diseases, birth deformities that prevent their development and why do they have to die in our wars?? Nancy was a seasoned operating room nurse yet at night I have seen her sobbing over some little girl that lost her arm and leg from stepping on a landmine. We were not supposed to give up, we got discouraged, we got overwhelmed, we got run down and we were scared. Yet even helping one person gives us strength to keep trying. Jesus asks us what is the worth of just one soul? As bad as it was in Biafra seeing a child smile helped make things bearable, even if it was for just a moment in time.

Ever since Nancy and Jane hooked up together at the medical center at Landstuhl, they became instant friends. Now the plot thickens as they joined the Doctors Without Borders and got involved with the relief efforts in Biafra. But back at the hospital they were working at distributing drugs and medical supplies to update the hospitals in Germany. Nancy and I were able to distribute these supplies into East Germany and that is how we got around both sides of Europe. Nancy and Jane started to see that their supplies were not getting to the destination they were sending them to. This looked like something was going down in our own shipping department that involved the flight team. The supplies were leaving the base but getting intercepted somewhere before the clinics and hospitals at the tune of $10,000 a shipment. Our nurses started to investigate the whole thing and they discovered that the medical supplies were taken off the manifest so there was no record of them being delivered. They were all supposed to be delivered for the nurses to educate the medical staffs on the new drugs and medical procedures. Apparently, the black market redirects them to sell to the highest bidder as these drugs were the new cutting edge. So now it was our job to find out how to bust them. How my world has changed now that I am hooked up with the Colonel. We are slowly realizing that the Colonel is more involved with the CIA as nothing is what it seems. I guess that the Colonel knew that I was familiar with the shipping of drugs and medical supplies on both sides of the spectrum so I should be able to figure some of these things out.

We had a lot to figure out how this whole process went down. We figured that Nancy and Jane would investigate how the drugs were distributed back into the system by following the drugs and I would follow how they were shipped. Whatever they were doing, we did, so I should have some experience finding out their MO. We had to find out who was stealing this stuff and how they were doing it. We decided to make up some fake manifests to send out as decoys and see how they shipped. We made some pallets up just like the original orders and sent it to a few more destinations. They were shipped out of Landstuhl by truck to a hub at Hamburg to a hospital in the city. Nancy and Jane were waiting there to intercept the order but it arrived missing the medical supplies that we shipped. It seemed that during the first part of the route our West German allies already made their strike and erased the entire order. We had to go with the fact that it was an inside job as we were the only ones that knew the scoop. Somebody was stealing the meds and medical supplies and had people working right within our own systems. We have to investigate both the shippers and the medical team to find out who was taking our classified cargo. Nancy and Jane were always suspicious of these two doctors from The Hamburg Medical School that were still working in General Admissions and should have been on to their specialty in Internal Medicine. The nurses felt something just wasn't right with these two Doctors, they should be in a medical fellowship at a prestigious hospital. Instead they worked part time in an army hospital with average pay. We are supposed to follow the money or lack of it and it just didn't seem that these young Doctors were donating to the cause. We kept trying to infiltrate their paper trail. Someone was getting to erase the manifest documents. Our big break came when we got a couple of tracking devices to pack in the next order. I shipped them from the medical supply unit at Hamburg to the Landstuhl Hospital Pharmacy. That is where they were received and then erased from the route. Within the week we found out that the shipments were rerouted to a warehouse on the Hamburg harbor. The NATO special police busted the entire team of thieves including the two Doctors. Maybe they can open a little practice in prison.

The Gideons were having these guest speakers telling us about how the Word is being spread over the world. They spoke the Word to anyone who listened and they organized fellowships to pray and study the bible. They were studying the book of Acts to see how the first century church moved the Word. Everyone prayed for the work that Brother Andrew was doing smuggling in bibles behind the Wall. One of the gentlemen gave us exciting news of a few groups trying to bring bibles and classes on tapes, translated in their languages, to some of the Communist Bloc countries. The bells went off when he told us that the name of the one group was called "The Ambassadors". This group was not a bunch of boy scouts, more like a paramilitary group of vets that were committed to spreading the Word over the World. We stayed for a closed meeting to learn more about their goals and objectives. We figured that they might want somebody that knows how to ship anything from pencils to "air to air" missiles. And they definitely will want a combat nurse and a great believer on their team. I sure would like to keep our husband & wife team in action, we could be Boris & Doris Breckenridge visiting family in Prague.

I got invited to an officer's dinner and dance to escort my beautiful surrogate wife and to help her celebrate her promotion to First Lieutenant and get some service medals for her work on the medical team. She looked absolutely vivacious with her silver bars, her new medals and her two combat stripes on her forearms. Her dress blues looked so good and she was the hottest gal on the base. We planned on taking a few days of R&R cruising up to Copenhagen and then to Brussels to take in the sights. Nancy was a great driving companion and she was always looking for a beautiful spot to have a picnic and have some sweet time together. She always liked to drive and she sure could drive me crazy as well. We sure had a good time together and we were always keeping things exciting. We were young and in love and we had the entire Mediterranean Sea and Europe to play around in.

The holidays were coming up and we were looking to go to a chalet in the Swiss Alps with some friends at our bases. We were scheduled for another trip down to Biafra before Christmas so we could deliver more food, drugs and supplies. We were bringing the "Doctors Without Borders" and picking up some children that needed special surgeries back at Landstuhl. Nancy will be on the medical team for these two kids badly burnt in a fire. The medical team also wanted our assistance to airlift some of the children back to hospitals in Germany for special surgeries for birth defects and treatments that needed the advanced operating rooms. She also had time to organize a trip to an overcrowded orphanage to give out goodies and clothes. She wanted to give as she knew that giving is receiving. The visit to the orphanage was rough to take as the they were trying to feed, clothe and take care of 200 young souls without homes and families. A very bittersweet moment was when the children were sad that they had nothing to give back to us. They came up with an old oar that they wrote their Christian names on and it is one of our best trophies. We later varnished the oar and have it on the wall with a group picture of all of them with the staff. Nancy would love to open a shelter or an orphanage someday and I could see myself spending some of my Red Lobster cash on a good cause. It's been said that life is wasted on the youth and Nancy and I had plenty of time to make those serious decisions. But on certain nights I start getting these feelings that I never want to let her go and I know that when she leans back on me, she feels the same. This is more than a physical feeling as it comes from within our hearts and God wants our hearts.

I have not told anyone about my stock investments, my accountant advised me to keep business close to my vest. There is nothing illegal about investing in overseas companies and it is all done in my corporate name, Sunshine Shipping. We made certain that everything was on the up & up as things have to be nowadays. Everybody that knew me, knew I had a rich grandad, and I have a nice trust fund from him that got me interested in the Dow Jones. When I was growing up with him, we would go to breakfast every morning and read the Wall Street Journal together. He would ask me my "take" on things and then tell me how stupid I was if I didn't agree with him. I guess I learned a few things but I also know that it had a lot to do with him giving me his DNA. I told Nancy I had an investment in the Red Lobster franchise. It was just starting to take off last year. Don't get me wrong, I wanted to be honest with Nancy from the get go but I didn't think I had to give her my financial statement at this time. If we were getting married, I would put her name on all I have. When the market tanked in 1929, big time bankers and investors went belly up and were jumping off their roofs and we were thrown into the Great Depression. Nothing is certain (but death and taxes), so it is said that playing the stock market is like playing the ponies and it is all just a crap shoot. Everyone that is betting that their stock is on the rise is playing against the guy that believes the stock will fail. The Dow Jones has continued to rise and is a safe investment. It gets a little more complicated when they want the stock to fail?? Money is not the root of all evil, it is the LOVE of money that is.

We started taking a language course given on the base by Communications and it was given to teach the students basic skills. We were already working German and in class and at home we were trying to speak it exclusively. Nancy was so fricking smart that she was talking to the local people already and I was still working on my pronouns. The Ambassadors wanted us to know Russian and we could get certified from the communication school on the base. I didn't sign on the dotted line yet and they haven't accepted me yet either. I was thinking of messing with Nancy by asking her to tell them that if I don't go, she don't go. But I don't think at this point she would join without me, and at this point I don't think I would want to live without her. I went on a wild rollercoaster romance ride with Ann Marie and Tony that was beyond words. Except it was crazy. And here I am loving God, and one of His daughters. One of my favorites scriptures is Jesus being asked" Master, what is the greatest commandment in the law?" Jesus answered," Love the Lord your God with all your heart, mind, soul and strength. And love your neighbor as yourself. On these two commandments hang all the law and the prophets."

We hadn't heard from Charlie in a few months, we left messages at his base. We wanted to get him over to our Christmas party. Our friend Jane was coming to the Christmas get-away with her kids. We thought that because her husband was a helicopter pilot and had a similar love affair as Charley for their Hueys that maybe they would want to meet. We were wondering if we should try to hook them up at St Moritz. We finally got a call from him before we were getting ready to leave. We had not heard from him because he was hospitalized so he could dry out from drinking and driving. He was found sleeping off a bender in a two-ton transport until it ran out of gas in front of a bar near his base. It looked like it did him some good as he sounded in good spirit and he wasn't drinking. He was back to work and hadn't lost his sense of humor. We are hoping that somehow this would be a good wake up call for Charlie-son and his fight for his own sobriety and his sanity. He certainly was a lot of fun and he could be charming at times. Nancy said that Jane certainly could use a good laugh or two. Jane and her kids could be a stabilizing force in Chasworth's life.

We had a few more people going so we decided on this charming old inn at St Moritz. We felt like we were on vacation with the Von Trapp family. I cooked my traditional 7 Fishes on Christmas eve and we had a turkey dinner the next day. Our special guest was Col. Thompson and we had a midnight fellowship outside around a big bonfire with about 20 new people A lot of the gang that came with us for this Christmas to New Year's break were digging our bible fellowships. We were meeting at our cottage on Wednesday nights and we met at the base chapel on Sunday mornings. We hung out with the Colonel and he told us all about the gospel moving around the world. He said there was a big revival going on. Col Thompson was taking over the duties of the European and African NATO Chaplain services and was looking for some new assistants to work with him. He told us about some good stories of the Word moving and how the signs, miracles and wonders follow those that believe.

It is a great joy to see a person, or a family or even a group of people get turned on to God and go through that transformation from a caterpillar to a butterfly. To start getting to know God and His word and to walk by his spirit gives you the manifestation of holy spirit. For me that was a big deal as that was the "cosmic-consciousness" that us hippie types were looking for. I knew it was available but I didn't know that the bible was the handbook for that spiritual life. I am so much higher now and the wisdom, the knowledge and the understanding, blows my mind. I can see miracles as I walk with the Lord. Our little group was praying together and Christ tells us that if two or three are gathered in his name, he is in the midst of them. On a sad note the Colonel spoke of the communist's oppression of Christianity and any other religious beliefs. The Berlin Wall, the Iron Curtain, and the Communist Bloc represented barriers that inhibited any energy to flow through those schisms. Castro's Cuba was over 90% Catholic yet the new communist regime took the crosses off of the steeples. Like the Nazis before them, the Communists tried to censor Christianity by confiscating the bibles and had public bonfires burning them. By closing the churches and taking away the right to assemble, the Communists tried to stomp on any belief in God. We believe that when you trust in God, he will take care of your land and your country. We even pray for our leaders that we can live a peaceful life in all honesty.

It was beautiful to be out on the water being able to see the sights and it was unfair to try and compare one place from the other. The wide-open places cannot be categorized, they were infinite. The miracle of sight and our senses let us observe incredible things and here we are able to look through a microscope of single cell life, all the way to peer through a telescope and capture other galaxies. Our senses can see things in thousands of shades and colors. The Eskimo people have over 100 words just for the color white. Back in time, way before electricity and burning fossil fuels, the people read the stars. The Prophet Daniel read the stars and taught the people about God through them. In fact, the wisemen from the East knew when to look for the star to lead them to Bethlehem. The Magi knew the whole story of the birth of the savior as told in the scriptures. They came from Persia where Daniel established a school years before. They came to see the One born King of the Jews, the messiah. That is why they brought gold, frankincense and Mir, the gifts for a King. The star of Bethlehem guided them. Now we can map the stars and they figured out that Jesus was born to a Virgin in Virgo, while the shepherds were still out in the fields. The window for the star passing over Bethlehem was from 3 B.C. to 1 A.D. This was all worked out that Jesus Christ was born on September 11, 3 B.C. in the evening, when the star of Bethlehem shown right over the stable.

When we were out together at night the waters were magical. There was the feeling that we were detached and smaller than a grain of sand, out floating in space. There were times we felt so connected that everything made sense and we had that Great Truth phenomenon that gives us a stream of consciousness. Now we can see through electron telescopes that there are thousands of galaxies so that words like infinite, eternal and forever can really blow our minds. How can God always be with no beginning and no end, the alpha and the omega? When Nancy and I are out cruising in the night, we are drifting in space. The strange islands float by like the stars in the sky and we get disconnected from land as the stars are reflected in the water.

The Bible grounds us that we will not be spirits floating in space as heaven will be here on earth. We will have new bodies and new minds and we will go through a metamorphosis from death to eternal life. Christ was the first to be resurrected and when he comes back, he will raise up his church. We will then understand these great mysteries of life. We can now get these streams of consciousness through the Holy Spirit that gives us snapshots of further paradise and life with God and his Son. We can receive revelation by the spirit via Word of Knowledge, Word of Wisdom and Discerning of Spirits. We have the power to walk like Christ and we can pray for miracles. There is a lot to believing and thinking positive and our faith gives us the courage to make it happen. The nine parts of the manifestation of Holy Spirit are spiritual tools to walk by the spirit. One of them is Faith, so you can gain the ability to pull off the miracles, the gifts of healing and to understand the prophecies and the spiritual world. This spiritual faith is made available so we can gain the power to do the impossible.

Nancy and I are connected to God through Christ as we both share God's Holy Spirit. It is good to believe that God has our backs and that Christ is our wingman. God's Word says that he has us under his wings like an eagle. These are some of the things we share as we rush through the night. The Holy Spirit we have is so much purer and higher than anything we ever experienced. "And it shall come to pass in the last days", says God "I will pour out my spirit to all flesh: and your sons and your daughters shall prophecy, and your young men shall see visions and your old men shall dream dreams." When we pray together out under the canopy of the stars rushing through the water with the wind in our faces, we felt one with God. It is power and energy fueled by God's love, and the tears ran down our cheeks, a catharsis of emotions.

St. Moritz is everything you can imagine of an alpine resort elevated 10,000 ft. with surrounding peaks reaching 13,000 ft. It was home to 2 winter Olympics and year-round activities and is a great place to celebrate the holidays. We went skiing a few times and we went ice skating while we were ice fishing the lake. Nancy was the best skier but since I was playing hockey since I was a kid, I was still ok out on the ice. I got to play a couple of pick-up games with some of the local skaters and got my ass handed to me! In winter sports, the Germans and the Swiss were great as were most of the Europeans. Charley-son was a good skater but this local-yokal kept fouling him and trying to trip him. Finally, our boy gets up off the ice and checks the guy into the boards. We had to break them apart before Chaz gets really mad and bashes the guy's head in. Things cooled down and they shared a beer in the pub and we were all singing and dancing. Charley took the stage funnier than a barrel of monkeys and his Vietnam stories were just insane. Everywhere we went, Chasworth had a group of people sitting around listening to his tales. We figured that Jane liked hairy chested guys that made her laugh; she didn't stop laughing all week. At one point we noticed Charley walking by with Janes kids and her son was riding on his shoulders. Nancy gave me an elbow of approval like she is excited for romance to bloom. I did not tell Nancy that old Charley-son was married for 68 days a few years ago?!! He thought things were going pretty good till he came home for lunch and found his wife in bed with her old boyfriend. To add insult to injury

Charley-son said that she was going down on the guy like it was her job yet he had to beg her for any of that action. Poor Charlie just couldn't catch a break and I wondered if that is why he became such a dog.

I know we just don't "fall" in love as it should be an interactive mutual decision that two people can experience together. But the chemistry needs to activate too! The funny thing is that for centuries marriages were arraigned and they still are all over the world. In our culture more and more couples are just living together or getting divorced and it isn't unusual for a person to be divorced a few times. Because we do talk about marriage, and divorce, Nancy and I want to take our time. Late New Year's Eve we both talked about tying the knot when we get out of the service, but when we woke up, we came back to our senses, sort of. We liked to say that we've already gone through a war together, so what could be the problem? After celebrating New Years together, the people that stayed the week wanted to do it again on Easter, Nancy said we are going to need a bigger place! CB & Jane were being sweet with each other and it seemed that they were good together. Charles was only stationed 160 kilometers north from us so if they took different sections of the Autobahn, they could make it in an hour and a half. Our German lessons were going over directions and reading maps and road signs. My fraulein was making me look retarded and I thought it would be great if she just became my translator. Speaking German was tough and some of the words were a mouthful. The word for the Autobahn is Bundesautobahn and the word for the speed limits was Richtgeschwindigkeit!! So, it was nuts to try and go fast, no pun intended -. Fortunately, everybody in Europe was learning English as well. The Colonel had left right after Christmas and said that as soon as he set up his quarters, he would be in touch with me, and I knew that this can't be good. We finished the year with a great party at an old chalet up in the mountains overlooking St Moritz. The Swiss Alps were so magical that it looked like time stood still.

It was good to get back to our cottage and back to work. We signed out of our rooms on our bases as we never used them so we took a big step in our relationship. We have been together for over a year and a half and still held our passports and different identities. We got the word that we would be out of Africa soon, the mass exodus was tailing off as it was being taken over by the private sectors. I am sure that we were going to be kept busy at the base and hospital. There was no shortage of death and misery. We kind of thought that Colonel Thompson had some sort of plans for us. It was now the spring of 1972 and we were hoping that Nixon was going to keep his promises and get our troops back from SE ASIA. It seemed that he ordered more bombing in Cambodia and Laos and went after Hanoi with a barrage of sorties constantly. We were bringing our troops back home as the numbers came down from over 500,000 to 100,000 so things looked promising. We were trimming back our troops. We were increasing our power in the skies as we bombed the hell out of them. If we fought this war on our terms and strengths it would have been over years ago. Instead we chose to fight them down in the jungle against their strength. Basically, we were fighting with one hand tied behind our back. The United States Military was the strongest force in the world but we were held in check because nobody wanted another Hiroshima & Nagasaki. Back in America the country was in its usual turmoil. They wanted to stop the war and dump Nixon. The Mideast was a hot spot as Iran, Iraq and Syria were all involved with Israel and the oil producing countries were banning together. The OPEC (Oil Producing-Exporting Countries) nations were putting a kibosh on the industrial countries. The price per gallon rose up to $5 and gas was being rationed with long lines and no gas. There was unrest all over the world. The Cold War went beyond Europe as it seemed that the Soviets were always backing whatever country we were against.

We did one more goodwill mission to Biafra and then it would be handed over to the Red Cross and other international aid and relief groups. The Doctors Without Borders organization has grown and had a lot of work in third world countries. Nancy was going to be on call from Landstuhl and join the staff at the NATO headquarters. The Colonel met me for breakfast and we had our favorite SOS and he told me his plans. Now that he was in charge of the European and African theaters, Chaplain and the Ministering Services, he had to oversee the priests, ministers, rabbis, and the Muslim cleric as well as the spiritual needs of any soldier. He wanted me to work for him; he would need my work as an assistant as he had both continents to take care of. The Colonel told me he needed me to keep things moving and to get things done. He also told me we would be getting into some clandestine work that Nancy and I were being recruited for. He told me I was becoming a strong man of God and that he was proud to serve with me, the man of God thing blew me away. I always considered the Colonel to be a man of God but I didn't think it applied to me? I have served with Col. Thompson for two years now and I know his passion for Christ and he has to help meet the needs of the other faiths as well. We saw that a big opposition was the lack of faith in the communist countries as we see the cold war was trying put a wall around their hearts and minds. The only hope for the communist countries was for the people to be able to worship God again. This was one of the main themes in Alexander Solzhenitsyn's writings about his belief in God verses the Communists view that there is no God. The bible tells us we are to speak the gospel to the four corners of the earth and when we do Christ will come back to resurrect the church. It was working in Africa as it seemed that half the churches from the States had work going on. For our last relief mission, we made sure to bring toys and treats for the orphanage. My last job was delivering the food and supplies and to bring back some of the medical equipment that we still needed. Nancy was still giving out vaccinations, birth control and nutrition materials. Africa was going through so many changes that it must have driven the map makers crazy. By the time they printed out the new maps they had to make another one. Boundaries were changing all over the world.

One of the biggest concerns of the military on having woman go into combat is that the male soldiers will be overcompensating trying to protect them. Women and children have always been the spoils of war yet there have been certain women like in the Israeli Masada that could be ruthless and could drop you in a second, and with one smile melt your heart. Much to my amazement Nancy was all of these things and yet she was tender and warm at the same time. And it wasn't something that she turned on and off, she just reacted as her reflexes were so well trained that she was automatic like a jaguar ready to strike. To my constant amazement Nancy loved life and somehow could deal with the sick crap and injustices we lived with. How she could be so damn sweet and loving was one of life's mysteries and I don't want to figure it out, I just want to love her back. I think the fact that we believed (in God) and that we believed we were working for a righteous cause, covered a multitude of sins. Another great scripture for our bathroom mirror was "Be not overcome with evil but overcome evil with good." We know that all the fears we have will only slow us down and retard our energies and can freeze us from taking action. Fear is the sand in the machinery of life but a little bit does help keep us on our toes. That is why our training puts us on automatic pilot so we don't have to think about it. Like I have said, some people run away from danger and some people run towards it. Nancy always runs towards danger if she can help someone in need. Another practice that Nancy has me doing is fasting for a day or two and staying a little hungry to get sharp and focused. Like she says, I became a lean, mean fighting machine, and a caring lover!!!

As a soldier getting to see some of the world these past three years, I've seen some beautiful sights and met some great people. The problem is that we see mankind (minus the kind!!) at his worst, killing each other viscously without reason, not that there is ever a good reason to kill. It doesn't seem like there is any rhyme or reason. Being stationed here in Germany I see the past wars as far back as the feudal wars with the castles and moats. The city walls protected the people of that kingdom. The word for police comes from the root word polis which means city walls, like Indianapolis. The city walls protect the people as the police do, and when the bells ring every citizen comes in for protection. Translating the root word polis from Greek to English we get city, citizens, citizenship and then police and politics all stemming from the city walls, the polis. A citizen of a city or a kingdom has the rights to all the benefits like water, sewers, waste collection and police protection. The bible tells us that we are citizens of heaven and it ends in the book of Revelations where the New Jerusalem will be established and the Tree of Life will be restored for the healing of the nations. It says that Abraham wandered around in the desert because he looked for a city whose founder and maker was God. These walls are a big deal as we have been making these lines in the sand since time began. Now we have Berlin being called the walled city (but that is really Jerusalem), and this line of oppression going all the way through Eastern Europe. They not only put up these walls and boundaries but they put them up in the hearts and minds of the people.

Our own fears and limitations put boundaries on our mind and spirit but when the government does it, walls are built instead of bridges. With the ruins of past wars and seeing the buildings that were shot full of holes, it gets even more weird to realize that just 25 years ago we hated these krauts and fought an all-out war against them. The Russians were our allies and we had to drop two atomic bombs on those "dirty Japs" to end the war. We helped rebuild West Germany and Japan and now we hate the Russians. Not only are the words "civil war" an oxymoron but most insane was that in our own civil war more Americans died than in any war we fought in. We have Catholics fighting Protestants in Ireland and the Christians have been fighting the Muslims since the first crusades. I have to laugh to myself when we say that we are sending a group of highly trained peacekeepers to some fucked up place. We send guns and weapons to back the side that we hope will become our allies. This again can be all summed up in our old hippie slogan “KILL FOR PEACE”.

Back in the states the whole hippie -free love -peace thing was being put to rest. The communes and places like Haight Ashbury or the Woodstock Nation were all but a memory. It was still about sex and drugs and rock and roll and the college campuses replaced the peace signs with the money sign. Our own great schools were filled with foreign students learning medicine and technology to bring back to their countries. I am sure there are some students studying atomic engineering so they can bring back the ability to make nuclear weapons. America had over 1,800 nuclear warheads and the Soviets and the US decided nobody else should own them!! The Chinese can’t build a better mousetrap but they can build them 5 times cheaper! I thank God all the time that I believe that He raised Jesus Christ from the dead and when he returns on that white horse, he will raise me up to meet him in the air. And I will help him restore the earth back to Paradise.

It looked like we would both get to finish active duty together. We were working for the headquarters of NATO and Nancy was still a nurse at the medical center. I am still working as a Loadmaster it is just that I was on special detail to the US Army Chaplains

Corps. We were still learning languages and Nan was already working some Russian, she is a whip. I took 4 years of Spanish but made my grandfather sad, he was a language professor at NYU and I couldn't roll my Rs!! I felt that the Colonel was trying to groom me for something special and that it would be with Nancy as a team. A couple is so much more unassuming travelling and checking into places. On the highway two guys can be running drugs or up to something no good. Nancy definitely has my back and she is sharper than a knife. We have been getting pretty good at this married couple thing and we have been a good compliment to each other. Nancy is just an amazing woman who believes that God and her can do anything. Nancy and I believe in the power of prayer so we have been praying together since we first met at Cam Ron Bay. We wanted to do something exciting and on the edge. We had some incredible special forces, we have Green Berets, Navy Seals, Airborne and special teams that don't even have identities. They are deployed all over the world to intervene with all the many problems and skirmishes our country is involved with. Nancy & I are not on that level but we have been getting around a little. We haven't had the training but Nancy is a combat nurse specializing in the operating room and she has been doing relief missions in central Africa after spending a year in a MASH unit in Vietnam. And now she is learning Russian and we have passports from Canada as well as being GIs. Ever since my training at tech school I have been learning to hide weapons in pallets of food or special deliveries of our fallen heroes that lost their lives. With all the subversive activities and downright smuggling going on and the fact that I have been doing this on 4 continents with a woman that looks like she could be in a Bond movie gives me a real thrill.

Nancy and I were starting to look to the future and all the options we could have. We still had at least 6 more months of active duty and there was a lot of things to do. The Mideast was always in turmoil as the Israelis would send out it's F-114s to blow up a Syrian factory if they even suspected foul play. Jerusalem has its biblical roots and it is divided between Christian, Jewish and Muslim faiths. Then the espionage between the American and the Soviet cold war participants were fighting for the friendships and alliances of every country in the region. Africa had every type of war available from tribal wars with arrows and spears to trucks full of mercenaries or paid assassins fighting for gold, diamonds or minerals. These are some of the things you get involved in being sent to a place to make peace or war. We talked about all the cool things we could do together, and we definitely wanted to be together. We thought of taking time to finish our education as I wanted to get my degree and Nancy wanted her masters. We could do that while in the military and continue doing what we have been doing. Or we could move out to the civilian life and go for some of our dreams. We know the Colonel had something brewing and it was something to do with our new orders. We also knew that we wanted our lives to be living for God.

The Coronal was a wise man, something like a sage or even a profit. Sometimes he had the step of a young man and then sometimes he had a certain look like a twinkle in his eye that made him seem mystical. Nancy said she felt a lot of love for him like her own father. I added that the Coronel was like a biblical character like King David or the Apostle Paul. We settled that he was a little like a lot of our favorite men in the bible. It dawned on Nancy that the Coronel's main goal was always trying to teach us to be like Jesus Christ. That was our true calling and we get those "aha" moments where everything starts to make sense. We used to call it the great truth phenomenon but now we know it to be revelation from God through his holy spirit. That his how we learned how Moses was inspired to write the first five books of the bible. Then it continued on with the great men and woman of the bible as God gave them the inspired words to write. It is all about Gods spirit working within us. It takes a person that knows the truth to teach us the bible, Gods Word.

Now Nancy and I can be inspired to learn the bible through our holy spirit and even teach and share it with others. This is why at certain times I can see that twinkle in the Coronel eyes that tells me that we know that we know the truth. The Coronel has continued to get Nancy and I to live a more holy life. Going through these wild and crazy times and the Vietnam War, not to mention the civil discord and the hate all over the world, we live in such evil times. It makes us rationalize our sinful mistakes. I make excuses for everything so I don't have to deal with all my faults. Now the Coronel tells us we need to get honest which greatly messes with my pride. Proverbs 16: 18 - "Pride goes before destruction, and a haughty spirit before a fall." Our own pride prevents us to get honest with God. When we are alone with God and we look in the mirror it is time to strip off all our B.S. that we hide behind. It is time to quit making excuses and get honest. If you have to get down on your knees, ask God to help you. This is why we can be renewed by your spirit in Christ. Only Jesus Christ was a man without sin, but when he returns to raise the dead we will be born again and cleansed from all our sins. That is why Jesus died on the cross for us.

I am far from being like Christ, I sin a lot and fall so far away. But the shed blood of Jesus Christ cleanses me when I do get honest and ask for forgiveness.

The Stuttgart and Landstuhl area were exactly what you would picture the reconstructed West Germany to be. A modern industrialized city rising out of old-world charm. Companies like Mercedes Benz, Porsche, Volkswagen, Bosch and Stith Tool are all around as well as thousand-year-old castles and churches. It would be a great place to live if it were not for the California coast or the Long Island shores. Easter Sunday was approaching and our gang wanted to spend a couple of days back at St Moritz in this mountain retreat famous for its sunrises and views of the Alps. We planned for a sunrise service and a nice Easter dinner and some sightseeing of St Moritz. The lovebirds, as Nancy calls them, were coming and they have been having a real good time together. Chaz bought himself a Triumph 750 cc so they could tool around Germany together and Jane loved to go riding. If old CB stayed out of the bars, things could work out.

Nancy and I spent a lot of evenings taking rides out in her BMW with the top down touring the countryside. We decided to just keep praying together and being thankful for all we have together. We tried to communicate our hearts knowing we are young and have so much to learn. But on the other hand, God will bless us big time if we make our marriage about Him. "Two are better than one; because they have a good reward for their labor. For if they fall, the one will lift up his fellow: but woe to him that is alone when he falleth; for he hath not another to help him up. Again, if two lie together, then they have heat: but how can one be warm alone? And if one prevails against him, two shall withstand him; and a threefold cord is not quickly broken," (Ecclesiastes 4: 9-12). The threefold chord is the union of God and a couple and it is represented by the wedding ring. The wedding ring is a braid of three strands that gains strength when woven together.

At Travis AFB we had the commercial airlines bringing back soldiers and military personnel. The anti-war protesters were becoming more heated and violent and we had to block the terminal so our guys could get off the planes. Other bases had bad trouble with the protesters trying to attack the GIs as they came back to the states. Can you imagine how our GIs felt as they made it back from the hell-hole they had been through only to be dishonored by Americans that they sacrificed their lives for. We were called baby killers and war mongers and guys came back with a lot of problems and with no jobs or honor. A famous battle at that time was a bloody week-long shit show for

Hill 937 that was so messed up that human flesh was being turned into hamburger, thus named Hamburger Hill. A hundred marines finally stormed the hill and turned back the VC only to have the enemy retake it, days later. We lost 47 lives with over 300 injured. The NVA lost close to a thousand with no count of how many injuries. The marines counted 680 bodies that the NVA left dead on the ground so it really looked like ground up hamburger. One day later we moved on only so the North Vietnamese could retake the hill. This battle was wildly publicized and the American people protested to the waste of lives and money. So those brave American soldiers were being spit on and disrespected by the people they were sacrificing their lives for.

President Nixon kept promising to pull out and end the war but it still took years- it was hard for de-escalation when everyone was dug in for years and all the fighter jets and helicopters zig-zagging the sky. When the platoons were losing casualties, the soldiers got involved in a more personal focus as it did get down to kill or be killed and you had your brothers back. No one was left behind was an army slogan but we still had to deal with the MIA & POW horrors. There was a strength in that and some men would jump on a grenade for you, and that is a strong bond that is very powerful. This bond is like the bond we have with God and that is through our believing in Christ and following Gods Word. For Christ died for us so that we will live. Meanwhile the marines that were heroes for their bravery and lifesaving sacrifices had to come back with a truckload of war related problems to try and assimilate back into our society that was going nuts. They had civil discord at the Democratic Convention, killing at Kent State, large demonstrations where they were burning flags and draft cards and carrying coffins & effigies of Nixon and even Uncle Sam. The big marches on Washington had the Doves waving peace signs and 'End the War' posters. My personal favorite was "War is not healthy for children and other living things."

I was torn between what was right and wrong. I was serving my country and we were involved in war that we were shipping home hundreds of bodies a week. The amount of injuries made it even more horrific as our people were sent home in pieces. The amount of human lives we were annihilating was staggering; we were good at what we did. The demonstrations were taking place all over the world and most of the big college campuses had ongoing protests and demonstrations. The nightly news was all about the war and the protests against it. America was torn between increasing the fighting and the bombings and ending this war and pulling out. President Nixon vowed to end the war when he took over in 1969 but it still took 4 1/2 years for the US to get out with more than 50,000 American casualties. A big issue was what to do about our men that were captured which became prisoners of war and missing in action. In 1969 we had over 500,000 troops involved and now our casualties were hundreds a day. A lot of our battles seemed senseless as if any death had any purpose at all. The plan was to start bringing our troops home and arm and train the South Vietnam to take over. During this time the bombings increased, especially along the Ho Chi Ming trail running north and south through the country. It was reported that more bombs and firepower were used in those two years then all of WW 2. The Tet Offensive of 1968 - 69 was the big campaign of our forces with our jets, bombers and helicopters bombing with all they had.

Morale was getting low. So much of this war seemed senseless, a lot of our troops were dying and they felt that we were being held back. Because of the American political problems between Hawks and the Doves the Vietnam War was our number one issue as well as all over the world. Big demonstrations and protests were in the streets, on the college campuses and all over the news media. It was very common to see our guys with peace signs, as everywhere the two-finger peace sign flashed as a sign of the times. Our Generals wanted to be given the ok - thumbs up to give the enemy an all-out attack and get this war over with. The House & Senate were behind split decisions to start pulling out of the war which looked like a defeat to the patriots. Then Nixon finally promised to withdraw and let the South Vietnam Army fight their own battle which will mean that the communists will take it all over. So, either way the whole thing was a total waste of life. One of the battle cries was that if we didn't stop the communists in south east Asia, we will have to fight them in North America, and that is not the Democratic or Republican way. Anytime we gathered together these issues were discussed and argued. We still had all the camps divided between the heads vs the straight shooters, sometimes the blacks vs the whites and then we had the pro-warriors vs the peaceniks. Just like back home the night time news showed the images of war in their living rooms and we saw the violent resistance against the war. When the Japanese and the Nazis attacked us, it was a pretty easy decision to fight back. We always hear those doomsday theories that President Roosevelt knew about Pearl Harbor and let it happen to gain American support. We all felt that to be absurd as Roosevelt would never let 3000 American soldiers die in an ambush by "those dirty Japs". Our hate for them was so bad that our Japanese American citizens were detained in Detainment Camps until the war ended, for their own protection and ours, as if they had plans to attack us from these encampments in southern California? We started involvement in Vietnam as advisors and 4-5 years later we are in an all-out shit show as we called it -

Just a little over three years ago, before I was drafted, I was involved with being a part of the demonstrations and the protests against the war. It was also about making the scene seeing the music like the huge concert in Washington to see the Grateful Dead & the Allman Brothers. I got to go to the Woodstock Festival for 3 days and songs of protests from performers like Joan Baez, Richie Havens and the Jefferson Airplane were the voice of the times. After a while our soldiers were getting drunk and high on pot and some were doing the hard drugs like speed, cocaine and heroin. Some say it was all a communist plot to keep us high on drugs so we couldn't fight. A lot of men used the drugs to try and cope with the horrors and it was a part of the counter-culture society of being turned on and dropped out of the hippie and new age thinking.

Many guys I knew were so messed up that it was amazing that they lived and got home. A lot of the troops came back as addicts and alcoholics and they had to live with the horrors that they went through. Of course, the majority of our soldiers fought through a lot of this shit and made it home to live normal lives even though there is nothing normal about what they went through. Regardless of all the scars of war our soldiers were tough and well trained and fought for each other and for our country and sacrificed their lives. To see our soldiers who sacrificed so much coming home and being disrespected was deplorable. America was reeling and we lost this war and we were living in violent times. At least we had groups like the American Legion, the DAV (Disabled American Veterans) and the VA to help give them honor. Most hometown families and patriots welcomed their heroes back home with parties, picnics and parades. We might have gotten out of Vietnam but the Cold War still kept us close to another World War as it seems like we have war in our blood, and we were the best at war and killing and we had the most bombs.

Chapter Five

THE CIA

"The secret of their success is the secrecy of their moves."

We flew to Dulles in DC and got to stay in Georgetown at the National Republicans Club. Nancy's uncle was a Congressman and he had a dinner for his goddaughter's return from combat and her missions in Africa. Since this was the National Republicans Club, we wore our dress blues and took pictures under a huge portrait of President Eisenhower. Every republican in the place was admiring just how beautiful Nancy looked. I think she is filling out her skirt, her tight ass was so shapely that it made me bite my finger like the Italian that I am! I don't know what I did to deserve it but Nancy was about the best-looking women in uniform and she is actually getting even better looking. Of course, I think she is so fine, her eyes were a hazel blue that melts my heart. When she dyed her chestnut hair blonde in the summertime, her bronze tan was downright sexy. We got to stay at the Republican Hotel and worked out at their gym and swam at their Olympic pool. Staying so close to the Capitol and Pennsylvania Avenue gave us a good sense of pride and patriotism. Sitting together on the Lincoln Memorial, looking down the mall at the Washington Monument is so very glorious. We were to start training at Langley and we would be housed at CIA headquarters for a couple of months.

Langley was like an enclosed city and seemed to be hallowed grounds. Between Langley and the Pentagon, it was the heart of the American influence and power connecting the entire world. The CIA was everywhere and then it was nowhere as once again things were not what they seem. The CIA was connected to the military so they could coordinate any clandescent maneuvers all over the world. The first few days of processing was surreal, we were attending briefings and given many documents to study. We were given a small suitcase of official documents, passports and identifications that seemed so official yet the whole thing was bogus and completely fictional. In fact, the entire agency was a mystery as everything was done in secret. We had to get recertified with our new pistols so we both chose

9mm Glocks. When I saw Nancy admiring her small pocketbook model, it did give me a shiver to realize that these were the preferred handguns for the Agency and the spies. Just the feel of the different kinds of metal molded into our hand, even our rifles became a part of us. They came with silencers that gave them a special mystique and my undercover wife was a Marksman in a few weapons. I remember the instructors stating the difference between a military assault rifle and a 32-caliber hunting rifle. The hunting rifle is designed to hunt deer, the M-15 is made to kill people who are shooting back at you. Now these small handguns were designed to be concealed and to kill with silencers on them. I couldn't help but to joke with Nan that we really do have a license to kill. My thing so far was to get to defuse situations rather than to escalate them. But if someone was coming at you with an AK -47 you had better have some good firepower of your own.

We started back with some PT so we got back in the gym to do some training. Just hitting the heavy bag for a few days pumped me up to feel like a monster and working the speed bag helped me get my timing back. Then right away they had me sparring with some of the boxing team and I held my own. Nancy was doing some road work as she wanted to do some long distance running and work her way up to marathons. We took a

Martial Arts class and we got into motion and inertia to learn how to focus and transfer energy. We practiced trying to be fluid and not tensing up so we didn't resist the flow of energy. Like riding a wave or sky diving we tap into the flow of energy around us. We learned to focus to be able to break a board with our knuckles and our reflexes became even sharper. They had us doing some meditation exercises and by the time we were done we were feeling pretty good about ourselves. They set us up with language tapes to get at least a basic understanding of the Slavic languages. At least I had Nancy who could actually speak Spanish and some Latin and she was working on some Russian. Our second week was spent going over the layout of the land and the checkpoints and the various routes. We learned the value of a good bribe; it could be a carton of Marlboros all the way up to good old American cash. We had a lot to memorize and we had tons of things to know about all the connections, we had to be good actors and ad libbers and we had to get it down smooth. Smooth is experience and an innate ability to be cool, and nobody can teach being cool. But if you train and practice enough you can get to be smooth.

Part of our training was to go on a three-day pass and practice being out together as a couple. We were going to go to London and take in some shows when we went back to Europe. It wasn't that we had to practice getting along but we had to get our new identities down. We had to get use to all the various borders and the paperwork needed as some countries were only the size of some of our states. We were being trained by the CIA but we were still government issued (GIs) assigned to the NATO forces. Our new positions were brand new so we were all making it up as we went along. We would be on our own but the CIA was still involved in the entire process. They gathered all the intelligence and called the shots on our activities and provided all our documents. We were now Eric and Gisela Hartmann and we had dual citizenship as we lived in Montreal and have family in Hamburg as well. All this was worked out by the CIA and we had to make it all our own. They even set us up with a Renault that had compartments that had places to hide paperwork and any small item to smuggle. The plan was to drive right through the checkpoints and border crossings to meet up with our contacts on the USSR side. This is why we had to know each other's histories to get through some checkpoints with suspicious guards. It was all about our paperwork and our Passports, everything was made perfectly by the agency. Last year over 100 people were shot on sight trying to cross the borders and hundreds were detained and arrested. We were also learning the train and bus routes as I guess my work as a loadmaster will help me become a smuggler again. Nancy was so good at everything she does and she does it all. As a nurse she had a great cover to go anywhere in the name of medicine.

The last couple of weeks at Langley was spent going over the different connections and we studied the Hamburg area and the importance of it being a hub for our activities. Hamburg was the second biggest city in Germany with almost 2 million people and only 30 miles from the wall. It was located on the Elba River leading out to the North Sea with Leningrad to the north on the Baltic Sea and Copenhagen to the south west and out to the North Sea to the Atlantic. Hamburg was a leading port city and a lot of materials were smuggled by the thousands of ships going along these waterways. The Soviet bloc countries wanted everything from the west, clothing like Levi jeans and our Pro- Keds were a very hot commodity. Drugs were still the main desired contraband as both illicit and prescription drugs and medical supplies were hard to come by. The things we took for granted like a radio or a toaster were so scarce that people were put on waiting lists for them. Because of the blockade on free trade the food stores and retail stores in the East were bare-empty.

As formidable as the wall was there were great accounts of people able to go back and forth without the CIA behind them. We learned about things like kids that were able to go back and forth to drink some good German beer and buy a pack of smokes. Brother Andrew was smuggling bibles all by himself for years and whole families were being smuggled through all the time. It wasn't like you could just throw things over to people on the other side. The double wall built by the communists in 1961 was as wide as 100 yards with armed sharpshooters and German Shepherds on patrol like the enormous prison that it was. But if the local kids could find ways to cross just for sport, then we can figure it out, or die trying. With the agency giving us all our documents hopefully we will have smooth sailing but we will be prepared. Like most of our military training, we practice until we get it right and we keep doing it until it becomes a habit so we can do it in our sleep.

We spent the afternoons learning German and seeing more training films of life behind the wall. We were working out at the gym and I tried to keep up with Gisela doing some road work. After dinner at night we would watch films or look at the crap that the KGB and the Russian Foreign Intelligence Service put out. There was a whole lot of propaganda going down. One of the biggest tools we had was Radio Free Europe., it was able to be heard as far as Moscow. RFE was broadcast in various languages and was considered anti-communist propaganda. They broadcast from Munich but it was all funded by the CIA. They had topics on the American values, rights, and freedoms and debates about communism vs a democratic republic. Nancy's favorite program was the Medical Hour when they cover first aid, preventive medicine, women's issues and health care. Many broadcasts were backed up with the distribution of pamphlets delivered by balloons to places such as Poland, Czechoslovakia and Hungary that never got news from unoccupied countries. Over 600,000 balloons with 600 million pamphlets were delivered. We would be somewhat involved in Radio Free Europe in moving intelligence and government secrets. Bu heh, we were just couriers following orders and trying to fight for our freedoms. Back in Vietnam Charlie-son would throw out the Jack of Spades because that would freak out the NVA.

When we finished up the training, we were able to take a few days leave and drive the couple of hours to Baltimore and then up to New York. My mother thought that Nancy was the greatest and it didn't hurt that they were both army nurses. We didn't tell her that we were Eric and Gisela Hartmann and we were playing house with the NATO forces in West Germany. Our last nights in New York we had dinner at the newly opened Windows on the World restaurant atop of the World Trade Center and we watched the sunset over the harbor. We then saw the play Jesus Christ Superstar and loved it. We stayed the night at the Marriot Towers in the theatre district and just as we were making plans to fly back to Munich, we got new orders to report to FT Benning in Georgia. At the last moment the Colonel had put in for us to get some special survival training that was starting up for the Special Forces and we got invited. We were privileged to get to train in survival tactics for a month and the last week we went out in the woods on our own.

Nancy and I got to train as a couple which was very special to take part in and getting to train with the Special Forces was incredible. Nancy did amazing and at 130 lbs., she was almost as strong as me but way more mobile, she could do more pushups and pull ups and she ran faster. The only thing I could do was out swim her and out box her but on the range, she had the eyes of an eagle. She qualified as a Marksman in the M-16 assault rifle, the M-50 automatic sub machine gun and a few handguns. We were issued a couple of Glocks and a couple of 357 Magnums and we had our M-16 assault rifles so we were loaded for bear. Our enemies have all stepped it up a notch with more powerful weapons and high-tech toys so we had to keep pace. Nancy could make one hell of a good spy, she looked more like a college cheerleader then some kind of special ops soldier. I couldn't help but to buy her a small ladies Colt that she could keep in her purse or on her ankle. We got some cool toys to play with, we had two Montblanc pens that were really one shot 22 caliber guns.

During our training we got to see the real Special Forces going through their routine and it was an awesome and inspiring experience. They had a training program going on that our elite attack units were all getting trained in. Our special forces were groups of SEALS, Delta Forces, Airborne, Green Berets, Rangers and various trained teams that were the best trained soldiers in the world. Earlier groups were demolition teams and the SEALS (sea, air & land) came from the WW2 frogmen and was established in '62 by President Kennedy. Most people forget that Kennedy didn't just establish the Peace Corp but was a decorated Navy man as well (PT 109- Profiles in Courage). Kennedy had the balls to tell Russia and Cuba to take a hike. He stood up to Khrushchev and Castro during the Bay of Pigs and the Cuban Missile Crisis in a very tense time of the threat of nuclear war. I was only in 6th grade at that time but I still remembered the night we thought we were going to war with the Cubans and the Russians. President Kennedy initiated the Navy Seals and first deployed them as military advisers in Vietnam but soon became a part of the combat by 1964-65. These soldiers were in continuous training and were deployed all around the world, especially in Africa and the Mid-East as there were clandestine operations going on against terrorism and skirmishes everywhere. Most of these operations were done in secret and nobody knew of them except the CIA and the Pentagon. The secret of their success was the secrecy of their moves.

Seal Team # 6 was the name given to the very elite of the teams. They were the alpha dogs and they were all close to being wild and insane, they were fearless. There were only 3 teams, # 1, 2 & 6, just to make it seem like there was a # 3, 4 & 5. Back in the middle 60s they sported beards and long hair in defiance of the military's code and they even rode motorcycles like the Hells Angels. Most of them have been to hell and back. Nancy and I were not in this category for we were more involved in espionage and surveillance. We were adapting to the missions for NATO and the Cold War and we were being trained to be sleuths and spies. We were developing skills to get around and to travel underground and the whole world was our stage. We learned how to change our identity and to work together in secret with the CIA. There was no way I was the right stuff to be on the level of the special forces as these people were the best of the very best. Most of these teams started with the best men and women in the service and by the end of training only a third of them remained as the top trained soldiers in the world. They were the elite of the very elite. Between these special op's teams and the CIA, we had connections and muscle in every country in the world. The many things we were involved in all over the European continent and the Mediterranean Sea were all part of American diplomacy in which we proudly served. I was very lucky to be serving with Nancy as she had what it took to be a very special agent and yet she was the most loving and caring woman I ever knew. She had very special skills. I guess with God's grace we were quite a team.

We got to train in survival techniques with a lot of physical training and even urban tactics. We worked on how to clear a room, set up surveillance and blow things up. We got to take some paratrooper training and we got to do some night jumps and the final week we were dropped into the forest to fend for ourselves. I really messed up by trying to make a fire as I must have burnt some poison ivy that Nancy breathed in and it closed up her throat. I picked her up in my arms and started to run her out of the woods. I had to get to the main road and to a hospital before she stopped breathing. It was about 5 miles through the woods and something incredible started to happen as we were running. Nancy was holding me tight with her hands around my neck and our bodies were pressed against each other. All of a sudden it seemed that we were molding together as one person. Our heart beats were synchronizing and our breathing was regulating so that Nancy seemed to be getting more air. I felt as if I was getting stronger and more graceful and we were starting to go into a bubble. It was like getting that high from that second wind in anerobic running or swimming but a lot more powerful. I felt like I was a gazelle able to leap and abound over the brush and downed trees. Nancy became so light that I could not feel her. The poem about footprints in the sand came to mind and Nancy told me later that she had the same visions. The ending of the poem asked God how come in the times of need we see only one set of footprints when God promised to never leave us. God replies that those were the times that God carried us. We both felt that we were flying and I could not feel my feet were touching the ground nor was the prickly bushes cutting my legs anymore. We later discussed all the sensations that were rushing by and that God was carrying us. We also felt an incredible feeling of love for each other. We got her to the hospital on a Huey so they could get her some Benadryl injections and oxygen until the swelling went down. She was very close to asphyxiating when she started losing consciousness. We stayed overnight and we got back to training in the morning. Something very magical happened that probably saved Nancy's life.

It was something I was supposed to know when learning about eating edible berries, nuts, mushrooms and grasses. It must have been poison oak or poison ivy but I just didn't see it and I was supposed to. Like the guy walking point couldn't say whoops if he set off a trip wire and blew up his squad. He is trained to know what he is looking for and I should have been more careful. It would be great to catch a rabbit or a quail because grubs and bugs just weren't my cup of tea, we could make some berries and root teas with enough nutrition to stay alive. If Nancy drank some poison ivy tea she would have probably died. I guess we learned the hard way and I am sure the whole incident would be part of the training in the future. We also heard that the training was so intense that some of the trainees did die from accidents, snake or other bites and poisons. A few trainees every year fell off the mountains due to bad footing or bad gear. Our instructors told us that last year, a couple of men got badly hurt when they were hit by falling rocks from the guys repelling above them. We had to constantly look over each other for leaches, tics, mosquitoes, spiders and other pests. The entire training was a great experience for us as we could learn to adapt to a lot of situations and environments. My buddy Rex Hillman, the marine, was in his foxhole during the monsoon season worried that he would drown. He had to constantly check to see if the leaches had crawled up his butt or into his urethra. Not only did he have to worry about the enemy killing him but all other dangers in the jungle.

Anytime we got to jump out of a plane was still an awesome exercise as it was always thrilling, scary and the biggest rush we could possibly experience. We felt like we were Batman & Cat Woman, with our training and abilities. As we talked about what we just went through as we both felt some powerful emotions as we trained together. I guess all this training was working as we gained strength from each other. We did some repelling down the cliffs and we learned to make shelter and some tracking maneuvers. We learned about reading various footprints and animal tracks and how to not leave our own. When we finished two months of training with the CIA, we felt like we were ready to get busy and fight for our country in this so-called Cold War. We landed at Heathrow and checked into the London Hilton as husband and wife to start our assignment. Many times, we felt that these wonderful places would be a nice place to get engaged. When Nancy came out of the shower at the London Hilton with just a towel on her head singing into her hairbrush how she loved me more today than yesterday, but not as much as tomorrow, who was I to resist? But we were going to wait until we got some divine inspiration to start planning a wedding, but at least I took off her towel before we went out for breakfast.

We rented an old apartment with a view of the Hamburg harbor and we picked up our new Fiat that blended in with all the other small cars in the city. It came with some modifications that were made to store a few items in compartments built into the chassis that could not be detected by any visual inspections. I brought it to a German performance shop to soup up the engine and the suspension so it had more kick and better handling. We spent the first few weeks driving around north Germany getting use to the area and driving north and south along the wall. We took some overnight trips all the way to Italy to check out the Adriatic Sea and Yugoslavia and then back up to the North Sea. I was thinking that almost every destination was accessible by water and I wished I had a black 18 ft Donzi with a 300 Merc Cruiser to fly through the night in. A Donzi would run circles around any Soviet Coast Guard cutter, just like they did in the Caribbean running from our own Coast Guard. I put in for a request for a speed boat and I think the Colonel will approve it. But since we will have all the right paperwork, we will be able to drive right through Checkpoint Charlie in downtown Berlin. We will be transporting documents and intel so we will not be concerned about larger items like my days in California. A lot of what we were delivering was on microfilm and easy to conceal. On all our trips we were trying to keep talking German and working on reading all the signs as some signs were in Polish, Russian and Romanian. Thank God that English was spoken at the banks, hotels and all the terminals and money was spoken everywhere. The CIA had already given us the right papers so we went back and forth without any problems so we were ready to get busy.

Now we are very close to the wall dividing Europe in half with its own DMZ with tanks and sharpshooters, barbed razor wire and land mines. They had their German Shepherds and guards and even the young KGB boys in training to be good little communists. Nothing changes as walled cities and walled kingdoms have been around since the beginning of time. The Bible speaks of Babylon as being the kingdom of the world opposed to the Kingdom of God in Paradise.

The United States, the NATO Forces and their allies are standing against the Soviets and other communists to tear down this wall and unify Europe again. Our assignments here in Germany could get as hot as the war we left in Vietnam. What the heck is a Cold War anyway? Is it like a Hot Firefight or a lukewarm border skirmish? We called it a Cold War but thousand have been killed just trying to escape and only God knows how many were sent to Siberia or killed in the night. As good little hippies we thought we were going to change the world but it is actually getting worse.

We were getting ready to take off for a few days up to St Moritz for Easter when we got a call from Col Thompson. I thought that he was calling to wish us well because he couldn't be with us for the Sunday mountaintop sunrise service. Instead he tells us that we have a meeting with Lt. General Bilking, second in command at NATO, and be on time! We met the General and a group of military men and some suits that were CIA and some West German brass. The General told us that on Col Thompson's recommendation we were being recruited to a new special operations assignment. They told us that we were exactly the couple they were looking for to join a team of military and NATO agents to be able to travel across various borders including the Soviet Union. One of the agents went on to say that they have some records and files on us and that 1st Lieutenant Nancy Barrett is an excellent combat nurse. The report said that her service in Vietnam was lifesaving and her missions in Africa were exemplary. Then they proceeded to read me reports from Travis AFB and handling all the shipping from the busiest base in the late 60s. They had reports of a lot shit that Tony and I did and the report said that it was all ex facto because they never could catch me doing anything wrong. So, they told me that I had the right instincts for the job. They did catch GIs trying to smuggle stuff and they did catch Tony and his friends. The thing I put in my head was that their report stated that Tony died trying to escape, so I guess they don't know everything. And I, by the grace of God, was able to get out when it was time. The big deal was that we would be given another identity as Canadians again, newly married and visiting family now in East Germany. Nancy and I are again being paid by the government to travel and see the world together. How many couples are travelling into the USSR nowadays? The only problem was that if caught, Nancy and I would probably be sent to different gulags in Siberia unless they shot us onsite as spies.

We were so looking forward to getting back to St Moritz and spending a few days in the Alps. The theme for the sunrise service was three of the greatest words ever spoken, 'He is risen'!! Since the Colonel wasn't coming, it was up to Nancy and I to coordinate this event. We figured that we would share about Christ' resurrection and how we will meet him in the air when he returns to right the world. Up in the mountains when the sun rises, we will go over all the great stuff about Mary going to the tomb and then Mary hearing and seeing the resurrected Christ talking to her. And Peter running back to the tomb and realizes that it was all true. The Apostle Thomas was not there to see the resurrected Christ and stated that unless he sees the holes in Jesus' hand he will not believe. When Jesus showed Doubting Thomas his hands and feet, Thomas fell down in humility. What a glorious time that must have been and not unlike when we get to that place that you know that you know, that Christ is coming back. The whole bible was written so we could believe that these things were true. It was not for the doubters but for the believers to believe and manifest the power. Nancy has been working on a banner that we are going to display up on the gazebo at the overlook, "HE IS RISIN". This place is famous for sunrises and we wanted our banner to show as soon as the sun rays peaked over the mountains.

The North Atlantic Treaty Organization had 23 European countries plus Canada and the USA and opposed the Warsaw Pact of the communist countries.

It boils down to the US vs the Russians. My home base was the NATO headquarters and housed personnel from all over western Europe. Technically we were now being reassigned to NATO and we picked up a packet of info we were supposed to start studying. We said goodbye to our people and could only say that we were reassigned to NATO and that is all they needed to know. We figured we would get to see Charlie and Jane later when we are set up somewhere north near Berlin. From what Nancy told me, Jane was planning on transferring to an army medical center up near Hamburg to be with CB. Most of the bases are joint West German and US ventures that fall under NATO's command. The Warsaw Pact countries such as Romania, Poland, Czechoslovakia and Latvia are all fortified to stand against the forces of our allied countries as another way to balance out the power. Now we will be a part of NATO and a part of a very real Cold War and the Iron Curtain runs north & south right through Europe dividing the continent and its people. Hundreds of people were killed trying to escape every year and just as many were caught and dragged off to jail. Not too many were caught trying to go back in, except people like Nancy and me??

It was great getting back to St Moritz; the mountains were so magnificent and the Olympic sights and the mountain lakes were still full of skating and hockey games. The skiing is some of the best in the world. We were all excited to spend a few days together and celebrate Christ's death and his resurrection. Later on, Saturday night, Nancy and I had a big fire going and we took some time to just be thankful and we all prayed together. Nancy and I thanked God for His protection, His love and his grace. We met in Nam and quickly fell in love in the middle of the war. We sat under the same moon and stars whether we were looking over the South China Sea or looking over east coast beaches. We saw the starvation and death in Biafra. We dove in the Florida Keys and toured a lot of Europe in an old sports car and here we are up in St Moritz high in the Swiss Alps again. I can only hope that our love will continue to grow and that the closer we get to God the closer we will get to each other. Predawn up in the Alps is incredible as the glow of the early morning sky with the stars and then the snow caps looking as if they were illuminated by the early light from the sun.

We had about a hundred people gathered around the gazebo overlooking the mountain peaks and the valley and lake below. Other folks came and there were other gazebos that had services up here too. We even had a podium, and the banner looked great as the sun shone through it and illuminated the letters. We sang some songs and said some prayers. We were teaching the Resurrection just as the sun finally lifted off the peaks. The angel told Mary "He is not here for He is Risen "!! Now I have seen a lot of great sunrises all over the world, but that morning we all felt that some angels and Jesus Christ himself was with us. A couple of people from the Gideons were with us and they told me later that they got extremely blessed. We finished off the day with a great dinner in the lodge. We had a roasted lamb swiss style and we spoke about Jesus being the Passover Lamb and the Lamb of God. It was a great final day with all these believers and now it was time for us start another exciting adventure

We spent the first month at Hamburg getting use to our new home so to speak. The Colonel and the CIA had our training all figured out. First, we got a good indoctrination of the way it was in the east and then we got more training in some of the things we needed more work on. Nancy had our place looking good as she kept me busy painting, hanging shelves and staining old furniture. Nancy got a job at the nearby hospital as a per diem nurse so she could have something to keep close to her cover as a visiting nurse from Montreal. I was an exchange student studying at the University of Hamburg as I was able to take some classes to give ourselves a normal existence. The Colonel connected us to a group like the Gideons but was connected to Radio Free Europe. The group was called The Crusaders and they were involved in moving the Word and its values. So now it was all about practice makes perfect and we were going over transfers as the most important part of the process. We used these aluminum attaché cases so we were all on the same page so to speak. These cases locked up and were indestructible so making the swap is about the location. The agency taught to go to an open public place so you are far away from cameras and bugging devices. The KGB were the biggest and best at this espionage and secret intelligence game as they went beyond any restraints that our CIA was governed by. The KGB did not need a warrant to bust down your door.

Ever since I was a kid playing soldier I loved to sneak around in the woods or build caves or secret forts to hide in or to bury treasure. When I got to stay out all night we would spy on the girls or take them to the haunted houses or local cemetery to scare them so they would hold us tightly in the darkness. We had an abandoned NIKE missile base out in the woods that we would sneak around at. Out past the old barracks was a big clearing that had these huge metal doors that opened up the four silos that held the missiles that were designed to protect NY City. We use to go down about

30 ft underground and it was so dark down there that if you weren't holding the flashlight it got pretty creepy, especially when the guy holding the flashlight starts messing with everyone. We got the idea to start taking out these huge spools of copper wire, but it was too much work getting it out. The next time we went down there the entrance was bulldozed over so that was it for trying to mine all that copper. Soon after we started going to the city to buy and sell drugs and soon, we were driving down to Florida to pick up pot or coke. Getting drafted put an end to all that for a little while until I got hooked up with Tony at Loadmaster school and got trained to smuggle (I mean to ship) things!

Since the wall and the DMZ was built in 1961 it is estimated that 100,000 escaped all across the wall. The KGB claimed that only a couple hundred escaped, they said that the border guards shot most trying to get through. There was a lot of accounts that whole groups of people escaped by boat or trains and even long tunnels dug right under. Now Nancy and I were fighting against the people that built a giant wall to divide a continent and all of its citizens. So, we felt like some kind of freedom fighters in this cold war and the stakes were high because if we got caught, we could go to jail for a long time or be shot as spies. During this period of time we never actually fought against the

USSR so that is why we called it the Cold War, because it never got hot enough to explode. The Bay of Pigs, the Cuban Missile Crisis and the construction of the wall all came to face-to-face hostilities and conflict, yet no war broke out. The eastern bloc had death strips of electric barbed wire, minefields and booby traps set up backed with machine guns and attack dogs. But it was called a war of words, and we called the wall "The Wall of Shame" and they called it "The Anti -Fascist Freedom Border." I would say that espionage on the highest level was our own failsafe system. It had high altitude supersonic jets flying around the world programed to strike and if the restraints "failed" only a call from the president could turn them around. The Chinese Communists overthrew Chiang Kai-Shek and Chairman Mao Zedong took over in 1949. The Cold War involved the NATO forces against the Communist forces as we battled over all the emerging countries in Africa, Asia, South America and here in Europe. The CIA & the KGB were all over these countries and no one could trust anybody as double agents were giving it up to the highest bidder.

Nancy and I were both officially short. We were within a few weeks of completing our 4-year commitment. We never thought we would be considering re-enlisting but we were both committed to this whole campaign.

We had a choice to reup for 2 or 4 years or take an assignment with NATO as civilians. We decided to continue for 2 years as Nancy will be up for Captain next year and I could still take courses for my degree. We talked about getting engaged by the end of this year and getting married when we completed this assignment. I told Nancy my good fortune with the Red Lobster stocks and how great it could be if we took a long honeymoon on a sailboat around the world together. We certainly had a lot of opportunities and as long as we kept our heads down and stayed out of a Soviet prison, maybe we can stay alive to enjoy it all. So much has gone down in these last four years and we both have seen a lot of crazy things. We thought that as Americans we were doing the right stuff for God and country. But how can we make sense out of dropping bombs on kids and families. Nancy felt that our trips to Biafra were truly a peacekeeping mission as we didn't kill anyone and did bring them aid. And for that she was given a service award. I still pray that I can get through 6 years of war time service without having to kill someone.

Colonel Thompson sent us another letter to tell us more about this clandestine mission we were going to be involved in. Because of the bases in North Africa shutting down, all operations were based in Germany and the Colonel was put in charge of much of the work going on in Europe and Africa. The Mideast was a hot bed and Europe was having major terrorist attacks so there was plenty to keep us busy. The Colonel told us that he was coming to Ramstein for meetings and will tell us about everything when he sees us. He finished by letting us know that Nancy and I were being called the "dynamic duo" as we have been doing some good work on 4 continents now. The Colonel said he was proud to be working with us and he wanted to meet up with us for more plans. I think it was more about Nancy being Wonder Woman than me being Batman. Having a new identity and passports did give us a secret agent type status and the feeling that we were doing something important. The Colonel was a 28-year combat veteran who had degrees in psychology and philosophy and he had 25 years of ministering to the troops and their families. When he came to take care of his business with Headquarters, we invited him over for dinner. He told us that he will always be indebted to us for pulling him out of that swamp and saving his life. We tried to be humble but it was the greatest thing I ever did. Nancy was a nurse and was all about saving lives and we were training to go out and save some more.

We ate in our gazebo on the river and then we opened a good local Liebfraumilch and sat around the fire. We shared the Word and then we heard about the Colonel's work in Africa. He was assigned to coordinate the various goodwill groups and give support to the clinics and schools. He had a staff of military and civilian volunteers and members of the Peace Corps and the American Red Cross to help stop the insanity. In Africa, Christianity and the bible were on the rise and had more followers than the Muslim religion and the teaching of the Koran. Both religions have their roots in the Abrahamic covenants as Abraham is considered to be the father of Judaism, Christianity and the Muslim faiths. The various voodoo practices had the third biggest followers in Africa and their beliefs and their customs were passed down from generation to generation by the shamans and the witch doctors. The main common beliefs similar to both Christianity and the Muslim religions was the belief in a monotheistic God as many of the other cults and practices believed in many types of gods and spirits. The shamans believed they were the guides and mediums between the dead and the living and these spirits can possess people and the animals. I was thankful for all the prayers and to be working with all these great believers and I thanked God for Nancy's strong faith and commitment. The Colonel then told us all about what we were really involved in. Ever since we met Colonel Thompson in

Vietnam, he was involved in a lot more than we knew. He was involved with the army brass, NATO, the CIA and many clandestine operations. We knew he wore many hats but we did not know just how deep he was dug in. We were working for the Pentagon and its top agents and spies and our "soon to be" General was taking over the field operations. We were now big time connected.

Back in Germany a few guys invited me to a breakfast fellowship they held at this old inn in Landstuhl. They met twice a month for a breakfast prayer group and they met all over the world. Gideon was an old testament man of God and a judge over Israel and the Gideons International was a bible fellowship that was founded in 1899. It started with 2 businessmen meeting in Wisconsin to read the bible and pray together and then it became the organization that raises money and distributed bibles to hotels, schools and hospitals. About 20 men and women met, mostly servicemen and some local German citizens. They were working on distributing the bibles in Africa and the Mideast so Nancy and I were recruited and excited to get involved. The Gideons used the King James bibles and had 10 translations in all the major languages. It was more rewarding than shipping guns and weapons and I get to work with Nancy. The agents with the CIA set us up with new passports again and this time we were a newly married couple from Montreal travelling on our honeymoon. We were registered as Mr. & Mrs. James Fox and we were on TDY and now we had the government paying for our meals and lodgings. Now we felt like we were playing house for real and our lovemaking was getting more and more intense. I loved her so much and I started worrying about her as she was always in the danger zone. She liked to write a scripture on a small blackboard until we memorized it. It was my turn to write a scripture and since I was starting to get anxious about Nancy's welfare, I wrote Second Timothy 1:7 "For God has not given us the spirit of fear, but of power, love and a sound mind." I had to just give it all to God and ask Him to take care of us.

From us pulling extra shifts on base and destinations in Africa we were getting run down and needed a break. It was time to take a few days off and take the trip on down to Italy. I had been working on a big surprise, I bought a 1951 MG to give to Nancy. I had it hid away at a garage on the base and some of the motorheads from the base motor pool were cleaning it up and going over the engine. It was in original condition and even the leather and paint were pristine, it was red with a tan interior. It had the long front fenders and running boards and the classic front grill and rear spare tire boot. The mechanics all thought it was very cool, and it ran and handled great. I wanted to give it to her when we left and let her think it was rented, until she got behind the wheel and drove it with the top down.

I pictured her driving through the winding roads of the Alps downshifting through the turns wearing her scarf and her leather gloves. It made me think of the twins driving the California cliffs at 100 mph without a care in the world. The difference was that Nancy liked to go fast but she didn't like to scare the shit out of you by doing 100 in a 50 zone. But out on the Autobahn she would drive like she was Nancy Andretti. She was going to look so good and was going to turn heads everywhere she went in her slick roadster. Nan was so giving and she did everything with all her heart, she just loved life. As we were planning our trip to Italy, I mentioned my favorite book was "The Agony and the Ecstasy, "about Michelangelo and the renaissance and the next day she was reading the book. That is how she rolls and that is how she made me feel so loved and important. We truly could share our thoughts and our dreams together and with God's love and spirit we will be "blessed". In Ecclesiastes it speaks of the threefold cord as a braid not quickly broken. The braid is the union of God and a man & woman that gains strength as it is braided. That is why a wedding band is braided to represent that 3-fold cord. The Colonel has been reminding us of the blessings that await us when we do tie the knot. He was trying to gently show us that when we make the commitment to get married God will bless our lives even more and we will be that threefold cord not quickly broken.

We started off slow by making some runs around Europe delivering a few packages to Amsterdam and to Stuttgart and then to Munich. We thought that this was the life as we were like tourists vacationing in Europe. The problem was that everyone was a suspect or an agent or a spy and no one could be trusted. Just a few months ago they busted a Navy captain that was a Russian spy. Our chain of command was still Col Thompson and our CO (Commanding Officer) at the NATO headquarters, but now we made our contacts out on the field in Hamburg. All the phones were bugged so all our communications had to be made on the fly. Whatever we were doing we usually didn't ask about it, only on special assignments did we need to know. We had to treat it all the same and it was all confidential and it could get us all killed if we didn't do our jobs right. We practice all our moves to get it down and we were both blessed with steady nerves and some of our training was to be able to write our names and addresses while we are being screamed at in Russian. Things did not change too much; we were still being called FUBAR but now in German or Polish. It was all about being cool & confident but now we wanted to blend in and not stick out. Even in sweats and running 10 miles Nancy still looked good enough to turn any red blooded Russki 's head around. When she got dressed up, she was stunning and could be a secret weapon, so sizzling hot in this cold war. When she dressed in her nursing uniform or her dress blues with her hair pulled back, she made my heart sing (she made everything groovy).

So much has changed in the last four years and my biggest achievement was starting to learn how to walk closer to God. We have been studying the bible and practicing how to live like the Lord. I have found answers to most of the things I've been searching for, God's Word is God's will and His holy spirit is given to us to manifest his power. I have this woman of God to further experience God's love and his blessings for us. As we put this Word on in our hearts and minds, we are transformed into the mind of Christ and we have that spiritual connection. It is God, in Christ in us, the hope of glory. We were still trying to put God first and we were serving our country and standing for what we believe in. To see this wall going around Berlin and dividing the continent was so oppressive, the citizens were locked up and they were not able to enjoy the freedoms or the abundances of the West. In 1972, West and East Germany opened up trade agreements which opened up the borders for more activities and movement. Since we had the proper paperwork, we just had to show a reason for our business and our visit. We had Nancy working with the medical clinics on family planning and nutrition. She had set this all up as a visiting nurse from the Hamburg Medical Center.

Our first few trips across the wall were at Checkpoint Charlie and it was routine, for Nancy's cover was excellent and no problems were found. We had approval from the border guards to visit a few of the hospitals in the city and we had to keep applying for Visas. Sometimes the paperwork was held back so we had to wait at the processing centers to get the papers right. The whole process was a can of worms as every place had different rules and requirements. Having a couple of cartons of Marlboros or some jean jackets on the back seat worked well. All of Germany loved Beethoven, Bach and the Beatles and West Germany hosted many great concerts with bands like the Beatles, the Stones and The Who playing big stadiums and live recordings. We saw Van Morrison in Munich and Santana at Frankfort and the Germans and the Japanese were big rock & roll and jazz fans. I am not a music critic, but I know what I like, and good music is purely subjective. So, let me just say that German rock is insane, the musicians are hypnotic, robotic and strangely melodic. It was commonly believed that wiretapping, bugging and encrypted messaging was being channeled in all different ways from Morse Code to using stencils to encrypt the Berlin Daily's front page. Even the Radio Free Europe guys were being threatened for the espionage in their broadcasting, they were the energy behind the thousands of balloons being flown every night. With the right winds they can send the pamphlets all the way to Moscow and all-over East Germany, Poland, Romania and Czechoslovakia and up north to Latvia and Lithuania. They even used carrier pigeons that could carry notes and microfilms. If Nancy was sitting out at a cafe I could sit and watch people taking pictures of everything and everyone. So many things were being put in film canisters. They were also a sign of the times for a person's private stash. I have gotten so straight and clear that "I can see for miles and miles", and the only thing in my film canister is film.

On the day of Pentecost, Peter prophesied old testament scriptures that summed up what had taken place that day. "And it shall come to pass in the last days, saith God, I will pour out my Spirit upon all flesh:

and your sons and daughters shall prophesy, and your young men shall see visions, and your old men shall dream dreams." That Holy Spirit connects us to God and His Son and gives us understanding beyond our 5 senses. Nancy and I pray together and for each other that God does take care of us. We believe what the bible says that God sends angels if you need help. Now that we are doing our jobs, we were taking on the work with the Radio Free Europe and the International Christian Fellowship (as it was now called).

At a meeting that Col. Thompson called together, he urged us that being involved in this war of words was as important as the ongoing SALT conferences to limit the arms race. The Colonel said that it was important that the Poles and the Czechs who still believe can get filled with God's Word again. Because the wall was built to block our hearts and minds from free thinking and the ability to fellowship together the people suffered. We were reminded that we were still crusaders fighting that spiritual battle against the wiles of the devil. For these people not to be able to worship God, it was a travesty. The censorship of ideas, the book burning and the demolition of church steeples and statues were all designed to attack the people's beliefs. They even changed the name of their beautiful city from St Petersburg to Leningrad and they took away a lot of art and public works, especially if it glorified God. Jesus taught the apostles the right way to walk with God and to live an abundant life. We are taught to share our possessions and goods and give them to those who had need and that God loves a cheerful giver. Communism believed that the state was everything and everything was given to the state to share communally. Christianity shares all things common, big difference. The bible urges us to share our plurality for as we give, we shall receive. When we learn to put God first and trust him with our hearts, He gives us that Holy Spirit to comfort and guide us.

The most important reason for all of this is that we believe that God raised up Jesus the Messiah from the dead. In doing so we will be meeting him in the air to help him to make this world right again. Then we will meet YHWH (Yahweh in translation) face to face without any sense of sin or condemnation. We needed to get this information past the iron curtain so they can make up their own minds as the government tries to control the way they think. If you tried to go outside the lines or rock the boat you could be fined, lose your job or be sent to a work camp for your beliefs. The people feared what the KGB could do and the paranoia of all the wiretapping, surveillance and dirty deals and payoffs were a part of the government way of life. Most of the citizens learned to keep quiet and blend in with the crowd so they did not tip off the informants. The reality was that big brother really was always watching.

We were on a trip to the city of Leipzig to a hospital in the heart of the city. I was picking up Nancy from the hospital. I was sitting out front in my car waiting for her to come out. Just as Nancy was walking out of the main entrance, I saw a man I knew! I immediately dropped down in my seat in hopes that he didn't see me. The last time I saw this guy was 2 years ago at Travis AFB. I would see him all the time in the airport cafeteria. I thought he was working for the airlines as he was always dressed in a suit. I even sat by him at the lunch counter so what the fuck was he was doing here, in East Germany? I didn't want to know! He walked right by me just as Nancy got in and he went to his Mercedes in the lot. I told Nancy to check this guy out as I knew him from Travis. She got out her camera and off we went to see if we could see where he was going. Nancy got his plates and told me she knew that the guy was a sales rep for medical equipment and she has seen him around the hospitals. I had no idea who he was and what was he doing but when we send our report in, we will find out. He drove fast out of the city heading north and we had to let him go, for there wasn't any way for him not to see us on the single lane back road. But Nancy said she sees him a couple of times a week. I don't know what's going on but I have a good idea he is working both sides. We heard about agents that were working multiple countries and also for large companies in industrial espionage. Behind the curtain and in Russia, big brother was definitely watching. They didn't need search warrants or court orders to break down your doors or tap your phones, and they liked to come in the middle of the night to make you disappear.

We found out that our man was actually a double agent working for the Russians and for the Israelis on big time arms deals. His cover was medical supplies that he could deliver as well as ensure weapons and ammunition to various mercenaries fighting around the world. We didn't have to be told to stay as far away from him as we could. We couldn't figure out how this guy was working for the Israelis and the Russians but stranger bed fellows have been formed in our world of 175 countries. President Nixon was trying to keep his promise to get us out of Vietnam by the end of the year. This is why the Cold War was still a war, we were not actually fighting the Communists up and down the wall but plenty of people were still dying. I can remember how I felt when I was sent on a detail in Cam Ron Bay to help pick up the wreckage of a downed

MIG. The plane was all written in Russian without any signs of Chinese or Vietnamese. We couldn't tell sometimes if we were fighting against the North Vietnamese, the Russians or the Chinese. My point is that when our astronauts looked down from space, they could actually see fighting going on all over the world as large explosions and fires could be seen from space.

If we weren't fighting the Russians right now here in Germany, we were in Asia, Africa and the Mid-East. The Palestine's were fighting the Israelis now as they were 3,000 years ago. When King David stood up to the giant, Goliath the Philistine, it was the Israelis against the Palestine's. Nothing new under the sun, Jesus said there will always be war and rumors of wars, (until He returns and ends all wars and takes away our tears). What we have to understand is that the devil controls the world now, when Jesus returns in the new millennium, He will take back our world and make it right again.

We spent a lot of time together driving around Europe through some incredible lands and places. The landscape would be so pristine as the farmlands looked like a Van Gogh painting. Then you go through an old village with cobblestoned streets and people sitting at little cafes like they did years ago. But then we would pass a space age building of some corporate headquarters that brought us back to the future. We would downshift and fly out of the village only to stop for the cows crossing the street and getting that overwhelming smell of manure. We shoot past rows of grapes and it is a beautiful day! Nancy looks so content with her tan face and her hair flowing in the wind. In a little while we will stop for lunch and have some bread and cheese with some vino. Nancy is raring to drive the backroads that were exhilarating and thrilling and she was fearless. We were probably more like Maxwell Smart & Agent 99 going against Boris & Natasha. It is times like these that we stop to think of what we have been doing for our country as we are just busy doing our jobs.

I have been smuggling for 3-4 years now, I am a professional Loadmaster, courier, soldier and a married spy!! We have transferred information and classified materials all over the world and I am with a fantastic lady who has my back big time. We live a thrilling life as we serve our country and we try to give God the glory. We have to walk with God and trust in His Word and "believe that He is, and is a rewarder of those who believe in Him". With Nancy being such a strong believer, we are energized by the Father and his Holy Spirit. Life is good! This whole relationship with the spirit gives us peace, joy, love, kindness, patience and goodness as we tenderize our hearts and make them pliable. With this ongoing war and rumors of war we certainly need Gods help. In the Bible they have so many accounts of God protecting His people like King David, Moses, Abraham and all the great men and women of God. In the New Testament we see that Jesus as our Messiah came to speak the Word and deliver us from our sins so we can have that spiritual connection with God. I was just thankful that I was connected and I was thankful that I had Nancy as without them I couldn't do all this alone. "If two of you should agree on earth as touching anything that they shall ask, it shall be done for them of my Father which is in heaven." Mathew 18:19

Just like the way Radio Free Europe was involved in broadcasting our slant on the Democratic way of life, a lot of Christian ministries were trying to spread the gospel across the Eastern Bloc. They smuggled bibles and thousands of tracks and other pamphlets and even bible classes on cassettes. Some of the countries like Czechoslovakia and Poland still had people who could worship their God freely, until the communists shut them down in 1968. Many Christian churches felt that this was a spiritual battle as communism was against the free worship of God and the major religions. It was only 40 years ago that this whole area was under Nazis control and they still dig up bombs that haven't been detonated. Fascism and communism opposed the right to freely assemble and doing so was another way to get hauled off to Siberia. The book of Ephesians tells us to put on the whole armor of God, that we may be able to stand against the wiles of the devil. For we wrestle not against flesh and blood, but against principalities, against powers, against the rulers of the darkness of this world, against spiritual wickedness in high places.

We smuggled in a lot of Christian materials to run bible classes and help people believe and give them hope for the future. I don't know about changing the political and social structures but I do know that the Word of God can change a person's heart and life. One by one the gospel can free people by knowing the truth and the truth can set you free. We are trying to turn people on so they could truly believe that God sent his Son to save us. Through this connection we get a complete package of being resurrected when Christ comes back to change this world. Paradise will be a beautiful place with no more wars or death and we will be with God. By believing that God raised Christ up from the dead we will be saved from this life, so this is so much greater than anything we can imagine. When the Messiah comes back to raise us from the dead we will be born again. When we first believed that God raised Christ from the dead, we received His holy spirit.

It is a fantastic duty to protect people and to help save lives but if they die and not make it to Paradise then it is all short lived.

Some of the materials we smuggled in helped set up bible classes which started bible fellowships. God's Word was starting to take off again. The fellowships were held at a different location every night so the authorities didn't catch up to the them and shut them down or arrest them. It was against the law to assemble for anything against the communist manifesto and you could end up in the Gulag like what Solzhenitsyn spoke and wrote about. In Berlin there was always government vehicles driving around broadcasting over loudspeakers about some political agenda, they were broadcasting in German then repeated in Russian and then in English. Since it was against the law to assemble all resistance was done in secret and there were a lot of informants working for the KGB. Some of our deliveries were equipment to be used for surveillance and counterintelligence.

We were making a connection in Berlin with an agent to deliver an attaché case and it went smooth. We knew the man and we met him at a park across from the train station. We planned on driving north to cross the border closer to Frankfurt to go visit Bonham and Jane when we were done. As we were driving north out of the city, all of a sudden two BMWs were right up our ass with their headlights flashing. They didn't look governmental but we didn't know who the hell they were. I downshifted to third and floored it so they would not catch-up to our sides. Nancy took out her camera but this time we were the ones being chased! Now it was time to drive like I was driving through Monaco or on the Autobahn with my lovely copilot equally adept at downshifting and flat spins. We shot out of Berlin and did a couple of back tracks and left them in the dust. But this was far from being over for we, believe it or not, are now on the run behind the Iron Curtain! We got out of the city and drove straight to a small lake that we had been to near some farm land and close to the border, about 30 miles north of Berlin. We put our stuff in a couple of backpacks and buried the rest of the stuff in the woods. I had modified the car when I first got it as I removed the car's insignias and model numbers so you didn't really know what make it was. We pushed it right in the lake and it quickly sunk like a rock and we covered the tracks with some pine branches. This was why we spent so much time going over these procedures so we knew what to do when things went bad. We knew our next couple of moves to get through the woods to the next checkpoint and went on our way to meet Bonham at the border.

Whoever was chasing us knew who we were and it was time to go underground. We had to walk together in the cover of the night through the forest for about ten miles so we could call in the morning to meet Charlie at the border town of Ruine, that was safe to proceed to into West Germany. We used a backup set of papers in case all the checkpoints had our numbers and we got across with no problems. Charley picked us and drove us up to the mountains to a cabin we knew of so we could chill for a few days. We didn't want to go back to our apartment until we found out what was going on and check in with headquarters. Nancy and I made some wild love up in that cabin as it was ignited by our thrilling escape from East Germany. In this spy vs spy espionage, there wasn't a trace of us, except on their surveillance cameras that only proved we were there as visitors. And now we were back in a free country, with Charley and Jane for a long weekend and then we had to go send in our report. We drove down to Stuttgart to see the Colonel and spend a few days back on the base. We did not know just what went down but we knew our cover was blown and it was time to relocate. The Colonel was glad to see us and asked us once again when we were getting married. With all that was going down we thought it strange that his first thoughts were when we were going to get married. What about the fact that we just got chased out of East Germany and had to ditch our car and escape through the woods? The Colonel said that he knew that we could run circles around any agents and we were the best trained team that he had. We told him our plans of leaving the service and moving back to the States and going to school and we were thinking about studying Theology. Then we could start planning our wedding and starting some kind of "normal" life together. But so far it has been far from normal and if we commit to walking with God it will be an incredible trip.

Chapter Six

THE BIG BLUE MEDITERRANEAN SEA

Moses said to Pharaoh,
"Let my people go." Exodus 5:1

We went over our new orders and it was time to mix it up a little. We just didn't put our roots down anywhere as a rolling stone gathers no moss so we wanted to keep things moving. Once again, we had our belongings shipped out and stored as we were headed to the coast of Italy to continue our work there. We spent a week at Headquarters going over the various objectives and activities that we will be involved with. We had some military, CIA and veterans and Nancy had medical staff to meet. This just could be the best assignment yet as the Mediterranean Sea will now be our avenue and we will be based in southern Italy. The

Mediterranean was basically wide open and the flow of refugees trying to flee the communist countries was practically causing a traffic jam at certain ports and waterways. The port of Brindisi was active for a couple of thousand years as a port serving Greece and the Mid-East. The two-thousand- year-old Appian Way ended at the Brindisi docks and was built so well it was still intact today. For smuggling, the Adriatic Sea had over 1300 islands and enchanted coves and rivers to hide in and they say that there is an abundance of treasures still unclaimed from the years of travel and smuggling. Out in the Mediterranean there were thousands of islands and thousands of years of history. We were headed for places like Cypress, Turkey and Israel as we could skirt around the southern Soviet bloc. We had an old Air Force base in Brindisi and we had NATO and the United Nations headquarters that Nancy was hooking up with.

"Doctors without Borders" was all over the world and Nancy loved the work. She could travel with me and run with the medical team so she was excited to be able to get around. Using Nancy's nursing experience and nursing license gave us great cover to go into Soviet Occupation.

Living here on the cliffs overlooking the Adriatic was a dream come true for I have been fascinated with all the islands and ancient waterways as long as I can remember. Even as a kid I liked maps and globes and liked to study geography and history. The Mediterranean Sea has thousands of islands and we had over 1300 here in the Adriatic alone. It is not unusual to find an ancient Roman coin or a piece of pottery from Africa. We have various cultures piled on top of each other. The Florida Keys and the Caribbean were a smuggler's paradise and the islands all along the trade routes were famous for buried treasures and ship wrecks. The Mediterranean Sea has such a vast shoreline with so many thousands of islands, rivers, bays and coves that led to more seas and lakes that you couldn't cover in a lifetime. The islands came in all sorts of sizes and shapes, some were huge and jutted up in solid rock. Some were so small that they had one tree or bush and were the size of a small boat. With shipwrecks from all different periods of time so that the artifacts are mixed together in a potpourri of cultures. There are hundreds of shipping logs and documents showing shipwrecks from centuries ago and more treasure maps and exciting tales. On some reefs there were old sailing vessels rolled on top of World War I and WW II War ships. Some of the cargo could be medical supplies and vials of morphine still sealed after all these years. The Appian Way was built by the Romans over 2300 years ago and ran from Rome to the port of Brindisi that was guarded by the Roman army against thieves and robbers for a thousand years. The Romans built so many big aqueducts hundreds of miles long. The Appian Way still runs all the way to the docks right near our cottage overlooking the cliffs.

Being here on the Mediterranean we are in the heart of the cradle of civilization dating back thousands of years and these islands are just full of incredible history and fascinating stories. There are great accounts of hideouts and secret caves and passages and many a tale of treasures not recovered. There are hundreds of caves carved out by the tides and some of the caves have grottos and underground passageways. The cliffs along the coasts had so many exotic towns and villages with steps and pathways leading down to docks with gaily panted buildings and boats. Some cliffs had gondolas or lifts and some had donkey trails thousands of years old. About the most incredible place we got to visit was the island of Capri off of the Italian coast. Capri has it all, beautiful views of the sea and quaint towns and villages and flowers growing everywhere. Capri just smelt good with all the gardens filled with flowers and the smell of sauce cooking all through cobblestone streets. The island had steep cliffs and underwater grottos and the Mediterranean could not be bluer. We could look down and see the water taxis and boats ferrying people back and forth to Naples. Naples was a whole other story, the best food in the entire world.

We decided to take an R & R to nowhere to have the time to catch our breaths and focus on our roller coaster ride we have been on together. The Navy had the slogan "Join the Navy and See the World "and the Airforce had the "Up and Away into the Wild blue Yonder "but we had no idea that we would see and experience all we have been through these last few years. The biggest discovery was that we found God and his spirit and we have opened up a whole new existence and knowing these truths has set us free. The military life grounds us to its rank and file, chain of command and order of daily life and gives us a common bond to work together. But the incredible things we were involved with has evolved to us being able travel all over the world in service to our country. Somehow Nancy and I have been called together by God and our country and hooking up with the Colonel has given us a supernatural team to be able to go against the evils of mankind's maturations. I can't say if fate brought us together but we know that God called and we answered. And now our connection with the Colonel and NATO has given us an incredible assignment and responsibility. We took some time to energize and make new goals to achieve the objectives we wanted to accomplish. As we looked over the southern Adriatic and the mouth of the Mediterranean Sea, we prayed for Gods protection and guidance and we started making plans to go back out to do some good.

On our time off we were able to talk over all that has gone down and the whirlwind of events we have been involved in. Things were happening so fast that Nancy and I were not able to keep up with all our reports and the CIA had most of it classified. We were not supposed to be in most of our destinations as it was. The great thing about our involvement was that we were not in this alone. We were backed by and connected to some good organizations, the UNITED STATES OF AMERICA, the USAF, the CIA, The North Atlantic Treaty Organization and the Garruto Olive Oil Company!! We had boats, planes, cars & trucks and we had connections and reconnaissance all over the Mediterranean. We had a big connection with an import- export company that dealt with Greek & Italian olives & olive oil and figs from Lebanon. Our connection dated back to the 40s when the CIA took over the whole operation. It kept tabs on and infiltrated the Sicilian mob and their associates in New York. Now my work would be in shipping all over the Mediterranean and it would be a lot like my work as a Loadmaster but with ships, small planes and my new pride and joy, a 26ft Donzi powerboat with twin 300 hp Volvo inboard/ outboard tuned up engines with top speeds at over 60 mph. We also got our new car, we got an Alpha Romero roadster that was just confiscated. They had it painted black to match the black leather interior and with only a few thousand miles on her, it looked brand new. We hopefully will not have to ditch her in tough times- I envisioned us running the coast with a whole family down in our bow driving them to freedom as the Soviet boats were policing the waters off the Croatian coast. The Israelis Coast and the entire Turkish coastline has been the center of civilization for thousands of years and war has been a part of life since Cain killed Abel.

The Soviet Union is trying to dominate the whole region. They push for a communist world take over. The NATO alliance and many United Nations countries were going to stand up to the Communists until we knock down the wall. Nancy and I were going to do our best to just do our jobs but we were hoping to actually help in getting people out to their freedom like a modern-day Underground Railroad worker. We will be involved in making deliveries all along the Soviet southern borders that stretched around Europe, the Mid East and Southern Asia. So, we were wide open for plenty of action and movement. No matter how we got down to it, it was still the United States of America against the Union of Soviet Socialists Republic and together they control thousands of nuclear warheads and they had enough firepower to waste the entire world. Because of the so-called balance of- power the two superpowers walked softly and carried big sticks. It is incredible that we somehow split an atom causing a chain reaction that can level a million people in the blink of an eye. The thought of seeing the huge mushroom cloud and the complete annihilation of everything for miles is staggering. The fallout from the radiation continues to kill life for years and the birth defects weren't pretty. But we made that commitment to help protect Israel as the holy wars were going on and on and the Christians, the Muslims and the Jews have been at it since the days of Abraham that trace back 4 thousand years. I look at things according to the Bible as now it seems to be like one side has God believers and the other side the unbelievers. But the spiritual battle is way bigger than that as eternal damnation vs eternal salvation in paradise, is the big deal. When Satan is thrown into the fiery pit and the last enemy (death) is destroyed. Then we will be with God and Christ in Paradise.

Some of our key destinations were Athens, Split, Croatia, and Yugoslavia, Istanbul (formerly

Constantinople) and Crete all bordered around the USSR. The other hard fact was the increasing spread of terrorism all around the entire world as suicide bombings and hijacking of planes, trains and buses were becoming common disasters. Smaller speed boats were running down big vessels to board and hold hostage. We had Strategic Attack Bases all around the region and Israel didn't play as they had their jet fighters out 24/7 and would attack their enemies like a pack of angry hornets. If the Israelis thought that their enemies were building any fortifications, they would send their fighter jets out on a midnight sortie and take the target out just like that, they had attitude, they had to play it tough as there was no other choice. Like every target, they were camouflaged as schools and hospitals and visa-versa to further add to the confusion, hate and destruction. The news would show a devastating scene of a mother holding her dead child in front of the rubble from a stray missile. The Mideast countries seemed to be stacked on top of each other and border wars went on and on. Places like the Gaza Strip or the Suez Canal were in constant turmoil and Jerusalem is considered the future capital of the world, when Christ returns.

Hopefully we will be targeted to our work in the Soviet Bloc, as this Cold War has to be stopped or the Soviet Union will continue to try to take over the world. All up and down the Iron Curtain the tensions were great and out in the water around the coast the big shipping routes were guarded with all the many country's navy and coast guards. There were pirates and the large shipping companies from Greece had their own coast guard and security. Hopefully, our little speed boat could get around and under the radar and we could hop around and hide in the many islands of the Mediterranean. We could hop flights via our Air Force and Navy and there were ferries going everywhere. The many ports were around for centuries as shipping was the transportation that was the only way to get around, unless you were traveling on a caravan of camels or wagons! We've only had the iron horse for 150 years and now we have trains, planes and automobiles, and rocket ships! It used to be that the empire that had the biggest army won the wars and then it was the biggest navies and now it is the United States because we ruled the skies and now the space above. That was JFK's goal to place our Stars & Stripes on the moon and claim the heavens for the United States of America.

We were able to rent an old cottage on a cliff overlooking the Adriatic Sea. Right behind us was the 2,000-year-old Appian Way running all the way down to the Brindisi Docks. Our cottage had a front porch with a love seat swing with a fabulous view of the sea and some of the many islands. We would sit out in the morning watching the sun come up over the water and at night we had a fire pit to look out at the stars. The place was quaint and old and we had a stone fireplace and big windows in the living room and bedroom. Our cottage was built in the mid-1800s with a slate roof and all stone with big exposed interior oak beams. The kitchen had a Dutch oven that Nancy wanted to bake bread with the semolina wheat grown in the region. We stayed in some fabulous places but Italy had it all. The beautiful blue Mediterranean was some backdrop to the amazing cultures of the old ruins from the Roman Empire to the Renaissance age, and to the modern-day beauty and style.

The Italian cities were a plethora of fountains and gardens with sculptures and town squares and fantastic churches and cathedrals. The big cathedrals were absolutely incredible. Some of the cathedral ceilings were over 50 feet high with magnificent columns of solid marble. These ceilings were amazing works of art with pictures of creation and depictions of bible stories. Some had beautiful frescos of God looking down at us and the stained-glass work radiated through the cathedrals. Some of these churches dated back over a thousand years and towered over the towns and cities. Two of the biggest and most famous were both called

St Peters, one at the Vatican and one at Leningrad, formerly St. Petersburg. The people still sat at little cafes sipping their demitasse and Sambuca debating the ongoing feud between the Catholic Church and the Fascists politicians. And the food was the best in the whole world. Nancy and I decided to try to take it all in when we could because next year we will be gone and unfortunately the wars will still be going on and on. It looks good that we will be able to seek God and do some sort of service. We had a great place to start our day on the cliffs in front of our cottage. We could pray and do some exercises and we started doing isometrics and meditation. Nancy had me eating better and I was feeling sharper so that we felt like we were super- conquerors.

First, we have some intense espionage to deal with, all done to serve our country and stand against those damn commies and fight in this crazy Cold War we are involved in. Nancy was happy to be able to continue with the groups like the American Red Cross and the "Doctors without Borders", and we will continue to move information and to help people to freedom. I will start working for the olive oil exporters that was actually operated by a group of guys that are ex-military and CIA operatives that use to be involved keeping tabs on the Casa Nostra from Sicily and New York. They have had been running cover from the late 40s and still use it to operate in the Mediterranean as olive oil is a huge business. The company is named the "Garrutto Olio d'Oliva" and we are importing in the entire region. We ship liters all way up to 55-gallon drums and figs from Lebanon and Israel. We have trucks, boats and planes to deliver and pick up all over the world so it should be something I am familiar with. As far as smuggling goes, I will get to go back to its roots as small boats island hopping and outrunning the authorities has been the way it is for centuries. We still have Island hideouts and midnight runs and secret codes and suspicious characters. Now I have the backup of Naval intelligence and surveillance to help me get through the maze of Soviet boats and planes out in the seas. From the small skiffs to the giant freighters we had every country keeping tabs on each other. Like we say, it was a jungle out there -

Once again, we got new identities and had to spend a few weeks going over things and learn the lay of the land. In studying the maps, it showed that the whole area was in constant change as countries and borders were different on every map. Were we looking at Yugoslavia, or Croatia or Romania or Serbia and was it now part of the Soviet Union or was it Christian, Muslim or communist? We were going out into international waters but we will hug the coast and the Balkan Peninsula to stay out of the shipping lanes and all the various surveillance equipment. Greece and Turkey were not under Soviet rule and was all part of our future travels. I was very excited to get out on the water but we will also be traveling by conventional forms of travel as we had trucks and even public transportation like trains and ferries. Besides doing my job I prayed for the opportunity to literally help people out to freedom, and tell them about how God loves them. That is the greatest thing I could do. Jesus did a lot of great things out on the water and so can we. I have the ability to speak in tongues while cruising through the water at 70 MPH and praising the Father all the way. In fact, these were the same routes that the Apostle Paul traveled on his way to Rome. Some people ask me how I can preach about God and the Bible and be fighting in these wars and then I get to tell them about King David who was a man after Gods own heart and a man of war. Just read the account of David and Goliath and the Philistines as David always prayed for Gods protection. As we did every day in Nam, Nancy and I pray every morning before we start our day. We also speak in tongues as it is a way for our spirit to commune with Gods spirit.

After we got all set up and got around a little, we took a little time off and drove our new toy up north to Roma and Florence. We got to visit the Vatican and saw the Sistine Chapel and got to view Michelangelo's great depiction of the finger of God touching man. At Florence we got to spend more time looking at the great Renaissance masters and their great bible interpretations. We got to see the great works commissioned by the Medici family and their influence on the church and the Renaissance. I had seen the Pieta at the '63 World's Fair in New York, but seeing the statue of David, the Pieta and stuff like the statue of Moses or Madonna & Child all together was just incredible. And we still got to see DaVinci, Raphael and Donatello as well as the Ferrari plant in Milan. We saw that the Ferrari was designed from the Alpha Romero and that is why our convertible was flying up the Italian coast like a big cat gripping the road. I might be a little prejudice but the Italian culture is so rich in history, fashion and in the culinary arts, and the architecture was absolutely incredible. We did go up to Venice again to meet some people involved in our assignment as Venice has always been a major port throughout history and now it is very close to Soviet Occupation. Just a couple of miles across the bay started the Soviet Bloc country of Yugoslavia and the Adriatic Sea. We took 2 more days enjoying the eastern coast as we headed back down to Brindisi to start our escapades in this Cold War crap! It is so sad that after all the beauty in the world we still have to live with all the hate and violence.

This entire area that we are now working in is really the cradle of civilization. The Mediterranean Sea had some of the biggest empires in history as the Persians, the Egyptians, the Greeks, and the Romans all had control of this part of the world. These old dynasties had navies that would send out a thousand boats at a time to attack, and armies that would have 100 thousand -foot soldiers. The landscapes had the scars of wars going back literally thousands of years so we would see beautiful bridges, fountains, churches and old mansions with missing pieces from so many wars. The invention of dynamite greatly increased the ability to destroy the landscapes and all the lives an explosion can cause. In just under 50 years mankind went from blowing up things with dynamite to splitting a hydrogen atom and wiping out whole cities from the face of the earth like we did to Hiroshima & Nagasaki. Now we have these two empires facing off with this wall dividing them. With thousands of these nuclear bombs available the ability to destroy the world has greatly increased. And in the old days it would take the Army & Navy weeks to get there as they had to row and walk. Now from the air and soon from space it could be all over with the flip of a switch-

A lot of the people were into this tropical pace and it wasn't all bad as we got to meet wonderful people out on the islands and at the local ports. People with a lot of color and a lot of history. We got to meet a lot of people making their living off the water and there is a very romantic feel out on the moonlit waters. The whole palm trees and tropical breezes with colorful birds and flowers were intoxicating to our senses. Small streams became rivers to the sea and wide-open waters then opened up the whole world. Everything was connected and the ports and shipping lanes, like the trade winds, connected the people. Importing & exporting was the main event and places like the Spice Islands and the East Indies were all about the goods being traded. My buddy Buzz's shipping business sent our American goods from Miami to the Caribbean and picked up fruit and bananas to bring back to Miami. The coke & marijuana piggy backed off of the big containers traveling by boat, plane and train. This is part of the life out at sea, something to give the sailors to spin yarns about. Smuggling, pirates, hidden treasures, shipwrecks, island hopping, rum running and drugs and then the horrors of human bondage was spoken about in all the seaside bars and docks. Something about a salty old man with a parrot on his shoulder or a guy and a guitar singing songs of the ocean romanticized the whole experience. Somehow Nancy and I were deeply involved in the whole damned thing. We just had to believe that we were doing the right thing and that the end justifies the means. I have been involved with this smuggling thing since the drug days and my training in the Air Force. Now we are chasing some very bad smugglers that smuggle and kill people. We try to keep busy and stay on the move so we don't think about all the bad. That is why it is such a rush to go speeding through the night with the wind in our face out on the waters or out in a speeding convertible. And having someone to share it all with is simply amazing.

My generation had a strong bond with the automobile industry, back in the 1950s, the Eisenhower administration connected all the super highways and the big cars could fly down the roads. As teenagers in the 60s we developed a very special relationship with cars and women. We started "going out" on dates and then going parking out at the local lover's lane. Double dating at the drive-ins fogged up the windows so nobody could see the picture and nobody cared. It seemed like the great American Dream was driving around with a car load of girls on a Saturday night. Two couples driving in a '63 Impala with the ragtop down on a country road was like a magic carpet ride. The couple in the front seat were sitting so close so they could play with the stick shift together. The couple in the back were flying together in the night. By laying down in the backseat out of the wind, they were in their own sensual cocoon. With the moon following us over our shoulders, I could see flashes of her face and body. All of a sudden, we are pulling into a gas station and the lights pierce our eyes. We have to sit up, what a rush. After getting some gas and snacks, my buddy throws me the keys so we can drive them around for a while. Soon we were back driving through the night feeling free as a bird. At 17, girls and cars meant everything, there will be plenty of time to be fenced in later.

The American Corvette was the epitome of sexy cars. The side of the Vette looked like a voluptuous woman and you could lay inside of her and hug the curves together. She was smooth and sleek and very responsive and she could give you the ride of your life. She was so powerful that she would drive your head back in the seat and you better be holding on to the steering wheel. Events like Monte Carlo and the Gran Prix circuit were a combination of super cars, speed & power, and beautiful people. In the winner's circle were Ferraris, Ford GTs, Chevrolet Chaparrals, Porsche and Mercedes racers and the big events all over the world made car racing the number one spectator sport. Nancy will look amazing driving around in her sports car touring Europe. Zipping along the Mediterranean coast with her will be quite a rush. We can also be out in a speedboat with the salty spray in our faces. Whether it was in a speeding convertible or out in a fast runabout, the wind brought tears to our eyes and helped sharpen our senses like a splash of cold water on our faces. It could be real tears as our emotions came to a head as well.

Nancy and I got to share these amazing truths from Gods Word and there are so many great things with the revelations through the spirit of God in Christ in us. We get knowledge and discernment and the working of the Holy Spirit, even miracles and gifts of healing. The whole package operates with speaking in tongues, interpretation of tongues and prophecies. We also get the fruit of the spirit like love, peace, patience, joy and faithfulness. We are encouraged by the scriptures to walk by the spirit and let our light shine. We pray that we can get through this darkness and help more people get to the promised land. The job at hand is to help some of these victims get to freedom so they could pursue life and a possible relationship with God. We have been involved with moving a lot of things and moving Gods Word is the most noble endeavor. We can really help to save someone. Everywhere we went there were all different religions and ministries involved with trying to convert the "savages and the heathens", as they were called for centuries. Actually, the Bible says that before we believed we were without hope and separated from God and His Kingdom. In every airport or town gathering place were groups trying to evangelize or proselytize their slant on God or Nirvana. Even in Italy the age-old discussions were between the Church and the political Socialists. The biggest issue was the Communist view that religion is the opiate of the masses and that there was no God. Our country had "In God we Trust" as a national motto as we are "One Nation Under God". Most of our founding fathers were big time believers and our constitution shows it. Nowadays there are a lot of Americans trying to tear down those beliefs and it makes a lot of GIs wondering what we are fighting for? Having God in our hearts comforted us through these very tough times.

I was still working on the maps and the destinations and studying the cities on our routes. A lot can be done with our travels on our olive oil business and my regret is being apart from Nancy when she is gone doing her medical stuff. We will have plenty of great times together cruising the Mediterranean under the full moon with the water looking turquoise with the silver spray on the waves. Some nights when it was calm, flying through the night sky, the Milky Way reflected in the water. At times there were luminous jelly fish that lit up our wake making a long neon stream behind us. When we found an awesome cove or an incredible view we would stop and take it all in. Sometimes we could open a bottle of Chianti and make love under the stars out off of the Iberian coast. I don't know how it could be more romantic then this and sometimes Nancy would whimper with tears of joy as I held her trembling in my arms. We were young and in love and getting to travel around the world on the governments dime. I had one of the greatest jobs in the service and Nancy was practically Wonder Woman and she had that healing touch and love for her patients, especially the kids. She sure could heal my heart with a touch or a soft word and her energy was pure and clear. The Word tells us that God is not the author of confusion, but of power, love and a sound mind. The Devils mission is to steal, kill and destroy. Right now, it is Satan's world. When Christ returns, he will take back the world and turn it back to Paradise. By believing in Christ we are connected to God through His Holy Spirit. That is our ticket to Paradise.

This part of the Mediterranean was so incredibly beautiful with its thousands of islands and inlets and the cliffs were magical as they towered over the blue waters. Then they had these villages and towns carved into the cliffs with awesome ports and colorful buildings. The landscapes were abundantly blessed with its 3 main crops, olives, grapes and semolina wheat. This area had been harvesting these crops since before Christ and it was cool to see 2,000- year old shipping manifests from the Roman & Greek times. The trade routes we will take were around since the Phoenicians with their sails and rows of rowers in those boats that looked like majestic sea creatures. We were going on fantastic voyages along the Iberian coast from Venice all the way around to Athens delivering olive oil and whatever NATO wanted us to deliver. The guys I was hooked up with were all a bunch of characters, mostly ex- servicemen and CIA and a lot of tough guys working the docks and they all had that sense of adventure. The open waters and the massive coastline were quite a backdrop to the imposing dark kingdom of the Soviet Union and their satellite countries. Through Greece and Turkey and the open waters around the Black Sea we had access with our legitimate import -export company. These patriots I was hooked up with all had their duties as well as we all worked together for our government. We were more like a combination of smugglers, couriers and high seas buccaneers as our cargo was always in question. With all the human trafficking going on we had refugees that we took to their freedom as we also tried to stop the sex trafficking going on in any direction. We had access to the entire region and our boats and trucks blended in with all the traffic that was coming and going on their daily routines.

It was so exciting to be out with Nancy driving or boating Eastern Europe making our deliveries and rounds. We had a great job as our destinations were so awesome. Places like Venice and Split in Yugoslavia or Athens and Istanbul were a maze of espionage and subversive activities. Out on the water the activities were a part of the countries that shared the region for centuries. Smuggling was the way some old cargo ships were operating around all these ports as a way of life. But Nancy's involvement with the humanitarian efforts was even more important then what I was doing as it was hands on saving lives. The medical team was doing relief efforts for various orphanages and street clinics along the Communists Bloc. The whole area was politically controlled and some children and certain ethnic groups were practically imprisoned. A big group of people that Nancy was working with were Armenians that were caught up in a continuous mass exodus for over 50 years. The Turks have been trying to drive them out of Turkey and Greece since WW 1 and thousands have been killed. Somehow during the Cold War these Armenian people have been detained by the communists and thought of like gypsies, Christians or political dissidents. Nancy's team is working on getting some of them out and they want us to use our resources to sneak them out. We started to make plans to be able to ship them with our cargo ship, like the Underground Railroad and the years of people smuggled in the hulls of freighters going around the world. We certainly had enough ships to take them on and if we took one person or twenty, we were trained and equipped to get them to the UN in Italy so they can help them settle somewhere. We now had thousands of miles of coast and that many islands as well as rivers, and inlets to get lost in. The Black Sea north of Turkey was another hot bed of Soviet activity, we had international waters but the ports were all in communist countries. The entire Mediterranean Sea was lined with countries with hundreds of ports and shipping routes so there was so much being shipped and smuggled.

I know that war tests the good and the bad in people but human trafficking is one sick practice that has been going on for centuries. Children are preyed upon and young girls are scooped up and enslaved in the sex trade and certain nationalities are specially targeted. Because of what the Armenian people were going through we were seeing the orphanages getting ravished by these sleaze-bags as they steal these girls for the sex trade industry. They are shipped all over the world like a commodity. In some countries in SE Asia they recruit woman for modeling and the high life never to be heard from again. Young kids that weren't even 10 years old were the desired age for a lot of these freaks. So, my Nancy as a woman, as a nurse, as a humanitarian and as a NATO spy was involved in this sick problem to do all she could to fight for these people. We can't change the world but we can take a stand against the evil (as in the devil) in this life. We were going to start working together to move these unfortunate people out and to a free country and away from this sickness and madness. Because of the genocide taking place against certain people there is a lot of children left homeless and therefore preyed upon. There was a lot of people and groups behind us and praying for us and for all we have done so far. We will need a lot of prayers and Gods help. Why can't God just open up all the orphanages and the dungeons and set all these poor souls free?

Greece and Turkey were the two countries that stuck out from the entire communist bloc. The Mediterranean, Adriatic, Aegean and the Black seas all separated the countries with thousands of miles of coastlines and islands. The Greek coastline was enchanted with its old world -charm and fantastic views. Athens and then Istanbul are world capitals and hubs of shipping and trade. The Greeks ARE the shipping industry and Istanbul is a center of trade and commerce for thousands of years. The history here is incredibly old as Istanbul use to be Constantinople and was always the gateway to China and India. Greece was the center of the world 3,000 years ago and both countries are now a mixture of international mayhem and secret deals and trade agreements as it seems like no one can be trusted. Alliances and agreements are made and violated daily so the ports were tangled with every type of ship and boat as trading connects the entire world. But the KGB and the CIA were still the lurching sea creatures in the coastal fog as the entire Mediterranean area was under suspicion and surveillance. With all the different countries all sharing the Mediterranean coast and trading from port to port, the shipping lanes were a big mess as there were so many different types of vessels in all different sizes. There was ships and tugs, barges and sailboats and the various navies and coast guards had guns and weapons that could blow you out of the water. But with the spirit of the Trojan Horse we were going to play our style of espionage and sabotage. To catch these pirates, we were going to act like pirates, just smarter and with the backing of the United States Armed Forces and the CIA.

Our cover in the olive oil business was brilliant as we had access to the entire area and we had the ability to go by land, air and sea. Olive Oil is still called "Liquid Gold" and it was traded on the Italian stock market. We could even ship our car or our boat aboard our cargo ships if we needed to get around the inner boarders. We were getting ready to make some big moves to coordinate the efforts of Nancy's medical team to get some of these refugees to freedom. We were not the only groups involved in all this movement but since we were working for the United States, the CIA and NATO, we had a humongous backing and support system. This period of time was a most exciting adventure and we had so much going on delivering our information, running cargo and olive oil and smuggling our precious cargo out of the Soviet Union and other slave trading regions. Nancy and I were being called the "Dynamic Duo" in Greek, Russian, Italian and Arabic as well as a lot of bad names in languages we never heard of. It was more about Nancy's looks and the fact that we were still so young driving around in our convertible or our speed boat. When we were in some foreign port having dinner together it felt a little like Bogart & Bergman in Casablanca and our romance was a whirlwind of energy and love. I don't know how all this happened but we prayed to God that he was taking care of us and protecting us from all the evil around us. And again, our prayers were being backed by our people all over the free world. Ever since we started getting into God together, back in the makeshift chapels in Vietnam, we prayed that great prayer of Psalm 23; "Yea that I walk through the valley of the shadow of death I will fear no evil, for Thou art with me, Thy rod and Thy staff they do comfort me ".

I know I am a soldier but I would rather save people then kill them, after all we are supposed to be PEACEKEEPERS. We kill for peace to protect our country and stand against evil and tyranny. The big problem is that our enemies think the same things about their countries and world views. Through the eyes in the skies we must all look the same and I am sure it hurts God's heart that man continues to kill his fellow man and that there has always been wars and rumors of wars. We believe that the United States and its allies stand for the right stuff and the right principles and stand against the policies of our enemies. I am glad that we can be free to worship God and our Lord Jesus Christ. Nietzsche penned that religion was the opioid of the masses and the communists went after the churches and the temples and changing the names of all Christian cities, towns and landmarks. They persecuted the Jews and resisted Christianity and Islam as the Communist STATE was everything. There was no God, and their commitment was to the Motherland. Try to imagine that, no heaven or hell, no religion, no country-

After a cosmic purge that will eventually restore the earth to paradise as the highs will be made low and the desert places will become more tropical. I think the pineapples are going to be awesome and the avocados are going to be huge with a smaller sized pit. And the melons and the strawberries will flow and taste like milk and honey. Paradise will be beyond our earthly imagination; everything will be wonderful. The biggest deal will be that after we help Christ restore this sad world back to Paradise, we will be face to face with God and there will be no more tears or death. The Tree of Life that has been hidden away for thousands of years will be put back for the healing of the nations and there will be no more darkness. We get to live with praises to God on our lips. This is the Kingdom of God spoken by the prophets and by Christ, that we get a little token of now through Gods Holy Spirit, as we believe. The truth is that Paradise is a place on earth and everything goes around and round and even the whole Bible goes right around as it starts and ends in Paradise. The book of Revelations ends with the earth restored to the way it was in the beginning in Genesis.

We will once again be able to walk with God in the garden.

So many religions think that when we die, we go floating around out in the universe or up to heaven somewhere. But the Bible shows us through Jesus Christ's return, his disciples will help to restore the earth and defeat Satan and death. At the end of the thousand years reign, Christ will present the new earth back to YHWY. Joni Mitchell's song about getting back to the Garden was actually true. With all we are trying to do in protecting our country and now trying to rescue people from torture and death we will still all die. It is always about free will; it is your faith that unlocks the gate to paradise. By following Jesus Christ, we are led to the holy land, the new heaven and earth. The Holy Spirit and the love we get to receive now is a token of what we will experience when we get to see God face to face in Paradise-The greatest love and blessings we experience now is just a small snapshot of what lies ahead when we get back to the garden of Eden and Paradise with God and His son Jesus Christ.

Ever since Nancy was working with the medical team I was in better shape, thinner and stronger than I was in boot camp. I was getting so clear and sharp as I didn't even smoke any consei anymore and I had a real desire to walk with God. With all Nancy and I have been through it was by God's grace that we could manifest his love and share it with others. Our hearts and our bodies were healing but it was a challenge to clean or renew our minds for we have a lot of bad thoughts from all we have experienced and have seen. The medical team was working together with nutrition and natural treatments and now they are taking classes in nutrition. She had me trying to eat healthy and we were training in exercises and aerobics and we were swimming and running. I had to draw the line as no way was, I doing yoga as the guys in the gym would call me a Mary and next, she would have me wearing tights. It felt like Nancy was a positive force in this negative world. Seeing young children being so abused or seeing human skulls or jewelry made out of the VC's eyes was not something you see every day yet we saw shit like that all the time. In time the crap we have in our heads will either be suppressed into the subconscious or we somehow dealt with it. We cannot change the past but we can change how we look at it.

Being a part of this war can give us certain clarity on life and death issues, as we fight to stay alive, we also have to kill or be killed. I don't know the answers of how it all works but one of our sayings is that death is inevitable and we are all going to die, eventually. I don't know if our lives are measured by the length of days or the quality of the days we do live. When we see a young child die, we know that it was way too early, we can accept it if the person was eighty- something. I guess in our country we must feel that 18 is an okay age to die because we are old enough to get drafted and to go fight. Even then some guys go through years of combat without getting a scratch and others die the first night out. I don't know how it all works, only God does. In the Bible we see stories of men of God that believed in His protection and His power. Men like King David were involved in war and death all their lives. King Saul, who David honored and loved, got jealous of David's greatness and tried to kill David for years. Later, when David became the King, he had Bathsheba's husband Uriah sent to the front lines to die in battle. One of the reasons that made King David special was his heart for God and his humility to ask God for forgiveness. When King David was confronted about these sins from the prophet Nathan, he truly repented and he begged God not to take away his Holy Spirit. The Bible said that David was a man after God's own heart so although David made a lot of mistakes God still forgave him. There was only one perfect man, our Lord Jesus the Messiah. This is why the bible calls Jesus the Lamb of God (perfect- without spot) to be the perfect sacrifice on the cross. Not until

Christ returns to resurrect us, to eternal life, we are all going to die.

Faith is still the key that unlocks a lot of these mysteries as you shall know the truth and the truth shall make you free. There is a lot of different kinds of prayer but the reality is that we are having conversations with God. Through our holy spirit we have that connection to God via Jesus Christ, that is what believing is all about. To hear from God, we just have to keep talking to him and He will answer, we just have to learn to listen. Courage and bravery are high forms of believing as fear and doubts are on the low side. I know that fear is a part of our makeup as we have that inherent fright and flight reactions to protect us, but we can train ourselves to overcome certain reactions. That is why we train to be sharper so we can be ready for adverse conditions. Even our muscles and movements can be trained and we can get stronger and faster. The Bible teaches us that we can put on a renewed mind to have the mind of Christ. This means that we can share in the revelations and knowledge that comes from the power of God in Christ in us.

Arnold Palmer is considered the best golfer in the world and the reason he was so superior was his mental toughness. He would play the course the day before and then that night he would play the entire course stroke by stroke in his mind. He would visualize his swing, where he wanted to hit the ball and the physical feeling of his motions to the point of developing some muscle memory. We can strengthen our minds to build neurological synapses that literally imprint in our memory centers. Our core knowledge like our name or address is so imbedded in our heads it would take a traumatic incident or a physical injury to unloose them. That is what can happen when getting a concussion or electric shock therapy that can alter our mental and emotional pathways. Arnold Palmer trained his mind and body to play the game as was already won in his mind, that is what believing is all about. The Bible teaches a lot about the mind of Christ and how we can manifest the same thoughts giving us that connection to God. Romans 12:3 - And be not conformed to this world but be ye transformed by the renewing of your mind, that you may prove what is that good and perfect will of God.

The Colonel's son was a soldier and is a big-time believer. Ever since he was a boy, he wanted to be a soldier and he excelled as a student and made it to West Point. After graduation he enlisted in the Green Berets and went through all special forces training. He has over 200 paratrooper jumps and has had a few tours in Nam and other special missions around the world. As a Captain he has led his men in many firefights and saw much devastation and at the same time prays with his men and tries to encourage them to believe in God and the Bible. He was out on a jump one-night training his men on a high altitude jump with oxygen masks and all black jump suits with grease paint on their faces. One of his men couldn't open his chute at 10,000 ft. Rich glided over to help him and as he was doing so the soldier was holding on to him and somehow, he opened Ric's backup chute. When Ric opened his main chute, it got tangled with his backup chute and he tumbled down to earth. Richard fell two miles out of control spinning around and he hit the ground at 125 MPH. With over 200 jumps both his chutes malfunction and while saving another jumper he falls out of the sky and lives to tell about it. He said that on the way down all he could do was pray. He broke most of his body and the doctors said he would never walk again because he broke his back. Within two years Major Richard Thompson Special Forces, walked out of the VA hospital and now helps others to believe that they can overcome their disabilities.

Richard defied all the doctors and they had to admit that it was a miracle that he was able to walk again. He now works with the Wounded Warriors Project and has a ranch and horses to help these veterans get back to their lives. They also train guide dogs to work with veterans and people with special needs and the dogs and the bonds formed with the new owners is absolutely incredible. The dogs not only can learn hundreds of commands, they can learn how to sense out people with seizures and other opportunities. They are trained to smell a change in the physical makeup of their owners and can call for help. The dogs are able to smell physiologic changes in their owners and can alert to seizures, diabetic problems and other problems that they can smell internally. It is just amazing what Ric is doing with these people and these horses and K-9s. These animals and the trainers are way beyond Lassie, Rin Tin-Tin and Fury combined. Major Richard Thompson is another one of our heroes.

When we were in a war zone, the prayers we shared were so real, the black and white pages of the Bible became living technicolor when we believed and walked out on them. We prayed for protection, we prayed for safety for our families. We prayed for each other and during dark times it gave us peace to give it all to God. When I first heard Psalm 23 out with a bunch of soldiers it gave me chills and got me all choked up.

> *"The Lord is my Shepherd; I shall not want. He maketh me to lie down in green pastures. He*

leads me beside the still waters. He restores my soul; He leadeth me in the path of righteousness for His name sake. Yea that I walk in the valley of the shadow of death, I will fear no evil. For Thou art with me; Thy rod and Thy staff shall comfort me. Thou prepareth a table before me in the presence of my enemies; Thou anoints my head with oil, my cup runneth over. Surely goodness and mercy shall follow me all the days of my life, because I dwell in the house of the Lord forever"

This prayer and the Lord's Prayer are being prayed at most of the Christian services everywhere we go and means so much when the soldiers are literally in the valley of the shadow of death. To hear a bunch of soldiers singing Psalms 100 out in the bush is an awesome privilege. When we cry out to the Lord for His love and power, he will protect us by putting us under his wing.

Nurses had to deal with all the blood and guts and Nancy would have to help our soldiers that looked like they just fought at Hamburger Hill. Things were so horrible when the pain and suffering were causing these poor souls to shout out to put them out of their misery and all we could do was give them more morphine. We thanked God that we were on the mend and able to continue to serve God and country. By trying to live in God's love and live a healthy lifestyle we do all we can and give the rest to God. We saw so many people so messed up with injuries and with all the death and destruction that they experienced they had a hell of a time dealing with reality.

The VA hospitals were getting filled with veterans that left a lot of their vitality back in the war and many vets were still going through their own personal hell. The only treatment available was more medication and the drugs basically knocked them out and made them gain weight. The side effects of the antipsychotic drugs like Thorazine, Mellaril and Haldol were as bad as whatever they were good for and caused the patients to look like zombies, and constipated zombies at best. When the patients started checking their meds and saving them, they would usually start climbing the walls and really start acting crazy. It was a no-win situation as these types of drugs kept them in suspended animation. They would shuffle around without much purpose.

Mental illness was no joke. If the meds weren't strong enough then the Doctors would try ECT, Electric Shock Therapy, and if the patient was still very violent, they were given lobotomies!! Nobody recovers from a lobotomy as they severe the frontal lobes and it is pretty much lights out, nobody's home. To see people that were still alive yet not able to respond questions the very definition of what is life, it seems that they are buried alive. We had VA hospitals that were Psychiatric Hospitals and a lot of veterans were coming to the day clinics or they were hospitalized. A lot of these vets had multiple diagnosis of alcohol or drug abuse along with neurotic or psychotic behaviors. American Legion and veteran groups would take them to baseball games and picnics and the medications settled them out a bit and it was a long way to recovery.

All the medical team gave 100% and I so admired Nancy's heart and dedication. Part of her work was helping her patients deal with the physical pain and then it all becomes a part of the psyche in dealing with the recovery. Nancy says that working in surgical nursing was easier than psychiatric nursing because the patients that did live had hope of recovery. The psychotic patients were in their own hell and reality was hard to attain. Part of Nancy's mental and physical health was good living and eating and working out so she could maintain a positive attitude. In the law of attraction good energy attracts good energy and repels negative energy and karma means that what you give is what you receive. The Bible says that we should give with our heart and it will be multiplied back to us.

What Nancy's people were involved with was the monasteries and the orphanages that were taken over by the State to detain the refugees, the orphans and the runaways. Even in Greece and Turkey these lost children were retained in institutions. They retained the old churches and monasteries in Greece and the Turks were basically Muslims and their prisons were open to all people and a very horrible place to be. These people were being enslaved and the woman were being taken as sex slaves and sold to some very bad people who had no regard for human rights or human life. Some of the most disturbing things I have ever seen in all the horrors of war was the so-called snuff films that actually showed these monsters raping and killing the woman and were highly valued on the black market.

In countries like Afghanistan and Saudi Arabia and other Muslim countries they abduct young boys from the age of 12 to 16. Since adultery and homosexuality is against the law and against the Koran, by some sick reasoning the boys are made to look like girls to please the men. You see this isn't considered to be elicited sex as the young boy- girls are just taking care of the men. They are even forced to lick butts and drink urine as part of their sick -disgusting practices, and then there are the men that even have sicker appetites then we can even imagine. The things we have seen and been showed literally made us sick and it gets ingrained in our heads as scenes of abductions, rape, dirty nasty sex, sex with animals and then murder is not easy to forget.

Sometimes we questioned what we were doing especially in the unpopular Vietnam War and just who was our enemy. The Mei Lie incident where Lieutenant Calley ordered that his men kill everyone in the village of woman, children and old people because he was ordered to terminate the enemy. They killed and piled up and pit buried 280 at one village and slaughtered many more around the surrounding countryside. The big question was just who was the enemy? Some of the surrounding villages had guns and ammunition buried with enough rice to feed an army. The question was, did these villages have a choice and if they didn't cooperate with both sides would the whole village get torched? These types of war crimes so enraged the country, specially the liberal left and the college students already protesting the war. But this type of genocide that was going on against these girls and boys was so evil that we had to take a stand against it, and everyone in their right mind was on our side. To trade human lives and treat them like garbage and then kill them grabbed you deep inside and twisted your guts out. There was no grey area here as we had to send these fuckers to hell.

We learned in the Bible that compassion is a verb that evokes a person to act. Christ was moved with compassion to touch the leapers and forgive the sinners. The word compassion was translated from the term "bowels of mercies" as it did come from deep inside our hearts and was a motivating life force so we can get involved with another person's life. The thoughts and feelings to go against these evils were compassionately motivated to help these unfortunate prisoners, but it is hatred that motivated us to stop those sick bastards at all costs. I wanted to try and help save these souls from a horrible life and death and we wanted to fuck up those sick and twisted ghouls really bad. These fiends were so evil and it didn't seem that they were looking for any forgiveness or for God. In fact, some were worshipping Satan and were possessed with demons (DEVIL SPIRITS). We know our God forgives to those who asks for forgiveness. Only God knows what is in our hearts. We just continue to pray and give God our hearts.

Being here on the Mediterranean we are in the heart of the cradle of civilization dating back thousands of years and these islands are just full of incredible history and fascinating stories. There are great accounts of hideouts and secret caves and passages and many a tale of treasures not recovered. There are hundreds of caves carved out by the tides and some of the caves have grottoes and underground passageways. The cliffs along the coasts had so many exotic towns and villages with steps and pathways leading down to docks with gaily painted buildings and boats. Some cliffs had gondolas or lifts and some had donkey trails thousands of years old. About the most incredible place we got to visit was the island of Capri off of the Italian coast. Capri has it all, beautiful views of the sea and quaint towns and villages and flowers growing everywhere. The island had steep cliffs and underwater grottoes and the Mediterranean could not be bluer. We could look down and see the water taxis and boats ferrying people back and forth to Naples. The water was so clear that we could see the boats floating like they were suspended in mid-air. Naples was a whole other story, the best food in the entire world.

We decided to take an R & R to nowhere to have the time to catch our breaths and focus on our roller coaster ride we have been on together. The Navy had the slogan "Join the Navy and See the World "and the Airforce had the "Up and Away into the Wild blue Yonder "but we had no idea that we would see and experience all we have been through these last few years. The biggest discovery was that we found God and his spirit and we have opened up a whole new existence and knowing these truths has set us free. The military life grounds us to its rank and file, chain of command and order of daily life and gives us a common bond to work together. But the incredible things we were involved with has evolved to us being able travel all over the world in service to our country. Somehow Nancy and I have been called together by God and our country and hooking up with the Colonel has given us a supernatural team to be able to go against the evils of mankind's maturations. I can't say if fate brought us together but we know that God called and we answered. And now our connection with the Colonel and NATO has given us an incredible assignment and responsibility. We took some time to energize and make new goals to achieve the objectives we wanted to accomplish. As we looked over the southern Adriatic and the mouth of the Mediterranean Sea, we prayed for Gods protection and guidance and we started making plans to go back out to do some good.

On our time off we were able to talk over all that has gone down and the whirlwind of events we have been involved in. Things were happening so fast that Nancy and I were not able to keep up with all our reports and the CIA had most of it classified as we were not supposed to be in most of our destinations as it was. The great thing about our involvement was that we were not in this alone. We were backed by and connected to some good organizations, the UNITED STATES OF AMERICA, the USAF, the CIA, The North Atlantic Treaty Organization and the Garruto Olive Oil Company!! We had boats, planes, cars & trucks and we had connections and reconnaissance all over the world. Nancy was connected as a combat nurse and as a member of Doctors Without Borders and since we had the proper papers, we traveled all over forbidden lands. Of course, the greatest thing we had is Gods spirit and guidance. We had a lot of training and support and the men in the import business had our backs and would take a bullet for us. Nancy was so sharp and so smart and she was a great nurse and she could run the mile under 6 minutes, and knowing martial arts wasn't too shabby either. More than having great looks and a bodacious body, Nancy was very strong and athletic. Being in love and being able to pray together is priceless. Even though we could be caught and fed to the fishes we were living in a dream.

My worst fear was that these scumbags would get a hold of Nancy and have their way with her and drug her up like the people we were trying to rescue. When I think of these possibilities, I get sick and I want to take her far away and hide her from all this crap. The thing is that she is confident and fearless and ready to go on attack and when she makes up her mind she can't be stopped. We are making quite a team and we just got to pray for our safety and believe that God is, and that he is a rewarder of those that seek Him. The evils we are up against is so sick that I probably could be raped and tortured and chained in some dungeon as well. The sick fucks we were up against liked boys as much as girls and some even liked animals as they were sub human animal themselves. We were reminded that syphilis came from the shepherds doing their sheep. Mankind was so deranged that the bible said that God regretted making man because he was full of evil continuously. The Old Testament laws starting with the 10 commandments was given so people could know the difference between good and evil. Now we are working against people that seem to love death and sickness with the most horrible perversions. A normal healthy mind can't even imagine this shit, piss and destruction. These cretins are possessed with devil spirits.

In 1972 we were in a brief period of detente when both sides were trying to reduce the arms race to abide by the SALT treatise, The Strategic Arms Limitation Talks were held twice in Helsinki to discuss the probability that the United States and Russia had enough ICBM and ballistic nuclear weapons to knock the earth off its axis. Coincidently, in Stockholm the

Nobel Peace Prize was being awarded for literature to Alexander Solzhenitsyn, one of the great writers of the 20th century. The problem was that the KGB banned all his works and labeled him Public enemy # 1 against the USSR. He could not even attend the ceremonies in Sweden to receive his Nobel, as he feared he would be expelled from the country. His two most famous works were "A Day in The Life of Ivan Denisovich" and "The Gulag Archipelago" were about life in the Russian prison system and the KGB that put him there. He was a Russian patriot who loved Mother Russia and the people loved him. He served in the Red Army and taught at the university but then he spent years as a political prisoner in various camps. He was an Eastern Orthodox Christian and had a famous statement that "Russia will not get far without God". The KGB tried to poison him and finally they deported him to West Germany in 1972.

The Soviet Union was directly involved with the incarceration and the censorship of Solzhenitsyn's works. The KGB confiscated all his writings and would not publish anything new. Radio Free Europe would read his writings and lectures and hold discussions of his anti- communist philosophies. Radio Free Europe was also responsible for distributing his books and sending out pamphlets by balloons as his ideas were a powerful tool to combat the oppression of communism. As soon as I heard about sending out balloons to deliver things over the border I wanted to get involved. The whole thing reminded me of sending cargo out the back of the C-141 jet planes to parachute them down to their LZ. Whether it is drug running or shipping pallets of guns and ammo disguised as food, it was exciting to sneak around in the night under the cover of darkness. Now Nancy and I were a part of some big-time deception as the CIA and the KGB were playing cat & mouse on the world stage. We were really just couriers delivering suitcases and information to the other contacts either CIA or military agents. To do this we had to be able to pull off a lot of shit. And now we were going after the smugglers.

Chapter Seven

OF HUMAN BONDAGE

What is the price of one human life?
PRICELESS

It didn't take us long to get motivated to go after these scumbags that are enslaving human lives. We saw files and films on the horrors of these sex atrocities and even saw a few "snuff flicks" that ended with the mutilation and slow tortured deaths of young kids for the viewing pleasure of the sick fucks that buy them. The shit we saw was far worse than this and we want to terminate the ones that did this evil and try to rescue as many of the young victims as possible. The problem was that this shit was all over the world and women and children were missing from all over and there were clubs and organizations dedicated to these horrible perversions. Nancy and I have been talking about ending our military commitments and go out together in the real world to start a life together. This situation and duty could be the last detail before we go home and get married, and that also will be a motivation to give it all we got against this absolute evil. We started to prepare for all the details as we studied the maps and the shipping routes. We went over equipment and actually went over our weapons as we knew that this was going to be dangerous out on the waters with a bad bunch of animals that held no value for human life. They raped and even killed their victims and thought nothing of throwing them overboard if things got hot. Just like what we see in the drug smuggling, if things get too hot, the drugs and contraband were thrown overboard and we know that the hostages would be fed to the sharks.

They were heavily armed so we went back to the firing range and worked out and did some combat obstacle courses. We got back in the gym and Nancy did her roadwork. She also wanted to run the Boston Marathon next year. I got back into the water. I use to swim miles in training. We had installed 2 new Mercury 300 outboards and had the Donzi painted a metallic black with deep purple highlights that made it invisible at night. The guys at the shop put some special gel coat on the hull and waxed it and polished it so it will glide through the water with least resistance. Our boat was going to sprout wings and cut through the water like a shark. On a calm day we could be having lunch over at Split, Yugoslavia in two hours. We checked out key islands for hideaways and connecting points and had NATO help keep tabs on the activities in the air and the sea. Nancy worked on the targets we wanted to try and liberate mostly in Greece and into the communist bloc of Albania, Bulgaria and Yugoslavia. Nancy was able to get us in. She was still working with the medical relief team and we could deliver medical supplies as our cover. We had to be able to quickly take a group out and transport them all the way down to the coast to the boat and then transfer them to our cargo ship and then back to Italy. We had trucks we used for transporting olive oil so everything had to be coordinated and we had to be sure the women were ready to go. If anything went wrong, the refugees would be slaughtered and we would be sleeping with the fishes, literally.

We were dealing with different groups of thugs who were good at smuggling human beings as slave traders and pirates. We were at a disadvantage because we had to try to rescue the captives without getting them killed. We definitely needed Gods guidance, protection and power to pull this off against people that were possessed by devil spirits and every evil power. For somebody to be able to rape and kill a young child without batting an eye usually means they are possessed with devil spirits. Normal people just don't do those things unless they need some serious help. In fact, we discussed how we could see visions and other phenomenon through our spirit like a smell of an animal or a feeling of fear that something is near. Sometimes the whole room would get deathly cold or the hair on my neck and arms would stand up, and I knew it was time to pay attention. This is not something we can physically fight against, unless we have the "sword of the spirit". That fight was a spiritual battle.

We went back to the firing range a few times and worked on our hand to hand combat skills. Like the saying goes, you can't just bring a knife to a gun fight. We have to be ready for everything and we had to become invisible. We had our guys build a compartment in the panel truck under the barrels of oil and behind the cab and it was insulated for the cold and the sound. The outside wall behind the cab was two foot longer and the compartment was deep enough to hold four average size refugees, we had even more room behind the barrels.

Nancy was going to be delivering vaccinations, vitamins & birth control and I was going to be the aid and the driver. The good thing was that these orphanages were not high security areas and we had to have the element of surprise to get in and out fast. We were going to work on one mission at a time and if we are successful, we will start the next one. Every job will be different and we will mix up the targets within the 3 countries and areas. We are going do the same procedures as the pirates that are smuggling them and we pray that we will be even better at it. A problem we will face is that we can't take them all out so we had to start with the kids that were in prime position to be taken first.

These young women were a combination of Armenian and Greek and Russian Jews so they were so beautiful to begin with. These young girls were desired by these creeps all over the world and they wanted young boys as well. Some of these pig's plan was to share these women and even build elaborate, soundproof underground rooms so no one could hear their screams. We saw the remains of some horrible mutilations from the sick masochists that got off with this kind of rape and torture. We have seen a lot of sick shit in Vietnam and in Africa but nothing as heinous as what was going on here. The voodoo and black magic and the witch's covenants and the sadomasochistic clubs were all looking for human toys to play with to satisfy their sick desires. This stuff had to take the cake and these people were not even human and worse than any animal. We could freak out the exorcists and the shamans from places like Africa, Haiti or New Orleans with what we see now. Our new enemies were not only necromancers but they were not opposed to eating flesh or drinking blood for their initiations and rituals. They had many various sickening appetites to boot. Videos that showed these shattered souls all doped up having sex with dogs or horses was as bad as you could possibly imagine, but I am sorry to say that I've seen even worse shit then these fucking monsters. I would frag them in a second. If you want to chain a young woman in a dungeon to live out your sickest fantasies with your buddies and then when you wear them out and then finish them off so you can get another human play toy to torture and kill, then you don't deserve to live. Nancy and I are forced to be the judge, the jury and the executioners. We saw victims getting various surgeries to have body parts sewn together and other sick sadistic things to see how much torture a person can take before they die. Similar to the sick Dr Mengele, the Nazi Butcher. I have no remorse in sending them all back to hell. What more can I say, just telling people about these atrocities doesn't seem right as they can drain your soul. Writing it all down, reporting it and taking the proper actions to go against it, is war.

We were GIs, we were soldiers and when we were sworn in, we took the oath to serve and protect our country. Some volunteered, most were drafted and many had to fight against the enemy whoever that may be. Even in our own country people fought and killed each other. Now that Nancy and I were out on our own, our enemy seemed very personal and the evil loomed around the entire subculture of smuggling human beings. There were clubs and organizations devoted to all this horrible insanity and they were able to ship them all over the world. In order to save these victims, we had to kill some of the cretins that were enslaving them. As part of our duties we all had to go commando as the dangers needed to be faced with force.

We had yet to go out on our own. With our training we were armed and dangerous and well trained. Of course, I worried about Nancy but then again, she is well trained and she knows what we got involved in. As we got to drive around by car and boat, we had time to share these wild thoughts as our thoughts rushed like the wind in our faces. It was a catharsis for us to be out together so we could let some of the bad thoughts and feelings go as the bad energy hurts our whole being. To concentrate on holding a gun up aimed at a guy's head and then dropping him and splattering his brains all over is so messed up yet it had to be done. These bastards would slice our throats without blinking an eye. That was another one of our brilliant sayings, "It just had to be done, death is inevitable!" These are the things we have to let go of and replace it with the positive thoughts and feelings of the lives we are trying to rescue. There is a fine line between having to kill someone in self-defense and murdering someone. If we were warriors or gorillas, if we were on a search & rescue helicopter mission or on patrol in the jungle it was all war and death. Now we are going to go on attack to save the victims and we will be ready to do whatever we have to do to meet our objectives.

One of the serious problems of trying to free these victims is that under this type of confinement and abuse the victims can form strong bonds towards their captors. The captives have to learn how to survive by pleasing their captors. This is what happens with the prostitutes and their pimps, as the women even compete with each other to be the number one girl. We saw tapes of Patty Hearst as she sympathized with her kidnappers and even joined in on robbing banks. In Sweden, at the time when the victims tried to get the anarchists out of jail and support them through the trial, is when the phrase "Stockholm Syndrome" was coined. One of the worse cases in history was the holocaust. The Jewish women had developed feelings for the horrible Nazi guards as they held their lives in their hands in the concentration camps. The Jewish women were haunted by what they had to do to survive and the Nazi bastards would promise them that their children were being kept alive, although the children were the first to be gassed. They couldn't work or produce. Years later these poor women still went through the guilt of having those feelings towards those monsters.

We had to be concerned that the people we were going to liberate were not already attached to their captors and would resist our actions so they can protect their masters. We will have enough to worry about without worrying that these girls will jump on our backs as we are trying to get them away. I was involved in a free for all back at Travis with the MP that got jumped by the pimp and his girls, so I know how faithful they can be. It was a sick relationship as the captors had all the power and they were able to get their subjects to do anything they wanted. The people being enslaved had to do anything they had to do to stay alive but then they had the sad transference of their feelings for the monsters that were making them do very sick things. Young girls were tied up in dungeons in the dark for months being treated like animals and then they start to desire a strange kind of love for their captors. It was some kind of sick symbiotic relationship that both sides attach to each other. We have people who love Satan and want the darkness and the power that will enslave them so anything can happen. Seeing pictures of the horrors of the concentration camps and the Doctor of Death (Mingles), we can never forget those horrors.

Nancy and her medical team had been to a place on the Greek - Albania border that was an old monastery that was turned into an orphanage. It was a work farm and a holding pen for children that were being exploited for all bad reasons. Nancy's team was able to bring in some medical supplies and she found out that some of the girls were Armenian refugees and they were further being sold to be abducted to be used and abused. On Nancy's next visit to the so-called orphanage she spoke to four girls that were refugees from the same town in Armenia and were all cousins and in their early teens and already been through hell and back. She told them that she would be back for them soon and we were going to get them out of there and take them to Italy and possibly to America. She said that they will wait and see as they have been told and promised many things for years since their families have been killed by the Turks. The girls told Nancy that they were going to be taken soon because men had come to see them and they were picked like they were livestock. They were told to strip naked so the creeps could poke and prod them like they were at the stockyards. When they got pregnant the local horse doctor came and did the abortion. Our first target was in north Greece outside of the border town of Katina, a hundred miles north of the Adriatic Sea and a hundred miles across to Italy. Since these atrocities were all over Europe and the Mediterranean the CIA and NATO had to take action.

Part of our first plan was to get the girls to the infirmary and then out to the truck to travel south to the coast. Sounds easy doesn't it.? We had 4 orphaned girls that were young teenagers that we were going for outside the town of Katina, not more than 10 miles from the border. There was an island just off of the mainland named Corfu with a good port and even an airport, so if we could get the girls there, we would be home free. The orphanage that was really a work farm, the children were required to work in the fields 10 hours a day, every day and still do the daily house chores (as much as 5 more hours). The fruits, vegetables and dairy products were sold in town and the kids didn't even get to eat the good foods as they ate oatmeal, leftover cheese & bread, and soup for dinner. Their dessert was old sour buttermilk. Nancy made sure to pack some fresh fruits and some chocolates and orange juice.

All through the Soviet Bloc the food stores were bare and tools and appliances were hard to come by.

Gasoline and oil were being rationed and most things were traded on the black market. On the Greek side of the border things weren't as bad but the corruption was still rampant. Unfortunately, these kids were being sold on the black market, even the boys were abducted for sex (the younger the better) and for hard labor. Some were able to escape as they were on the run most of their lives and they drifted from place to place. Some were taken to other countries and they were purposely disabled to keep them from running so they could be controlled to do the dirty work. Some could be blinded or their feet were maimed so they wouldn't be able to run away. They were given drugs so they had to rely on their captors for a fix and do tricks for money for their pimps. They were sent out to beg and bring everything back to their "masters." As long as they could produce, they lived and the so-called lucky ones were for sexual pleasure to all the perversions. There were obviously no child labor laws and the poor people just didn't have any human rights.

This is why as Americans and part of the United Nations we stood for the code of ethics and for the human rights to emancipate all people being held down by their governments. This is why we fought against the governments that oppressed, jailed and even tried to euthanize their people. At least this is how Nancy and I saw things literally first hand and we were putting our lives on the line to defend these rights. Unlike the opposition and ambivalence to the Vietnam War, this was black and white and screaming for us to do something. We continue to prepare and every time we got more reports from the CIA our rage was fanned by these atrocities that we were going up against. At least we could pray.

We were ready to go so we packed up the truck looking like any other truck carrying produce through Greece. We took a ferry from Brindisi to the port of Preveza and then we headed north to the town of Katina where we checked into an inn for the night. We were running right along the Greek and the Albanian border along the Communist Bloc. We had a nice dinner at an old cafe in the town and then retired to go over the final plans before the big day. We were too excited to sleep so we laid in front of the fire until we passed out in each other's arms. Nancy was so sweet and tender, at least we had each other as we both were having nightmares about all this horrendous crap we were dealing with. We got up in the morning, had some breakfast in town and then we were off to do some ambushing and abductions of our own. We were scheduled to arrive at 10 am so we parked in back by the loading dock and took a little time to pray and to ask God to guide us and protect us. We checked in with the so-called infirmary where they performed illegal abortions and we sent for the girls. They brought the girls to see Nancy and we immediately had a bad problem. Two girls were missing. Apparently yesterday the two were snatched up and going on a boat to the Suez Canal. The orphanage got 50 bucks for them so apparently in 1974 a human life was worth 25 dollars and you could rape them, and torture them and kill them if you so desired.

Nancy told the two girls what was going to go down and they quickly showed us that they were wise beyond their years going through the school of hard knocks. They told us that the two men went to town to pick up supplies and just two old women were inside and one old man was out on the farm, so now was the time to take off. One of the girls made the sign of the cross as we quickly made a dash out the door and into the truck before the old woman came back. We stopped out of town and got them situated in their little cubby. They spoke pretty good English (as well as Greek and Armenian) and we told them we will drive a few hours before we stopped for lunch. We doubt the orphanage would even report it because of all the illegal activities they were hiding. But the word will get around.

We stopped on the roadside and had a little picnic to stay out of any public place. The girls were devouring the food and goodies. There was plenty since half the party was missing, we told them our plans. We told them we were headed to Italy to the United Nations Headquarters and they were eventually going to live in America. The excitement in their eyes made Nancy cry and she hugged them both and everything was worth it for that moment. The whole thing was so damned glorious and I felt alive with Gods spirit. Hopefully they will adapt to their new environment and they will become Armenian-American teenagers (instead of the inhumane life they were facing.) Most of these kids in this system have already been raped and abused as it is, and now they are being abducted to be treated like animals, but way worse as it is hard to believe someone would even treat their animals this way. Even the people involved with dog and cock fighting, as bad as it is, doesn't come close to these violent crimes against humanity. We can only pray and hope that these children can start a better life and adapt to their new circumstances. Somehow these kids who have been through so much hell can still be cleansed with love and that positive energy that can drive out all that hate and violence. God knows that even back home we have major problems with the treatment of our children in our systems, that is why we have child protective services and social workers and health care people to help protect them. And even these systems fall short. But first we have to get these two girls to Italy, and it seems like we are only scratching the surface, but then again, what is the value of even one human life? It has got to be more than 25 dollars!!

We made it down to the coast and checked into a beach side motel with cabins and snuck the girls in for the night. I went to a market to get more food and Nancy helped the girls shower and change into new clothes. They loved their new blue jeans and Pro-Keds, and Nancy's makeup. We told them stories about American life; they thought that we were all rich and movie stars. We all finally fell asleep dreaming about nicer things and a new life for these young teenagers. It was amazing to see them this way after all the shit they have been through. In so many of the nations that Nancy and I have been to, we have seen these children used and abused. In Nam the kids were used and abused by soldiers on both sides and the population of half white and half black Vietnamese babies was a growing into a phenomenon. In Africa most of the young girls already had babies of their own as it wasn't uncommon to have an arranged marriage at 12 years old. The spread of disease was rampant as they had the first reported autoimmune diseases that were killing people like a plague. Birth control and prophylactic protection were handed out as the birth rate and the spread of sexually transmitted disease was out of control. Nancy was called to help with the medical team to try and treat these epidemics.

Here in Europe the children were the flowers of war and war has been going on forever. In the morning we were going to catch the ferry back to Italy and to get the girls to freedom. Nancy and I discussed what we knew we had to do. We were going to go after the two girls that were on the way to SE Asia. The girls were all cousins from the same Armenian town. Our two girls were sisters and their names were Valerie & Lena Kazerian and they had those big almond eyes and fair skin that made them so beautiful. As soon as we got these girls to Headquarters, we were going to make tracks to intercept the slow boat to China (so to speak) as we were able to track the cargo ship through our eyes in the sky. We were going to fly to Port Said in Egypt before it headed south to the Suez Canal. Our men from our shipping business were going to help us out and provide all the transportation so we could steal back the two girls. Our guys were setting us up with a small runabout so we could strike from the harbor as the boat waited to be admitted to the canal. Fortunately, the traffic in the Mediterranean was backing up the entire entrance. The port was bustling with ships coming and going and there was about a day's wait to go forward.

Port Saad probably had 100 ships in its harbor so we could be ready to go the next day when we get our special cargo back and safely in Italy. Now we had to devise a plan to get the girls off the boat and away from these monsters without getting us all killed. These people were not the Boy Scouts nor was their ship a cruise ship so we had to strike fast and hard. Once again, we had to have the element of surprise and catch them off guard. We got the skinny from Headquarters on the ship and its crew. It was a Greek made and registered 85 ft flat deck boat that looked like a large tug boat with a 30 ft cabin and twin Diesel engines. It had a crew of 5 and there was over a thousand of these types of boats all over the oceans everyday going from port to port. We learned there was three men smuggling the girls and the manifest destination was registered for Manila.

We already had surveillance on the boat and we were going to hit them at around 9 PM. Some of the crew should be up at port drinking some ouzo and hopefully the dock will be quiet. Our plan was to take the runabout right to the dock like it was nothing new and sneak right on and do whatever we had to do. We both were going to wear flak jackets and carry two Glocks with silencers. In the 5 years of service I was lucky to get through without a scratch, but now we were going on the attack and it was going to get very serious. In all we have been through I think that Nancy and I had the ability to stay very cool under pressure. Not that we didn't get scared but we were able to turn this fear into a sharper energy as we tuned into the fight or flight nervous system response. Nancy was sharper than a tack and there was nobody that I wanted covering my back more as we have been working together for over three years now. I don't think anyone that knew us thought us to be just a young girl and a young kid as we were well trained, confident and well prepared.

We brought the girls to the NATO Headquarters so the UN people could take care of them and even fatten them up a little. They were like our prize victory and the staff was going to take care of them, we wish we could take care them but there was no way we could with our lifestyle so we hope we could see them again. We said goodbye for now and prayed for their safe voyage to their new world. We caught the next flight straight to Port Said, Egypt, our olive oil importers were quite familiar with the port and will be there to back us up and run surveillance. We arrived at 4 in the morning and went over our plans and took possession of our skiff. We got some rest but we were way to keyed up to really sleep, we could not even cuddle with each other as we were fueled by the hate that we had for these murderous bastards. We docked and went into the town plaza and got something to eat and Nancy bought some goodies for the girls we were going to liberate. We had a few more hours before nightfall so we actually went for a jog to keep loose and burn up some anxiety. We came back to our small cabin cruiser, a 23 ft skiff with an inboard and a small cabin, just big enough to hold a few castaways. We got dressed and secured our gear and weapons. At times I stopped to take in Nancy's focus and commitment and it makes me shutter that I was with a Wonder Woman and a Woman of God. Some people try to question how we could love God and be involved in these wars but that was their problem. The Bible was full of people like King David that was a man of war and a man after God's own heart. Moses killed an Egyptian and went on to lead the people out of Egypt. So here we are asking God to protect us and help us to safely make our own exodus out of Egypt! We said a final prayer and we started what we came for.

We docked the boat on the same pier and quickly boarded the small ship. It was quiet and we went straight down to the hold. We drew our guns and went into a small room and we were met with a hideous scene. Two men were busy having their way with the girls as they had them on their knees and violently screwing them in their butts. But we came in on them from behind and I hit the first guy with my pistol but I did not see that he was holding a knife to her throat as he was brutalizing his 15-year-old captive. He was able to swing around and slice me in the shoulder and then it was over with a couple of muffled shots as Nancy took both men out with two shots into their turbaned heads. I must have been in shock but I heard Nancy yelling "Let's go, let's get out of here, quickly!" We grabbed some dirty blankets and wrapped them around the girls and beat feet up the stairs. I met the third guy coming down the steps and he was carrying an assault rifle and I let him have it right between his beady eyes. I kicked him to the side of the stairs and we climbed over him and out to the deck. We came to a door on the forward deck that had a padlock. I blew the lock off the door and we went down a passageway to a dimly lit room. Once inside we found 4 kids tied up to each other. Then we realized that they were two sets of twins. We had two identical sisters about 15 and two 12 years old twin boys. They told us how some sick fucks that bought them for some very sick activities. Nancy and I saw films about the insane tests the Dr Of Death, the Nazi Butcher Mengele did on twins back in the concentration camps. That sick bastard would run his so-called medical test to see how much these young children could take. Putting burning instruments in side of them or electric shocks especially in their genitalia was one of his favorite experiments. A horrible sight was the mounds of teeth, the eyeglasses or the wedding rings that were confiscated before they were gassed. Now here in the 1970s we have the same evil shit to deal with.

Fortunately, the rest of the crew wasn't around and we made it out to our waiting boat and we took off like sleuths in the night. Now we had our girls from the orphanage and 4 more kids that were Romanian Gypsies. We were going to drive about ten miles out through the harbor to hook up with a sea plane waiting for us to take us back home. We started to catch our breath as the whole thing only took about 10 minutes and then I started to feel the pain and the bleeding in my left shoulder.

I wanted to push to our rendezvous to meet up with the sea plane but Nancy insisted we stop so she could take care of my shoulder. I was going on blood and guts and now I saw that my entire left side was soaked with blood. Nancy grabbed her first aid bag and tried to clean me up, I had a nasty gash from my shoulder to my neck, but thank God it missed my jugular vein. It is just incredible that she was a MASH nurse and she had the sutures to sew me up. She gave me a dozen stitches and it was hard going because the surf was bad and our small boat was rocking in the waves. She bandaged me up and gave me some pain pills that she pulled out of her bag. God, I love this woman, and I was going to tell her when we are back in Italy. I fired the engine back up and took off into the night. The four girls and two boys were huddled together in the cabin and still under the filthy blankets. Nancy went to comfort them and to try and tell them about these crazy events that just went down. We told them we were taking them to the United Nation Headquarters in Italy. We told the girls from the Greek orphanage that we have their cousins waiting for them. It was still an explosion in my head and it still wasn't over until we were safe back in our cottage in Brindisi.

Our veterans were waiting with the sea plane and we took off in the rough surf. We landed at the port at Brindisi in a few hours and we decided to bring them all to our cottage until we could take them to Headquarters in the morning. I am sure they were in shock as they were rescued in a predicament that I will never be able to forget. We felt no remorse in sending those sick bastards to hell. It was hard to believe that these children had any sanity left, but somehow the human spirit heals and helps them cope with the evil that they went through. Nancy got everyone showered and cleaned up and I made a nice fire and we put out blankets and pillows. Fortunately, we were all wiped out and they all fell asleep watching Italian TV by the fire. When we all woke up in the morning, I made them my famous blueberry pancakes with lots of hot syrup and butter. The kids were instantly addicted to commercial TV as they had not watched anything good, ever. We took them to Headquarters and said our goodbyes and they were able to meet up with the other kids. Once again, we all cried and thanked God we were safe and sound, except we will all be troubled for the rest of our lives.

Nancy and I have not had the time to get the full realization that we just shot three men at point blank range. We finished up at the base and put in for 21 days of sick leave and told them we would put in our reports later. I had a nasty gash that needed to heal and we needed some R&R to heal our heads. We were going to spend a few days home recovering and then we were going on vacation to America. The staff at Headquarters threw us a surprise party and the Colonel invited all our friends. He told us that we were getting a medal of freedom and we thanked all the team for their help and support for we did not do this alone. The Colonel spoke about how much we all trusted in God throughout this whole adventure and that we have been praying together since we met at Cam Ron Bay. The Coronel never lost an opportunity to speak about trusting God. We were humbled and embarrassed and we still felt the horrors of all the evil shit we went through. Soldiers like Charley Bonham had done this for years and had to frag hundreds of Vietcong and even some of our own men as he had to save his chopper from crashing at the LZ. I probably already told you that he was a true hero and the VA should take care of him for the rest of his life.

Nancy had to take care of me, I had a nasty infection from the guys knife and I had to take antibiotics and pain pills. It hurt like hell when I moved my arm so I had to wear a sling for a while. We were changed as life will never be the same again. We sat in front of the fireplace and spent a lot of time reading the Psalms together. Our favorite Psalm was Psalm 51 as it dealt with David's sins with Bathsheba and having her husband Uriah killed in battle. David went to God begging for forgiveness and asking God not to take away his Holy Spirit. This helped us to reaffirm that God loves us and forgives us and we will eventually be okay. Within a couple of days, I was itching to get out even though I had to let Nancy drive. We took some trips around southern Italy and we booked a flight to New York for some decent R & R. We were still looking over our shoulders and we had to comfort each other during the night from the horrendous nightmares. A lot of mine were sick and twisted with visions of rape and torture and Nancy would wake up shaking and crying. Sometimes I had this crazy dream of the Devil screwing Nancy like that movie "Rosemary's Baby "and everything was totally whacked out. Some nightmares were so real that I could see myself in the dream and at times I felt as if something was on top of me holding me down. These damn dreams would bother me all day like they were real. With all the LSD I use to do, I now felt like I was slipping in and out of reality but the fact that Nancy never did acid further confirmed that we were under a big -time spiritual attack.

Nancy and I started realizing that we needed help as these mental and emotional problems were getting out of control. We didn't want the Air Force getting wind that we were having these problems in fear we would be taken off of active duty. Seeing these young children getting abducted, raped and killed was more then we could take, at times. Nancy seemed a little tougher than me, I think she saw so much in the OR, all that blood and guts. The thing is, I was starting to feel like an emotional blubber head. A grown man, a special trained soldier, shouldn't be seen crying. It is just that these victims were just precious little children.

Even if they were teenagers or adults, they were still Gods children. It was starting to rip our hearts out and I was breaking down. We went to see the Colonel and he used his experience in these matters to minister to us and to speak the Word with us. We spent the final day with him and we both felt a big weight was lifting off our hearts and shoulders. Colonel Thompson was definitely another one of our heroes and he was a man of God. The Colonel prophesied over us and sent us on our way with his blessings. He assured us that God will heal our brains and our hearts and we needed to take some time to let it happen. He assured us that if we spend time together in the bible and in prayer, it will heal our hearts, the renewed mind is the key to power. We knew that if we shared Gods love we could gain back the strength we needed to get back to our mission. Our mission is to help save these tortured souls caught up in these vial acts of evil.

We arrived back at the newly named Kennedy International Airport in New York and checked into the New York Hilton so we could take some time to get it together before we see any family or friends. We had cart blanche and we spent time in the bathtub as we could not seem to get clean enough. Nancy hung a scripture up on the mirror like she used to do, it was Romans 12: 2 - "Be ye transformed by the renewing of your mind that you may prove what is the perfect will of God." We will be transformed like the metamorphosis of a caterpillar to a butterfly - we couldn't get that intimate yet but we did start to hold each other and be sweet with each other.

We took in some great dinners in the city and spent an afternoon at the Metropolitan Museum of Art spending some time with the Impressionists. We liked to see people's faces as they looked at a great piece of art like a Van Gogh or a Monet. It was great to see a person get inspired and then go get their friend or partner to share in their experience. My favorite painting was a huge picture of Joan of Arc receiving her commissioning with the angels Michael and Gabriel behind her in the trees (Jules Bastien-Lepage, 1879). Nancy stared at it for 20 minutes, Joan of Arc looked like she was right there standing next to us. We ended up at one of the beautiful chapels in St Patrick's Cathedral. St. Patrick's is a cathedral on par with the great ones in Europe and you expected that Jesus himself would come down from the cross and do a backflip for us. We loved the smell of the incense. We walked around the city into the night and got a good sleep without any night terrors and woke up somewhat rejuvenated. We ate brunch at the Top of the Sixes and were ready to try to get back to reality. We still had two more weeks to rehab and enjoy our great country and we had to start to make some decisions on our futures. All we knew was that we were going to get married and continue to do Gods will. We wanted to move on to civilian life and continue with school yet we had a lot of opportunities to consider. We were still committed to our mission to save as many of the refugees as we could.

Colonel Thomson was up for Brigadier General and he wanted us to stay with him or join the CIA. He was going to retire soon and he too could do anything he wanted to do. We joked about taking a year off to sail around the world together but we knew that we had too much to accomplish. Maybe we could fit in some shorter adventures and if we do retire, we had months of vacation time accrued to take before we did go. We decided that we wanted to spend some peaceful time alone so I told her about my favorite place growing up in the New York Adirondacks. For at least 10 years my grandparents had a cottage up in Lake Placid, host of the Winter Olympics and Olympic Training Center and the future sight of the 1980 Winter Olympics. I have been to a lot of great parks and beaches but something about upstate NY is the most beautiful. It is a combination of the mountains and the thousands of lakes and rivers. I knew of a cabin on Lower Saranac Lake that we could rent for a week and it had everything we would want.

Fireplace, boat & dock, hammocks and great views of the lake and mountains. Oh, by the way the fishing was famous, Largemouth and Smallmouth bass, Northern Pike & Lake Trout along with an abundance of pan fish. We can watch the sun rise out in the canoe and catch them when they are most hungry. When the sun was coming up it burnt away the morning mist as it gently rolled down the lake. We were 15 miles from the town of Lk Placid with all its great restaurants if we did want to go out to eat. We caught some big whoppers and spent a lot of time mending in front of the fire watching the flames dancing in the dark and listening to the call of the loons and the roar of the bullfrogs. We sat back and watched the sparks of the fire turn into stars, it was a magical and healing place.

On the 5-hour ride back down to the city we talked about the girls, the fiends, the communists and the battles we were in. To try and save the young girls we knew we had to get armed and dangerous and we both were Marksman with rifles and hand guns. As the saying on the rifle ranges reads; "DO NOT BRING A KNIFE TO A GUNFIGHT". We actually did sign up for this shit and we took an oath to defend the United States of America at all cost, even our own lives. Nan and I spent a lot of time going over this to reassure each other that we are okay and asking God to forgive us and restore us. We were starting to move on and look to the future. We tried to think of some of the beautiful places and the people that we met along the way. I think that our psyches protect our conscious minds as it is easier to remember the things that make us feel good and we suppress the bad ones into the unconscious so we don't have to deal with them. But the problem is that what is suppressed continues to haunt us, that is why the Bible teaches us to put on the mind of Christ and the real issues are in our hearts. Then we can ask God to give us a clean heart so we are open to manifest the spirit he has given us. Jesus Christ came to save us and heal our hearts, minds and bodies. The heart represents the deep seat of our personal lives and is the combination of our thoughts and feelings. We also pray to our Heavenly Father to keep Satan and his demons away from us. A good benefit of praying as we go to sleep is asking God to help us get a peaceful sleep and keep the devil at bay. WHY COUNT SHEEP WHEN WE CAN TALK TO THE SHEPHERD. When Nancy and I pray together we give it all to Christ and ask him to take care of it. The Bible shows us that we have the ability to "put on the mind of Christ" as we could ask each other "What Would Jesus Do?" Jesus also tells us that greater things can we do because he ascends to his father. Nancy and I are committed to the belief that the black and white pages of God's Word become living color when you believe that God raised Jesus Christ from the dead. This is why we believe that God will continue to take care of us and if God be for us, who can stand against us? NO ONE!! This is why we called ourselves believers.

When we got to Manhattan, we finally felt good enough to visit our families and we took my mom to go meet Nancy's family in Maryland. We took her to a special treat at the US Naval Academy at Annapolis to see Nans brothers and we were all invited to the officers dining room for dinner. My mother was thrilled as we gave her a toast for her service in Korea. Nancy's brothers started heckling us that I was dating my mother as they were both army nurses and it was a little weird. The thing was my mom might have turned some heads in Korea when she was Nancy's age but she was my mom for gods' sakes!!? At least I think that I did not have an Oedipus Complex!?

Nancy looked so sharp with her new gold Captain bars and her new braids on her visor. I looked like her driver as a noncommissioned officer (a NONCOM!). Her parents were so proud of her and my mom already loved her, and we hadn't told them our plans as we had not made any yet. I guess they all assumed since we brought our mothers together it was time to make the announcement. We had a lot of decisions to make but for now we had to get back to the Mediterranean and try to get more children out. Our team of veterans like to use the terms like liberate, reconnaissance and termination and our spying was always surveillance and gathering intelligence. We changed the terminology of the words to dehumanize them so they lost some of their emotional impact. We now have to plan on doing what it takes at all cost and the ends justified the means. We knew we would do it all again to save a life. We said our goodbyes and although we didn't talk too much about our work, our family knew we were involved in some bad shit. We took my mom back to Long Island and told her that next time we meet her could be Washington DC.

We flew back to Headquarters and finally put in our report and went to check in with the newly commissioned General. I told him that he was also one of the bravest men we knew as he was in combat since WW 2 and he was my mentor and spiritual advisor. Our new orders were a lot like our old ones, to seek out and to rescue the children who were kidnapped and plundered for sex and discarded like trash. We went back to our cottage on the cliffs and started gathering information on a new target to visit. We received reports that there was an entire holding camp in Soviet Armenia accessed by going into the Black Sea deep in occupied territory. We did have access into the Black Sea in international shipping lanes but this is all the way into communist Georgia and Armenia with only one way out through the straits of Istanbul. We would have to devise a way to get a boat to get us to the coast of Greece so we could avoid the entrance to the straits where we would be sitting ducks to the Soviet controlled port of Istanbul. The only solution was to make a water transfer to a sea plane and make the jump right over the entire area. To pull this off we would have to coordinate a second water transfer to our boat waiting in the Aegean Sea.

We had the boats and planes, the problem was getting to the detention camp and getting the detainees out without getting us all killed. Because this wasn't in any active military zone, we couldn't get any special ops team in or get any planes or choppers in to just swoop in and pluck them out. So, we went to our NATO Command and worked on the various possibilities of sneaking the kids out. After a few days we were starting to think of shutting this mission down in fear of collateral damage to the lives we were trying to save. But like an act of God we received reports that a Greek trawler was going to be deployed to take a group of victims out to sea and over to Columbia, South America. We are able to get this technical information because in all international waters we had satellite surveillance, surveillance planes taking pictures and charting the activities and Italian coast guard cutters with radar roaming the coastlines. And like in the Air Force they had to show an account or a manifest document of the cargo being shipped that was part of the devious game being played for thousands of years. Things are just not what they seem to be.

So now we hoped that we can intercept the ship just like the Nigerian or the Angolan pirates have been doing since sailors like Magellan have been sailing around the Cape of Good Hope. We hoped to be able to intercept the trawler as it left the Straits of Gibraltar and at the Canary Islands was the refueling port of Los Palmas about a hundred miles off the Moroccan Coast. Except for the big tankers most ships had to stop here to refuel as it was a long ride across the ocean. In the days before engine power the Canary Islands were right in the trade winds so they had a few great ports and islands to dock at. Just like we did at Port Saad in Egypt, we wanted to strike them at the port of Los Palmas. We could get a few boats out from Italy ahead of the trawler chugging through the Black Sea as they haven't even left yet. We were very excited to get this rolling but we had to remember that things can go wrong in an instant. If we got too confident, we lose our edge and start to rely on our own ability and forget about Gods abilities.

We have to never forget that God has it all figured out and will take care of us. If there wasn't a higher power in control of things how could we get through the day in one piece. We should be thankful for miracles every morning as we open our eyes to see or to smell the coffee. What about the colors of the flowers or the tropical birds we can see in all their glory? How did Nancy get through all the horrors of war and still be able to love and show compassion? How could a fuck up like me still work for the USAF and the CIA and get to stand for the God and Father of our Lord Jesus Christ? Well the answer to all these life questions is that there is a God and he is a rewarder of those who diligently seek Him.

We started to devise a plan that would involve the help of our olive oil importers. The men that volunteered were actually all veterans and CIA and they were committed to the cause as most of these guys had children of their own and hated these bastards with a passion. We all had a couple of days to come up with a good working plan. They still wanted me to call the shots and their support and experience was awesome. All four men had worked with me as they showed me the ropes in our trips around the Mediterranean. They were all Nam vets, two were ex-Rangers, one a Green Beret, and one a Navy Seal, so these guys could kick ass and take names. They had no problem in terminating the entire crew and feeding them to the sharks and then setting the ship on fire!! Our primary objective was saving the young women without anyone getting hurt and getting us all safely back to Italy. If the trawler was under sail it would look like the hundreds of slave ships traveling all over the world in the 17 & 18 centuries. We planned to wait until their ship left port in the Canary Islands and hit them late in the night with two high powered skiffs. We had a cargo ship waiting for the transfer back to Brindisi and we were going to be loaded for bear. Hopefully these monsters will not know what hit them, as we appeared to be just another cargo ship traveling the big ocean.

The Canary Isles was an Archipelago of eight major islands and a few smaller ones and of course the weather made for a tropical paradise. We planned to wait at a smaller port called Santa Cruz and our men were all Alpha males that were seasoned soldiers and itching for some action. They were all family men so I hoped I didn't have to worry about them putting moves on Nancy. Men are men and some will go after their best friends' girl or their sister in law. We all arrived early and we had a couple of days to prepare as the trawler was reported to have just left Armenia. We spent the first day in town buying things and Nancy had a footlocker filled with clothes and supplies for the young woman we were liberating.

That night we got all suited up in our black fatigues and we put on the grease paint so we went on a midnight practice run. Our crew had full combat gear on and they had all sorts of weapons to get the job done. They had been telling us about plans to go back to SE Asia to help get our troops out from the POW camps as far away as Laos & Cambodia. They told us that our men were held outside in bamboo pits eating bugs and we have their prisoners housed in summer camps eating better than they ever did. The Geneva Conventions were only being observed by our side and that could be questionable in certain interrogations. These patriots wanted us to join up with them as they are looking to form a crack unit and they certainly wanted a combat nurse; our soldiers were reported to be in very bad shape. With all our options that Nancy and I were considering, mercenary work was not on the top of the list. I was appreciating our crew more and more and I was very excited and thankful that we had these heroes to help us to pull this off. These are the guys that aren't afraid to run towards trouble instead of away from it. We split in to two teams and took the motorboats out into the ocean for a run. The stars were out in force and we seemed to be floating out in space, for a brief time everything seemed to be okay. But in 24 hours all hell was going to break loose. We had rented two rooms in a cabana on our island to spend the rest of the night and day, until the night we were set to go out and raise some hell as the guys like to say. We also like to say that preparation is the highest form of believing so we were getting "ready to rock & roll!"

We spent the afternoon going over everything and we all shared some of the horrors we knew about our enemies. Not that we didn't need any more motivation but one of the guys saw a snuff flick that the woman was forced to have sex with animals. And if that wasn't bad enough, they were slowly dismembering her because there is a whole club around the world that likes having sex with amputees. Can you even imagine that there are clubs and organizations that are formed for this kind of shit? It made our skin crawl but we had to know what we were dealing with. Even the Bible has accounts of evil kings and kingdoms and thousands of years ago God said he regretted creating man as they were continually filled with evil all of the time. Thank God that there were a few good men like Noah, Abraham and Moses or mankind would have been history. The book of Ecclesiastes tells us almost 3,000 years ago that there is nothing new under the sun. We knew we were up against an evil that was so big that our efforts were just a drop in the bucket. Nancy and I also knew that death and destruction will be getting worse until the Lord returns to restore the earth back to paradise. Then there will be no more tears, no more death and the devil will be thrown into the bottomless pit and the lake of fire. We will not be giving up as even the mighty oak eventually falls after enough chops of the axe. We are committed to rescuing these people even one life at a time, we just couldn't give up. We still had to take one step at a time and now we were all focusing on the mission at hand and we were ready to engage.

We got our two teams together and set up the two rescue boats on the dock and we waited for the trawler to set out on its cross Atlantic voyage. We were one island away and our team was able to get a tracking device stuck on the stern of the no name ship so we could follow it in the night. We had one of the ex-marines with us in our boat, his name was Al Rosco from Brooklyn and he had three tours in Nam and still was one tough son of a bitch. He was loaded with enough stuff to blow the whole ship out of the water. He was able to dive under the dock and slap the tracker on the stern of the trawler. The other team had enough fire power to send the entire ship to hell so we just have to pray that the women didn't go down with the ship. We finally got the signal that the trawler was underway and we were going to push off and vanish into the night. It was pretty calm out with a good moon and a lite breeze and surf. I looked over at Nancy and she gave me a little wink and a thumbs up and the three of us gave each other the big nod that this is going down, now! When we started getting close, we both turned our running lights off and tried to sneak up on them as the waves and the chug of the trawler's diesels drowns us out.

We boarded the vessel on both sides right by the cabin and we climbed the stairs straight up to the wheel house. Our second team took off down the stairs as I ran up the stairs, I saw 2 Arabs lying on the deck with parts of their faces missing. We busted into the chart room and I put my pistol right on the back of the Captain's head. As I did so I heard two shots that dropped him immediately. Blood and brains sprayed all over me. Al was right next to me and yelled "let's go, let's go "and he was gone down the stairs. Nancy and I beat feet down to search the kitchen and the living quarters as we could hear our other team was down in the cargo area. Only about 15 seconds went by and 3 thugs were down and more on the way. Two more of their crew came flying down the hall with rifles and as the lead guy went to shoot me, Nancy and I nailed both of them. I remembered seeing blood all over the walls and we kept running downstairs to the cargo area, it was so dimly lit but Nancy had her flashlight out so we could see a few open doors. We heard all the noise coming from the forward compartment, we ran in to see a real shit show. There were 5 guys, maybe from Turkey or Iran laying on the floor screaming and crying as our guys took them all out at the knees. One of the scumbags was dead as he had been shot right in the forehead and he was naked. Just then we heard a small cannon going off a few times as our man Al had pumped two more guys from the hallway as we heard him yell "A-TWEET-MOTHERFUCKERS", a term we heard in Vietnam for anything outrageous.

Our focus was now back on these kids and how bad off they were. Our men said that these animals were already getting their jollies as the dead guy was caught in the act and his pals were all getting started. They had a few girls untied and undressed and they had a few more naked and tied to the wall. The rest of the group were all tied together on the filthy floor; they must have had livestock in here. We could only imagine what was planned for the nighttime activities. Four or five of the men were ripping the woman's clothes off and bashing them around and our men came and broke it up. We worked on untying the captives and getting them dressed the best we could, Nancy had their new clothes on our freighter along with blankets and plenty of food. Our survivors were begging us to let them shoot their balls off before we kill them, but we got it over with and fragged the four still alive in one swoop. We were only on the ship about a couple of minutes and the whole gang of thieves were history. We gathered the ten girls and 4 other women along with 5 boys that were probably not more then 10 (that was the way they liked them). We took them out to our two boats and got them situated and we waited for Al to set the explosives and then we took off. No more than 10 minutes later we saw, then heard, a hell of an explosion on the horizon and the sounds could be heard echoing across the waves. Just like that the night got calm as the moon and stars were out and the Milky Way looked like we were suspended out in the cosmos. It was again calm. The distant lights faded away and you would have never known that a cargo ship with its crew just vanished in thin air. The only trace that was left was a small flicker on the horizon and the 19 souls that were heading to a better life.

We headed for Spain and the straits to meet up with the "OLIVE OYL" as she was chugging out of the sea to meet us. We met at the port at Tangiers on the Moroccan side of the straits. We traded ships and the crews split up to take the other ship and boats back to Sicily. We then were able to take our rescued squad back to Brindisi. All 19 of them had new hooded sweatshirts and sweatpants along with sneakers and they have been eating nonstop all night and day. American clothes and foods were like a godsend to help these poor bastards from wanting to scream bloody murder. Most of these kids seem to be in shock. They have all been through hell and we prayed that they will be taken care of. These evils are contagious and only Gods love can start to heal us. The problem is that we didn't feel as bad as we did on the second time around. Guys like Al from Brooklyn were seasoned warriors and still he wore his heart on his sleeve and his crucifix around his neck. He is the example of why we say that we have to kill for peace. His main objectives were to protect his fellow soldiers and get back home in one piece. Back in Country we had platoons of our troops that were sent to flush out and be sitting ducks for the NVA. Some of our men were so courageous that they sent in the jets to bomb their own coordinates to save what was left to save, and kill the rest. War what is it good for? Absolutely nothing!! But we had to defend our people and again the ends justified the means.

Everything that Nancy and I have been going through is so different now. I went through Vietnam for a year without having to fire my weapon and Nancy was a combat nurse trained in the operating room to stitch people up and put them back together again. We got through another year in Germany and behind the Wall with only minor scratches. I did have to fist fight but I never had to kill anybody. But now because of the missions we were on we had to defend and protect the victims from monsters that could kill them. My sweet Nancy is now a killer and I am over the shock of taking somebody's life. We have trained to be good at it. We talked about the goombahs back in Las Vegas that killed people and threw them in the trash. We thought that our actions were righteous because we were trying to save the victims. Out here in the field we had to be the judge, jury and the executioner. One amazing truth was how Nancy could wear her Hippocratic Oath Pin and her Marksman Medal on her chest to both save and kill life. It seemed that we were killing people that were trying to kill us, was it self-defense? So, were we killers or murderers and was it all the same no matter what we call it. Conscious Objectors take the bible literally that "Thou Shall Not Kill" as one of the ten commandments. But my bible also says that God forgives sins in Jesus Christ's name. That is why Jesus died for us.

We got everyone back to NATO Headquarters and spent a few more days with the General and the staff.

He ordered us to take a few more days off and then he assigned us to the base for a while until we got our new orders. We wanted to get right back out but we will stay and get refocused and go over some new plans. Nancy started working at the base infirmary and I checked in at the flight line. We spent some quality time together at our cottage and we attended some of the Christian fellowships and churches in the area. I put the Donzi in dry dock so we could hook up a new radar system that was out, it came with a fish finder and we planned on testing it all out at least a few times while we were home. We made a few pots of tomato sauce and put some of the local shellfish in. Our favorites were scallops, crabs and clams with macaroni and Italian bread. It was our opinion that Italian cuisine was the best in the world. Even the base cafeteria was awesome. The cooks were all local aficionados and served some great delicacies. When we weren't working, we had time to get out and tour the country side and get back out on the water.

These were good times for us, the Vietnam War was ending as the Geneva Conference had ordered the American Forces out by January of 1973 and the war was handed back to the South Vietnam Army. We were still guarding the Wall and dealing with the Mideast and North African tensions and the ever-pressing threats of nuclear war. We had time to catch our breath and enjoy the Mediterranean summertime. We toyed with the idea of getting transferred back to the States and finishing out our active duty on the east coast. But we were still being pulled to stay and help the kids to freedom and the vets were already working us to get involved in the rescue efforts to go back to SE Asia and help get the POW's out. If we put our paperwork in now it would still take months before we got discharged and we had a lot of leave time to use before that. Like the Moody Blues song "The Question," we felt something calling us and we knew it was God. Life has certainly been an adventure.

The newly appointed Brigadier General called us in for a big staff meeting to go over the changes and the new orders. We then met with both military and civilians about a joint venture to open up a camp and a rehab center to work with disabled veterans. The project was to be headed by General Thompson's son, Major Richard Thompson who was still healing from falling two miles out of the sky. The group was called "Vets 4 America" had purchased 40 acres along the Gunnison River in Gunnison, Colorado. It was a beautiful ranch and camp with handmade cabins and a dormitory with fantastic views of the mountains. It was complete with a rodeo and stables that bordered on thousands of acres of state land. The camp use to be a bible camp so we all felt that the place was holy grounds to begin with. The Gunnison River went right through the camp and was famous for trout fishing and elk hunting. The place was going to be a rehab center to work with horses and guide dogs to help the vets get on with their lives. We all signed up as investors and volunteers. Having Richard Thompson heading the project was exciting. Camp Gunnison was going to be a healing place.

Countries such as Iran, Iraq, Syria, Libya and Saudi Arabia were going through constant turmoil and their history goes back thousands of years. Israel as a kingdom was around before the days of Moses. Jerusalem is the center of three religions and some say the future capital of the world. The Bible tells us there will be a New Jerusalem when the Lord returns to reestablish the earth back to Paradise. The country of Israel newly re-formed in 1949 was backed by the US and then an enemy to most of the Arab countries. The Soviet Union was locked in a battle in Afghanistan and border wars were raging all around the planet. We had civil wars and the Catholics were killing the Protestants in Ireland. Tribal wars were raging in many Third World countries and violence in the streets was in our urban areas. Our prisons and our psychiatric hospitals were filled to capacity and our prejudices and hate was nonspecific and open to all. Another great scripture that Nancy put on our bathroom mirror was "Be not overcome with evil, but overcome evil with good." (Romans 12:21). If we don't look up to God we can sink with the adversary. A great account is when Peter saw Jesus walking in the heavy surf, he asks Jesus to have him come out to him. Jesus simply said "COME". Peter got out of the boat and walked to Jesus but when he looked at the storm he began to sink. Jesus grabbed him up and walked him back to the boat. This is why we're constantly being encouraged to fasten our eyes on Yahweh, His Word and His Son. If we look at the circumstances and it takes us away from our creators' energy, then we can walk away from his protection and we start to sink.

We got new orders to meet in Venice with the Italian authorities and their special police unit. We had some suits from NATO and even a member from the Vatican so we knew this wasn't going to be good. Venice is an old-world-class city state famous for the canals and waterways with over a hundred islands and bridges. Saint Michaels Cathedral and Parish was built in 995 A.D. on the Grand Canal and ran a large orphanage. Venice is famous for the morning mist that shrouds the city as only the steeples can be seen through the fog. It is also famous for its underground catacombs and tunnels connecting the city with southern points. Venice is considered the gateway to the East as the end destination of the trade routes of Marco Polo and Genghis Khan. Venice had miles of underground passageways and tombs of Church and important Venetians. Just recently they replaced all the torches and oil lamps with electricity. Just the wind tunnels whistling and screaming made the entire place seem like Satan's Playground. Sometimes the insane murmuring running behind us would just scare the crap out of us. The whole place smelled like dust and death. We have experienced so much darkness and death but here in the church we could feel the bad energy. We felt pulled in two directions as good and evil were at war with each other. This war was the big magilla, more powerful than all the atomic bombs we could ever imagine. The war called the Armageddon, at the end times, will be the final battle between good and evil. Then the heavens will rain down fire and brimstone and the volcanos will erupt and the earth will be remade. When Christ returns, heads will roll.

We were called here to investigate bad reports from St. Michaels Parish. The orphanage was run by two older Priests that were doing very horrendous activities to the children and some of the nuns. We were set up by the CIA as a couple from Montreal looking to adopt a Catholic baby. We checked in with the Hotel Venetian right on St Mark's Square and then registered with the church. We were introduced to a Filipino priest named Father Miguel. He was going to show us around for a few days and give us a tour of the city. He started the tour by taking us by gondola to all the great places of interest. Some of the bridges had these beautiful little houses and walkways through the gardens. Other bridges had drawbridges and ferries and the waterways and canals had every type of boat you could imagine. When we toured the orphanage, we could see that the children loved Father Miguel and followed him around like he was the Pied Piper and that said a lot about him. The two old priests were never around and there were so many rumors about their subversive activities. Father Anthony and Father Salvatore were getting ready to retire but from what we know they are running a big racket from the orphanage. We just felt that Father Miguel was a good man and he was training to take over the orphanage when the two old priests get put out to pasture soon. This is why we have to get to the bottom of this mess. Behind the main building was a 4-bay garage that was connected to the underground and late-night activities. The children all thought it to be haunted because they could hear screaming late at night.

In the catacombs beneath Venice there was these very creepy passageways carved through the limestone that were made to resonate and echo throughout the tunnels. These hallways were sources of energy as colors of light were reflecting off the rocks inlaid with human bones. Sounds and colors were distorted to create a most eerie atmosphere. We could hear something like a deep dark evil chanting that made the hair on our neck and arms stand up. We didn't know if it was the echoes of the spirits from long ago or something from our own imaginations. These tunnels were a source of some very dark twisted secrets dating back a thousand years. The walls seemed to breathe and sweat and the floors shook and trembled. The air reeked of strange smells that made us gag and there was rats, spiders and creeping things. The entire place was haunted with dirty foul spirits from all sorts of beliefs and practices. There were places where the walls looked like they were bleeding blood red from the sulfur and the rust and the sounds of rushing water played with our senses and our imagination. The entire place screamed absolute insanity.

Father Miguel had a file cabinet in a closet that was filled with old lead skeleton keys. He was trying to go through them to open up the locks down in the catacombs and sub floors. He took us right down through a passageway from his fireplace. We went down a spiral staircase two flights into a large dungeon that was as evil as they come. The room was a torture chamber with all sorts of apparatus to hurt and stretch a poor soul till they slowly rip apart. A favorite activity was to make a person drink a couple of gallons of water and then tying his John Thomas with a chord. We are talking about evils going back to the Roman emperor Caligula. Father Miguel took us through a passageway that went to both the dock and the cathedral. The wind started whistling and howling and the tunnel started screaming like a banshee. The faster we ran the faster the spirit was on our back and it took our breath away and froze us in fear. I felt like I was running in quicksand and got punched in the gut. I tripped and fell down on Nancy and it felt like we were falling into an abyss. I started to feel Nancy's breath on my neck and I realized we were laying on the floor and at least we were still alive.

Father Miguel was on the floor behind us and he was shaking like a leaf. There was such an oppressive feeling of gloom that made us feel we were overcome with grief and death. The three of us made it to the hut on the dock and sat out under the stars for a long time. We all prayed together and thanked God for His protection. As we were all laying out in the grass, we saw a small skiff pull up to the dock with two men and a boy and they went into the front door of the garage.

We waited for some time and said good night to Father Miguel and went back to our hotel to sleep. Laying together was still a challenge and we could still hear the insanity in our heads. We felt like we just got home from a Led Zeppelin concert. It felt like I was delirious with a fever and everything was going from big too small or it was turning upside down. Reality was spinning around. The entire place felt haunted, not very good for a cathedral and a place to worship.

The Vatican sent a Jesuit priest, Father James to investigate some of the phenomena going on at the parish here at St Michaels. The Jesuits were the strong arm and the guardians for the church. He was assigned to look in to possessions, curses, cults, Devil worship and even miracles. For years the catacombs and the tunnels were believed to be haunted and full of supernatural activities. We knew that the two old priests were involved with some very dirty sick things and we were going after them to bust them for it. Rape, torture, sex trafficking, dungeons and drugs were all organized by the priests and certain townspeople for their sick perversions. They made a lot of money selling sex and drugs and importing girls and boys. Since Nancy and I were believers in the bible we were learning to fight with the sword of the spirit and the whole armor of God so we can stand against the wiles of the Devil. The Jesuit priest was a formidable looking man probably in his mid-thirties. He dressed in a black shirt and pants with just a small white collar. I saw him out early running and then sitting in the garden praying. He spent most of the day meeting with parishioners and the children. We met him one morning and we shared some of the things we knew. We all said some prayers together and shared some of our favorite bible passages. We both knew that the whole operation had moved out of the basement and the underground. Still the catacombs and the tunnels were full of some evil spirits. We could hear screaming and footsteps and a heavy weight on our shoulders. There was an oppression that made the walls seemed to breath and there was a pounding in our heads. All the residents complained that at night the whole place came alive. A lot of the kids were so scared that they wet the bed rather than go down the hall to go to the bathroom. Some of the sub floors were ten stories deep going down over 100 feet. It had escape routes all over the sea and land. There was so much bad here that everyone was tormented.

We slept late because we too felt drained and we needed to chill out a little. In the late morning we went down for some brunch and at the main desk we had a note from a nun from the orphanage. Her name was Sister Mary Theresa and she lived with a couple of nuns at the rectory. Her note asked us to meet her at the fountain at St Mark's Square at noon. We met her and she was wearing jeans and a sweater and she was shaking like a leaf. She said that if Father Salvatore found out she was here he would kill her. In her best broken English, Sister Mary Theresa started trying to tell us about her years of abuse by Father Salvatore and Father Anthony and their compadres. They used her and abused her and got off hurting her. They made her take drugs inside herself to be a mule bringing product back from the Mideast. They filled her with drugs so she could service them for hours and still take a beating. She was forced to have abortions and she gave birth a couple of times but they took the babies right away. She tried to take her life a few times and she thought that it was Jesus who was punishing her for her sins. Her only love was for the children that she took care of and she loved them like they were her own. We couldn't let her go back to the church or the orphanage so we got her the room next to us until we could get her some help.

In the evening we took a boat ride around the harbor to investigate what else they had going on. The dock at the orphanage had a couple of boats tied up so we anchored out in the harbor to see what was going on. Within the hour both boats left and they went out to another island out in the bay. Sister Mary Theresa told us that they had a new hangout that they moved most of their operations to. There were a lot more boats tied up with more people coming and going. When the doors opened, we could hear loud music echoing across the water. We made plans to come back the next night loaded for bear and on attack. We hoped to literally catch them with their pants down and bum rush the place. With the element of surprise and some formidable firepower we could shut the whole place down. We tried to get a good night sleep and spent the day going over our plans. A bad problem was that we haven't seen Father Miguel or Father James since yesterday morning and we were worried about their whereabouts. We took precautions by wearing our flack- jackets and grease paint and black jump suits. As the sun was setting, we went out for a swim to burn off some of our pre-attack jitters. We got dressed and said some prayers and pushed out into the night.

We pulled up to the side of the dock all pumped up and ready to party, it was Friday night and the place was hopping. With a force of two we stormed the front door and dropped a smoke bomb and an incinerating bomb to get the party started. There were a few strippers dancing on the bar and they let out screams as they ran for cover. A couple of bouncers and some cops pulled out their pistols so we let them have it and we dropped them in one motion. Men came running out of the backroom trying to get dressed and we shot the first two in their knees and put the rest of them on the ground. A man came running up the stairs with a shotgun and as he took aim at us, we both just about took his head off. We ran down the steps to a horrible scene of sadistic sex and torture. The entire basement was a big torture chamber with women chained to each other and men getting off on all the perversions. In the corner was a man badly beat up, naked and tied to a chair. When he picked up his head to see, we were shocked to see that it was Father Miguel. Nancy took out her knife to cut all the chords to free him but he was so messed up that he didn't recognize her. He was so full of cocaine that the white powder was all over him.

Everywhere we looked was mirrors, straws, glass pipes and drugs. They were all snorting speed balls that was a mixture of amphetamines and cocaine. We heard a woman scream from down the hallway so we kicked in the door to see the two old priests roughing up this young girl and raping her. We beat them within an inch of their lives and stopped so they will rot in prison for the rest of their miserable lives. We brought everybody upstairs and Nancy helped Father Miguel to walk. The people upstairs were all still doing the drugs so we had to practically wrestle it away from them. The strippers all had their personal stash so we had to get tough with them. The Italian SWAT team finally came to take order so Nancy and I took Father Miguel Torrez to the hospital. Six people were dead, four were badly injured and ten were hauled off to prison. The problem was that Father James had been missing for two days. We got Mary Theresa Bucatti into a treatment center and a lot of the kids into group therapy. The orphanage has been through so much evil that killed some of the children. The main activity was to ship them all over the world.

We stayed in Venice for another week to visit with Father Miguel and Sister Mary. By now we realized that Father James was probably dead. After a few days, Father Miguel started getting a little better so Nancy started taking him to his office to get acclimated to his purpose. When he started putting everything in order, we knew he was recuperating. As soon as he came to his senses, he told us the bad news that they killed Father James. He was about to put in a report that would shut the place down but they got to him and chopped him into pieces and threw him into the bay. We felt so bad that we couldn't do anything to get him out of there. We spent some time with Sister Mary Theresa trying to tell her that God loves her and that Jesus forgives her. She was going to get help at a Catholic hospital that hopefully will share some of God's love with her. We started praying and reading the bible with Father Miguel and after a few days he was getting back to reality.

All of Venice was celebrating Shove Tuesday and the Mardi Gras. They had these outrages costume parties at the big mansions and everybody came by gondolas and carriages. We were right in the center of it staying at our hotel at St Mark's Square. Nancy rented an 18 century Parisian gown and I rented an old French military uniform complete with sash and saber. Nancy had her hair done up in little French curls and she was the Bell of the Ball. We drank Moet and ate strawberries dipped in chocolate and we danced the night away. After all the horrible activities we were involved in, it was good to let loose a little. Seeing all the babies had Nancy in a tizzy and she wanted us to make our own. Who was I to argue?

The port city of Split is a beautiful combination of harbor, bays and awesome cliffs on the southern shore of Yugoslavia (or Croatia, depending on what period of time and how the communist occupation divided the area). Split is a popular destination with a bustling harbor protected by surrounding islands in the Adriatic Sea. Ferries and water taxis connected all other ports from Venice to Greece and the entire Mediterranean region. It had a huge commercial fishing industry and important shipping trade business as a hub for the Soviet Bloc. It was also famous for smuggling anything of value from the West as Italy was close enough for a small speed boat to make it across in a couple of hours. From our cottage on the cliffs in Brindisi we could see ferries and freighters going back and forth. The entire area sported hot destinations for hotels and casinos with island resorts and private clubs. A popular place was the Mediterranean Club and Casino called Club Paradiso that we called Cub Med for short. You could get anything you wanted and they entertained many various services depending on your taste or perversion. They catered to some very special so-called social clubs, one being the S&M club for sadomasochistic practices. People from all over the world could come to act out their fantasies. It was more than just people wanting to be spanked and tied up as there was a society of dominatrix and slaves with wizards and many types of weird practices. They practiced witchcraft and used all different potions and drugs to take over a person's spirit. They had dungeons and plenty of old equipment to be tortured and raped with. If your pleasure was to be stretched on a rack and have people in masks and costumes have sex with you then you came to the right place. But if you just wanted a fairly normal experience then you could have a private time in your own room with a champagne glass hot tub and views of the ocean. These resorts catered to the rich and famous and people with a lot of needs and desires. They also tried to please and protect their guests so it was hard to investigate.

During the height of the busy tourist season a young girl about 15, was found washed ashore on a nearby beach. To add to the horrible discovery was that the girl's hands and feet were hacked off and it showed that she was tortured, raped and drugged. Since she was found floating in International waters, she was considered just another runaway lost in the prostitution ring and discarded like a dead fish. Nancy and I started to investigate the hotel chain and the casinos and found out at Headquarters that it was an international outfit from South Africa controlled by the wealthy white supremist all around the world. Nancy and I decided it was time to take a little vacation at the Club Med on Fantasy Island off of Split to see what we could uncover. We checked in to a honeymoon suit and started to check out some of the activities available. We signed up for fishing and scuba diving and we took in some gym and spa time. One of the concierges told us that if we wanted any of the more intimate activities to speak with the masseuse to set up an appointment. Everything was set up rather business like as if we were looking to buy time shares. The place was filled with beautiful escorts and services all willing to please. There was champagne flowing and fine cuisine and the pot and cocaine was out in the open. It all was like the sex club Plato's Retreat famous in New York City or the Playboy Clubs opening up in all the big cities. The whole state of Nevada was compared to Sodom & Gomorrah with the legalized gambling and prostitution. Out in the Mediterranean similar rules or the lack of rules applied as anything goes and people could act out their fantasies even if at the cruel expense of their victims. Money could buy you anything you wanted and the love of money was the root of all evil.

We spent the first evening at a restaurant on the beach with a marvelous view of the cliffs across the bay. We ended up dancing in this cabana to a cool band and mingled with some of the guest until we went to the casino to play some cards. As it was getting to the bewitching hour it seemed some of the couples were starting to hook up as if the night was still young and there was a lot more to come. I know by past experience that the drugs were starting to call the shots and everyone was getting excited for more action. Drugs and alcohol not only acted like an aphrodisiac but it broke down one's inhibitions and fueled their desires. In other words, they made you extremely horny.

Unfortunately, it helped some people to act like animals and some like the maniacal monsters that they were. There were international societies that were devoted to child pornography and getting to participate in mutilation and murder. We were just on the edge of a deep dark underworld of man at his worst and we needed to walk circumspectly with Gods guidance. We were in such a dark place that we needed some sort of positive energy to push through the evil around us. Our ends justified our means, saving these victims was our goal. Once again, we were dealing with people that had absolutely no regard for human life and just being here put our lives in jeopardy. There were some serious reports that some the tourists went missing from time to time. Since the girls were moved around from site to site it was hard to keep track of all the activities.

Because of what we were involved with, I had my Glock on my ankle and Nancy kept a Colt in her purse and she knew how to use it as this was no joke. If we were somehow discovered we would be chopped up like chum and fed to the fishes. We needed help so we contacted our buddies Kenny and Al and they brought 2 more ex-Rangers to pose as fishermen and their skiff was loaded for bear. One thing we had to go on was that the women were shipped from hotel to hotel so we had to figure out the route and then who we could be saved. Some of these victims were so drugged up that we couldn't pry them from their captors. The motivation factor was the hell and torture they wanted to escape from. This was such a big organization so we had to figure out how to break it down so we could get in and out to do some good.

Kenny and Al and now Joe and Artie were the guys that you wanted on your side. They were highly trained operands and for now we all ran surveillance to see how things worked. A great way to run surveillance out on the water was to actively fish. We could move about the waters and even catch some dinner. We were sure that the fiends had hideouts among the hundreds of islands to hide their cargo and drop off the human traffic to transport them to other locations. This we hoped would be the weak link in this big chain of activity we were up against.

The mutilated body of the young girl that washed ashore was probably floating in the current from the southern Adriatic so we had our guys fishing that area. Nancy and I continued our stay at the resort and we tried to stay away from the sex clubs and other compromising situations. We were sure they had surveillance and we didn't want to draw any more attention to ourselves. We were able to rent a boat to go out on our own fishing and diving adventures so we could get around

the harbor and other points. Some fishermen made another gruesome discovery when they netted a big 5 ft barracuda in their catch. Back at the docks when they cut the big fish up, they found some human flesh in its stomach. They had caught the fish out by where our guys were and it gave us more clues that we were on the trail. These body parts and the young girl were lining up that somebody was throwing things in the waters nearby. The coroner reported that the body wasn't in the water very long, probably dumped in that morning. With the current it could have traveled 10-15 miles. Our guys started working their way down the coast and we worked the maps and the surveillance we had on the area. Another problem is that many more islands and open water routes intertwined as we traveled south. The Adriatic had over 1300 islands but only 100 were populated so there were plenty of places to hide shit.

The next night we had dinner with these two rich good-looking ladies that Nancy met at the steam room at the gym. They were probably in their late thirties and they had been traveling around together and they were from Serbia. They spoke English as well as Croatian and Romanian and we enjoyed our dinner conversations. After dinner and a few more drinks, they told us a remarkable story about their journey around Europe and the Mediterranean Sea. For the past two months they have been to many ports and cities staying in these resorts and hotels looking for their missing daughters. The girls were on the way to Belgrade to visit a museum for the day and at the bus station they vanished. The mothers got together as soon as they realized that the police were not going to help. We always hear about the maternal instincts and super strength of a mother and her kids. An elephant can fight off a pride of lions when protecting their young and these ladies were no different. The mother's names were Silvia and Dorcas and they have been literally doing anything they can to find their missing girls. They have been to every hotel, resort or casino that had young girls for sale. These two mothers were getting so desperate that they started reaching out to people and were in danger of going missing themselves. Somehow, they ran into Nancy and trusted that she was someone that could help them. Could God have set up these coincidences as how else can we explain these circumstances. They did speak to some brave and sympathetic prostitutes who had told them that the girls were still alive, at least they were 2 days ago. They showed us the pictures of these very cute young ones and I finally exhaled when I saw that they weren't the girl found on the beach. But as the barracuda told us, the girl found mutilated on the beach had company as more bodies were out there floating around. It was a very rough realization that these young girls were fucked up so badly that they were already thrown out with the bath water like garbage. Our little team had to do something to find these girls before they were shipped out to their next destination or lost forever. The big break came when we were studying the maps, we discovered a registered 27 ft. Wellcraft, with a cubby cabin and twin Volvo inboard- outboards that operated as a water taxi. Most water taxis run about 15-20 mph and don't have twin Volvo's pushing 600 HP. It made weekly stops at the hotels and resorts and the big deal was that it stopped at an island out in the suspected area. There wasn't much to the island but it had a small dock and a refueling station with what looked like a small house on the property. Our faithful fishermen, AKA our federal agents, kept surveillance on the island and during the night they saw what we were looking for as smaller speed boats came and went in the night. We deducted that this depot was a way station to store any contraband or human prisoners.

We had to work fast so we pulled back to Brindisi in our fishing skiff so we could make some plans. We contacted Headquarters and gathered what we could but we had to act fast as the ghouls were on the move. The next destination on our proposed route was another small island down the coast just off of the old city of Dubrovnik, the old part of the city was a walled city on the Balkan cliffs. It was a big tourist destination and had a few bigtime casinos and hotels. After that it was quite a way south to Albania, so we hoped that we can make our move in this span. We had to leave as fast as we could and we had to devise a plan as soon as we could come up with one! Our best scenario would be to intercept the boat after it picked up any girls from Dubrovnik, but how could we intercept the girls that get dropped off. The thing we understood from the beginning was that we had to pick and choose as we can't save them all. We can't just raid the resorts and abduct every woman who is enslaved. We have to strike them like we are the pirates and gorillas and we will need some firepower to pack a punch. We worked with all four men in the cover of the olive oil business as we got around together and made our connections. These guys were all trained operand's, mercenaries and soldiers and now all six of us are considered paid assassins. They told us a great story about an attack and rescue they called the Trojan Horse. They had to intercept a boat out in the open waters before it got close to port, where there was nowhere to hide. They decided to set their 60 ft Cape Hatteras adrift. The boat they were chasing came along and when they bordered the boat to see what they could find our guys were waiting in the cabin. They were able to save the two Americans being held hostage and locking up the kidnappers in the abandoned yacht. We all met at the Brindisi docks to put our two boats together, we split into two teams as we took Al again in our boat. Silvia and Dorcas begged us to take them to the resort at Dubrovnik so they could get in and see what was up. No way did we want two civilians involved in a possible firefight. They argued that they got this far in the past two months so we decided to bring them and take them straight to the Dubrovnik docks. Kenny, Artie and Joe had a very fast Scarab that was confiscated by the CIA in some drug war so we could make it to the Yugoslavia coast in less than 2 hours. Our Donzi could go 65 MPH the entire way, as fast as anything out there,

We had to make the decisions on how we were going to attack our dilemma. We knew that the women were all being moved but we had to make the decision to go after the Wellcraft water taxi when it left Dubrovnik so we would have more time out at sea and time to get away. The guys wanted to frag the boat and go back to the fueling station and look for more girls and then set fire to the place. These guys really liked to blow stuff up and they filled the boats with enough explosives to start a tidal wave. We took off that evening and got out before sunset, a good-sized moon was already out and it was a beautiful night. Nancy and I loved being out when the moon was shining on the sea so we could run without our running lights on. The moonlight shone on the deep blue sea and lit it up and made it glow. Rushing through the night at 80+ knots, with every one of us filled with adrenaline gave us a lot of focus and mental strength. We just hoped that we could save the women before we sent some of the smugglers to hell. Through all this nasty crap we were involved with the main point was to save these women and children. This is why we were here and what motivated us to fight against these enemies.

We made it to the Dubrovnik harbor and dropped off Silvia and Dorcas at the docks so they could go to the hotel. We found the Wellcraft we were looking for at the casino marina so we docked and waited. It was magical as the cliffs and town twinkled and it all reflected in the water. At about 2am we see a group of people being escorted to the water taxi and it was time to go. Al radioed Kenny to tell them it's going down and we slowly followed the Wellcraft out of the harbor and into the night. If we were just going out to frag the boat it would be easy but we had to be a lot slicker then that. When we got out in the open waters, we caught a huge break as they headed back north going towards their depot. We both stayed back and turned off our lights so we could follow them. When we were certain that they were going back to that island, we took off to meet at the back of the island. Now we could steal the woman back and pick off their captors. We beached our boats and got into position and waited for the group to come back out. We setup our snipers on both sides of the little channel so we could hit them hard and then board the boat.

After about a half hour the group came back out and there was more woman and men. There was 8 woman and 5 men and I figured that 2 of the men were with the other boat. They loaded up and 2 guys pushed them off. We were 100 yards down the channel and as they floated by, we took out the guy driving and the other guy on deck with two shots to their heads. We jumped on board and as the guy in the cabin came running out, we clipped him too. Al took over the controls and put the boat in reverse and we went right back to the dock. The two Russian men came rushing out with weapons drawn but we blew them to kingdom come. We went inside and took some maps and radios and Kenny and Artie set some timers up so in 10 minutes they would blow the whole place to smithereens. We had saved 8 young women from a short life of hell. The very cool thing was that Silvia and Dorcas's daughters were battered up but alive. We told them that their mothers were waiting for them in Dubrovnik. The other six young women were all abducted from Yugoslavia and one of them was an Italian on vacation with her parents at a resort in Split. We took them all back to our NATO headquarters so they could be taken care of. Nancy and I took a joy ride back to Dubrovnik to get Silvia and Dorcas and bring them back to Italy and to their girls. It made everything we did seem worthwhile and our ride through the Adriatic was glorious. All four of us rode back into the sunset with tears of joy streaming down our faces in the rushing wind. The world was a beautiful place as we felt so alive for a little while. Later on, Silvia and Dorcas started an international foundation to go after the missing girls as there were creeps at every big train and railway station waiting to abscond them.

Nancy and I laid low for a while but we did keep working on a few deliveries and pickups and Nancy went to do some work at the base clinic. We got to spend a few weekends out in the baby blue Mediterranean and we cruised around in the Donzi and toured the islands. With over 1200 islands just in the Adriatic Sea the area was stunning, between the old-world charm and the cliffs, islands, harbors and coves it has to be one of the most beautiful places in the world. The entire Mediterranean from Spain to the French & Italian

Rivera to the Greek coast and islands is just stunning and you could spend your whole life and not be able to take it all in. So far, the California coast, the Caribbean, the South China Sea and of course the Mediterranean are the best places I've seen. But there is a big world out there that we still want to see. On closer inspection we could spend our lifetime exploring just the Great Lakes or the Gulf of Mexico so we have to make the time. I will be happy just to go out exploring, as long as I am with Nancy.

Evil catches up to us when we allow it to bring us down to where we cannot function in our so-called normal way. It makes us fear what will happen and can hold us back from accomplishing our goals. Nancy and I had to help each other so we could try to stay positive because the killing and rape literally made us sick. It is more than a physical sickness as it affected our whole being deep down in our souls. Now we have this blood on our hands and we knew we would never be the same. We justified our own evil because we were at war with these criminals and someone had to stand against this violence and death. Only in times like this when we talked about these miserable acts did we allow our psyche to deflate and we were left naked and guilty. It was easy to have such hate for our enemies and therefore to protect the innocent we had to kill the guilty. The slogan to "Kill for Peace" is really more than an oxymoron, it is a grim reality. So much killing and wasted lives for nothing and that is why we concentrated on the lives we were saving.

When the two Russian cops tried to attack Nancy on the train, I actually took pleasure in driving the guy's head into the wall. But I didn't kill him. The sadists that were brutally raping the young girls, we shot on sight. Most of what we did was reflexive and it fell into the category of kill or be killed. It was basically what we were trained to do but dealing with it day to day in our head and heart was on our own. That is why having Nancy as a sounding board, we could help each other deal with all the sickness we were going through. Again, we concentrate on the positive side of the emotions we had. When we got weak, we suffered more like being half asleep or when we tried to relax, we let down our guard. Our trainers always yelled for us to drive our minds. The Bible really helps in so many ways, it helps us deal with our sins and we can ask for forgiveness. It talks of how we can renew our minds and even gain the mind of Christ. We can attain peace even when our surroundings are in hell. The apostles sang songs of praise even while chained down in the Roman dungeons. Joseph spent years jailed for crimes he didn't do to eventually be promoted to be in charge of all the

Pharaoh's kingdom. He eventually saved the people of a famine that was going to starve his own people. His people were the Jews that had the Christ Line that is recorded in the book of Mathew. We tried to think of these positive affirmations rather than be so torn down by the evil around us. The bottom line was the love of God we got to share with each other. Without this love we were up shits creek without a paddle. Without God we were definitely FUBAR.

We learned so much from General Thompson about the bible that first year and we studied it with zeal. It opened up a whole new consciousness that I had been looking for since I was a kid looking up at the stars. It certainly changed Nancy's life and helped us to deal with all the bad stuff we were going through. Learning about the connection between God and Jesus Christ was the big deal. The bible teaches so many truths that contradict some of the things that the big religions teach. We studied and read the bible and tried to interpret it just like how it was written. The key to our learning was to connect the entire bible so that it was perfect, written by God. No contradictions' we just read like it is written. For instance, over 50 times the bible says that Jesus Christ is the son of God and not once does the bible say that Jesus Christ is God. God did not die on the cross, the son of God died as our sacrifice. The word trinity is not even in the bible, (the concept of the trinity was first introduced in 325 AD at the Treaty of Nicea). Holy spirit is the gift of God that ties us together with God and Christ.

Christ was a man born of a woman (Mary) and the miracle was that God was his father. He is the only one that is resurrected from the dead as everyone else is awaiting his return when he comes back to resurrect his church. So many religions believe that when a person dies, he goes straight to heaven, or hell (or even some kind of purgatory?) Great believers like the apostle Paul or St Frances of Assisi or any other person that loves God is still dead. Jesus Christ our Messiah, must first return to make things right and then there will be a new world here on earth. This will be paradise. The Coronel urged us to study the bible to see if these things are true. He said to prove it on our own, not to take what someone else tells us. The bible shows us that everyone that dies is just sleeping until Christ comes back to get us up. And the Word tells us that there is no memory in the grave, so your next thought will be with the resurrected Christ! It is a nice thought that our relatives are up in heaven now but the bible doesn't tell us this. There will be a final judgment when everyone will stand before our creator, if you believe in Christ you get a free pass. In fact, the bible shows us that there will be two resurrections, first the resurrection of the just, that is us. And after a thousand years, the resurrection of the unjust. That is when everybody else will stand before God and be judged.

I was raised Catholic and they believe that the saints are in heaven now, but only when Christ returns to raise the dead will this happen on earth. Jesus has to first come back and raise the dead and then begin to restore the earth. At this time, he will send the Devil (Satan) and his devil spirits into the bottomless pit. Then there will be no more death or sickness and no more tears. The world will be made whole and we will be in Paradise. Then we will be with God like it was in the beginning in the garden. We are the saints; the only other beings are the angels and the fallen angels. There is a big difference between what the bible tells us and what some of the major religions teach. It is truth vs traditions and we try to make the entire bible fit without contradictions. The original Word of God was written by the holy men and God told them what to write through His spirit. Moses wrote the first 5 books of the bible, the Pentateuch, as God told him what to write up on the mountain. He started with the ten commandments and continued on with over 600 more. Before that mankind did not really know the difference between right and wrong and what was sin!?

The bible starts in the book of Genesis in the Garden and ends in Revelations in Paradise.

We found a beautiful island with a small cove and a sandy beach that we could pitch a tent and camp out on. We spent the first evening out on the water doing some fishing and we caught some sea bass and witnessed a great sunset. We baked some bass over the campfire and cuddled up around the fire and saw the heavens in all their sparkling glory. It was a calm night and the sea was as calm as glass. Late in the night we could hear a few boats cruising off in the distance, noise can really travel over the water but the boats didn't seem to be more than a couple of miles away. The boats were definitely both coming and going to an island nearby. We figured it would give us something to do tomorrow as we go out fishing and sightseeing. We can look for some secret rendezvous for hidden treasures or contraband, we just can't help ourselves sometimes. We made love on the beach by the fire, under the stars and it was so healing to our damaged souls. We fell asleep right on the beach and it was so perfect that there wasn't even any bugs or mosquitoes. We got up with the sun and flew out to the port of Malala that we could have a great breakfast and buy some goodies to spend the day out on the water. We checked out the map to see what local islands we could explore. In the

5-mile radius of our little island we named Paradise, there were 22 islands with only one being inhabited.

It was a beautiful calm day; 85 degrees and we were flying through the water at 65 MPH. Nancy had her binoculars and her camera to survey the waters, she was working on a map to mark off some of the nearby islands. We drove around all morning and we saw a few islands that could have a cove and/or an inlet that would have a place to dock. We decided to fish off of a small island that we could look around the area. We caught some nice size tunas and after a couple of hours we saw a skiff going around to the other side of the bigger island and leave an hour later. We got a little excited that we could have uncovered something interesting and we started to plan on our next move to find out what was up. We went back to our little camp and ate and went for a swim. We took a nap and went back to our port at Brindisi to pick up some things for the night. First, I picked up some baby eels for some midnight bass fishing and Nancy picked up some food from the market. It was exciting going out for a nighttime adventure and bass fishing on a full moon can be awesome. When a 50-pound striped bass starts running with your line and then it jumps out of the water it is such a rush. I was so wanting for Nancy to land a 70-pound monster to make her night and then see if there is any more activity at Mystery Island, as we named it.

We were out for about an hour when the Bunker fish were jumping out of the water and the water started to boil as the big bass were ripping through the Bunker turning the water red. We both got a strike at the same time and the fight was on to reel them in. Just as I got the net ready, we saw two boats come streaking from behind the island headed towards the big port of Split on the Yugoslavia coast. We managed to land two 60-pound Bass and then we took off to follow the boats up the coast. We stayed back at least a quarter of a mile and sped along with our lights out as we could see the lights on the cliffs and the canopy of the Milky Way above us. When we turned off the running lights, the new paint job made our boat invisible. When we got to the port of Split it was still hopping on a late Saturday night and we tied up at the dock near the two boats. We saw four guys walking down the dock to town. We took pictures of the two boats and their registration numbers. We stayed the night at an inn and we left after breakfast in the morning. We took a fast ride back to our camp and packed up to get back to Brindisi and then to our headquarters.

We checked in with the brass at NATO HEADQUARTERS and put in requests for some surveillance and any pertinent information that we could gather. We found out the two skiffs were registered to a Greek line with shady dealings with importers from North Africa and South America and they dealt with the Soviet Union hauling anything that had a value. With 1246 islands just in the Adriatic Sea alone there were many places to hide and even the bigger inhabited islands had some rogue history and colorful ports. Our Mystery Island was a part of a row of large uninhabited islands called the 5 Sister Islands. Like in the Caribbean Sea, these waterways were a smugglers paradise. We now wanted to find out what was going on here at our Mystery Island and since it was just a 45-minute ride from our cottage we figured we would continue to fish the waters and gather info of any activities. Our eyes in the sky saw nothing as they probably had everything under wraps. We found that most movement was in the night and there were days where there was nothing happening. We wanted to find out if there was any weapons, drugs or worse, human captives in their secret activities. Small boats like ours could move a load of guns, a couple of hundred pounds of drugs or a family of refugees. With what we suspect of this shipping company they could be involved in all three, plus God knows what else. We spent a few days out fishing for more than fish and we would take the ride across to the port of Split for that was were a lot of their boats were moored. As we already knew, Split was a major port for the communist block and the Mediterranean Sea and just about everything was being moved on the black market.

Nancy and I spent a couple of days taking in the sights and enjoying the fine restaurants and the nightclubs all to find out what we could uncover about our mystery island. We found out from local fisherman and dock workers that the Five Sister islands were considered to be off limits as it was restricted by Yugoslavia as government land. But the biggest rumor was that there was human trafficking going on all over the region. This time we heard that young woman in their 20's, have gone missing and there is no trace of them again. Most of these victims were taken from the University or they were young woman working in the travel-hospitality industry. There were so many islands that were smuggling all sorts of contraband but we were starting to think that this island was the one we've been looking for. The coincidence was that we heard the boats late at night from our little no name island we called Paradise. We spent some days out fishing and looking around the area. There was no surveillance available as the islands did not show any structures or activities but we were certain that boats were coming and going. We figured that there were camouflage covering up whatever they had going on.

We set up a plan to have our buddies Kenny and Al come out with us at night so we could get close enough to scuba dive to the island. Nancy and Kenny were going to be out fishing and get us close enough to the west side of the island so that Al and I could swim on to the beach. We could then see what is going on and see if it was what we thought. Nancy and Kenny dropped us off within a couple of hundred yards off the island and we snorkeled the rest of the way in. We were able to walk a little way through the island as it wasn't much bigger than a few city blocks. We came upon a cove with two structures and a small cabin and a dock. It was all under a canapé and there was one of the skiffs we saw in the port of Split tied to the dock. At two in the morning everything was quiet but we saw footprints going to the cabin that were smaller and not the prints of the men's boots. The prints were fresh and I figured we had to strike soon before whoever they were shipped out. We snuck off to the other side of the island and we swam out to meet our boat. The paint job was so good that we swam right up to the boat and still couldn't see it. We knew we had to go right back that night before it was too late. Because usually it was a boat in and a boat out, we figured only 4-5 guys were guarding this little cove. We planned to bum rush the place late at night and catch them napping and haul out some victims. Hopefully we will get in and out and save some lives.

We spent the morning gearing up and going over various scenarios and we planned on going in at 3 am. All four of us were going in our boat as it had to be the fastest and sleekest speedboat around. Later in the afternoon we took a break to eat and rest but we were way too keyed up to get any rest. We all took a walk around the Brindisi docks and packed the last things on to the boat. Then we huddled up and we prayed for Gods protection and for some wisdom and courage to pull this thing off. We couldn't sit around any longer so we set out into the night. It was another clear calm night with a half moon and plenty of stars. The little islands would appear out of nowhere and some were just big enough for a tree or a bush and others were big enough to hold a few beaches, bays and coves. Then there were islands like Malala that had towns and villages. When we got about a couple of hundred yards away, we shut off the engines and switched to the electric engine we use for trolling. We snuck up inside the cove and we drifted in to the shore. Nancy and I were going after anyone we could find and Al and Ken were going after the smugglers. There was a dock with one of the boats tied up and a cabin with a couple of sheds and we ran up the dock through the front door. We were in the main room and the kitchen, on the right was two doors and one was locked. On the left side of the hall was two more rooms so Nancy and I went right and to the locked door and I blasted the lock off and kicked in the door. With our guns drawn we find 4 good looking young women that were dressed in nice clothes. We told them we were here to rescue them and take them to Italy and that we were Americans. Just then we hear BLAM- BLAM -BLAM and we knew our guys found their targets. The four women had been locked in the room but were untied so we escorted them right out the door and all eight of us got in the boat and we took off out of the cove.

Just as we got away from the island, we saw we were not alone as two boats were bearing down at us from the Sister Island next to us. I pulled back on the throttle and went left but the two boats had the momentum and caught up to us as I was just getting up to speed. We could hear the bullets flying across the water and one came in and dropped Nancy right in front of me. She fell down holding the side of her head and just then I felt a sharp pain in my bad shoulder and I held on to the steering wheel as I gave the boat everything she had. All of a sudden both Al and Kenny jumped up from behind their seats and chucked some kind of hand grenades in both boats and the explosions blew both boats out of the water. I pulled up quickly and jumped down to see Nancy as she was bleeding and holding the side of her head. When I pulled her hand away, by the grace of God she was cut on her ear, it appeared to be badly cut by some flying glass. Once I saw that Nancy was going to be okay the pain in my shoulder hit me like a jackhammer. Al took over the wheel and we put some ice on Nancy's ear and bandaged her head as she looked like Van Gogh's self-portrait. They took us to the hospital in Brindisi and they had to cut 2 slugs out of me and my shoulder had to be reworked and put together with two rods. Nancy had plastic surgery to put back some of her earlobe and she covered it with her hair as it healed, so we were lucky to all get out alive. The four young women were all students at the University and were abducted to be taken to Ceylon for white slavery, as they called it. It was not safe for them to return to Yugoslavia so the CIA was going to relocate them to America and they all wanted to go and try to get some of their families out later. They had been shipped around for days and had all been abused so we were actually happy that the scumbags were wiped out by our team. In this war our end results definitely justified our means. Somethings just had to be done.

Nancy was released from the hospital after two days but she had a concussion and stitches on her ear. I wanted her to go back to our cottage and start to recuperate but she refused to leave my side and slept with me in the room. At first, she slept in the chair and later she curled up with me and she took away a lot of my pain. All the guys from our team would stop by and the General would come in and pray with us, somehow his prayers seemed to make the angels chide in and we felt that God was still taking care of us. After ten days in the hospital we went back to our cottage on the cliffs so we could look out over the sea that we just spent an incredible mission on. We decided this was it as my shoulder was going to need months of rehab after it heals and it was time to use up our vacation time and start the next chapter of our lives. Nancy was going to start planning our wedding and after a long honeymoon on a sailboat we wanted to start school. The trouble is our buddies were trying to get us to go with them to Cambodia. There were reports of a lot of American troops that needed our help and it has been hard to say no. With all our training and adventures, the men still trapped in the jungle were screaming out to us. It was hard to ignore, especially when we saw it on the news. We figured that we could join them as civilians if we wanted, as long as my shoulder heals. Once I could go for rides on the cobblestone roads without pain, Nancy took me out and we started taking trips around Italy and France. We could travel through France again as De Gaulle opened up the borders so we spent a few days on the French Riviera and then to Paris. We decided to stay at some incredible places, some as old as the hills and some brand new with fantastic views. Our plan was to work our way up to say goodbye to Charley and Jane and see some of the friends we made along the way. We stayed in Europe for a few more weeks and made our final plans to start our discharge from active duty.

We decided to sell our MG and the boat rather then put them in storage. We took a trip all the way through France, Switzerland, West Germany and back through Italy. I could start driving again with the steering knob attached and with the top down our senses were alive with the onslaught of spring. Our final celebration was to take the boat out for the weekend and camp out at our little Paradise Island. We caught fish and cooked them with corn and sweet potatoes on the campfire. After dinner we bathed together as the sun was setting and we dried ourselves around the fire. The last time we were shopping in Naples I was able to sneak away to pick up the diamond ring I had ordered. I opened up a bottle of red and we raised up our glasses to God. I got down on one knee and asked Nancy Barret to marry me. I had the band inscribed with the scripture, "A THREEFOLD CHORD IS NOT QUICKLY BROKEN". She said yes and we spent the rest of the weekend together on our island paradise loving God and each other.

We finally said goodbye to General Thompson and we discussed him coming to Washington to marry us in a few months. We signed out for the last time and we took a supersonic flight on the Concorde from Rome to New York. Once we were up in the air, we toasted each other and thanked God for starting a new life together. We had a lot of options and we were looking forward to becoming civilians. But first we had a lot of vacation time to use. Our flight on the Concorde across the Atlantic was amazing, supersonic speed with the sky and the ocean blending in a sea of blue. We held hands and looked out the window and the world looked like a beautiful place.

THE END

Printed in the USA
CPSIA information can be obtained
at www.ICGtesting.com
CBHW020055180824
13348CB00026B/28

9 781489 733764